P9-DEQ-236

noah's wife

Lindsay Starck

G. P. Putnam's Sons / New York

PUTNAM

G. P. PUTNAM'S SONS
Publishers Since 1838
An imprint of Penguin Random House LLC
375 Hudson Street
New York, New York 10014

Library of Congress Cataloging-in-Publication Data

Starck, Lindsay Rebecca.
Noah's wife / Lindsay Starck.
p. cm.
ISBN 978-0-399-15923-7
1. City and town life—Fiction. 2. Interpersonal relations—Fiction. I. Title.
PS3619.T37335N63—2016 2015007435
813'.6—dc23

Printed in the United States of America
10 9 8 7 6 5 4 3 2 1

Book design by Meighan Cavanaugh

This is a work of fiction. Names, characters, places, and incidents either are the product of the author's imagination or are used fictitiously, and any resemblance to actual persons, living or dead, businesses, companies, events, or locales is entirely coincidental.

For my parents

who keep me afloat

I thought then
I should save
one
small
warm
true
thing
from the flood

—Zbigniew Herbert, "Elegy for the Departure
of Pen Ink and Lamp"

PROLOGUE

In the beginning it was not raining, but it is raining now—and steadily.

It has been raining for so long that even though it has not always been raining the townspeople begin to *feel* as though this is the case—as though the weather has always been this way, the sky this gray, the puddles this profound. They feel, sometimes, as though the sun has never risen over their town at all, not ever; that its very existence is nothing but a rumor: a product of the same sort of fallacy and telescopic inaccuracy that had everyone thinking for so long that the world was flat or that the constellations were arranged in patterns.

"There are no patterns!" they say to one another now—and darkly. "There are no stars. There is only the rain, and the clouds."

They divide their lives into two sections: the time that came before the rain and the time that will follow it. But after a while the rain soaks so thoroughly through their consciousness that they begin to feel as if there is no time but the present.

"Today is the only day!" says Mauro to his neighbors when they enter his general store.

"You mean—there is no day but today," they say. They propel their arms in circles to rid their sleeves of rainwater.

In the beginning they had all believed that it would end because whenever it had rained before (as it rains everywhere), it had always ended. After a few weeks, when it didn't stop, they tried to find a scientific explanation for it. At first they congregated in the library to seek counsel from written accounts of great rains of the past, and rotated the rabbit ears of their television antennae in a vain attempt to find a weather station that would illuminate their situation. As the rain continued, the transmission of their televisions and their radios grew worse and their sense of isolation increased. They turned the damp pages of their books, and when they met on the street they exchanged theories about the rain as some sort of meteorological quirk resulting from a change in the winds or the tides. Later on, as the vitamin D drained from their blood and a damp despair seeped deep into their hearts, they decided that there was nothing that could explain it and so they stopped trying.

"It is not something to be explained," they say to one another, philosophically. "It is merely something to be endured!"

They endure.

What is more: they take pride in their endurance. They strive to see the rain as something that sets them apart, makes them stronger, wetter, wiser. "If this had happened to anyone but to us," they remind each other, "those people would not have been able to bear it. They would have left long ago."

Thus *staying* becomes the quality that singles them out. Staying becomes the symbol of their strength, their response to clouds hanging heavy and low, the mantra that they mutter when they find their outlook to be especially gray. Sometimes, on the days when they believe they cannot bear it any longer, the rain seems to let up—but the clouds never scatter, and a day or two later it has begun to fall again in earnest.

The water pours down roofs and rushes through gutters and falls in silver arcs from the eaves to the ground. It collects between the cracks in the sidewalk and then spreads in pools across the pavement. The townspeople postpone school picnics and town parades, put away their bicycles, carve ditches through their lawns, take baseball bats to knock the rust from their cars. They purchase special light boxes from a mail-order catalog because the description promises that the bulbs will cheer them by simulating the sun. They look at the sky so often that they become experts on the many different shades of gray. They collect ponchos and rain boots and wear them with self-conscious style. They learn how to walk two abreast on the sidewalk while carrying open umbrellas. The trick is in the tilt: a slight movement of the elbow toward the side of one's body so that the spokes do not collide.

"How lovely the streets look with the colors of all the

umbrellas!" says Mrs. McGinn to her neighbors with a fierce and dogged optimism. "How pleasant it is not to have to water our lawns or wash our cars."

In short: they adapt. They are, in fact, surprised to find how *fluid* their lives are. They are surprised to discover how easy it is to make these alterations, how simple it is to shift their daily habits to fill the empty spaces and restore balance. Weeks become months and years. By the time the new minister arrives in town with his birdlike wife, it seems as if it has been raining forever.

"There really is a certain beauty in it, isn't there?" exclaims the wife, examining the jeweled drops that cling to the windowpanes. She looks attentively to her husband.

"My cup runneth over," says the minister, watching the water topple out and over the edge of a brimming rain gauge. His voice is hard and bright.

"There are good days and there are bad days," explain the townspeople—and this is true. There are days when they wake full of pristine joy, when the town outside their windows seems cleansed of trash and filth and old muddy dreams. But there are also long hours of mildew and frustration; there are moments when they lash out at their friends with bitter words or threaten each other with strong resentful shakes of their spiked umbrellas.

They are not always happy, or at peace. They miss their shadows. Sometimes when they step outside in the morning the first drop of rain on their plastic ponchos echoes in their ears with the resounding toll of a funeral bell. Sometimes when they return home in the faint gray light of evening, they cannot bear the hoarse whispers of their rusted wind chimes and they cannot bear the sight of the water rising in their rain gauges. They despair; and they are sick of despair. With swift and sudden anger they take up the shining cylinders and they hurl the water into the grass and they fling the gauges with great force toward the concrete, standing and watching while the glass shatters and breaks. At the moment of impact they feel something crack within their very souls and then they go inside—repentant—to find a broom to sweep up a pile of pieces that are jagged and clear.

In the rain, the wreckage shines like diamonds.

one

It was raining on the day that Noah's wife met her husband.

The sky was plum-colored, the sea wrathful and wild. The wooden planks of the boat wailed in the wind as the storm tossed it across the sea and pitched her to one side. Noah's wife would have fallen if she had not thrown out a hand and accidentally struck Noah's shoulder.

"Whoa there!" he had said with a cheerful flash of white teeth, lifting his own hand and grasping her forearm. "Are you all right?"

That had been her first impression of him: thick dark curls smashed flat to his head by the rain, open face wreathed in a smile, eyes that were soft and black as coal. His face was craggy, his beard coarse and closely trimmed. He was, she guessed, eight or ten years older than she was. She could tell by his expression that he was pleased that they had been thrown together ("by fate," he teased her later), and the pressure of his fingers was warm against her skin. She was tall but he had a good six inches on her, and when the boat rocked again she was thrown so close that her cheek slammed against his plastic slicker. For a moment—before she pulled away, embarrassed—she heard his heart pounding through a chest as solid as the hull they stood upon.

"I'm so sorry," she murmured, withdrawing her hand. He continued smiling, assured her that he didn't mind. She took a few unsteady steps toward the pilothouse, looking for something to hold on to. As she went she could feel Noah's eyes on the back of her neck, beaming through the hood of her raincoat.

She had never liked boats. She would not have set foot on one on dry land, much less on a stormy sea, but the choice was not hers. The photographer who usually took tourists' photos for the whale-watching company had called in sick that morning, and so the studio had sent her. The water was too rough for her to set up her tripod, so as far as work was concerned it was a wasted trip. The anger of the ocean took her by surprise, reminding her of the stories of the vengeful Greek gods she had pored over while in middle school. She remembers watching the buildings in the harbor grow smaller while the little boat rocked and churned, thinking to herself that, if nothing else, at least this would be a dramatic way to die.

The passengers careened from side to side with their hands shielding their eyes, looking for whales. No one could find any. They didn't know if they should focus their search over the left side or the right side of the boat—"Port or starboard," she heard someone correct them pretentiously—and so they kept switching back and forth, stepping quickly across the rolling decks with arms outstretched for balance.

Made drowsy by the pair of pills she had taken to prevent the onset of seasickness, she settled down on a ledge between two lifeboats and rested her chin on her orange life preserver. She looked out at the water, watching for whales from half-lidded eyes. After they had been at sea for about fifteen minutes, the rain fell harder and she could feel the wind picking up, could hear it whistle through the railings. The lifeboats were lashed close to the pilothouse and in brief moments between the gusts of wind she could hear the captain talking to his first mate.

"Pretty rough," said the captain.

"No kidding," said the first mate. "Probably shouldn't have come out."

Noah was among the throng sliding from side to side when the ship rocked, and he happened to catch her eye at the moment of this exchange. Even back then, he had been able to read her as easily as one of his psalms. He told her much later that from the minute he saw her he loved the way her emotions tumbled across her face, genuine and bare. He said that he fell for her right there, right on the heaving deck of that boat when he saw her gripping the straps of her life vest with her knuckles white, her expression at once fearful and composed.

"Don't worry!" he had shouted over the wind. "It'll be all right!"

She lifted one hand to tighten the straps on her life jacket. Her coat was pale green and soaked through to her shirt and her skin, the hood plastered to her hair and stuck to the sides of her cheeks. Noah had beamed at her then, and she felt a little warmer.

"Really! We'll make it back just fine!" he said again.

"How do you know?" she yelled back.

He shifted a coil of wet rope and sat down beside her. Then he grinned. "I just do."

The storm was too loud for them to speak very much after that, but she snuck sly glances at his profile and kept her leg where it was when the boat rocked perilously to one side and caused her to lean and to slide, to press her thigh against his. Out of the corner of her eye, she saw him smile. When another wave knocked their shoulders together, she smelled peppermint and soap. He leaned in and promised her that once they got back to shore, he would take her out for lunch and she'd forget they ever nearly died at all.

She liked him, instantly. He reassured her. Over the months that passed, she grew to love him for that confidence, for his unwavering faith that no matter how high the waves or how strong the wind, they would all make it safely back to solid ground. By the time he asked her to marry him (she said yes before he had finished the question), the rain and the wind were so deeply embedded in the story of their romance that she didn't mind the fact that it rained on their wedding day; she saw the inclement weather, in fact, as a good omen. When she thinks of the wedding now, she remembers the soggy tangle of her veil, the streaks of mud that her guests carried into the church on the heels of their galoshes. She recalls the thunder that shook the steeple, thrumming through the pews, and the lightning that lit up the altar after the power had gone out. Noah had laughed at the whole thing and she followed his lead, wandering gaily among their guests while they waited for the worst of the wind to die down so that they could drive to the reception. Even after they had arrived at the restaurant to discover that the power was out there, too, she remained unfazed. Everyone drank warm beer and passed around cold plates of cheeses and meats, exclaiming at the flickering beauty of the dining room by candlelight. There was no music, but when the meal was winding down his friends raised their glasses and sang, Noah's baritone bellowing steady and full through the chorus. She tugged his suit coat off the back of his chair and draped it across her bare shoulders, and then she leaned back and took large bites of her cake, feeling warm and at peace. Noah had frosting in his beard and she loved it, loved that he ate as he lived: with gusto. She was expecting him to teach her how to live with gusto, too.

And she was right about the luck of the rain. The first five years of their marriage have flown by in a haze of celebrations: a steady succession of weddings and baptisms, anniversaries and birthdays. True, she has heard the rumor (passed around at coffee hour) that Noah brings in so many new members not on account of his righteousness—although he *is* righteous—but simply because he is so handsome. No doubt it would be better if people adored the Lord at least as much as they adored the assistant minister, but Noah's wife understands as well as anyone that it is easier to believe in a God who would choose someone like this for his instrument: someone with such rich hair, with such a straight nose and dignified jawline. When he preaches, his dark eyes shine and his teeth glint through the space between his mustache and his beard. His congregants hunker down in their pews and, even if most of them do not heed the actual words that he is saying, they wait for the low gravel of his voice to tumble over them and then they believe—for the time being, at least—as though they have been saved.

Noah's wife always sits in the front row with her shoulders back and her hymnal open on her lap, although she never sings. She grew up without ever having set foot in a church, without any strong opinions about God or heaven or much else, for that matter. And yet there is something persuasive about Noah. Whenever he speaks, whenever he leans over his pulpit to close the distance between him and his congregation, she finds it much easier to accept the world as he sees it: benevolent and just, full of mystery and unfathomable beauty. His congregants, she supposes, must feel the same way. The pews are always packed.

Noah's first call out of seminary had been as an assistant minister to a large church in the city. His wife edits his sermons and collects petitions from his congregants; she distributes the newsletter and organizes picnics. At church functions she takes photographs, arranging group shots in front of the building or setting up her tripod behind the banquet table to snap candids as people serve themselves. Noah's congregants like her macaroni salads and her dry humor and her open devotion to her husband, but most of all they like to see her pictures. She develops them herself. In the weeks following the event they gather around the bulletin board in the nave to exclaim over their favorite prints and to compliment one another on how healthy and happy they look. Noah's wife has a way about her, they all agree; she has a talent for bringing out the best in people.

THE SUN IS BRILLIANT on the day Noah receives the call. His wife is waiting for him to come home, sitting on the gritty concrete of the front stoop with a mug of tea cupped between her palms. Spring is nearly over—the leaves are darker every day, and the air feels dry and taut. She stands when her husband pulls up to the curb, watches his shadow lengthen as he strides across the grass with steps that are swift and certain. She has always loved the way he moves.

"I've been called!" he tells her. "I'll have a congregation of my own."

His skin is flushed with energy. She would not be surprised to hear his beard crackling with excitement.

"That's wonderful, Noah!" she exclaims. "Where is the church?"

The news is unexpected. She had not known that Noah was looking for another church; she had assumed that he would eventually take over the lead position at the church they are attending now. She is further disconcerted when, instead of naming a neighborhood she knows, Noah tells her that the church is a half day's drive from the city—nestled deep in the northwestern hills.

"So—we're leaving?" she asks him.

"We're leaving," he confirms. "We're expected there by next week."

Of course he can tell that she is staggered by the thought of it; she has lived her whole life bound within the borders of this city. Before she can respond, Noah draws her close to reassure her. He kisses the top of her head and leaves his lips there, so that when he speaks his voice is muffled in her hair.

"I know it's huge," he says. "I know it's unexpected. But I believe that we can really do some good out there. I believe we are needed, that this has happened for a reason." He kisses her again. "And I promise that no matter what, we'll be together."

She rests her head against the shirt that she had pressed for him that morning, feels his heart beating through the linen, and remembers the whale-watching boat in the rain. He is happy, and so why should she be troubled?

That evening she goes directly to the public library, determined to learn all there is to know about the place where they are headed. She stays until the building closes, riffling through the card catalog and paging through brittle newssheets, but there is little information to be had. She finds one yellowed profile on the businessman who had established a zoo there and a few articles on the animals they had acquired afterward. Noah's wife peers for a while at the faded images of exotic birds and wildebeests, but she fails to locate anything written on the town in the past ten years. Even the librarian whose assistance she requests finally has to throw up his hands and admit defeat.

"We've got nothing here," says the man, unbuttoning and rebuttoning his cardigan several times in evident distress. "It's as if that place has fallen out of our books."

SHE REFUSES TO LET this faze her. "That only makes it more of an adventure," she tells Noah as they are leaving. His body is tense in the driver's seat, but his face softens when he looks sideways at her.

"You're so beautiful, my dear," he says. He pulls their battered station wagon away from their old life and turns toward the new, and as they head up the highway she rolls down her window and feels the sun on her face, removes the map from the glove box and unfolds it across her lap. She looks for the crease that marks the spot of their new town, its name faded, the print almost too small to read. The drive takes them along the rocky western coast, hugging the sea before turning toward the mountains. There is only one highway that leads into the town, the road as smooth and sloping as a dragon's back. For most of the way they ride silently, and although it is not like Noah to be silent, his wife is too full of her own thoughts to press him into speech. She tries to focus on where they are headed rather than what they are leaving behind; she deliberately does not think of the photography studio where she has worked her whole adult life, nor of the owner who tried to persuade her not to go. She even turns her thoughts away from her best friend. Noah's wife has made up her mind to be as delighted as her husband about this sudden change in fortune.

Indeed, when she first sees the charcoal-colored clouds that have collected over their destination and hears the rain begin to patter against their windshield, she takes it as a good omen. As their car growls into town, she considers the clouds curling thick around chimneys and the jumble of roofs obscured by a beaded veil of rain. Along the main drag she can make out the hazy shapes of the inhabitants ambling along sidewalks, umbrellas blooming in vivid bouquets wherever they stop to meet on corners. They turn to watch the car go by, their faces sullen. She squeezes Noah's hand and tries to smile at them. She continues smiling as the car chugs down the road and up the driveway of the empty parsonage, a rambling, gray-blue house with shuttered windows and three slightly tilting stories. She smiles even while they are unloading boxes from the back and setting them down in a dining room that smells of mildew, the dust rolling in soft whorls across the groaning hardwood floors. She does her best to smile the whole evening through, and only dares to let her face relax when the lights are out and she can hear Noah snoring beside her in an unfamiliar bed. The rain taps all night on the shingles above her, eventually lulling her to sleep. It is still raining when she wakes.

two

Two days before Noah was called to this church, the previous minister walked into the river and didn't walk out again.

When Noah arrives to take his place, the town is still debating the nature of his death. It is true, people say to one another, that after so many months of rain, the river has become higher and faster than it was before; and yet it has not become so high or so fast that anyone would have expected death by drowning to be a very real possibility. This is a town of strong swimmers.

Then again, as Mrs. McGinn observes in hushed tones to her daughter on the morning of the burial, one can die just as well in two feet of water as in twenty. It's a fairly simple matter once a person sets his troubled mind to it, and everyone knows that that's exactly what the poor man was. Troubled.

God rest his soul.

It is a blessing, at least, to have the town cemetery on the high ground behind the church. Most of the townspeople grumble about having to slosh up the muddy hill in their worn-out galoshes, but Mrs. McGinn is glad to do it because she is determined to get a better look at the new minister and his wife. She only caught a glimpse of them through the foggy windows of their car as they rolled through town last night. The woman looked beautiful, Mrs. McGinn admits to herself, but she is hoping that the beauty of the minister's wife will turn out to be something like the beauty of a fine impressionist painting: lovely in certain lights and best when seen from farther away, but a muddle of colors and textures when one stands with one's nose right up against the gilded frame. It has been years since Mrs. McGinn was in an art museum—whatever museums this town once had have long since closed up shop and taken their objects elsewhere—but there was once a time when she was quite interested in art and she likes to think she still knows a thing or two about beauty.

She would not begrudge anyone a beautiful wife, but in truth she would prefer for the woman to be a little plainer so that her own daughter would look a little better in comparison. Mrs. McGinn is not worried about herself; when it comes to good looks she has certainly had her day, and she is reassured by the belief that if she were twenty years younger she would not pale in comparison. Indeed, when she glances in her most trustworthy mirror at certain times of day, and especially when she applies a touch of lipstick before doing so, she doesn't believe that she pales so much even now.

"It's not a competition, Evelyn," her husband reminds her gruffly when he sees her craning her neck for a better view at the cemetery.

Mrs. McGinn sees the flicker of his irritation (she is always on the watch for it), and so she falls back on her heels and lowers her chin. "I know that it's not a competition, Jackson," she retorts. "But I feel as though they're looking down on us."

"That's because we're all standing on a goddamn hill," he snaps. He waves his hand at the minister and his wife, both wrapped like seals in slick black raincoats while the steeple looms pale and solemn behind them. The cemetery runs down on an incline from the backyard of the church, weeds creeping across the graves, puddles collecting at the bases of the tombstones. The minister and his wife are standing closest to the church's whitewashed siding while the mourners range unevenly across the drowning grass below them, all sheltered beneath the nylon canopies of their umbrellas. Mrs. McGinn swivels her head to count her neighbors, surprised to find that nearly everyone is here. She nods at Mauro, the silver-haired Italian who owns the general store, and watches Leesl, the former music teacher, pace the ground beside her father's grave. Mrs. McGinn's daughter is leaning back against her fiancé, wrapped up in his arms. Mrs. McGinn shakes her head and turns away.

"The whole town turned out for this," she mutters to her husband.

He shrugs, glowers at his neighbors. "No one cared enough to check up on the old man when he was still alive," he replies, "and now that the guy's gone, suddenly everyone feels sorry enough to make the trek up here and stand in the goddamn rain and hear the new one tell us that all is forgotten, our sins are forgiven." He spits into the grass to show his wife exactly how he feels about this.

"What sins, Jackson?" she demands, her whisper fierce. "What do you mean by that?"

Her husband spits again. "Why would a *minister* walk into a river, Evelyn? What could have driven him to it?" He starts to say something else, but Mrs. McGinn snaps at him to keep quiet and tells him she doesn't want to hear it.

The truth is that she has, in fact, already heard it. For the past few days her diner has been buzzing with speculation over the death of the minister. Was it an accident or not? Did anyone know anything about the old man—what he was thinking, how he was doing? Had anyone seen him since they stopped attending services at the church all those months—years?—ago? Was he happy or not? And if not, why not? Many of the townspeople admitted that they, too, were largely unhappy in this place. They looked out the windows of the diner at the river, the water shoving at the crumbling banks, and a collective shudder ran through them.

Mrs. McGinn is grateful that the new minister begins to speak right then. She peers at the woman standing behind him, trying to get a better glimpse of her face.

"Good morning, everyone," says the new minister. His voice is booming, his stance wide and self-assured. "My name is Noah. I haven't met most of you yet, but I'm glad to be here with you. Of course I wish that I had been called to this town under happier circumstances, but I am certain that we will make it through this difficult time together. None of us is ever given a heavier burden than he can bear."

He has a speech prepared. With the calm and practiced grace of his vocation, he lays out his plans for the church and the congregation, his hands fluttering like swallows and his face shining as radiantly as the future he describes for them. Grace and faith; light and life. Mrs. McGinn dismisses these words as they reach her and waits for Noah to say something more concrete, something more helpful. She waits for him to acknowledge the rain, at least, or to say something about the nature of his predecessor's death. Her neighbors wait, too—she can see them all leaning slightly forward, their gazes flicking between the ruddy face of the new minister and the open grave of the old one. They look as disappointed as Mrs. McGinn feels when Noah wraps up his speech, shivers a little in his damp clothing, and steps away from the headstone while the grizzled undertaker and his son shovel dirt over the coffin.

"That was it?" exclaims Mrs. McGinn. "That's the extent of his advice to us—*hope* and *pray*? For God's sake!" Before her husband can growl at her to stop, she has stormed her way through the throng of colored umbrellas and come to a halt in front of the minister and his wife.

"Noah," she says, jamming her hand into his. "Evelyn McGinn."

"Evelyn!" repeats the minister with evident delight, beaming at her. "Yes, I've heard all about you! People say that you're the one who keeps this place afloat. Is that true?"

Mrs. McGinn leans backward, disarmed. Noah's grin is more engaging than she had anticipated. "Well," she says, "I do my best."

Noah nods, looking past her to the jumble of gray buildings that squat along the river below them. A drop of rain falls on his nose, and he wipes it away with impatience. "What a charming little town!" he exclaims. His stilted enthusiasm reminds Mrs. McGinn of a candidate for public office. "The downtown looks exactly like a postcard. When you have some free time, I'd love to have you tell me more about it."

At this, Mrs. McGinn snorts. No one cares about this place anymore. The only reason Noah is expressing interest is because he feels that, after only two days, he already has a claim on it—but this is *her* town; not his. Mrs. McGinn is the one who has spent a lifetime here. It is she who was elected to head the town council (the first woman, by the way, to ever serve on it), and she will not have her authority undermined by this man's ignorant enthusiasm.

"Really, Minister?" she says, her voice sharp and unforgiving. "Well, what would you like to know?"

Surprised by her tone, Noah doesn't answer immediately. In the silence that follows, his wife takes a step forward.

Mrs. McGinn's eyes rake across the woman's paperlike skin, coming to rest upon her steady, slate-gray gaze. She is good-looking, but in an unremarkable way. Average nose, average ears. The only feature that might stand out in a crowd is her hair: glossy waves the color of ravens' wings. At the sight of it Mrs. McGinn reaches up to pat her own carroty curls, piled high into a loose bun on the top of her head. She dyes her hair herself at least once a month but even so, she still finds fresh silver strands every few days and then she yanks them out, unhappily, clamping her mouth shut to keep from crying out. No one ever said that beauty would be painless, her mother had told her on her sixteenth birthday as she unwrapped her first pair of high heels. The same thing goes for love and for marriage, Mrs. McGinn has told her own daughter time and again when the girl walks into a room to find her sweeping up a heap of broken china. No one ever said that love would be painless.

Noah's wife makes a broad and graceful gesture with her arm that seems to take in the clouds, the umbrellas, mud, and the river in the distance all at once. "Is it true what we've heard about the weather here?" she asks Mrs. McGinn. "Has it really been raining for so long?"

Mrs. McGinn hates this question. "Yes," she says curtly. "It's been raining a long time."

Long enough to drive the mayor away, after all; long enough to lose most of the old police force, many of the shopkeepers, the artists, the businessmen. The sheriff has kept his office in the decaying town hall and there are still two firefighters with little else to do but play poker in the empty firehouse, since most everything is too damp to burn. A few years back they were so short on teachers that they started busing children to a school a few districts over. It is Mrs. McGinn's husband, in fact, who drives the bus there and back on muddy roads, one trip in the morning and one in the afternoon, an hour each way. He doesn't like the job, of course; he claims that the crying of the children nearly drives him off the road.

Worst of all was the effect of the rain on the zoo. That zoo had been what placed them on the map; it was what made them famous, what provided their income, what gave this town its character. There are exotic animal tracks in the sidewalk, for goodness' sake; there are statues of polar bears and elephants at intersections. The walls of the diner are crowded with wildlife paintings, and most of the townspeople sport zoo paraphernalia on their key chains, T-shirts, and jackets. In the old glory days, items such as these would fly off the shelves faster than Mauro could stock them, but lately he has been giving them away for free. The townspeople used to find it hard to believe that what had started out as a two-goat operation in a businessman's backyard had grown into a two-hundred-animal operation that drew high-rolling tourists all the way from the other side of the country. Now they find it hard to believe that the institution that allowed them to flourish for so long has wilted and waned to such an extent that no one but the zookeeper and his fiancée will set foot in it. They shake their heads, disgusted by their situation. And what is there to do about it? they would like to know. Nobody goes to the zoo in the rain.

"Is there any explanation for the weather?" Noah wants to know, taking over from his wife. "It's amazing that so many of you are still here, with conditions like these."

Mrs. McGinn frowns, and her entire face puckers. "Well, there used to be a lot more of us," she says finally. "This place is nothing like it once was."

It hurts her to admit this, as it always does. Mrs. McGinn understands perfectly well that this town has its problems, and that these days it is difficult to scratch out a life for oneself here. She knows that when her daughter's classmates and friends decided to establish careers for themselves in teaching, in business, in law, they looked elsewhere because this town had no real future for businesses more ambitious than her own diner, Mauro's general store, the dwindling demands on the single pharmacy, the department store, or anything other than the very bare essentials required for life in a small gray ghost town. She suspects that even her own daughter is champing at the bit to leave this place, and she is well aware that once the girl is gone, there will be little reason for her to return. Mrs. McGinn is a woman of strong convictions, but she is no fool. She knows how the world works.

"What we need from you, Minister, is some kind of action," she says now to Noah. "The rain has kept us too low for too long. We don't know why it's still raining, and we don't know why Reverend Matthews did what he did. People are looking for answers, and now that you're here, they'll be looking to you. I hope you won't let us down."

If Noah's face loses some of its enthusiastic color at her words, Mrs. McGinn does not notice. She is gazing instead at the town that lies below her, the buildings battered and weary. She knows that many of the town's former inhabitants—indeed, even many of those malcontented souls still living here today—would tell her that it would be wiser to give up on this place, to pack her bags and try her hand at life in a place that isn't forever haunted by its own past, that needn't live within the shadow of its former glory. But who among us is not haunted by her past? Mrs. McGinn would like to know. Who among us is as bright or as full or as strong as she was, or as she could be?

three

In the town where Mauro grew up, the showers were brief and radiant.

When he remembers Italy now, he remembers the sun beaming through sheets of rain that slid in colored panes from the clouds to the ground. He remembers indigo skies and salty gusts of wind and the crisp, clean air at the end of thunderstorms, when standing water shimmered in piazzas like small and shallow wishing wells. He has been to Rome many, many times, and he has heard the legend the tour guides feed the tourists between slices of street pizza and cups of handmade gelato, so he is well aware of the connection between water and wishes.

What he wouldn't give right now for two scoops of pistachio!

The legend goes like this: By throwing one coin in the fountain, the tourist is guaranteed to return someday to Rome. The second coin promises marriage; the third is for charity.

When he was a child, so cynical of superstition, it was easy to scoff at the foreigners and dismiss the legend. As he has aged, however, and as his return trip to Italy has become more and more unlikely, he has found himself wishing that he, too, had the assurance of knowing that he would one day set foot again on Italian soil. When he thinks about the untossed coin, he realizes that this simple act of faith, the flinging of the token, would have been of great comfort to him. Perhaps it would not even have mattered whether he returned, as long as he could remain happy in his hope. Now that he is older and, as he would say, wiser in the ways of the world, he tends more toward the superstitious beliefs initially impressed upon him by his grandmothers because it reassures him to feel as though he has some control over his fate, as if he possesses the knowledge necessary to crack the code of an enigmatic and exasperating cosmos.

How was he to know what fortune had in store for this place? When he arrived here, the future shone like a silver river in the sun—and now all the hope that is left in this town is rotting in the rain. Mauro tries not to think about it, for what good does it do to dwell on these things? He makes wishes on puddles and wards off bad omens. He has been betting on this town for years, and when the situation begins to go from bad to worse, he has little choice but to hold his head high and continue to bet on it still.

True, he also has a plan that is more concrete. At the end of every month he transfers the remainder of his profits from his cash register into sealed plastic bags, which he then carries down to the river and tucks under the seat of his old fishing craft. He knows this is a senseless place to hide his life savings, but that is what he likes about it. It is illogical, unreasonable. No one would think to look for it there. He has not yet saved enough to buy a ticket to Italy or to reestablish himself at home, but one day he will. He is sure of it.

In the meantime, he has the general store. Perhaps he shouldn't have it, but he does, thanks to one of the few lucky hands he's been dealt in his life. The owner of the store was drunk on Mauro's wine when he made up his mind to gamble it, and the day after he lost it to Mauro he packed up his wife and his kids and took off. No one has heard from him since. Mauro believes that the man was planning to leave anyway, that there must have been some other, underlying reason for his behavior, something else that was distressing him—why else would he have been so careless with the store?—but Mauro never found out what it was. And then he was gone. Mrs. McGinn blames Mauro for the family's departure, but Mauro tries not to let this bother him. That woman is always blaming somebody for something.

"But only because she is loving this town," he explains to the minister and his wife when Noah tells him what she said to them. "Her love is a rough love."

"Do you mean tough love?" asks the minister, a bit perplexed, but Mauro has already ambled away.

It is the day after the burial, and Mauro is walking through the old church with Noah. The new minister requested his advice for fixing up the building, which has fallen into disrepair. Rain is seeping in beneath the windowsills and dripping through a leaky ceiling. As he goes, Mauro marches through the moss sprouting plush from soaking carpets, swinging his arms through cobwebs, stepping over broken glass, and compiling a mental inventory of everything that needs to be cleaned or repaired. He speaks aloud for Noah's benefit.

"The benches, they are seeming okay," he says, rapping the back of the pew with his knuckles. He climbs the steps to the altar. "The carpet up here, maybe we need a new one, because of the things that are growing. Painting, we do that. We fix the windows and dry the basement and check the pipes and the wires and the fans."

"But the birds?" asks Noah's wife from the back of the church, gazing up into the rafters. "What will we do with them?"

Mauro glances up, and then down. The ceiling is high and dark and the white plaster is cracked, crossed with oaken beams that are lined with scraps of leaves and hollow pieces of yellow straw that the birds have carried inside to construct their nests. The floor is littered with twigs and halves of broken blue eggshells. Some of the birds perch on the backs of empty pews and peck at hymnals while others fly from beam to beam in great swooping arcs, diving at Noah's head when he accidentally steps below their nests. He ducks and hurries to join Mauro at the altar, where the Italian proceeds to point out the warped wood of the pulpit and the rust eating away at the chain that bears the eternal flame. The flame has long since gone out.

"There's certainly a lot to get done!" exclaims Noah, lifting a hand and wiping it across his brow. It is cool in the church, but his forehead is beaded with sweat. He turns to Mauro with a smile so broad that his face could have buckled with the weight of it. "Well, as Solomon would say—let us arise and be doing! Fear not, be not dismayed!"

"What?" says Mauro.

"First Chronicles," cites Noah's wife, still at the far end of the aisle.

"Ah," says Mauro. He shoots a toothy grin back at the minister. "What the optimist! How full are your glasses!"

"I'm sorry?" says Noah.

"It's an expression," Mauro explains. He loves nothing better than a good idiom. "You and me, Minister, we are like the two beans of the pod. We are the happy ones, the hopers. I am hoping that one of these days I will be going home, and you are hoping that if you can be fixing the roof and the lights and the carpets and the windows and the pipes and the—"

"Yes, I get it," says Noah, a little more sharply than before.

"You are hoping that if you are fixing those things, then everyone will be coming to your church!"

"Why wouldn't they?" presses Noah. Mauro sees him glance

toward the silhouette of his wife, her face tinted blue in the wet light of the stained-glass window. "Why wouldn't they come for me, if they were coming for Reverend Matthews?"

Mauro shrugs, waves at the moss in the carpet. "Why do you think this place is looking this way? We have not been coming to the church for a lot of time now."

"But you did once?"

"Of course," replies Mauro. "But then the rain was coming. And then it was raining here for a long time. So long that nobody now is remembering when it was starting. And finally one day the old minister said, enough and enough, we will all go to the church and we will pray for the rain to end. So, we all went to the church for the praying. Even the people who were not really believing in God were praying because why not? And we prayed and we prayed. For a long time we were going up to the church every day, and we were praying and we were singing and we were lighting the candles. It was beautiful, the church with all the candles."

"And what happened?" asks Noah.

Mauro shoots him a wry grin. "Look to the windows!" he says. "What do you mean, what happened? Nothing happened. No one heard the singing, no one answered the prayers. After many days some people stayed home, and were not climbing up to the church anymore. Then more people stayed home, and more, and finally no one was going to the church at all." He peers at Noah, his gaze keen and kind. "It is good to believe about your God. It is a beautiful dream, and it helps some people, it gives them strength in heart. But it is harder to believe about your God when we are asking and asking and asking for help and it is turning out that no one is listening to us. Then we are thinking: What is the bother? Maybe there is no God up there, or maybe He is there, and He is hearing us, but He doesn't care."

There is a pause. Noah moves to the splintered bench behind the pulpit, his limbs heavy. He drops down to the bench and takes a long, slow breath. His wife is by his side before Mauro has a chance to speak, flitting around her husband with worried hands.

"Noah," she says. "Are you all right?"

He shakes his head as a dog would shake off water. "Of course I am," he says briskly. "Of course. This church will be even more of a challenge than I had expected—but it's nothing I can't handle."

His wife agrees. "Right," she says. "It's nothing we can't handle. You helped double the congregation in the city, remember? People here will love you just as much as they did there."

She slides into place beside him, opens her leather satchel, and removes a pen and a softcover notebook. While Mauro watches, the two of them sit together with their heads bowed over the paper, speaking in soft, low tones to each other. After a few minutes they seem to forget that Mauro is there, and although he considers leaving, he remains where he is. He whistles to the birds in the rafters and pulls a stale cookie from his pocket to tempt them down, and when they alight calmly on the railing right in front of him, he wonders if this is how the old minister filled his time throughout all those rainy months while he was waiting for his congregants to return to him. When one of the birds pecks the crumbs from Mauro's palms, Mauro feels a quick stab of guilt. Why didn't he come up here to check on the man? Why didn't he invite him for a glass of wine or for a meal? What was the old man thinking about as he watched his church disintegrating around him, as he waited for the rain to cease its pattering against his leaky roof?

When Noah and his wife rise from their bench and approach Mauro with a list of supplies they will need from the general store, Mauro nods at them and accepts the list without comment. He shrugs, shakes Noah's hand, and promises to deliver the supplies tomorrow morning. Who is he to tell them that their plan to rebuild this congregation is a futile one? Would they even listen if he told them to get out of here while they still could?

The truth is that Mauro is not certain what he believes. He will not pray to Noah's God, but he will throw salt over his shoulder if he spills it and he will only have his hair cut at the new moon. His neighbors find him ridiculous, but that hasn't stopped him yet.

If, in order to avoid bad luck, Mauro refuses to set his hat on the bed, or step on a spider, or place his bread upside down on the table—where is the harm? If he deliberately does not tell a mother who enters his general store that her baby is beautiful because he fears calling a hex down upon the poor child's head—should that mother not be grateful? When Mauro left Italy for America he did not believe in any of this because he was immature and impressionable and he believed instead in things like justice and science and humanity and friendship. If he realizes now that these ideals are harder to come by in this country than he expected them to be, if he sometimes feels friendless or heartsick, why not place some faith in the other powers that could be? Why not allow himself to feel as though his small human choices (the placement of a hat or a feather), the actions that no one else notices or cares about, are not unattended but instead are witnessed and remembered by a highly responsive universe?

In any case, if he had thrown a coin into that Roman fountain, at least he would have more hope of returning. He didn't always love the rain in Italy, either, but at least there it didn't feel so heavy, or so dark. At least there, the sun shone through. This is how he remembers it.

He has never yearned so much for home.

four

The zookeeper became a zookeeper in the first place because even though he doesn't like animals much at all, he likes people even less.

He finds animals dull and people tiresome and the only person he can bear to be around for more than ten minutes at a time is Mrs. McGinn's daughter. If truth be told (as the zookeeper always believes it should be), she has her faults. For example: she sneezes all the time. Her toes turn slightly in. As an only child she is spoiled and aggressively competitive. She talks with food in her mouth. Finally, and not least, her mother has instilled in her a sense of distrust toward the world in general and lovers in particular that the zookeeper has had to work hard to overcome. If ever he speaks too long to a pretty visitor at the zoo (these are few and far between), to one of his female neighbors, even to a woman of the McGinns' own clan, he will catch in his fiancée's eye the same fierce gleam that he sees in the eyes of wolves or predatory cats. He is not afraid of much, but sometimes he is afraid of her.

"Don't even think about it," she'll say to him, her voice needlelike and cold.

"I'm not!" he says. "I'm not thinking about it at all!"

She will then plant a proprietary kiss on his mouth, satisfied. He watches the fluttering of her hair as she stalks away from him, certain that if she ever caught him with someone else, she'd take one of the toothy bread knives from the diner and come after him. He loves how perilous she can be.

Sometimes when she turns up to see him at work they will lounge together on the banks of the silver river where it runs through the zoo. Lately she has taken to bringing an oversized beach umbrella that she stakes into the mud beside them, providing makeshift shelter from the rain. He likes to examine her there, to trace his finger through the red-gold down that runs along her limbs, to watch one of her hands toy with the end of her meager braid while the other rests on the zookeeper's knee or on the knuckle side of his hairy fist. If she is there after hours he will often take her hand and lead her back to the long-abandoned gibbon enclosure, where he will push her up against the hard stucco wall and make love to her right there, the gray wolves howling in the woods and the rain rushing through the eaves above them, her feet off the ground and her legs wrapped halfway around his back, which is as far as she can reach. The zookeeper is not a small man. He is bulky and muscular and covered in a coarse dark hair. He towers over his neighbors and shows no fear of the animals, not even at feeding time when the wolves lunge toward the buckets of raw red meat that he hangs from thick, fleshy wrists. Mrs. McGinn's daughter licks the ridges of his ear, calls him her grizzly bear.

On his rounds he whistles in the rain and swings a pail of oats and overripe vegetables back and forth through the air. Later on he pushes a wheelbarrow full of hay from the barn to the cattle enclosure, one hand shielded over his face to keep the water from falling into his eyes. He dumps the hay over the fence while the highland cows consider him without fear, their gazes half hidden beneath their shaggy locks, their coats soaked. Behind them the antelope and the gazelle are grazing, their silhouettes soft and gold against the charcoal sky. The reindeer stands stock-still beneath a dogwood tree, his antlers caught once again in the branches. The zookeeper heaves a sigh, straddles the fence, and strides over with his garden rake to untangle the stupid beast. His boots sink several inches in the mud and it requires some effort to lift them. He grunts at the rain, exasperated and disturbed. The zoo was built in the lowest part of town, a piece of ground that used to be marshlands until it was filled in before construction. The triangle-shaped park juts out into the water, bordered on two sides by the river and on the third by a small creek that runs in front of the main entrance. At the time, the city planners believed that the site would attract native waterfowl and that the arching bridge to the entrance would soon become iconic. Now the zookeeper wonders how many more days he has until the entire zoo sinks back into the swamps from which it rose.

He trudges through the rest of his tasks while he waits for Mrs. McGinn's daughter to join him. As the daylight fades she comes to find him where he stands in the aviary, listening to the parrot and watching the toucan swoop in yellow-green arcs. In the corner is a mesh enclosure filled with butterflies, and on the far side of the room is the pen with the lone eagle. The bird shifts on its perch when she enters, and the zookeeper turns to greet her.

"Adam!" she says. She takes several swift steps forward to embrace him.

He pulls her against his chest, feels her heart hammering through her coat and her breath blowing warm on his neck. She presses her lips briefly to his and then pulls away.

The zookeeper reaches for her hand. Lately, she has been increasingly restless.

"Are you all right, Angie?" he has asked her, five or six times a day for the past week.

She will shrug and tell him she is fine. But a few minutes later she will inevitably ask him: "Adam, do you think it was an accident or not?"

To be honest, the zookeeper does not particularly care. He considers himself something of a fatalist, having shoveled out enough exotic animal carcasses to be more aware than most of the ever-present pressure of mortality.

"We'll all be gone sooner or later, Angie," he will tell her, "whether we walk into the river or not."

The zookeeper finds a strange kind of comfort in the thought, but his fiancée has not seemed reassured. Now she extricates her hand from his, stooping down to lift the pail of fish he has set out for her. As he follows her out the door and over the flat wooden footbridge into the simulated savannah, he notes that the water has risen high enough to cover the planks. When he catches up to her on the path he glances sideways at her, nodding without listening to what she is telling him. Like her mother, the girl is a serious talker—and yet he appreciates the simple fact of her presence, loping along at his side with her words running quick as a hummingbird's heart.

Taking a shortcut through the reptile house and the plaster cave for the nocturnal mammals, they head toward the Antarctic zone. Most of the enclosures they pass are empty of animals, choked with drowning weeds and littered with boards that have broken away from fences or feeding troughs. This zoo is becoming as spectral as the town itself. When the place was at its peak the dinnertime rounds would have taken the keepers three times as long, but now the zoo houses only sixty animals in total. Without a steady stream of visitors, the zoo's funds are running dry. The animals that die are not replaced and there are few new births. The zookeeper's home is on the grounds, in a spartan apartment above what used to be the gift shop, and at night he sometimes dreams he hears the hoofbeats and roars of beasts long gone.

At the penguin tank the zookeeper holds the pail while Mrs. McGinn's daughter reaches in to choose a fish from the heap. He looks away as she flings a clammy tail toward the birds. Dead fish make him feel seasick.

Mrs. McGinn's daughter takes great pleasure in feeding the penguins. They are exotic, comically formal, and monogamous. At the tank she remarks upon this fact and her hard face softens, her eyes warming to her favorite subject.

"Tell me the others," she insists, dipping a hand again into her pail. "You know—the animals who mate for life."

"Gibbons, swans, bald eagles," he says automatically, rattling off the list that he has rattled off a hundred times before. "Wolves, termites, beavers, pigeons, prions."

"Prairie voles, black vultures," she continues. Her tongue trips lightly over the names, and her tone rises and falls as if in song.

"That's right," he says.

He doesn't mind these pointed reminders of hers. As the daughter of a revolving set of fathers, perhaps it is only to be expected that she find comfort in stories of successful relationships and in the knowledge that the animal world is not completely devoid of constancy. There is such a thing, he is slowly training her to believe, as fidelity.

When the fish are all gone, she sighs and her head falls to his shoulder. He runs his hand through her wet and tangled hair, watches the rise and fall of her shoulder. The freckles on her face stand in sharp relief to her skin.

"When are we leaving, Adam?" she asks.

His heart thuds a little harder, and he hopes she cannot feel it. "Soon," he says.

"Have you had any luck finding a replacement?"

"Some," he replies. He swallows, thickly. "But I haven't found a perfect match yet."

"All right." She lifts her head and turns to face him, her green eyes gone suddenly dark. "You haven't forgotten what we talked about, right?" she asks. Her tone is unforgiving. "You haven't forgotten our plans?"

Behind her, two wild boars plod along the cracked and puddled sidewalk, shoving their snouts into the mud. In the distance the zookeeper can see one of the peacocks flaring his tail.

He doesn't know what to tell her. When she agreed to marry him, she did so on the condition that they would not stay here forever, that sooner (rather than later) they would leave her family and his animals behind and they would start over together, somewhere new, preferably in a place where it didn't rain all the time and where she would not be forever trapped under her mother's formidable thumb. That is the plan, and the zookeeper does not have the nerve to tell his fiancée that his heart isn't in it.

The truth is that when no one replied to the job listing he sent out to the newspapers, when not a single person applied for the position or showed up during the week he had set aside for interviews, he found himself unexpectedly relieved. It was then that he realized he has no desire to give up his job. He has a place here that he understands, a role that only he can fulfill. At the zoo there is a purpose for him.

The zookeeper considers his fiancée. When his gaze falls upon the long arc of her neck he wonders (as he has wondered before) how much of his attraction to her is founded upon this giraffe-like feature, how much upon her willowy silhouette, her long black lashes. Her chin is raised in his direction and she is glaring at him through the rain, blinking at high speed. Her drive to leave this place is instinctive, he knows—to her it seems like a matter of life or death. She will insist (falsely) that he doesn't love her. She does not understand that if he takes off now, if he abandons his post while the rain is still falling, the animals that do not starve will surely drown.

"Of course I remember," he says. "Patience, Angie. Everything will be fine."

And will it? He pulls her close again and stares out over her head into the distance, toward the single, crumbling highway that links this town to the rest of the world. There is only one way into this place, and one way out. The zookeeper has no idea what sort of life exists for them beyond these hills, and right now he has no interest in trying to imagine it. So instead he kisses her damp hair and comforts her, making promises he is not certain he can keep.

five

Dr. Yu had always known that she would be a doctor, and she had chosen long ago to become a heart surgeon specifically because she had wanted to be the kind of doctor who saves lives.

"Anyone can fix broken limbs," she often declared. "I'm going to save lives."

She had long, slim fingers with clean nails and a steady hand. She had perfect vision and a level tone, and although her ears were pierced, they were always unadorned.

Her best friend used to remark that perhaps she herself could claim to save lives by association because she was the one who helped the soon-to-be Dr. Yu become Dr. Yu. When other acquaintances marveled at her best friend's dedication, her best friend simply offered her most winsome smile, turned up her palms, and said: "What else is a best friend for?" She quizzed the soon-to-be Dr. Yu on anatomy diagrams drawn in red ink on the back of white index cards, she knocked on her door on the mornings of exams to make sure that she ate a hearty breakfast of scrambled eggs and toaster waffles, and if they made dinner together at night she asked the soon-to-be Dr. Yu to recount the lectures the medical students attended, and then she exclaimed very appreciatively over the heft of the textbooks and the complexity of the material to be learned by heart.

"It's a funny phrase, isn't it: learn by heart," her best friend had once observed.

"People don't actually learn by heart," said the soon-to-be Dr. Yu. "We should really say: to learn by hippocampus. Short-term memories, like names or numbers or insignificant others, we store primarily in the dorsolateral prefrontal cortex, and it's the hippocampus that is responsible for consolidating short-term memories into long-term memories, which are stored by the intensification of synaptic connections throughout the brain."

"Right," said her best friend, who had helped the soon-to-be Dr. Yu review notes for the neuroscience exam. "Extra credit: What animal does the hippocampus resemble?"

"A seahorse," recalled the soon-to-be Dr. Yu.

Her best friend nodded. "From the Greek: *hippos*, the word for 'horse,' plus *kampos*. Which means 'sea monster.'" She smiled at the soon-to-be Dr. Yu, who frowned sternly back.

"You're good at this," she told her best friend, tapping her pencil on the textbook for emphasis. "Why don't you try for an M.D., too?"

Her best friend laughed lightly. "I'm not like you," she replied. "We can't all save lives."

What was there to say to that? The soon-to-be Dr. Yu didn't answer, but for some reason the statement stayed with her. She was the only woman in her graduating class. She completed her degree and flew through her residency and now that she has been a practicing doctor for several years, she finds her best friend's statement to be more accurate, more prescient than ever. Although she is proud of what she has accomplished, she must admit that it is difficult to be the rare woman in a field dominated by men; it is exhausting to feel compelled to prove her worth at every step. Although she never says so to anyone—not even to her best friend, who is both impressed by Dr. Yu and baffled by her relentless ambition—lately she has found herself wondering if her decision to become a doctor was the right choice. She is not always happy, and she is rarely at peace. Mostly she is tired: so dead on her feet that there are many days when she steps out of the hospital and stares for several seconds at the pink sky above the parking lot, trying to determine whether it is dawn or dusk.

It is only two weeks since her best friend has been gone from the city, but already Dr. Yu feels her absence. They have known each other since they became roommates ten years ago, when the soon-to-be Dr. Yu placed an ad in the newspaper for someone to share her two-bedroom townhouse while she worked her way through med school. At their first meeting, the soon-to-be Dr. Yu found the young woman to be exactly as she had sounded on the telephone: soft-spoken, polite, disarming. As a roommate she showed a strong desire to make herself useful, and so Dr. Yu did not shy away from making use of her. By the time that Dr. Yu graduated, she had the feeling that her roommate knew as much about medicine as she did. They had become best friends within the first six months of living together—in large part, perhaps, because neither of them had all that many other friends to choose from—and when Dr. Yu took a job at the hospital nearby, they decided to carry on as roommates.

When Dr. Yu realized that in all their years together they had never once had a fight, she tried to stir something up—just to see what would happen. But her best friend never took the bait. She remained even-keeled, conciliatory. There were a few months when Dr. Yu deliberately stopped doing her share of the housework and waited to see how long it would take her best friend to bring it up. But her best friend never did. She merely redoubled her efforts (uncomplainingly), and if anything, the house was cleaner than it had been before. Cowed into admitting defeat, Dr. Yu finally picked up a sponge and went back to doing dishes. Apparently her best friend was impossible to irritate. Who was Dr. Yu to try to change her?

Dr. Yu became accustomed to her best friend's intuitive loyalty and her unswerving support. It wasn't as though Dr. Yu did nothing for her in return; on the contrary. She took her best friend home for holidays, since she seemed to have no family of her own. She helped her build a darkroom in their extra bathroom so that she could expand her work as a photographer. When her best friend had her heart broken—which she did, in those early days, quite a few times—it was Dr. Yu who cheered her, who promised that all of this was for the best and soon something better would come along. For all of her general good humor, her best friend was not an optimist by nature. In the darker, sadder moments of her early twenties she could tend toward melancholia, playing up the part with darkened nails and somber lipstick. Somehow she seemed to be constantly moving even when she was sitting still, solemn and straight-backed in a kitchen chair with Dr. Yu's notes splayed open before her. With her monochromatic wardrobe and the insistent fluttering of her hands and her feet, she reminded one of nothing so much as a dark, fretful bird, its wings forever beating against the windowpanes.

Although Dr. Yu doesn't like to admit it to herself, she thrived on her best friend's veneration. Perhaps that is the main reason why they became so close in the first place. It was always clear to Dr. Yu that her best friend was in awe of her, but it wasn't until after Noah came into their lives—and her best friend's full attention was displaced—that Dr. Yu realized how much she depended on her friend, and on that feeling of being admired.

Dr. Yu does not have a problem with Noah in particular. It is true that she is skeptical of Noah's zealousness and universal charm; she does not believe that it is possible to maintain such tenacious faith in a world, a being, an idea for which one has no evidence. Dr. Yu cannot tell, furthermore, if Noah appreciates her best friend for herself, for things like her clever comebacks or her fierce loyalty, or if he only loves her because she fits so naturally, so willingly, into the role of the minister's wife. In spite of all this, Dr. Yu is practical enough to realize that whomever her best friend married would have fallen short in her estimation. Noah is fine. Anyone would have been fine. The people we love, she believes, will never find matches that we consider worthy of them. This is what love means.

The sheer speed of that relationship and the announcement of the engagement took Dr. Yu by surprise. After eight years of living with her best friend, shouldn't she have seen it coming? Instead, the transformation was sudden: her best friend stopped helping Dr. Yu with her material, forgot to inquire after her patients. She smiled more often, took up cooking, and started going to church.

"Do you even believe in God?" Dr. Yu demanded, stabbing her fork into her best friend's attempt at a very unsophisticated tuna casserole.

"Noah does," said her best friend with a small smile. "That's good enough for me."

Dr. Yu had kept her mouth shut. She believes that she knows her best friend better than anyone in the world. Does Noah know, for example, every single one of her habits? The show tunes she hums when she is dusting the blinds? The way that she arranges canned goods in the pantry by color? Perhaps he has already realized that she is a troubled sleeper—she suffers through nightmares, sometimes sleepwalks—but how will he know to lock the doors and hide the car keys at night so that she will not try to drive while she is dreaming?

Dr. Yu found out later that her worries were nothing but a waste of energy: the sleepwalking stopped when her best friend met Noah. Furthermore, her other physical tics (the nervous movements of her fingers, her knees) also slowed, and trailed away. Something about Noah put her best friend at ease, and if Dr. Yu was sorry to lose her to the marriage, she was sorrier still that she had not been the one to cure her.

In any case, there was little for Dr. Yu to do but offer her support. Her best friend and Noah moved into the parsonage of a church only a half mile down from Dr. Yu, so they wouldn't be far. At the ceremony, Dr. Yu wore a coral-colored dress and stood at attention to one side of her best friend, gripping both their bouquets in her steady hand. She listened to the sound of thunder outside the chapel, saw the lightning illuminate Noah's eyes, and she watched the exchange of rings with resignation. Dr. Yu had given the bride a comb attached to a short veil studded in pearls, and beneath it her face was rosy and full.

The morning after the ceremony Dr. Yu awoke and staggered from her bed while the world outside her bedroom window was still black and solemn. She ate breakfast standing up in the kitchen, leaning her head back against the cabinets, listening to the clink of her spoon against the bowl and the rush of the occasional car passing on the street in front of her building. She took the bus to the hospital and when she arrived at her locker she slipped out of her sneakers and into her clogs and then she shrugged a white coat—only slightly crumpled—over her shoulders. In the operating room the radio was turned to a low hum and the lights were painful to her eyes. She fixed a mask to her face and took her place beside the attending surgeons.

Coronary bypass surgeries were a relatively new procedure. Dr. Yu had not yet performed one of her own, and so she should have been paying close attention. The patient's chest was spliced open and the surgeons were bent over their work, but she felt distant, drained. What percentage of cells would you need to replace to become someone else? she asked herself. Where does one person end and another begin?

She considered the tangle of organs and the shine of silver surgical clamps in the light over the table and she thought of her best friend asleep beside Noah, dreamless, at peace. Perhaps she never would have made it as a doctor. Dr. Yu has come to learn that working in a hospital means that one sees people when they are at their weakest, their most vulnerable, their most dependent—and although she believes that her best friend would have excelled at the coursework and would never have fainted at the sight of blood, Dr. Yu doesn't believe that she could have borne the sight of so much suffering. The only people who her best friend will allow herself to love are the strong ones: the ones who will never leave her, never let her down.

It is only natural, Dr. Yu supposes, for her best friend's focus to shift now that she has married Noah. She only wishes she had not come to rely on her best friend so; and she wishes that her best friend and Noah had not left the city when they did. With her mother now gone and her father swept up in his grief, Dr. Yu could really use a best friend. She could use someone to console her, someone to reaffirm her commitment to medicine, someone to remind her that the illness was never her fault, that she could not have done more than she did, that just because she became a doctor to save lives, it does not mean that she can save them all.

six

Noah's wife is not surprised by the enthusiasm with which Noah tackles this new project.

Her husband is nothing if not enthusiastic. There have been couples that hesitated over asking him to officiate their weddings because they worried that his excitement would outshine theirs. Noah's wife only knew this because the women would confess it as they were posing for their portrait on the church steps.

"We shouldn't have worried about it," the bride would say apologetically, her hand upon her new partner's lapel. "He was wonderful in there. But all that energy can be so overwhelming! How do you handle it at home?"

Instead of answering, Noah's wife would snap several photos of the happy couple. It was not until later, as she was developing the prints in the darkroom Noah built for her in the shed in their backyard, that she would have time to consider the faces more closely. As she agitated the photograph in the fixer, listening to the chemicals splash against the sides of the plastic tub, she would gaze at the colorless expression of the groom and feel a rush of gratitude and affection for her husband. His energy is exactly what she loves about him.

"How invigorating!" he exclaims to her now, running his fingers through his beard as he contemplates the white paint peeling from the siding of the church. "A real, tangible, sweat-and-blood way to pull a congregation together!"

Of course the task will be difficult, but he reminds his wife that he came to this town precisely *because* it would be difficult. He came to this town because he knew he would be needed.

Noah continues to meet with Mauro, who offers advice that is sometimes helpful and sometimes baffling. He calls in the town electrician and the town plumber, who happen to be the same person. One morning he visits the dank offices of the town bank to assess the state of the church's finances, and that afternoon he rounds up a pair of burly high school seniors to work as his construction crew. They roll their eyes and agree to his offer. With school out for the summer and the movie theater gone out of business, what else is there to do in this town?

"The situation isn't as bad as you might think," Noah tells his wife. "The floors and the fans, yes, we'll work on restoring those. But Mauro was wrong about the pipes and the electrical equipment—that's all fine. The windows and the roof we'll check. And the painting, sure. The mildew. You know."

Every morning he bolts down his cup of coffee and then heads up the hill to the church, his folder of notes tucked underneath his raincoat, to direct his sullen, ragtag work crew to various parts of the building. With them he carries in unwieldy boards of lumber and panes of glass. He ascends a ladder into the rafters, where he washes the windows with bleach and clears out the leaves and the debris. The birds watch him warily—a flock of bright button eyes in the dark. When one of the boys asks Noah what he wants to do about the birds he turns and gazes through the broken panels of stained glass, sees the rain falling coldly into the trees, and decides to leave them where they are.

"What harm are they doing anyone, really?" he asks his wife, who is kneeling nearby. She opens a can of paint and turns to him.

"No harm at all," she assures him. She moves the step stool to the wall, pulls out a small nylon brush, and begins swiping broad stripes of cream-colored paint around one of the door frames. Noah stands for a moment and watches her work: steady, even, silent. Her hair is pulled back and she is wearing one of his old button-down shirts, several sizes too large for her. Before he returns to his crew, he leans in and kisses the shirttail that hangs over her hip.

"I love you," he says. "I love that you're here."

Where else would she be, if not here? What would she be doing, if she were not helping him? As she paints she thinks about the job that she left in the city, remembers the displeasure that darkened the face of the owner when she told him that she was leaving the studio.

"Temporarily?" he pressed her.

"For good," she murmured.

"Well," he said, grudgingly handing over her last paycheck, "I want you to know that your job will still be here if you ever change your mind."

Although she left her work with some regret, she feels somewhat relieved now to be away from it, away from the disjunction between illusion and reality that photography implies. Sometimes she would hear couples screaming at each other in the parking lot on their way into the studio, and yet when they were in front of the backdrop, facing the lens after she had settled them down on their stools with flowers or props, they would kiss or lean into each other's arms as if they were always this content to be together. In one of her dresser drawers at home she has a framed photograph of her own family from when she was an infant: her sister perched upon their mother's knee, both of them smiling broadly into the camera, the baby cradled between them. The apparent tranquillity and the stability they present to the viewer are what Noah's wife marvels over time and again. In real life her family was reckless and desperate, and if she herself has turned out to be somewhat of a skeptic, if she sometimes finds it hard to reconcile the appearance of a picture with the reality of things as they are, perhaps this photograph is the reason why.

Her sister—a full five years older than her and born of a

different father—liked to remind her younger sibling that she was an accident, a mistake made by a mother who had never wanted the first child and who certainly hadn't planned on having the second. "You weren't supposed to be here," the sister would hiss at her at night, when they were huddled in the same bed with the streetlamp shining in the window.

She didn't want to believe her sister, but how could she not? It was clear that she didn't belong in this family. The memories she has of her prodigal mother and her profligate aunts are loud and brightly colored, full of music and the clinking of glasses. She remembers them as daring and laughing, while she herself was awkward and wraithlike, already taller for her age than she should have been. She learned to stand against the wall and make herself invisible until they forgot that she was there, hoping that her mother would not see her and whisk her away to her room, tuck her back into bed beside her sister, and kiss her good night in a rush of rose perfume. Her mother had been an artist and had lived an artist's life: wild, unrestrained.

She remembers her mother's efforts to discover her youngest daughter's hidden talent, enrolling her in drawing classes and singing lessons, handing her musical instruments only to take them away again; her mother even went so far as signing her up for sports, although she was never fast enough or strong enough to be of any use. Instead she spent most of her middle school and adolescent years on the sidelines. Somewhere along the way someone put a camera in her hands, and that was how she found her calling: to point and shoot at greatness, to sidle up close to the strongest or the smartest so that she could capture a little of their luminescence. Later on, after she had learned how to develop the photos by herself, she would bring the prints out of the darkroom and spread them out across the kitchen table and feel as though she had managed to acquire a fraction of that light for her own.

She liked to bring out the best in people, and it was true—she had a knack for it. She learned to look for it in everyone she came across. Indeed, it did not take her long after meeting Noah to realize that he had no "best" self; he was like his picture every day. She used to sit in her pew and look up at him, loving him for the way that he beamed out at his congregation as if they were, each and every one of them, pointing cameras at his face and asking him to smile.

Is she concerned that the people of this town do not seem to be as enthusiastic about the project as her husband is? No, not particularly. In the evenings as she and her husband hike down the hill and head home through town, they meet their neighbors on the street and Noah pulls up short to speak with them. He gestures to the church and lists all the changes he's been making; he reminds them that the building will be ready for services in two weeks. If the townspeople do not respond with the energy of Noah's former congregation, if they seem to gaze at the white steeple in the misty distance with more wariness than hope—well, then it is only a matter of time until her husband turns their hearts and minds around. And if Noah seems to grow a little solemn after these brief meetings, if his steps echo more heavily between the rain-soaked trees that surround them, it is only because he is so weary from his work. Who wouldn't be?

Besides, before he goes to bed he often gets his second wind. "You know, they said it couldn't be done," he calls to her from the bathroom. She hears him turn on the water and splash at his face. "They all warned me against it! They said this town had given up on God a long time ago and that I'd be hard pressed to change them."

"Who said, dear?" says his wife with a yawn. Her fingers are streaked with cream-colored paint. "Who are you talking about?" She undresses and slips below the quilt, trying to ignore the strange wooden carving on the unfamiliar headboard. Now that she has had a few weeks to hang photographs and rearrange the furniture, she doesn't mind this old house so much. It is spacious and warm. Still, it takes some effort to forget that the plates she sets out for dinner are the former minister's plates and the typewriter she hears tapping and chiming from Noah's study is the former minister's typewriter.

"But what's the point of a project if it doesn't have a touch of the impossible to it?" replies Noah, unfazed. When he returns to the room he bends over her and kisses her on the forehead and then looks toward the cheerless window, hardly seeing the rain at all, his countenance feverish with purpose. She turns her head on the pillow to face the same way, and from her position in bed she considers the church in the distance—a white stone figurine against an assembly of clouds that are both soft and ominous.

"Why do you think we came to this town, anyway?" Noah adds, as he slides into bed beside her. He grins. He means it as a joke, of course, but then again there is a little truth in every joke and now she understands that the broken church and broken spirit of this town are exactly what drew him to it.

If lately there have been times when Noah does not answer the questions she poses to him, if he forgets to bring home whatever it is that she asked him to pick up, or if he walks with her in meditative silence—in these moments she reminds herself that the only reason why he cannot hear her is because he is listening to someone else, and perhaps when a man is listening to God the voice fills to the brim of his mind so that it is much harder to hear the small and ordinary person walking in the rain beside him.

But when he is present, he is fully present—his affection palpable, his touch at once tender and electrifying. Under the sheets he reaches for her, his hands cool, and her skin tingles as his blisters—rough and new—graze across her side. He kisses her earlobe and her throat, sliding on top of her. She arches her back and wraps her arms around him, digging her fingers into the hard muscle of his back and feeling his body rock with hers while the rain pounds fast and thick above them.

seven

Leesl used to have a lover but she only ever loved him from afar.

Every day he would call her on the phone and when she heard his voice unraveling through the phone cord, twining in tight spirals across a distance of one thousand five hundred and nine miles, she would fall in love with him all over again. She would feel herself swoon—physically swoon!—and then she would need to clutch the receiver in order to keep herself from toppling to the kitchen floor.

"I love you," the lover would say to Leesl.

"I love you, too," she would reply.

"When are we going to live in the same place?"

"Soon," she would say. "Very soon."

After a few months of long-distance the lover couldn't stand it anymore and so he quit his job and moved to the town. But immediately after his arrival Leesl fell out of love with him and so a week later he moved right back to where he had been before.

He called her from a pay phone as soon as his train arrived. "Why didn't it work?" he said to her across the miles, plaintively.

"I don't know," she said—even though she did know. Her love had been linked to his absence. She did not miss him when he was near her.

When she hung up the phone she was sorry, of course, but not sorry enough to call him back. She lay down on the floor and she cried—Leesl believes that one should always cry at endings—but when she stood up again she felt better. As the days continued to pass she felt better still, and after two weeks she felt that she was almost entirely over the whole affair. When she thought of him it was not with love but with fondness. And some concern.

The townspeople were never quite sure what happened there. They assumed that because Leesl was so mousy (her face pinched, her glasses thick, her walk plodding), the lover had called it off. No one ever would have expected Leesl to call off anything. No one knows Leesl at all.

"She's been jilted, obviously," says Mrs. McGinn to her daughter. "And with her mother gone now to live in that group home in the city—Leesl's got no one. Not a soul."

"Do you think we ought to find her someone new?" asks the daughter.

There is not much to do in a town like this one but gossip.

With the weather so poor for so long, most people spend their time shut up in their own houses. There have been no outdoor art fairs, no markets, no family picnics since the rain began, and the only places people tend to meet one another now are in Mauro's general store or Mrs. McGinn's diner. Sometimes, when the rain lets up a little, they gather in great colored flocks of umbrellas in the town square and they start to plot, pulling at their neighbors' strings like so many marionettes. They do not mean any harm. They intend, in fact, only the best.

"We are only wanting people to be happy," says Mauro with a shrug and a swig from his wine bottle. "Who is to be judging? Who is to be throwing all the many stones?"

"She's clearly suffering from heartbreak," says Mrs. McGinn. "Which means she might *want* to be alone right now."

Although Mrs. McGinn says this with great conviction, she doesn't actually believe it. Each one of her divorces has devastated her. She is convinced that a person can only thrive when she is a part of something: a marriage, a committee, a crowd.

"I'm not alone!" proclaims Leesl, coming to her own defense when she hears them. "Look! Do you want to see a picture of my cats?"

The townspeople do not want to see a picture of Leesl's cats. They have seen all the pictures before.

Only Mrs. McGinn glances dutifully at the photo as she sighs. In truth, the main reason why she is so concerned about Leesl is because she believes that a place is as stable as its most unstable citizen; that one person's depression can affect the entire population, infecting everyone with a gray and dismal seed that, once planted, is difficult to uproot. Look at the old minister, and how his death has shaken the community. The townspeople have spent many hours worrying over his lonely life and his untimely end. Are they at all to blame? they want to know. Should they have been kinder and more patient with him? Could the rain have been sent as punishment? Mrs. McGinn knows that thoughts like these are foolish ones—how could anyone be blamed for something as fickle and as unpredictable as the weather? This is not the Old Testament—but they will not listen when she tries to reassure them. They seem to have conveniently forgotten that it was raining long before he died.

It was Leesl who knew the old minister better than anyone. She taught herself to play the organ as an adolescent and has been going up to the church to provide the music for services for years. She also offers music lessons, but over the past few months the last of her clients has fallen away. No one here feels all that much like singing.

But Leesl doesn't mind. At home she sits contentedly with her cats and her piano, paging through her music books while the cats stare into her fish tank with slanted yellow eyes and bat at the glass with tufted paws. The fish have fins that shine like bands of sequins. They rise from the jungle of their plastic plants and they drift upward with their mouths open, lips kissing the shifting surface. The cats purr and Leesl smiles, looking for songs to play at the new minister's first service. A geranium sits on the windowsill, sturdy and blooming in defiance of the rain.

When she has chosen her hymns, she prepares herself to climb the hill to the church. She slips the tuning knife into the front pocket of her dress and then she walks very cheerily through the streets with her red umbrella.

"Stranger than ever," say the townspeople, exchanging knowing glances. They remember how, in the days following the minister's death, they would approach her to ask what the man was like in those final days—what he talked about, if he seemed happy, if he ever mentioned them. Leesl's answers were always vague and disappointing. By the time the new minister showed up, they had stopped asking.

Someone suggests that perhaps Leesl is in love with Noah.

"You are thinking so?" asks Mauro, and Mrs. McGinn shrugs. The man is terribly attractive.

And yet Leesl is not in love with anyone—not even the long-distance lover, not anymore. The truth is that she likes the church; she feels safe there. She doesn't mind the slow walk up that hill, her boots filling with water and her umbrella pulling in the wind. She would rather be of use than stay at home, waiting to give music lessons to students who never come.

As she draws closer, she hears the sound of a hammer ringing through the rain. At the top of the hill she finds Noah on the roof, crouching over the shingles while the wind wraps around the steeple and the bells bang together. His wife is pacing back and forth on the ground below him, looking up at him and shielding her eyes in the rain. Leesl pauses to watch them. She is curious about the minister's wife, and has thought about befriending her (she knows the woman must be lonely in a town like this, where people are no longer accustomed to welcoming strangers); but then Leesl has never felt the need of many friends. Besides, how can she befriend a person who never leaves the house without her husband?

Leesl goes ahead and lets herself into the building. Once inside she hangs her slicker over the back of a pew and goes to stand alone at the pipes, tapping her tuning knife along the wood and fiddling with the sliders. It is a matter of temperament, she knows; each organ has its own pitches, its own quirks. Her task is to make this one sing.

It is important to Noah that the organ be perfect and the roof stop leaking. He told her so the other day. The buckets below the rafters are already halfway full, and the water is rising. She understands that the church cannot be in such a state when the congregants come, but what she does not want to tell the new minister is that she does not believe the congregants will ever come. They were not here for the last minister, and they will not be here for him. She only hopes that Noah will be stronger than the last one, that the failure will not break his heart.

Leesl knows what it is to have a broken heart, and she fears what can happen when the heart doesn't heal. She does not want to think of her long-distance lover, does not want to know how he is feeling because if he truly is in pain, she doesn't think she could bear to know it. That is the problem with love. That is why Leesl prefers to be without it.

It's true that she misses the part of her routine that the phone calls provided, and sometimes she misses the phone calls themselves, and sometimes she even misses the lover, a little bit—but then, that's how Leesl likes it. She likes to miss. She likes to be missed. She defines her love in terms of longing and therefore it is much easier for her to love when the object of her affection is nowhere near her. Not in the same town. Not in the same zip code, or area code. Not even in the same telephone directory.

"It's just so much *easier*," says Leesl to herself, "to love people when they are far away."

Leesl even loves her neighbors, but they would never discern this fact from her behavior. Her house is located on the outskirts of town. When she does attend gatherings she sequesters herself in corners, or stands behind wide wooden tables; and when she meets her neighbors unexpectedly on the street she answers their friendly queries in one or two words and then she steps away and quickly moves on.

The neighbors shake their heads as they watch her go. "That Leesl," they say to one another. "She's as eccentric as they come."

They do not know her; they do not understand her; and this is how Leesl likes it. She is still young enough and she has not yet seen much of the world but she has certainly seen this town, and she has certainly seen the intricacy of these relationships, and she has certainly seen how allowing someone close enough to know and to understand sets up both parties for disillusion and disappointment.

"People are never what we hope they are," said Leesl to her lover as she was breaking up with him. "If you get close enough," she adds, "you find that out."

She listens to the sound of Noah on the roof and rests her fingers on one of the keys. A throaty middle C echoes within the nave.

This is, perhaps, why Leesl will be such a devoted organist, and why it is that she has agreed to come to the church and play even though no one else in the town has expressed any interest in going to church at all. The townspeople do not understand the purpose of glorifying a being that they cannot see or touch or understand, because where is the sense in that? They find the whole notion rather difficult, but Leesl finds it simple, beautifully simple, because she prefers to love, to worship, to praise from a great distance, and there is no greater distance than that between this town and heaven.

eight

Mrs. McGinn wields her umbrella like a weapon.

The reaction is instinctive: a stranger has accosted her outside her diner. One might say that Mrs. McGinn wields her umbrella like a musket, but if she heard this she would (respectfully) disagree. Mrs. McGinn does not believe in muskets. Her mother was a Quaker—a real Quaker, with long hair and hands that trembled—but Mrs. McGinn is not a Quaker even though she still sings the songs that her mother sang and she still eats her baked oats with cream and dark brown sugar and sometimes she still feels a light shine out through her skin from her soul, but when that happens she holds her breath and sits quietly with hands folded in her lap and waits for the light to die away again.

It always does.

Mrs. McGinn is not a Quaker but she is a pacifist, she was born a pacifist and she will die a pacifist, in spite of her marriage to a man who is disinclined to peace; a man who—even if he is abounding in steadfast love—is not slow to anger. Mrs. McGinn learned early on that any harmless household object could become a weapon if it were thrown with enough emotion. Over the years she has dodged, among other things: lamp shades and soup spoons and melons and stuffed animals and plastic soap dishes and hard handfuls of cold cereal pelting the nape of her neck as she turned away. Sometimes, if she is mad enough, she will turn around and sweep the cereal up in her fist and then she will hurl it right back.

"Can I help you?" she demands of the stranger, the tip of her umbrella pointed squarely at his chest. They face each other three feet from the door to the diner. If Mrs. McGinn turns her head a little to the left, she can catch a glimpse of her reflection in the long windows that her daughter wiped clean before closing last night. She likes what she sees: her shoulders are back and her stance is unyielding. The rain falls in a rippling curtain over the side of the awning that extends across the sidewalk.

"Whoa," the man replies, his hands half raised in mock surrender. "At ease, soldier. I didn't mean to startle you."

His skin is sallow, his gaze translucent blue. He would be tall if he were not standing the way he is, with his shoulders hunched and his muscles tense, his eyes flicking up beneath brows as coarse and brown as groundhog fur.

"I asked several people outside where I could find the mayor," he says, deftly brushing the water from his sleeves. "And they sent me here."

Mrs. McGinn lowers the umbrella and immediately extends her hand. "Well," she says, flattered by the title. "We don't have a mayor, but I'm head of the town council. You came to the right place."

"A woman?" says the stranger. His chuckle sounds from deep in his throat. "In charge of the whole town? Well, there's something you don't see every day."

"Times are changing," retorts Mrs. McGinn. After they shake, she makes an attempt to soften her tone. "Please let me know if there is anything I can do to make your stay here as comfortable as possible."

The man looks appalled at the suggestion. "Oh no," he says. "I have no intention of staying. I'm only here to talk to you about the situation."

"The situation?" Mrs. McGinn's smile, though still fixed tightly to her face, decreases in sincerity. "What situation?"

"Let's go inside," the man suggests, "and discuss it."

Mrs. McGinn is not happy, but she moves to unlock the door to the diner and glances at the clock as she enters. Noah's wife will be arriving any minute for the meeting Mrs. McGinn had requested to discuss the photography for her daughter's wedding. Mrs. McGinn had been pleased at the prospect of this appointment because it would allow her the opportunity to bring out all four of her old wedding albums—ostensibly to share her vision for her daughter's nuptials but more truthfully to show off the pictures to someone who has not yet had the good fortune to admire them. She carries them in a waterproof tote bag, the albums wrapped in plastic for extra protection. Once inside she drops them on the nearest table, listening to the thud with a pang of satisfaction. It is clear that she has been through enough weddings herself to be something of an expert on the matter.

The door opens again behind them, the bell chiming, and the minister's wife steps across the threshold. She pushes her hood away from her high, broad forehead and runs her fingers through her hair. Mrs. McGinn greets her and then turns once more to the stranger.

"The diner opens in half an hour," she tells him. "I'll give you ten minutes."

The man moves swiftly to pull out a chair for Noah's wife, who thanks him and sits. Mrs. McGinn pulls back her own chair and pushes the albums across the table. She opens one for Noah's wife to peruse during this unexpected interruption. Noah's wife obediently turns a few pages, but she pauses as soon as the man starts speaking. For the remainder of the meeting she sits as motionless as she might in a pew, her lips slightly parted, leaning forward in attention.

"I'm with the state weather service," the man says. "We're aware of the unusual weather patterns in the mountains, and

I've been sent up to monitor the rain and to notify all the towns in the area that for the time being, there doesn't seem to be an end in sight."

"We're used to the rain by now," announces Mrs. McGinn. "If you're so concerned, why didn't you come years ago, when this whole thing started?"

The weatherman folds his hands together. "Because we've developed better tools," he says shortly, "and so we've got better information. Our radar reports are now computerized and colorized, so we can see and track severe weather patterns with more precision than before. This area in the hills has been of particular interest over the past few years, and from what we can tell, the rain will only get worse—much worse—before it gets better. I'd advise you to come up with an evacuation plan as soon as possible."

"Excuse me?" says Mrs. McGinn.

"An evacuation plan," repeats the weatherman coolly. "You need to leave."

Mrs. McGinn snorts, her fire-colored curls—stiff with hairspray—bobbing above her shoulders. "No one's going anywhere," she says. "Not on my watch."

The weatherman looks from her to Noah's wife, and then to her again. "I don't think you understand the gravity of the situation," he says. He removes a pack of cigarettes from the lining of his coat and pulls one out. Both women watch him light it up.

"Oh, I understand," says Mrs. McGinn. "And I don't know

about all your other towns, but here, we're not afraid of getting our feet a little wet."

"Your houses could flood," he insists.

"Then again, they could not!" she declares. "How do you know?"

"What about that river running through downtown?" he presses her, tapping the cigarette on the plastic ashtray that sits in the center of the table. "What do you think will happen if it rises much higher?"

"It won't," she snaps. "It never has before."

Although she arranges her features to maintain a stern expression, she is beginning to feel the flutter of panic in her gut: one hundred butterfly wings beating against the walls of her stomach. She takes a deep breath, does her best to swat them flat.

Everything will be fine, she reminds herself while the weatherman explains the situation in more detail. Soon the rain will end, as rain always does. In the meantime, there is too much here to lose. She has been witness to the exodus of this town for years; she knows that when people leave, they never come back. Those who have stayed have houses, lives, families here. Most of them have nowhere else to go.

"It's been raining here for a long time," she announces. "And we haven't had a problem yet. I appreciate your concern, but we're staying put. Now if you'll excuse me—I've got to open up the kitchen." She stands and shoves her chair under the table with an air of finality, hopes the weatherman will pick up on the hint.

"Fine," he says. He drops the butt in the ashtray and sways to his feet with lazy grace. "But you haven't seen the last of me. I'm being paid to get you out of here, and I'm not going anywhere until I've done it."

Mrs. McGinn makes no effort to disguise her contempt. "That sounds awfully mercenary," she says.

The weatherman grins. "Damn right it is."

At this, Mrs. McGinn spins on her heel and marches back behind the counter. "Thanks for stopping by," she snaps over her shoulder. Then she slams through the swinging doors.

In the kitchen, she flips the switch on the coffeemaker and places the griddle on the stove. She cracks a cartonful of eggs into a bowl with more force than usual, taken aback by her own anger. This man should not have had such an effect on her; she should not allow herself to be affected by his gloomy prophecies. What does he know?

She glances through the round window in the swinging door, sees Noah's wife gazing out at the street with an expression of relief. Like Mrs. McGinn herself, she seems glad that the weatherman has gone for the time being. Perhaps she is grateful not to have been asked to take a side. Her fingertips are resting on the open photo album, and Mrs. McGinn wonders which picture it is that she has paused upon; which husband is smiling up at her now. Abruptly she turns away from the door and whips at her eggs, the whisk gleaming in the ruthless white light of the kitchen. That is the problem with the photos, she knows—they are deceitful. They shine with the promise that a marriage will turn out to be something other than what it actually becomes.

Mrs. McGinn knows a thing or two about disappointment. She has had four husbands, and all but one have been unfaithful. Each time she has loved and lost she has retreated into her bedroom and lain down with her bowed head at the foot and her stockinged feet at the head and she has stayed there for hours, inverted in this way, while the world flips and her stomach lurches and her small calico cat purrs into her shoulder and licks at the salt that runs dyed with mascara from the crinkled corners of her eyes to the painted line of her mouth. Mrs. McGinn may be a real warrior (in her own peaceful way, that is), she may be strong and bold and quick at dodging flying fruit, but she is not invincible. She is, in the end, a human being—as breakable as any other—and it is in these moments that she feels the most broken, that she wonders what it is about her, what she has done wrong, why it is that each and every husband has strayed.

"Am I so unlovable?" she has asked the cat, time and again. "What is wrong with me?" She worries that her daughter, too, finds her unlovable and that her daughter sometimes asks herself: What is wrong with my mother?

What she wants most in the world—besides the former glory of this town—is for her daughter's marriage to be beautiful and painless and lasting. She does not know if such a thing is possible, but she refuses to give up hoping for it. She will not abandon ship so easily.

"You may not think so to look at me now," she tells Noah's wife upon returning to the dining room. "But I used to be very beautiful. See, that's me, can you see how that's me, years and years ago?" She jabs at the photograph in question.

Noah's wife looks, dutifully, and then looks again at Mrs. McGinn in order to evaluate the resemblance. She nods.

"You are very beautiful even now, you know," she says kindly.

And it is true that Mrs. McGinn is still striking, in her own way, even if she has lost the eyebrows that were once so distinctive (she has to draw them on now, with a brown clay pencil), even if her lips are closer to white than to red and even if her skin has begun to fold into small dark pouches below her eyes. It is true that she is still very proud and very pretty, even if she is not quite *as* beautiful as she was when she was twenty-five. But who is? she would like to know. Who is?

"It would have been nice," Mrs. McGinn declares, "if that *weatherman*, or whatever he called himself, would have given us some kind of prediction."

"Didn't he?" asks Noah's wife in her gentle way.

"A good one, I mean," retorts Mrs. McGinn. "I'd like to know how long the rain will last so that I know exactly how long we need to postpone the wedding. It's the uncertainty that drives me crazy. Those two have been engaged for two and a half years already, but I simply won't have it raining on my only daughter's wedding day. I'm not superstitious, but I know full well that marriage is a challenge. Every pair needs all the luck it can get."

"It rained on my wedding day," remarks Noah's wife. "And everything was fine."

Mrs. McGinn ignores this. She flips the pages of one of the albums in quick succession until she lands on one of her daughter dressed as a flower girl, her lips pursed in a grimace.

"Anyway," continues Noah's wife. "Couldn't you hold the ceremony inside the church? You should see what Noah has done to the place: it's gorgeous. And I know you haven't heard him preach, but he's very good. Really, he is."

Mrs. McGinn scowls down at her photo album. She doesn't care how well spoken the minister may be; she has no interest in asking his God for anything. Although Mrs. McGinn truly does believe in a higher power (at least on her better days), she does not need to sit under a stranger's vaulted roof in order to hear another man's opinion on the matter. Mrs. McGinn possesses conviction enough for twenty women; she has plenty of opinions of her own.

"We've all been up there before," she says to Noah's wife. "And the old man couldn't help us. Why would we go up there again?"

Noah's wife blinks at her, reflecting. "Noah is different," she says after a moment. "He could help you. He helps everyone. You're the leader of this town, and people look up to you. If you only gave him a chance—well, you might find that he could save this place."

Mrs. McGinn stares at her. What has gotten into everyone today? If she had known when she woke up this morning that ignorant weathermen and bored housewives would come waltzing into her diner to tell her how to run her town, well—she might have yanked the quilt back over her head and refused to come out at all. The people in this town do not need a minister to deliver them any more than they need a weatherman to rescue them.

"If I might be so bold as to ask," says Mrs. McGinn to Noah's wife in a brittle tone, "what *exactly* does your husband think that we need saving from?"

Noah's wife leans quickly back. For a few heartbeats, she is silent. Then: "The old minister—" she starts to say.

"Yes. The old minister walked into the river. But that doesn't mean the rest of us will," snaps Mrs. McGinn. "If we wanted to go to church, we'd go to church—but that isn't what we want. So if your husband is here to play the part of a hero, to shower us with truth and light, to bring us back to the proverbial fold, well—" she snorts. "We've got showers enough as it is in this town, and there isn't anything more truthful than that. So he might as well give up, and go back to where he came from."

"I can't go home and tell him that," says Noah's wife faintly.

"Then tell him something else," replies Mrs. McGinn. "That is not my problem."

Noah's wife apologizes. Soon after, she packs up her things and prepares to go. At the threshold she turns, hesitates, and finally speaks. "I wish that you would reconsider."

Mrs. McGinn sniffs, believing this to be unlikely. It is only later, in the middle of her morning rush, that she wonders if there might be a reason to climb up there after all. She pauses with a tray of pancakes balanced on her palm, her checkered apron slightly off-center, and looks into the gray faces of her neighbors. They bark orders at her and at her daughter; they change their minds halfway through their meals and then claim they are dissatisfied. They snap at each other, and when they are not complaining they are silent.

They weren't always this way, knows Mrs. McGinn. They used to be more patient. The whole place used to be so charming. That's what people loved about it; that's why the tourists kept on coming. She knows the change is due to the rain, but what she doesn't know is why it keeps on raining. Perhaps she *will* climb up that hill once more—not to ask for grace, of course, but to demand some answers.

nine

There are many things that Noah loves about his job.

Here are some of them: making a patient laugh in the stale hospital room; planting stout yellow marigolds over fresh cemetery plots; soothing the infant on his forearm as they bow together over the baptismal font. He told his wife once that he loves infants best of all because he loves the way that they can transition from crying to laughing so quickly—their line between sorrow and joy is so thin. Noah claims that this is something infants know and adults have forgotten: the fact that sorrow can so easily be transformed into joy.

There are no infants in this town—that is one thing he has noticed. There are families with young children, yes, who must be bused to an elementary school fifteen miles away. There are a few gangly middle-schoolers and a pack of adolescents whose favorite prank is to plaster their neighbors' cars with mud late in the dark and windy nights. But there are no infants. It is as if somewhere along the way everyone gave up, Noah has reflected to himself while making his daily trek from the heart of downtown to his church on the hill. It is as if when the rain started and didn't stop, the townspeople's vision of the future grew grayer and dimmer until they could no longer imagine it at all. They require every last ounce of their energy simply to endure the rain.

And it is impressive, he will admit, how they have managed to adapt. They have extended the awning over their sidewalks and stretched clear plastic tarps across the intersections so that they can walk the full half mile of downtown without getting all that wet. As the smaller shops have gone out of business and shut down, Mauro's general store has taken up the slack—his business sprawls across several storefronts, organized into sections: groceries, pharmacy, housewares, clothing, home improvement, radios and televisions. Last month, when the townspeople were informed that the trucks that carried mail and newspapers could no longer make it all the way into the hills (the roads were getting so bad that the route became too time-consuming), Mrs. McGinn held a town meeting and demanded that every citizen with a driver's license volunteer to help out. Every week one of them drives two hours out of the hills and two hours back, packing six days' worth of mail and papers into the trunk. Mrs. McGinn sorts the mail herself and stacks it on the counter in the diner for her neighbors to come and claim.

In Noah's stack this morning there are a handful of damp flyers and bills and a check cut from the church's bank account for his first month of service here. He also finds a letter to his wife (he recognizes the bold and angular handwriting of her best friend on the rain-stained envelope) and a brief note from the head elder at their former church. Noah stands just outside the diner while he skims the words, then he folds the paper carefully along the crease and tucks it into his breast pocket. He supposes he must answer later, although he isn't certain what to say.

Is he all right? the head elder wants to know. How has everything been going?

Fine and fine, Noah will reply. The questions posed are simple ones, but Noah can read between the lines. What the council of elders really wants to know—what they couldn't understand a month ago, when Noah volunteered to take the job—is why Noah came here in the first place, why he gave up his position and (most likely) his future with the most prominent congregation in the city in order to serve a community like this one: a community so stubborn, so disinterested, so taxing on the soul that it would drive a perfectly good minister into the river.

"That's not fair," Noah had protested when someone on the council made this point during their selection meeting. "We have no idea if that's what happened. It could have been an accident."

One of the elders had chuckled, his mustache trembling.

"Ha!" he said. "Noah! That's rich, isn't it? You already sound like one of them."

"Seriously, though," interjected the head elder. His eyes were green and vigilant. "Noah, what is this about? I can't believe that this is what you want. You have a congregation that adores you, you have a wife to consider. How does she feel about turning her back on the entire life that you have built together and being forced to start again from scratch?"

"This is my decision," insisted Noah. "I meant what I said. That church needs a minister, and I'm determined to be the one to fill the position."

There were several seconds of silence. Finally the head elder leaned back in his chair, and all the other men around the table followed his lead. Only Noah remained where he was, bent stiffly forward, his hands clasped so tightly together that his knuckles were turning white.

"I suppose it's decided, then," said the head elder with a sigh of resignation. "You're expected there by the beginning of next week. They'll hold off on the burial until you arrive." He scraped his chair back, stood up, and stepped away from the table. As the men filed out of the room, he approached Noah and gripped his hand. "I don't feel right about this, Noah," he said. "But I trust in your decision. If you need anything, promise that you'll call."

Noah had promised, but he has not been in touch since his departure. What else could he say to make them understand? He cannot tell them that for months now he has been feeling restless and troubled, or that he has been postponing meetings with his congregants because he doesn't feel he has the energy to pray with them. He cannot admit that he has been walking through his services like an automaton, mouthing the words and mumbling the hymns without feeling any of the old emotion stirring in his soul. A change of scene will do him good, he believes; the challenge of a new church will restore his old enthusiasm and return to him the passion for his vocation. He needs this.

Should he have told his wife the true cause behind their relocation? Perhaps; but if all goes as he has planned, there will not be any need to. Why tell her that his confidence has been shaken if he himself does not know the reason why, and if it turns out that he can solve the problem on his own? He has loved her from the moment he sat down beside her on the whale-watching boat, when he promised her that they would make it safely through the storm. He loves her because when he made that promise, she fastened her gray gaze on him and she believed him. She has never stopped believing in him since.

Noah knows that this is what makes her so good at her work—this is why people clamor for her photographs of them. She brings out the best in people because she believes that it's there, even when she cannot see it. That moment on the boat was only the first of many times that Noah would be thrilled and also a little overwhelmed by her faith in him. When she accepted their move last month without question, when she packed up her things and turned her back on her past without a murmur of complaint—once again, he found himself in awe of her.

He won't allow her faith in him to be misplaced.

And so with his mail in hand, he turns once again in the direction of the church, making his way through downtown to the hill. Outside the tattered city hall he pauses to observe a man he's never seen before attaching an oversized rain gauge to the side of the building. Once the gauge is properly secured, the man continues slowly down the road, pausing every few feet to inspect the water pouring out of gutters or running along the curb. He shakes his head and makes a note on the clipboard that he carries carefully sheltered below his black umbrella. This must be the man that his wife mentioned meeting, Noah reflects, and the one that he has heard people complaining about while checking out supplies at Mauro's general store. Only here two days so far, the stranger has made such a habit of inserting himself into the townspeople's conversations and harping on the importance of evacuation that he has already become something of a pariah. Noah shrugs and climbs in the direction of the steeple. Although he feels a little sorry for the man, at least this means that Noah and his wife are no longer the only new arrivals.

Once inside the church he shakes his head to chuck the water from his ears and then he flips the switch on the wall for the overhead lights and looks to the ceiling to count how many bulbs are still burned out. The lights that work crackle slowly into action, and once they are lit he can see with satisfaction that the building is not as dim, not as damp and musty and wrecked as it was when he first found it. Noah stands and stares for a moment, taking in a deep and thankful breath of air. He appreciates this church. He doesn't mind the disrepair. He loves that there is so much for him to do here. A swallow flies low from the altar through the nave, and when it brushes by his shoulder he ducks, a shadow of his famous smile flitting across his face.

Most days Noah likes to have his wife here with him, but as he walks through the church this morning he is glad to be alone, glad that the workers, too, are off for the day. The day before he had examined the warped sides of the pulpit and now he sets himself to the task of constructing a new one. He spends the hours until lunchtime cutting the boards and drilling screws into the wood, his spirit electrified by the power of creation. When he experiences the sensation of an object rising into being beneath his hands, he feels that this makes everything worth it—the roughened fingers, the blackened nails, the splinters that lodge in his palm just below the surface of his skin. Here, now, he can see the result of his efforts: he can see the change that he effects in the world, can see the level sides, the lines running through the lumber, the sturdy heft of the structure. It is on days like these when he feels as though he wouldn't mind changing careers to a carpenter or a construction worker, wouldn't mind if fixing up this church took him a hundred years so that he never had to preach again. He has always loved to work with people, but he's finding it much easier to work with wood.

He is quick to remind himself of his fondness for his

congregants to stem the tide of guilt that rises with these thoughts. People are so *interesting*, he reflects. If he has learned anything during his time as a minister it is that the human spirit can be broken in an infinite number of intricate, unpredictable ways, and while another (lesser) man would probably find the task to be daunting, he hopes that he will never tire of seeking out and mending that which is in need of repair. The only problem is that the rips and fissures in people—the broken hearts, the grieving souls—are so intangible as to sometimes seem unreachable. Over the years Noah has worked constantly, earnestly, inexhaustibly, and still both the task and the work remain invisible. Even if he *knows* (and he does! he tells himself—he does!) that progress is being made, still there are many, many moments when it is impossible to see it.

When his wife arrives with lunch, Noah is resting on the altar. She takes her seat beside him on the freshly scrubbed carpet, leans close to kiss his cheek, and hands him his turkey sandwich. When she smiles at him his gaze is drawn to the curve of her collarbone, a plain silver chain falling across the ridge. He stares over her head and imagines the space when it is finished, lit with candles and fragrant with altar flowers and full of congregants who turn shining faces toward him, waiting to be saved. Then she waves her fingers at him, laughing, and his attention snaps back to her. He grins sheepishly and takes his lunch. What he wants most in this world is to be the man she thinks he is.

ten

Dr. Yu's father is pleased to discover that he is finally becoming skilled at the art of escape.

"Here, will you tie this rope around my hands?" he asks his daughter when she comes to check on him at home. "I'll bet you five dollars that I can get out of it in ten minutes or less."

"I'm not tying a rope around your hands," says Dr. Yu with a sigh, setting a grocery bag down on his counter. "For the last time, Papa."

"April," he coaxes. "Please."

"No," she says. "I don't approve of this new hobby of yours at all. I wish you would just go back to magic. What happened to pulling colored scarves out of your sleeves? That was innocuous, at least. It didn't land you in prison."

"The art of escape *is* a kind of magic, my dear," he explains. "Illusion and escape! They're one and the same!"

He has a shock of silver hair and thick, tortoiseshell spectacles. He peers at her, squinting, owl-like and calm.

"I don't know what that means," she says. "But if you want to practice your card tricks, I'm willing to play along."

Dr. Yu's father would like to ask her when it was, exactly, that she became so condescending—she was so mild-tempered as a child!—but instead he purses his lips and keeps his mouth shut. The two of them have been fighting more often. Any defense he tries to raise with respect to his latest escapades will only result in her bringing up the prison incident. Indeed, she is likely to bring it up whether he provokes her or not.

"Here," he says, trying to sidestep an argument by distracting her with a trick. "I've got a penny and a half-dollar. Hold out your hands."

She offers him her palms, somewhat resignedly, and he places a coin in each one. When she opens them again, the penny has been transformed into a quarter. Her expression is frozen and unimpressed, and her face doesn't change when he reaches into the front pocket of her white coat to retrieve the missing coin.

"There you go," he says. "It's called a scotch-and-soda."

"Of course it is," she says and sighs, rising to her feet. She doesn't blink when he reaches under the table and produces a vase full of wilting daisies.

"For you!" he says with a slight bow and a flourish. "Out of thin air!"

"Thanks, Papa," she says. "Here—I should unpack these groceries."

His daughter visits his house on a semiweekly basis, bearing dinners that she cooks and freezes and divides into parcels packaged in bright aluminum foil. She stocks his cupboard with cans of fruit and beans and she stuffs the shelves of his refrigerator with fresh produce. Whenever he opens the door for a can of beer ("That is how I get my whole grains!" he informs her with annoyance when she demands to know the balance of his meals), heads of lettuce roll out onto the floor and bounce with a wet smack against the bottom of the stove.

"No red meat?" he asks, half joking.

"You're not supposed to be eating it," she replies. "I've told you."

While Dr. Yu arranges the food in the cabinets, her father stays at the table, sipping a glass of grapefruit juice that she has poured for him, and practicing the effect of the detachable thumb. When she has finished, she resumes her seat across from him and then pulls a stethoscope out from the deep pockets of her coat, pressing the metal disc against his rib cage.

"Knock it off," he says, pulling away. "I'm fine. If I wanted to see a doctor, I'd go to the hospital. Can't a grown man do what he wants with his life?"

"I didn't mind that you had found a hobby," she says. She yanks the prongs of the stethoscope from her ears. "I was glad, in fact, because I hated to see you so sad. I didn't say anything when you signed up to perform at the library, or when you started doing card tricks at bars. I thought: this isn't healthy, but if it makes him happy, fine. But I've got to draw the line now, Papa. You can't go around getting yourself arrested. Really—picking the lock of a cop car? What were you thinking?"

He shrugs. "It was right in front of the station," he says. "I needed to get their attention. And anyway, sweetheart, that was days ago. I haven't done it again."

"And you didn't even *call* me!" persists Dr. Yu unhappily. "I could have left the hospital, I could have come for you right away. Why on earth would you want to spend the night there?"

"Hush," he says. "April, try to calm down. It wasn't a big deal."

"Of course it was!" she exclaims. "You were *arrested*, for God's sake!"

Dr. Yu's father stands up from the table and strides toward the refrigerator, praying that his daughter has not hidden all of his beer again. He had not, for the record, intended to spend the night in prison. Yes, he had gotten himself arrested, but the whole point in doing so had been so that he could break himself out. He'd brought his lock-picking tools, his tension wrenches, his lump of lead. He simply hadn't thought the plan through; he hadn't realized that the first thing the police were going to do was to take away his belongings. The coat within which he had stored the tools was long and black, full of hidden flaps and pockets. It was an old magician's coat, he told the police when he saw one of them admiring it on the other side of the bars.

That was when they had asked him if he could show them some tricks.

Of course he could, he said, and he did. He was frustrated and bored and so he had gone in for some of the bigger effects: the suspension of one of the officers so that it looked as though he was floating in midair; the illusion of dismemberment; the first half of the Indian rope trick; and finally, a series of small escapes. He had the police handcuff him, tie his feet together, bind him to a chair, and then they watched him twist his way out. They applauded every time.

In retrospect, he has been studying books of escapism for long enough now that he probably could have found a way out of his cell without his tools, had he really wanted to. But it was more pleasant with the officers, he decided, away from home. He was relieved to have the opportunity to step out of his life, his house, his dreams—even if only for a moment.

Over the past few months, he has been making frequent trips to the library to check out books on the twin arts of illusion and escape. He stacks the volumes up around the edge of his desk, on the floor, constructing a small wall that he likes to think will help hold him in place as he pores over the tricks, the effects, the sleights of hand. He studies the diagrams and then tries to reproduce them himself, darkening the shadows with the flattened graphite tip of his pencil. The sketches never look quite as perfect or as professional as they do in the books, but this is the best way he can think of to memorize the many steps of the tricks. The collection of drawings is especially helpful once he must return the books to the library. He has always been a visual learner.

The other day he found a box of his wife's colors and brushes in the cabinet below the kitchen sink and sometimes, when he is feeling particularly brave or inspired or foolish, he thinks about adding a few strokes of watercolor to his images. He goes to the sink and hunches down and stares at the paints between the pipes for several long minutes. Then he shoves the cabinet door shut and retreats to his office, where he shuts that door, too, and he rests his head on the desk and waits for the feeling to pass.

He cannot bear to touch the paints, or the perfume, or the pearls that are left still coiled on the armoire. He cannot bear to open the closet door and see her coats or her dresses and so he does not open it at all. He wears button-down shirts and corduroy slacks from his dresser and sometimes he wishes for his tweed blazer but it is in the closet and so what is there to do? He must live without it. What is one more loss, he wants to know, among so many?

Life is one big disappearing act. Things vanish all the time.

That was the whole idea of it, anyway, that was why he had been driven to the study of this art in the first place. As he watched her coffin being lowered into the ground he had not been able to stand the thought of his wife lying in it alone. He had imagined himself inside it with her, and his dreams for weeks afterward had been nightmares, visions of entrapment in small dark spaces. He would wake right as his dream-self was on the verge of suffocation, and he would fling himself away from his pillow, his chest heaving, his nightshirt soaked with sweat.

Escape does not come as easily to him as illusion, however, and so far his efforts to free himself have been more difficult, more strenuous than they should be. What is he missing? He leaves his daughter and wanders back into his study, to sit himself down with his books and his drawings, to study again his sketches of the locks and the knots.

She follows him. He leans forward in his chair, suddenly too exhausted to work, his head slowly sinking down toward his desk. She stands towering behind him. She places her hand on his shoulder, curls her fingers around the knobby bones jutting through his sleeve. When did he become so small?

"You're not the only one who misses her," she says. He doesn't answer. His elbow is crooked on top of a leather-bound book, his forehead resting on his forearm. His daughter hopes that he will fall asleep.

She pauses for a moment, listening to the rhythm of his breathing, and then she turns toward the door, leaving his study and heading back through the cramped, low-ceilinged hallway to the kitchen, the living room, the dining room. She examines the entire house with her surgical eye in an effort to determine exactly how well he is coping on his own. The bedroom is dark and stale. From the doorway she looks toward the rounded oak armoire, its mirror reflecting the backs of pewter-framed photographs lined in rows across its surface. In the gloom she can see the quilt folded neatly at the foot of the bed, the sheets smoothed across the pillow. She steps closer to inspect the corners—tucked the way that her mother (and only her mother) knew how to tuck them. When her father made beds, the sheets were always arranged with quick and crumpled distraction. His end result looked like the work of someone impatient, someone who felt that he had better things to do with his time.

"Hey," she calls out. When there is no answer, she returns to the study to find her father still bent over his desk. "Hey," she says. "I was just in the bedroom. Have you—have you not been sleeping in there?"

He abruptly lifts his head and begins to turn the pages of his book. He doesn't look up. "I sleep on the couch," he says. "I don't sleep in that room anymore."

"But listen, Papa—"

"April, you don't understand. In thirty years I never slept alone in that room. I'll be damned if I do it now."

He reaches for his pencil, lifts it and holds it poised above the text. "You can stay for lunch if you like," he says. "I'll join you in a few minutes. Let me finish looking over this first."

There is a painful, protracted silence, and then her footsteps echo down the hall and into the kitchen. After a moment he hears the sound of running water, a pot being filled and set to boil on the stove. While she opens the refrigerator, removes something from the vegetable drawer and begins to chop, he turns again to his work.

In this house, where everything reminds him of his wife, the walls are closing in on him daily. Sometimes he imagines that the ceilings are sinking in with sadness, the furniture creaking beneath the weight of his ghosts. He feels trapped, and stifled, and old. White rabbits, flames, flowers, capes—the tricks are all well and good, but what he needs now is something more than the paltry task of slipping out of knots or fiddling with cuffs. He needs something much grander, more thrilling. He needs something that will get him out of here for good.

eleven

The rafters of the church are full of songbirds.

Noah's wife can see the townspeople watching them with some unease as they enter the church and choose their places. The birds swoop and dive, protecting their nests and trying to drive the crowd of waterlogged intruders from pews that have so long been empty. Noah's wife waves an arm to shoo the boldest of them away, while Mauro grins and slips into a seat beside her.

"Like bats out of heaven!" he declares.

She smiles faintly. To tell the truth, she had not expected to see Mauro here; she had worried, in fact, that no one from the town would come at all. She has spent the past week tacking flyers all over the lampposts downtown, but the ink runs in the rain and within hours the paper is too soggy to stay in place. Yesterday she and Noah staked out a booth in the diner so that he could approach everyone who ventured in. She loves to see him at his work, loves to watch the color flood his high cheeks when he throws his shoulders back and moves abruptly to the counter when a new arrival takes a seat. As she waited in their booth in the back, she could hear him speaking in low, fervent tones, alternately gesturing toward the hill and running his fingers through his beard. She ordered cup after cup of coffee, sometimes interspersed with pastries, and after a while she leaned back in her seat and gazed outside, watching the umbrellas parading past the windows.

Mrs. McGinn scowled at them both from behind the counter, but she didn't do anything to stop them; and while her neighbors patiently permitted Noah to finish talking up the service, none of them seemed particularly interested or pleased. Their faces remained the same ashen gray they always were, and Noah's wife watched them slide into their booths with the usual resignation and indifference that she has come to expect from them. She has issued numerous invitations to dinner over the past few weeks (Noah asked her to do so), but as of yet no one has accepted. Part of her worried—although she did not say this to Noah—that his church would be as empty as his dining room.

She is glad to have been mistaken, relieved when the first congregants come sloshing through the entryway while she is arranging flowers on the altar. She is grateful that all of Noah's hard work over the past month seems to have paid off, and that there are people here besides herself and Leesl who can admire as they enter how the building gleams. Once they step inside, the red wooden doors of the entrance swing open into the lobby that precedes the nave. The floor is laid with interlocking slabs of granite, and a narrow aisle runs between the pews down toward the threadbare carpet of the altar. The stained-glass windows have been washed and their cracks have been caulked; the ornate metal light fixtures, drifting from the rafters on bronze chains, have been cleaned and repaired. Noah has patched the roof, repainted the walls, rewired the fans, and built a new pulpit. The church is warm and well-lit, and as Noah's wife arranges herself and her belongings in the first pew, she has the distinct feeling of coming home.

The townspeople keep coming. By the time Noah steps out from his office and rounds the bend in front of the altar, the pews are nearly packed. His wife watches his long, familiar gait with the same attentiveness she always shows, and so it is probably only she who notices his slight stumble at the base of the carpeted steps. He rights himself quickly, and as Leesl begins the first hymn he makes his way to the chair behind the pulpit with his customary grace. When he trips over the first words of the liturgy, she chalks it up to eagerness—and by the time he ducks his shaggy head in prayer, he seems to have hit his stride.

It is her favorite thing to hear him preach. The first time she ever went to hear him was the first time she had set foot in a church in her life. She was struck by the majesty of the experience, by the sound of a hundred different voices swelling in song, by the light that streamed through to the altar and the fabulous stories spelled out in stained glass. She remembers her surprise when Noah told her afterward, over fresh fruit and powdered doughnuts in the church basement, that it was not his personal *choice* to become a preacher; sometimes he thinks he would have liked to be an architect or an opera singer. Instead, he is convinced that the church is tied up in his fate, that he was born to it or called to it the way that her best friend believes that she is called to medicine and Noah's wife believes that she herself is called to Noah.

"Called to me?" Noah had repeated when she told him this, shortly after their marriage. He seemed to worry that the thought was somehow sacrilegious. "What do you mean?"

How to explain it to him? She likes to hear him speak about the forces that are at work in the universe, about the great plan that she, too, is a part of even if she doesn't fully understand it. It was reassuring to feel, when she married him, as though her path had been predetermined.

During the first hymn she looks around to see who is singing. Most of her neighbors are paging confusedly through their hymnals as if they cannot find the correct page; others are sitting with the books unopened beside them, gazing sternly forward. One older man is clipping his fingernails several rows behind her. She hears people muttering to one another, their eyes on Noah and their mouths curled in smirks. When they notice her watching them, they stare back until her cheeks turn scarlet and she spins to face the altar. Only a handful of people near the back are singing, and Noah's wife feels so anxious about the meager performance that she parts her lips and tries to join them. She has never been a good singer (this is yet another talent her mother tried to foster), and when her voice cracks, someone laughs.

Thankfully, the song finally ends and Noah returns to the pulpit. Noah's wife slams her hymnal shut, dizzy with relief. She knows that he had worried over which readings to include for this first service, and she is curious to find out what he chose.

"Look at the birds of the air," Noah declares from the pulpit, tossing one arm toward the ceiling. A swallow dives as if on cue, and the people who are nearest cover their heads. "For they neither sow nor reap nor gather into barns; yet your heavenly Father feeds them."

Noah's wife gazes up in admiration. She knows this passage well; it was his grandmother's favorite. Noah told her how, when he was growing up, his grandmother used to offer the children nickels for every verse that they could memorize. Although his siblings had no interest in the task, Noah made a fortune every summer.

"Consider the lilies of the field, how they grow," he continues. His voice is resonant, assured. "They neither toil nor spin; and yet I say to you that even Solomon in all his glory was not arrayed like one of these. Now if God so clothes the grass of the field, which today is, and tomorrow is thrown into the oven, will He not much more clothe you, O you of little faith?"

The passage, Noah's wife recalls, is about the futility of worry and the promise that the Lord will provide. She remembers visiting Noah's grandmother in the hospital when the woman was in the final stages of her dementia, a year or two into the marriage. Her fingers were yellow and brittle where they clutched the sheets, and the wrinkles hung over her features like a fishnet. But her eyes were shrewd and blue, and her grip was strong. She clutched at Noah's arm as he leaned in to kiss her forehead, and when she moved her hand away there were thumbprints in his skin. In one of her last lucid moments, she quoted this passage to Noah, who sat on the edge of the bed and recited it with her. "Therefore do not worry," they said to each other, their voices low and comforting, "saying, What shall we eat? or What shall we drink? or What shall we wear? . . . For your heavenly Father knows that you need all these things." Noah's wife, perched on a wooden chair in the corner of the room, had been so moved by the scene that she had gone home and spent the evening memorizing the passage herself so that the next time they visited Noah's grandmother she would be able to take part. But the old woman died before Noah's wife had the chance to share this with her, and for several years the verses have lain dormant in her mind. Noah has not spoken them aloud again until now.

"Therefore," he concludes, "do not worry about tomorrow, for tomorrow will worry about itself. Sufficient unto the day is the evil thereof." He clears his throat. "Now, let us pray."

Noah's wife beams up at her husband, reflecting his glow. Leave it to Noah to come up with the perfect passage to calm his neighbors' nerves, to reassure them as he has always reassured her. She bows her head obediently and waits to hear his prayer, but before he can say another word, someone else speaks.

"Objection," a woman's voice declares.

There is the rustling of one hundred raincoats as all the townspeople twist in their pews to locate the cause of the interruption. Startled, Noah's wife turns with them to see Mrs. McGinn standing in the middle of the back row, her orange curls wild and her blouse untucked.

"Excuse me?" says Noah. He squints at her, baffled.

"Objection!" she repeats with overdramatic flair. It is clear that she has practiced this.

"That's not—" starts Noah. He pauses and considers her, reaching for his beard. "I'm not sure what other services you've been to, but objections are not quite appropriate here."

"Aren't they?" she demands. "Well, I've got some either way. What I want to know is—what sort of advice are you trying to give us? Do not *worry*? Take no thought unto *tomorrow*? What are we supposed to do with that?"

Noah shifts uneasily at the pulpit. "I know you have suffered a great deal," he acknowledges, quickly turning his head from one side to another in an attempt to make eye contact with as many of his congregants as possible. "But with patience and endurance I believe that your town can make it through these trying times. The passage—it's about having faith that you will not be given more than you can bear, faith that God will be watching over you. It's about trusting that the Lord will always provide."

Mrs. McGinn emits a bark of false laughter. "I am not a very religious woman, Minister," she tells Noah. "But if I believe anything, it's that God helps those who help themselves."

There is a murmur of agreement from the congregation. Noah's wife stares at them with growing concern. No one seems all that surprised to hear Mrs. McGinn speaking, and Noah's wife cannot help but wonder if this had been at least partly planned. Is that why so many people turned up for the service? Did the town matriarch put them up to this?

"The reason why we're here today is because we've got some questions that need answering," Mrs. McGinn says grimly, her voice carrying clear through the rafters. "If your God is watchful and good, if He listens to the prayers of His people and cares for their welfare like He does for the lilies and the birds—well, then why is it still raining? Why is it still raining here, when we asked your God to make it stop?"

Noah's wife pulls her attention away from Mrs. McGinn—it is difficult to do so, as that woman really can command a room—and looks to her husband, confident that he will have an answer. He always has an answer. But instead of stepping forward, he seems to fall back. His head drops toward his shoulders, making him look smaller than before.

"It doesn't mean God hasn't heard," he says, his voice weaker than it was when he was reciting his verses. "That's too simplistic. There are forces at work we aren't aware of, there are plans that are so much greater than our own. The direct answer that you're looking for—that isn't how God works."

"Please, Minister," says Mauro. He stands now, too, and Noah's wife leans half an inch away from him. "If He is not answering prayers, then how is your God working?"

"Yes," murmur others behind Noah's wife. She frowns at them. She hears them complaining all the time about the bumbling Italian, but they are certainly agreeing with him now. "Then how is your God working?" they repeat.

"And the old minister," calls the town sheriff from near the back. "What happened to him, anyway?"

"Was it an accident or not?" queries the librarian.

"Did it happen because he was unhappy with the rain?" someone else suggests.

"Aren't all of you unhappy in the rain?" demands the weatherman, trying to capitalize on their discontent. He catches the eye of Noah's wife before she is able to look away. She had not noticed when he came in.

"Why did it start raining in the first place?" asks a twiglike teenage girl. Before her father hushes her, she asks another. "Is this supposed to be a punishment for something?"

"What would it be punishment for?" growls Mrs. McGinn's husband, banging a hymnal onto the pew in front of him with more force than necessary. There is a splintering sound, and those who are closest to him start edging cautiously away. "What the hell have we done wrong?"

"Don't you think that God is telling us to get out of here?"

demands Mrs. McGinn's daughter with a scowl at her stepfather. Her mother spins and glares, but the girl glances at the zookeeper and presses forward with her point. "Before it's too late?"

"How will the animals survive if we leave them here, Angie?" retorts the zookeeper. "Do you want them all to starve and drown?"

At this, what was left of the service falls apart. The rest of the townspeople stand up, stomping and snarling at one another, hurling their questions at the minister. With increasing alarm, Noah's wife looks once more to her husband, willing him to restore order—but he doesn't even try. He merely steps down from the pulpit and slumps onto the bench behind it. Leesl, uncertain how to react to the scene, releases the pedals of the organ and begins to pound out the recessional hymn. When the townspeople realize that the music is too loud for them to air their grievances, they scowl and pull their hoods over their heads and storm out of the church into the rain. Noah's wife assumes that they have gone to continue their complaints downtown. By the time the hymn is over, there is no one left but Leesl, Noah, and Noah's wife—and Leesl is so quiet packing up her music that Noah's wife instantly forgets that she is there.

"Noah?" says Noah's wife, rising from her pew. He doesn't answer, and so she climbs the stairs to the altar and approaches him behind the pulpit. He doesn't move from his bench—the shadows etched into his skin make his face look eerie, masklike—and she places one hand gingerly upon the painted concrete wall beside him. "Are you all right?"

His gaze flicks up at her, and then down again. "I'm fine," he says. "I mean—I'm sorry. They completely overwhelmed me. I should have handled that better."

"No," she says instinctively. "No, you handled it fine. You did the best you could."

The words leave her tongue before she can process them, and it is only when she hears them spoken that she realizes she is lying. She has never lied to him before.

"You didn't know that they would ask you all those questions," she admits, attempting to modify her statement. "That's true. But Noah—" She hesitates, and finally continues: "Why didn't you just answer them?"

At this he lifts his head and looks squarely at her, his gaze quick and cutting. "And how would I have answered?" he asks her. "Enlighten me, please. What exactly should I have said?"

His tone has never been so hard with her. She shrinks back, but he reaches out and grasps her wrist. Then he gently draws her closer.

"I'm sorry," he says again. His voice breaks, and he tries once more. "I'm so sorry. I didn't mean to be sharp with you. It's just that they took me by surprise." He takes a deep breath, trying to steady himself. "For one thing, all those questions came so fast. I simply didn't have the chance to respond to them, even if I'd wanted to."

She nods, soothed by his answer. Of course—that makes sense. Everything happened too quickly. That's why he lost control. If they had given him more time, he would have been able to provide them with the answers they were looking for. He would have proven himself to be as strong and certain as he always is. Noah's wife hears the door to the lobby click shut and realizes that Leesl must have slipped away.

"Well," she says, aiming for a tone that's brisk and businesslike. "There isn't anything to worry about. Next time, you'll be ready to respond to them."

But Noah shakes his head. He releases her wrist and drops his forehead into his hands. "Oh God," he groans. "Next time."

"Yes," she insists. "You'll have another opportunity."

His voice is muffled, his face still turned toward the floor. "You don't understand," he mumbles. "To be confronted with all of that doubt, all at once, and to know there's absolutely nothing you can say—" He lifts his head and looks toward the window. "And who can blame them for feeling like they've been abandoned? It's completely dismal here. No wonder the old man walked into the river."

She starts at this. "I thought you said it was an accident."

"It probably was. But there are rumors." Noah shrugs. His gaze flicks up and fastens on her. "Do you think it was?"

There is a tiny splash on the bench beside him and they glance up automatically, see that the roof has once again begun to leak. Noah groans again and returns his forehead to his hands.

A shudder runs through her. "I don't know," she says. She folds her arms across her chest in an attempt to bottle up her distress. "No one does. But Noah—if the situation is as dire as they say it is, then why did you accept the assignment here?"

"Partly because I believed the rumors," he replies. He waits, seems to be choosing his words with care. "I've got to think that if a minister drowned himself on purpose, then there had to be a kind of darkness that drove him to it. And what if that darkness is still here? What if the rest of the town needs rescuing before the river swallows them up, too?"

And what if they do? Noah's wife cheers a little at this. Although her husband's tone is less than optimistic and his posture seems to radiate despair, this sentiment is something that the two of them can build upon. Noah needs to be needed; he thrives on a challenge.

"Yes," she tells him. She kneels down before him to be certain that he hears her. "Maybe there is a kind of darkness here. But you can lead them out of it, Noah. That's the reason why they called you here."

Perhaps this thought truly restores Noah to himself; or perhaps he hears the note of desperation in her tone, and realizes that whatever he is feeling, he must try to shake it off and rise to reassure her. Either way, she is pleased when he stands and puts his arm around her. "Of course," he says. He draws her head to his shoulder. "That's right, my dear."

She watches him closely as they shut up the church and she

remains vigilant all evening. It is true that he is not himself: that afternoon he sleeps for several hours, and when he wakes he is dazed and disheveled. He makes no attempt to speak with her at dinner, and he does not hum hymns to his reflection as he brushes his teeth. That night she lies awake while he tosses and turns beside her, listening to the rain increase its volume.

twelve

Mrs. McGinn's daughter hates fighting with the zookeeper. She doesn't like the tone he adopts, which grows softer and more wounded by the minute; she doesn't like his downcast gaze, the way he twists his hands together, or the pathetic expression that steals across his craggy face. Look at him, for goodness' sake! What a giant he is! One would think that he would have guts enough to stand up to her, a woman half his stature. But instead he cowers, backs little by little into corners, increasing her anger with every step and making it impossible for her to take him seriously.

If he had no intention of leaving this town, why didn't he tell her this before?

"There isn't anything for me out there, Angie," he says now, his voice sounding sad and low. "This is where I belong."

She snorts. "This?" she repeats. They stand outside the primate house, where the roof is caving in. With a sweep of her arm, she takes in the ruined gray buildings, the rotting signs, the field of sludge that used to be the African grasslands. The ducks are paddling through puddles in the roads while the peacocks slog past, their lovely feathers caked with mud and their eyes shut tight against the rain as if they, too, like their human counterparts, cannot bear to see what has happened to the former glory of this town. It has been weeks since anyone besides Mrs. McGinn's daughter has set foot inside the zoo.

"But there isn't anything for *me* here, Adam!" she snaps, dropping her arm to her side. "Do you think I'm going to work in my mother's diner for the rest of my life? Is that what you want for me?"

He shakes his head. "Of course it isn't," he says. "Come on, Angie. Be fair."

Mrs. McGinn's daughter scowls. What he wants, she knows, is the same thing that her mother and everyone else in this town want: for their lives to return to the way they were before. They are waiting for the rain to end, waiting for the town to regain its fame and fortune.

"After all," she hears them remark to one another in the diner as she refills their glasses with water, "who ever heard of a rain that lasts forever?"

They're dreamers, all of them, mutters Mrs. McGinn's daughter to herself as she spins on her heel and stomps away from the zookeeper. Her boots sink so deeply in the mud that when she yanks them out, they almost pull right off her feet. She pauses for a moment, wondering if the zookeeper will try to follow her. Looking up the road, she sees the highland cows huddled beneath trees that are bending under the weight of the water and force of the wind, leaning dangerously close to fences that look ready to snap if the branches fall. She listens, but there are no squelching footsteps behind her; only the doleful lowing of the cows and the rushing of the rain through the leaves. Is it her imagination, or is the rain growing stronger?

She continues on, dashing over the koi pond and through the waves that are sloshing over the footbridge. The koi watch her go with bubble-eyes, the water in the pond so high that in a day or two they could easily flop out and over her feet. The zookeeper claims that the zoo is in trouble—he has a *sense* about it, he says. But when she asks him if he has a plan to save it, he only looks more stricken and reminds her that the funds have all run dry. With no money, no staff, he is certain that if he were to leave now, all of the animals would either starve or drown. And would that be the worst thing? wonders Mrs. McGinn's daughter as she shoos a wild boar out of her path. What exactly is the problem with letting nature run its course?

The leaves on the dogwood trees she passes are pale and waxy, cradling stubborn flower buds that have refused to open in the rain. Another spring has flowed into another summer, realizes Mrs. McGinn's daughter. Hadn't she planned to be married this summer, if the rain was gone, just as she had planned to be married the summer before? She is tired of being engaged, quite honestly; she is tired of leaning forever toward the future, waiting for the rain to end so that her life can finally begin. She is not like the rest of her neighbors, who seem content in their belief—though it must grow dimmer by the day—that the future of this place will be as brilliant as its past. How can they not see it?

"If you really believe in action," she said to her mother yesterday afternoon as they stomped down the hill after Noah's service, "then why are we still here?"

She has asked her mother this question at least a thousand times before, but yesterday was the first time that her mother stopped in her tracks and spun around to face her, her green eyes blazing with the heat of her frustration.

"Angela Rose," replied Mrs. McGinn, grasping the sleeve of the girl's raincoat to yank her even closer. "Did I raise you to be a quitter? Did I raise you to be a woman who gives up on things when the going gets hard?"

She paused for several long, cool seconds. Her face was so close that their noses were almost touching, and her daughter only responded so that her mother would pull back.

"No," she muttered.

"No," repeated Mrs. McGinn, satisfied. "No, I didn't."

Then her mother turned and continued striding down the hill, and after a pause, the daughter followed—trotting to keep up. What was there to say to that? As she watched her mother's back descending, she was filled with fury at her father and at all the men who left her. If they had been faithful, then perhaps Mrs. McGinn would not be so obsessed with fidelity. If they had stayed, then perhaps Mrs. McGinn's daughter would not need to stay now.

Then again, she reflected, when her mother stopped to wait for her and wrapped an arm around her daughter's waist so that the two of them could walk beneath the same umbrella—then again, she understands that her mother is not an easy person to love. It is hard to love such a fiercely loyal woman, hard to admit that your emotion will never be strong enough to match hers. Everyone who has ever tried to love Mrs. McGinn has only fallen short.

She does not blame others for leaving, as her mother does. Two years ago, there were twelve girls who gathered at the McGinns' house for the daughter's bridal shower. They perched around the table in the dining room, the orange carpet soft and shaggy underfoot, the wallpaper alive with butterflies. Mrs. McGinn served them tea and scones on one of her many sets of wedding china while Mrs. McGinn's daughter opened gifts. Someone noticed a slow stream of water leaking in beneath the windowpanes, and Mrs. McGinn set out one of her floral serving bowls to contain it. There was a certain dogged elegance in the whole affair. But of those twelve girls, only four are left in town—and not even the ones that Mrs. McGinn's daughter liked best. Her friends promised they would write, but they don't and she does not blame them. What would she say in her replies, anyway? What news can there be, as long as it keeps raining?

The only news, in fact, is that it might be raining harder. She looks up as she crosses the wild grass of the former savannah, hopping the sunken fence with ease. They used to keep two elephants here—Maxwell and Rosabelle—but when it became clear that the zoo was in decline, Rosabelle was sold to a safari park across the country. Mrs. McGinn's daughter still remembers the day that the truck arrived to carry Rosabelle away, and how Maxwell tried to climb right in after her. It took all the zookeepers on staff at that time to drive him back—they waved brooms and hayforks, sprayed the elephant with hoses, tried luring him down again with treats and toys—she doesn't recall what finally worked. She only knows that when the truck with Rosabelle finally departed, Maxwell threw his weight against the fence and cried.

"He's not crying," one of the older keepers assured Mrs. McGinn's daughter. "That's the rain on his face. That's what you see."

She disagreed, and audibly: it had already been raining long enough by that time that she could distinguish tears from water. Maxwell moped for days, refusing food and drink. He twined his trunk around the fence and wouldn't leave the spot where the truck had been before it vanished. He grew weak and unsteady on his giant feet, and after ten days of this behavior the keepers had no choice but to call in a veterinarian from the city. The man checked the elephant over, peered into his eyes, heard his heartbeat, and pronounced the animal depressed.

"They can suffer sadness, too," he declared, to all the townspeople's surprise. "They know what it is to lose something." His prescription was that they send Maxwell off to join Rosabelle;

and since at this point the zoo needed cash more than animals, the owners were only too happy to make the sale.

That was how it went, for the next few months. The owners unloaded all the animals they could, and then they left the zoo for dead. The only person who stayed on was the zookeeper, who continued to draw his salary from what was left of the endowment and who cared for the animals who were not claimed or who had been forgotten. The townspeople, for their part, watched the slow dismantling of their zoo with increasing frustration. It had been what set them apart, what made their fortunes and provided them with a sense of civic pride. When cars and buses full of visitors rumbled into town at the start of the season, they used to come out of their shops and houses and wave until the sweat rolled down their arms and faces. They used to help the proprietors of bed-and-breakfasts air out all of the rooms, and those townspeople with bedrooms to spare would hang out signs indicating that they could be let. They opened up the windows of their shops and restaurants and were *happy* when strangers stepped in to dine or look around. This town used to be, remembers Mrs. McGinn's daughter, genuinely hospitable. It was a quality that tourists never failed to comment upon.

And now? She makes it out of the zoo and hurries through the dusky streets toward home, the drops beating ceaselessly against her shoulders. As she passes the minister's house, she glances sidewise at the rain that blows in sheets across their yellow windows and feels a pang of guilt for the dinner invitation she declined. For a few weeks there, it seemed that Noah's wife was inviting everyone—and although none of the townspeople ever spoke of it aloud, somehow they were unanimous in offering polite but cool regrets.

They do not trust strangers, not anymore. Not after all the uninvited men and women who came in and carted their livelihood away. They have grown cold and suspicious, hardened against newcomers—and even each other—as they have hardened against the rain. They do not want the minister here, or his wife; they do not want to be reminded that they might have played a part in the former minister's demise. They do not want the weatherman here either, tinkering with his strange tools in the empty apartment over the general store and telling them when he sees them on the streets that the end of this place is drawing near.

No, reflects Mrs. McGinn's daughter, tiptoeing through the hallway so that her mother will not hear her, climbing the stairs silently to her room—no, at this point they want only to be left alone. She curls into a ball at the foot of her bed, and when the calico cat comes pawing at her hair, she reaches out and pulls him close. As he laps up her tears (as he has lapped up her mother's tears so many times before), she closes her eyes against his sandpaper tongue and wills something to change.

thirteen

The rain picks up without warning.

Overnight, the sky splits open and the rain rushes down: swift and thick, black as velvet, invisible in the dark. It comes with such great force that in the small, murky hours of the morning the river rises over the lowlands and sends water roaring through the gates and cages of the zoo.

The zookeeper starts awake to the screams of primates and the shrieks of tropical birds. He shrugs into his raincoat and pounds down the stairs of his apartment, trampling through the gift store with its rows of stale stuffed animals. Outside the water is rushing so quickly across his path that it almost pulls a boot right off his foot. He yanks his leg back just in time and halts at the door, buttoning his coat and peering out into the downpour.

"Shit," he says.

He spins back into the shop and lunges at the telephone that hangs over the long-abandoned cash register. Cradling the receiver between his cheek and his shoulder, he tightens the laces of his boot while sounding the alarm.

"Evelyn," he growls, "I need some help down here."

As he slams the receiver back into its cradle, he pictures Mrs. McGinn on the other end of the line, flying out of bed with her hair still in rollers, padding down the hall to her daughter's room. The girl will be sleeping half on and half off the bed as she always does, her arms and legs at odd angles and her strawberry blond hair flung across the pillow. The zookeeper wonders if she will realize that this is exactly the kind of emergency that he has been waiting for. Will she finally understand that this is why they couldn't leave?

Mrs. McGinn will know that he would only call for help if it were a last resort. She will already be on the phone again, initiating the chain that she established many years ago in case of situations just like this one—a chain that she insists her neighbors practice every few months, despite their most strident objections. Right now, telephones will be ringing in kitchens and bedrooms all over town. The townspeople will be rubbing sleep out of their eyes as they pick up the receivers, will mutter curses at the zookeeper and at the rain as they stumble out of bed. They will struggle blearily into their clothing and their raincoats, pausing on the doorstep before moving toward their cars. They have grown accustomed to the rain, but not to rain like this. They will not like the look of this weather, or the feeling of the drops that the wind whips sidewise against their skin, reaching them even where they stand beneath the overhang.

And yet they will come. The zookeeper knows that they will come, knows that even those of them who have not set foot in the zoo for years still cling to the idea of the place as if it could yet provide the means of their salvation, as if it still holds the power to raise this town from the dead. If they hear that it is going under, they will come down here to drag it up again.

He spends the next half hour sprinting from one end of the zoo to the other—not to calm the animals (there is no time for that), but to determine where they are and how he can get them out. When the first headlights appear in the zoo parking lot on the far side of the river, the zookeeper dashes to the entrance. Traditionally visitors park their cars and cross the wooden bridge on foot, but the zookeeper waves a discarded yellow raincoat like a flag and shouts at the townspeople to drive all the way over. They can barely understand him over the pounding of the rain and they are still dazed with sleep and shock, but they keep their engines running and they file two by two over the bridge, their headlights beaming several feeble feet forward. Once they are on the other side they can hear the birds, the chimps, the high-pitched wails of wild cats. They shiver and rub clammy hands over their goose bumps, shifting on their feet and waiting docilely as cows for the zookeeper to break them into groups and call out their assignments.

"You!" he shouts to Noah and his wife, a red panda shivering in the crook of his left arm. "To the aviary! The cages are in the storage room around back. You three—any experience with horses? We've got to drive the hoofstock from the barns to the gate. Most of them should be out of the pastures by now. Careful! Watch that picnic table!"

The water has lifted park benches and overturned empty popcorn kiosks. Plastic furniture and old toys from the animal enclosures are floating on the surface. Noah watches the wooden cutout of an elephant tumble into the river, where the current sweeps it out of sight. He starts to go after it, but the zookeeper stops him.

"Too much to do," he barks, grabbing Noah's arm and propelling him in the opposite direction. "Trust me. That isn't the only animal we'll lose tonight."

The next four hours are as disjointed and as terrifying as a nightmare. The zookeeper works alongside his neighbors until the night begins to fall back, all of them knee-deep in sludge and chilled to the bone. They bail the water from enclosures and try to herd the mountain goats to higher ground. For half an hour the zookeeper holds the head of an injured tortoise above water, unable to lift her four-hundred-pound shell out of the muck on his own. Sometime later he follows the sound of screams from the feline house and joins a group attempting to coax a loose tiger from the deep end of the corridor. He shouts and waves broken tree branches, going as close to the tiger as he dares, but the task is impossible in a building that has lost all power and is slowly filling up with rain. The cat shows its teeth, snarls low in its throat, and stays put. Two hours later, when the zookeeper sees the striped and matted carcass bobbing up against a fence, he reddens in the dark and turns hastily away. He fears that he has lost the hippopotami as well, but he doesn't have the energy or the manpower to sound an alarm. Let them drift downstream; he only has two hands, after all.

With every step through the flooded enclosures, with every animal cry and every townsperson's complaint, the zookeeper's fury surges higher. He is as cold and tired as they are. He knows he should feel grateful that they are here, grateful for the fact that most of them have remained until now and that he is not trying to manage this impossible task alone. But instead he feels only anger: anger at the handful of his neighbors who snuck back across the bridge and returned home when they felt they had done enough; anger at the rest of them who stayed but whose efforts have been aggravatingly incompetent; anger at Mrs. McGinn's daughter for the resentful gaze she has been turning on him all night; anger even at the animals for still being here, for existing at all in the first place, for placing their deaths on his shoulders and making him feel as though this crisis is somehow his fault. How the hell could it be his fault? he demands of himself as he closes in on an armadillo. What could he possibly have done differently?

The reason why he took this job in the first place, in fact, was to escape the burden of responsibility. He grew up the oldest of four children, son to parents who loved him dearly and who desired nothing more than his success. But he was not interested in science or medicine, nor in history or law. He was smart and capable, but he hated the weight of all their expectations and the pressure of their stares. He left home as a surly adolescent, determined to avoid situations where people wanted more of him than he could give. That's why the zookeeping came so easily to him: because the animals expected nothing more from him except the routine of their daily feeding. This was something he knew he could provide. It was satisfying; it was safe.

And now? With the rain pouring into the grasslands and the penguins swimming over their tank and the monkeys screaming as the water rises in their cages—whose problem is this if not his own?

"Hey," says a voice from behind him. "Have you seen my husband?"

He turns. There in the rain is the slender figure of Noah's wife, her pointed face half obscured by her hood. "He said he wanted to round up the wolves, but I haven't seen him since," she says. "He isn't very good with animals, and I'm beginning to worry."

The zookeeper shakes his head impatiently. "I don't have time to go looking for lost ministers," he retorts. "Do you see that armadillo over there? I've got to get her into this crate before the whole damn field is flooded."

His tone is deliberately sharp, but to his surprise the woman refuses to be deterred. "If I got her for you," she presses him, "then would you have a minute to help me find Noah?"

The zookeeper narrows his eyes and considers her. Rain mingles with beads of sweat along her forehead. Her lips are drained of color, but her chin is set and her gray gaze is steady. In truth, he has not paid much attention to her since her arrival; in general he prefers people who are fiercer, brighter. But she is here now, and so he might as well make use of her.

"Be my guest," he grunts. He hands her his pair of canvas gloves, and swings the crate into her arms. She takes it and thanks him and then jogs toward the far end of the enclosure. The zookeeper loses sight of her in the dark. A minute later he sees the flash of silver armadillo hide, and a moment after that Noah's wife appears once again before him with the crate held out before her and Maisy hunkered down against the wooden slats. The zookeeper widens his eyes, impressed despite himself. Anyone else would be triumphant, but Noah's wife is only expectant.

"Nice work," he mutters. "Do you have another minute?"

She has all night, of course. Although the zookeeper knows that she would prefer to leave him and find her husband, she seems unable to refuse when he asks her directly for her help. As the darkness begins to peel away from the sky, she trots alongside him to the picnic grounds and helps him corral the rest of the elk. The task goes twice as fast as it would have gone without her, and since she shows no signs of tiring once it is completed, the zookeeper pushes her on in the direction of the primate house to collect the chimpanzees. For the first half hour, she follows his commands in some distraction, her gaze always roving the grounds for Noah. But halfway through the aviary, she begins to show more animation. She enjoys working with the animals—he can see that right away—and she is *good* at it. When the minister's wife talks to the wolves, they lie down in her presence. The toucan swoops to her shoulder and goes meekly into his cage. And after she sweet-talks the notoriously cantankerous zebra into his pen using nothing but an apple and a song—that was when the zookeeper could tell she had a gift. When he tells her so, she laughs at him. The sound carries in the rain and the townspeople look up from their tasks with some surprise. Mrs. McGinn glowers at the two of them as they dash past the penguin tank.

While waiting for the bats in the plaster nocturnal cave, the zookeeper asks Noah's wife how she came to be so good with animals. Briefly, unemotionally, she describes a solitary childhood. The zookeeper tries to picture her as a little girl, her dark hair uncombed and the bones in her pale face as delicate and as hollow as a dove's. He sees her kneeling on a chair at the kitchen table in the long afternoon hours before her family returned home, spreading peanut butter with great care into pinecones and building birdhouses out of shoeboxes. When she was older, she made a little money by walking her neighbors' dogs and feeding their cats while they were away.

"But it's not a *gift*," she corrects him, shrugging off the compliment. The zookeeper doesn't try to argue with her. Instead he watches the bats swoop in the shadows, listens to the dry rustle of their wings and thinks about his family for the first time in years.

Outside the nocturnal cave, the fish from the creek in the savannah float past with their dead bellies turned up, their silver scales reflecting the sky. The water has washed out yards and yards of fencing, and the animals are roaming the grounds, followed by exhausted townspeople bearing umbrellas or branches or brooms—anything they might use to herd the beasts toward the cars. A few feet away from the exit, the zookeeper leans down and scoops up an otter. The otter chirps indignantly and struggles to get free.

The townspeople are carrying out sheep and goats on their shoulders, holding the hooves clasped together as the zookeeper showed them. The tiger is gone but the other big cats and canines are safely tranquilized, rolled heavily onto tarps and then lifted into the back of the closest open van. Mauro tucks the tortoises into trunks; the last of the birds are coaxed into cages and draped in towels before being carried out into the rain. Leesl is wrapping the primates into blankets and buckling them into passenger seats while Mrs. McGinn uses an oversized metal rake to drive the barnyard animals toward the headlights. When the zookeeper sees Noah struggling under several bales of wet hay, he turns around to point him out to Noah's wife—but she is all the way across the yard leading a small band of townspeople out of the reptile house, all of them lugging glass aquariums. Under her direction, they load the tanks into the cushioned backseat of an open car and then turn around and trudge back to collect the rest.

"What the hell are *you* staring at, Adam?" demands Mrs. McGinn's daughter, her high-pitched voice slicing right through his reflection. "I thought I'd made myself clear."

"Angie," he growls, without turning around. "Don't be so stupid. I'm yours."

That is the trouble with love, reflects the zookeeper, pulling the otter more tightly to his chest and remembering the hard embraces of his father. The anger is draining out of him, leaving behind only exhaustion and the faint, insistent tugging of despair. That is why he has made a career out of avoiding people. Their expectations are too high. When they love someone, they demand that he be more than what he is; they forget that when all is said and done, he is just another animal—just as bewildered and beleaguered as the rest.

fourteen

Umbrellas bloom across the square in a field of colored canopies.

Noah's wife admires them as she approaches, following three or four steps behind Noah. Although she is soaked to the bone and more tired than she's ever been before, every muscle aching as she forces her legs forward, she is buoyed by the sight of the colors. The rain is less torrential now—it is lighter, more rhythmic—and in the delicate, gray light of morning, she finds that she feels better than she has since they arrived here. The long night is finished, the crisis has passed. The rain is letting up, and perhaps the worst of it will finally be over.

Noah, as he walks, shows more sign of purpose than he has in four or five days. Ever since the service, he has eaten little and slept fitfully. Several nights she awoke in the dark to find that he was not in bed beside her, and in the morning she stumbled up the hill to bring him breakfast in his office at the church. Even when he was in the house, warmly and bodily present, his eyes and mind returned insistently, incessantly to the window. The sky behind the steeple softened from black to gray at dawn, and the light slunk in through the blinds to fall across his head and shoulders. Yesterday morning he stood looking out, his clear, broad face reflecting the rain, and when his wife opened her eyes she felt as she always feels these days when she sees him standing at the window with the light streaming through him: that if she doesn't keep her gaze fixed upon him, he will disappear. What would become of her then?

The townspeople's cars are parked and double-parked around the square, all of them splattered with mud, their metal frames eaten away by rust. As Noah passes by a decrepit sedan he hears a shriek from inside the car and leaps back, instinctively, when a scarlet-feathered bird throws itself against the window. Most of the vehicles are shuddering from the wild movements of their occupants, and Noah's wife finds herself falling behind as she slows to gaze at the matted fur and feathers of the animals boxed up in backseats, their button-eyes gleaming at her from the other side of foggy windows. Noah turns around to call to her and she trots to catch up as a tinny voice resounds among the low brick buildings. The meeting has already begun.

"Good morning!" Mrs. McGinn shouts through her megaphone in the center of the town square. "Thank you all for being here! I know this isn't how most of you expected to be spending your Saturday morning. Well, Lord knows that no one expected the zoo to flood, either. But who can prepare for every crisis? Who can foresee every outcome? When plans change, we have to change along with them!"

"Come the high hell and water!" shouts Mauro from somewhere near the back.

Someone chuckles, and Noah's wife turns to see the weatherman standing two feet behind her. He flashes a sardonic smile and jabs his thumb in Mauro's direction.

"That guy is hilarious," he says.

"What are you doing here?" she whispers, her tone fierce.

"Town meeting." He shrugs. "I figured it would be entertaining."

Noah's wife looks away from him. The weatherman is by far the driest, calmest person in the square. The rest of the townspeople are huddled together, their ponchos rustling as they shiver. They are anxious to get home, but they cannot leave without unloading the animals and no one has told them where to put them. When they begin to mutter among themselves, Mrs. McGinn hoists her orange umbrella, luminous against the smudge of charcoal sky behind her. She has always been fond of rhetorical flourishes.

"Furthermore, we have a responsibility," she continues, "as the inhabitants and stewards of this town. Some of you might say that this town isn't what it used to be. Some of you might say that the rain has been falling forever and the zoo has been downsizing for years and what's the point of concerning ourselves with it now? Why should we care?"

The townspeople's gazes are foggy from lack of sleep. Some of them are reeling from side to side with dazed expressions, tightening their hoods over hair that is already drenched. The rain taps teasingly against their shoulders. A few people gaze longingly at the single highway in the gray distance, the only way out of here. Is it too late to make a run for it?

"Well, I'll tell you why!" declares Mrs. McGinn, really hitting her stride now. "It's not because this zoo is what put us on the map in the first place. It's not because we used to be famous once or because if we do this right, maybe we could be famous again. Although that might be true!"

"Evelyn!" snaps one of her neighbors. Noah's wife turns to see a man with a black umbrella and a face covered in claw marks. "Enough of your goddamn speeches already. We've done what you asked us to do. Just tell us where you're sending the animals so that we can get them out of our cars and go home to bed!"

"Yes!" shout the townspeople from various corners of the square. "What are we doing? Let's get out of here!" Noah's wife turns around again to see who is speaking, and finds the weatherman looking pleased.

Mrs. McGinn lowers her megaphone, her expression losing some of its luster. She turns to the zookeeper, and the two of them exchange a series of urgent whispers.

Noah's wife shakes her head. "They don't have a plan," she says, leaning closer to Noah. "They've got all the animals out, and now there isn't anywhere to put them."

The crowd is beginning to get restless. Their muttered conversations are increasing in volume, their rain-streaked faces growing red beneath the dirt. The optimism Noah's wife was feeling has already faded, and she reaches for Noah's elbow with some trepidation.

"Come on," she says. "Let's go home."

Noah shakes his head, his curls heavy with water. "What about *our* car?" he reminds her.

She remembers their backseat: the portable pens with the red fox and the badger, the one-winged eagle cramped into a birdcage in the hatchback, the otter at the foot of the passenger seat. Although she has no idea what to do about the animals, she wants nothing more right now than to go home, tumble down onto the couch, and rest her head on her husband's shoulder.

"We'll take them with us," she says to Noah, her tone slightly pleading. "Just for now. Can't we figure out what to do with them later?"

He turns to her with an expression she cannot read. She assumes that he is reliving last night: the rain, the exhaustion, the ever-present fear that one of the animals would run the wrong way and someone would be trampled or mauled or worse. She glances at the faces of her neighbors, still largely unfamiliar to her, and worries that after the night they have been through, there is bound to be an uproar. She would rather face the talons of the eagle in their trunk than the wrath of the mud-covered townspeople.

Suddenly her husband's countenance clears. She doesn't know what fresh hope has illuminated his expression, and since she doesn't have a chance to ask him before he speaks, his next pronouncement surprises her as much as anyone.

"We'll take them!" he shouts, spinning around and cupping his hands close to his mouth so that his voice will travel. "My wife and I! We'll take some home with us!"

The townspeople nearest him settle into a hush, their faces hard with disbelief. Others turn to stare.

"Noah!" his wife whispers fiercely. "What are you doing?"

"It's all right," he murmurs back, squeezing her hand. "I've got a plan."

In the sudden calm that has fallen over the square, he takes off toward the front of the crowd. His wife watches his black slicker weaving through the townspeople until he reaches Mrs. McGinn, who stands awkwardly on the podium with her megaphone dangling from her hand. Once there, he turns to address his neighbors.

"It's only a temporary solution," he calls out, "until we come up with something better." When the townspeople's faces remain blank, he shouts: "Fear not, be not dismayed— Arise and be doing!"

"What the hell?" mutters the town sheriff.

"First Chronicles," explains Mauro proudly, winking at Noah's wife. He taps the tip of his nose with his index finger. "The Solomon and the temple."

For a moment, the only sound is that of the rain pattering along the sleeves of their coats and the tops of their umbrellas. Then, from the weatherman: "That's the stupidest thing I've ever heard."

Mrs. McGinn shakes off her shock. Incensed, she whips the megaphone back up to her lips. "It's generous!" she informs them. "That's what it is!" Her cheeks flush with the thrill of a new idea. She is not about to let the new minister outshine her in his dedication to this cause. "We're *all* going to take the animals!"

While her neighbors erupt with disbelief and indignation, she swings down and confers briefly with the zookeeper. Noah stands to one side, looking out over the sea of angry figures with his face drawn and his fists clenched. Noah's wife tries to catch his eye, but fails. She wants to tell him that what she meant was for them to keep the animals in their car for a few hours and then return them before lunchtime; she did not intend to invite the beasts into their spare bedroom for an extended stay. Does he not remember how terrible he was with the animals last night? He didn't trust them, and they didn't trust him. He wandered through the grounds on his own, lost and overwhelmed. It was a miracle that he didn't get hurt.

"Ask the beasts, and they will teach you!" declares Noah, his expression illuminated and his poise suddenly returned to him. "And the birds of the air, and they will tell you. Who among all these does not know that the hand of the Lord has done this, in whose hand is the life of every living thing, and the breath of all mankind?"

Mauro turns and stares at Noah's wife. "Job," she tells him in a small voice. "Chapter twelve."

The librarian overhears. "Isn't that the man whose life was destroyed?" she wants to know. "Job? That's who the minister wants us to remember at a time like this?"

"All right," announces Mrs. McGinn, saving Noah's wife from the burden of inventing an interpretation. She straightens up and blasts her air horn. "Here's the plan. Do you see all of these vacant storefronts? We'll have the big cats, the wolves, the more dangerous animals divided up and settled down in those. The hoof-foots—"

"Hoofstock," corrects the zookeeper beside her.

"The hoofstock," she continues, running her finger down her checklist. "Most of them can stay in yards and gardens, if they are properly fenced. All the birds who can fly have clipped wings, but it would be best if they were kept confined. Since the penguins will need to be kept cool, we'll house them in our walk-in freezer at the diner. The tanks of snakes and turtles should not pose much of a problem—those can go anywhere, on any bookshelf or coffee table. I already have an idea as to who should take the most noxious reptiles, anyway." She smirks to herself and then pulls a pocket-sized notebook from the folds of her raincoat. "Now, what I'm going to do is to assign the remaining animals to specific households. The gibbons, the otters, the sloth, the seals, the ostrich, the peacocks—you name it. If you have any specific allergies or animal preferences, come see me, and we'll take that into consideration when making your assignment. Are there any questions? Do you all understand? We've got no other choice here, people! We need everyone to step up. The survival of our town depends upon this—depends upon *you*."

It is a foolish, dangerous idea, but the townspeople submit to the new plan with nothing more than a few low grumbles of halfhearted dissent. Is it because the weather has been so awful for so long? wonders Noah's wife. Has the rain deteriorated their ability to stand up for themselves? Or has the zoo been so deeply ingrained in the soul of this place and the hearts of its inhabitants that they honestly do not believe that it is possible for them to survive without it?

When Noah descends from the podium and joins her once again at the back of the crowd, his cheeks are so radiant with his success, his eyes so glassy, that she considers reaching up to touch his forehead to test him for a fever.

"Noah," she says, bewildered. "*What* is this about?"

He gazes over the crowd, his expression vacant and his smile slightly off. "Don't you see?" he says. "I came here to help these people, and so I'm helping them. Tomorrow morning we'll have another service. Look at the mess of this place—peace and order need to be restored. I need for them to see that the Lord is not against them, that we're all on the same side."

She stares at him. His face is gaunter than it was when they arrived only a month ago, his beard shot through with several strands of silver. The ravages of weather and worry over the past four weeks, it seems, have left their mark; but if his face is craggier and more melancholy, it is also more striking. He has always been a handsome man, and if anything, his wife now finds him handsomer still. This show of confident determination is not new to her, and in a way she is glad to hear the old stubborn tones of faith in his voice. This is more like the minister she married. She does not want to believe that his plan isn't sound; she does not want to see the shadow of doubt steal over his face again. And so she makes up her mind to keep her mouth shut, to nod and take his arm, to willingly accept the sign-up sheet when Mrs. McGinn brings it round to them. When they finally return to their car she lifts the otter to her lap as if she has been his keeper for a lifetime, and when she unloads the cages from the back and sets up the pens in the kitchen she does her best to act as though this is the most natural thing in the world.

Her best friend used to scold her for this kind of easy acquiescence, used to frown when she bent over backward to offer her help to coworkers, customers, strangers moving in or out of a townhouse down the row. When she threw out her back lifting an armchair for a woman she had never met and whom she would never see again, Dr. Yu prepared a heating pad and sighed.

"You know," Dr. Yu had said, "if you keep giving so much of yourself away, sooner or later there won't be anything left."

fifteen

Dr. Yu receives a call at the hospital from someone who informs her that her father has fallen down at the harbor.

"In the harbor?" repeats Dr. Yu, alarmed. She grips the receiver of her telephone, strides as far across the room as the telephone cord will allow. "How did that happen?"

"Not *in* the harbor, dear," says the stranger, whose voice sounds husky and female. "*At* the harbor. He stumbled over a loose plank in the dock while he was doing his sprints, and then he bumped his head on a mooring bollard. He's all right—a little dazed, is all, and he probably shouldn't drive."

"Tell him I'll be there in twenty minutes," says Dr. Yu. "Where can I find him?"

"We've got him up on our boat now. You won't have any trouble finding us. Look for a gold hull, with three orange sails. My name is Nancy. And please, try not to worry! He's in good hands. What a charming man! Has he ever shown you his card tricks?"

Dr. Yu hangs up the phone, worrying. On the drive to the harbor, she speeds and—though usually the most conscientious of drivers—she doesn't care. The scene at the boat is a blur of colors and sounds: a woman in a powder-blue pantsuit; a dark, quiet man shaking ice in his cocktail mixer while his mustache trembles; her father leaning back in one of their lounge chairs, finishing up an old-fashioned and telling stories to make the man and woman laugh. Dr. Yu thanks the couple briskly for their time and, after turning down their dinner invitation, herds her father off the boat and into the passenger seat of her sedan.

"That's Stan and Nancy," explains her father on the drive home. "I just met them. Aren't they the nicest people? I've got to say, I think I made a real impression on them. You should have seen how they looked when I told them to handcuff me and drop me off the edge of the pier. Pure amazement! They didn't do it, of course—said you were on the way, and all—but still. Maybe next time."

Dr. Yu grits her teeth, remains silent until they reach the house. Once inside, she sits him down on the sofa and pulls his arm forward. While she holds his wrist on her knees, her fingers pressed to his pulse, she says: "Magic or no magic, you're not in any shape to be going out to the docks by yourself. I wish you'd stay at home. What on earth would make you start sprinting out there, anyway?"

Her father sighs. "I've been telling you for weeks, April," he says. "To perfect these escapes, I've got to be in perfect physical condition. Take the straitjacket trick, for instance—that requires pure muscle. I've also drawn up a schedule to start swimming so I can improve my lung capacity. For the greatest underwater escapes, I'll need to hold my breath for three or four minutes."

"That's impossible," says Dr. Yu. "There's no way you can do that."

"Since when do you tell me what to do?" her father retorts. "Since when have I become the child, and you the parent? When exactly did that change occur, and why wasn't I notified?"

"Papa, please," she says.

"Don't 'Papa, please' me!" he says. "It's nice to have a purpose again. You should see the way those crowds gather at the docks to see me perform! The kids love me! And anyway, how else will I be able to take my escapes up a notch if I never try anything in the water?"

Dr. Yu rolls her eyes skyward and takes a deep breath. At first she had been pleased that her father was getting out of the house, going for walks along the water in the salty sea air. She hadn't realized that his main purpose was to take his scarves and cards and cuffs down to the docks to put on a good show for passersby. More people come to see him every week, and by now his shows have gained a loyal following. Although she knows that he is pleased about his popularity, Dr. Yu still cannot bear to see him. How has her brilliant, science-minded father become this crazy, wild-eyed street performer? Why must he insist on turning himself into a joke?

His escapes seem to be getting more and more complicated: he likes to ask boaters to tie his hands with their ropes, or to bind his legs together with fishing net. He isn't allowed to perform any tricks with fire on the pier, so he purchased a small skiff in which he rows out beyond the other boats. He'll transform seagulls into smoke or shoot sparks from his wand into the sky from out there. Dr. Yu is all too aware that recently he has spent several nights on his boat, snoring in fitful bursts on the damp boards that line the bottom of the craft, his ropes and keys in small heaps around him. It's only a matter of time until he does something more dangerous.

"You've been under such strain since Mama died," she says. "The best thing for you right now is to rest, to keep your strength up."

"Oh really?" says her father. "Says who? If it's the doctors who say that's the best thing, then I don't want to hear another word about it."

She considers him evenly, bites her tongue. This is what happens whenever she tells him a story from the hospital or urges him to take better care of himself. He will wave his hand condescendingly, dismissively, and inform her that he does not believe in doctors and he doesn't care a whit for what they have to say. He used to tell her that he was proud of her, proud that she had succeeded in a career where women were still so few and far between. Sometimes these days, in spite of her effort at self-control, his criticism will get the best of her, and her pained expression will show it; and although in these moments he looks as though he might be considering taking back his words, he never does. It doesn't matter, anyway. Once the words are spoken, they can never be retrieved.

Her mother used to tell him that the tongue is like a lion in its cage: once it is loose, it is bound to do some damage. Her mother used to keep him in line.

"I'm sorry, sweetheart," he might say, trying to soften the blow. "You know that I'm proud of you. All I'm saying is that pouring all of your faith into the miracles of modern medicine is a bad idea. You're bound to be disappointed."

Dr. Yu releases his wrist and reaches up to touch the coarse black strands of her hair. Whenever she is anxious, she chops some of it off. As her mother had grown sicker, Dr. Yu's hair had become shorter—half inch by half inch—until it was shorn into a bob higher than her chin, the ends flipping under her ears. Every time she cut it she collected the glossy scraps from the bathroom floor and threw them outside because her mother used to tell her that birds could use the hair to build their nests.

She considers taking the kitchen scissors to the bathroom and shearing it again now.

"Papa," she says, "you know that's not true."

"Do I?" he snaps back. "Do you?"

Dr. Yu wishes that her best friend were here; her best friend, who always knows what to say to make peace. They have not been able to speak as often as she would have liked in the month since her best friend moved away. The one or two times they tried, the connection was so awful that the two of them could only exchange a few pleasantries before the line went dead.

The last time they spoke, Dr. Yu believed that she detected something unusual in her best friend's voice: some kind of strain, tight and high-pitched. Is she upset because Dr. Yu has been so unavailable? Dr. Yu knows she ought to make good on her promise to go and visit them, but how can she leave the city when her work is so demanding and her father needs so much looking after? There is always next month, she tells herself. She will get to her best friend eventually. In the meantime, there is little she can do from where she is, and so she tries to put her friend out of her mind for now.

Her father has told her, in wounded exasperation, that he doesn't see how she can still profess such faith in her field after everything that has happened. He doesn't see how she could have stood beside him in the sun at the cemetery, staring down at the stone while her shadow tumbled into the grave and the sweat ran in streams from her stooped shoulders to her surgeon's hands—how she could have heard the words and touched the dirt and then thrown on her white coat and gone into work again the next day as if nothing had happened. As if she still believed that medicine had the power to save.

They have talked about this constantly over the past few weeks. They have fought with each other until they are both so irate that they go several hours without speaking. He has tried to explain to her about the silence in his house—how much it still unnerves him, how it makes him uneasy and uncertain. He devotes himself to his new hobby and his new audience in large part to keep himself out of the house. On the water, at the harbor, it is never silent. There is always the tender hush of the wind against the waves, the plaintive cries of gulls.

Dr. Yu, accustomed to his mood swings, doesn't respond to him now. What is there to say? She wishes that he were kinder, more empathetic than he is, and she tries to attribute his skewed opinions on her work and her life—one and the same, really—to the effects of grief and loss. She tries to remind herself that it isn't personal.

Since her mother died, he has not been himself. Dr. Yu is concerned for his stability, for his emotional and physical health. He should not be spending so much time on these high-energy escapes. He should not be allowing himself to become so excited. She wants him to ease up; she wants him to eat better. She wants him to read the large-print mystery books that she checks out for him at the library. She doesn't want him to be wandering around the harbor, falling down on metal poles, asking people to throw him into the sea.

"What if you had fallen in the water after you'd hit your head?" she says. "Did you ever think of that? Or what if you'd been handcuffed underwater and you'd knocked against something and fallen unconscious? You've got to be more careful!"

"Why's that?" he demands. "You're not going to save me from an untimely death, sweetheart. Every death is untimely. That's the nature of things. All you'll manage to do is prolong a lonely life, and I'll tell you what—no, don't interrupt me—I'll tell you what: sitting in this house doing nothing will kill me a lot faster than this will."

He leans forward, takes her hand in his and rubs her knuckles to calm her down. "I'm sorry it upsets you, of course I am," he says. "You're my daughter, and I love you. I know you don't understand."

"I don't," she says. She extricates her hand, picks up her stethoscope and slips it around her neck. The weight of the metal drum drops toward her heart like an anchor. She stands up and goes to the kitchen to heat a can of soup on the stove. A little while later, her father joins her in the kitchen and they eat in silence.

When she leaves the house she says good-bye to him and kisses his leathered cheek. Her lips are pale and dry. "See you later, Papa," she says. "Be safe, okay? Don't do anything stupid."

"I'll be fine," he says, somewhat vacantly. He smiles at her and pats her shoulder.

She walks down the sidewalk to her car, slides into her seat, drives away from the house. When she has gone a block and is out of sight of the windows she pulls over to the curb, stops the engine, rests her head on the steering wheel, and cries.

sixteen

Leesl is not surprised that Noah's second service is even less successful than the first.

But then, Leesl is never surprised.

Although she believes that Noah's heart is in the right place, the problem is that his would-be congregants now have other things to occupy them. As she walks through the silver drizzle this morning, she sees Mrs. McGinn's husband wrestling with large cages that he is loading into the back of his van; the sheriff is trying to persuade the habitually useless firemen to drive the elk into the town park; wild boars are roaming free, and Mrs. McGinn's daughter is chasing after the sheep. The zookeeper has been working through the night to transport the animal feed and supplies from storage units near the zoo to vacant rooms in the long-abandoned town hall. The plan is to distribute supplies to the townspeople several times a week.

When Leesl sees Mrs. McGinn poking a stick at a boa constrictor in the gutter, she pauses to ask if she can be of any assistance and then she says something—helpfully, she believes—about Noah's second service at the church this morning.

"Perhaps you would find a little peace up there," Leesl quietly suggests. "It might do this town a world of good."

Mrs. McGinn steps away from the snake. "That one's definitely dead," she declares. Then she turns on Leesl. "As for the church, Leesl, I don't want to hear another word about it. How can any of us be expected to worry over the next world when there is so much that needs doing in this one?"

The weatherman, crossing the street at that moment, hears her and snorts. "I've said it before and I'll say it again," he declares. "This place is a mess. If you people don't evacuate within the next week, your town is doomed."

A penguin struts out from behind Mrs. McGinn, making a beeline for the weatherman. When it reaches him it stops and gazes up with eyes so polished that they seem unreal.

"What does it want?" he says, disconcerted.

"What do you think it wants?" Mrs. McGinn snaps. "Fish." She whips out a can of tuna from the deep pockets of her raincoat, peels it open, and sets it on the pavement, where it promptly begins to fill with water. "Anyway," she says, "I told *you* before, and I'll tell you again. We're fine here. What makes you think we can't handle a little rain?"

"A *little* rain?" repeats the weatherman.

"That's right," she says.

Leesl squints between the two of them, hating the conflict.

"Listen," insists the weatherman. "Do you know how long it took me to get up here? I've never seen roads so terrible: thick with sludge, and some places several inches full of water. You need food delivered here, you need mail, you need supplies for your shops, and God knows what you need for these damn animals. It's only a matter of time until the river overflows and the rest of this place is underwater, too. How do you think you'll manage in a week when the trucks can't get through?"

Mrs. McGinn glares at him. "You think we haven't had bad winters in these hills before? You think we don't have a plan? Sometimes the pass into town is blocked up for days. We've got canned goods and gallons of water crammed into storage units down the road. We've got more supplies than we know what to do with. We don't get much mail even when the roads are clear. Anyhow, the rain's letting up. It'll all be over soon, so you might as well return to your car and go back where you came from instead of staying here and trying to stir people up into a panic when there isn't anything to be concerned about."

"And these animals you've got stinking up your shops and houses?" he retorts. "That's not something I should be concerned about?"

"They're *our* animals," she barks. "We can do what we like with them. I don't see that it's any concern of yours. In fact, if I were you, I'd get out of this town as fast as I could. We need someone to house the snakes, and if you're still here tomorrow, I'm planning to send them on to you."

Leesl murmurs a good-bye and leaves them while they are still fighting. She crosses the wooden planks that Mauro has been laying from curb to curb over the crosswalks. Although the rain has let up, the water is much higher in the streets now than it was before. It rushes quickly through the gutter, bearing loads of twigs and leaves along with it. There are broken branches strewn across the sidewalk from the storm two nights ago, and as Leesl climbs the hill she fears that the trees are leaning far too close to telephone poles. In the distance she can see that the river is running much faster than it was yesterday, its waves lapping like cat tongues at the crumbling banks. Well, what is there for her to do? She cannot move the tree branches; she cannot bail the water from the river to keep it contained between its banks, or force the rain back into the sky. For now, she simply continues on up to the church, her knees sharply bent into the wind.

There are only a handful of people in the church. Leesl sees Noah's wife waiting serene as carved stone in the first pew, her limbs crossed, her gaze fixed upon her prayer book. Scattered in rows near the back are six or eight haggard townspeople, most of whom get up and walk out when they realize Mrs. McGinn has not come to take attendance. The rest stay put until Leesl has finished the opening hymn, flinging bright, hard notes up toward the rafters. After several long, damp minutes have passed without any sign of Noah, those few remaining rise from their seats and trickle toward the door, one by one, until no one is left but Leesl and Noah's wife.

"Where is he?" asks Noah's wife once the rest of them have gone. Her flutelike voice is fearful, and she rises in her pew.

"I'm sorry," says Leesl. "I don't know."

Noah's wife turns and hurries down the aisle. "Maybe he went home to check up on the animals," she says. "It's so unlike him. He's never missed a service in his life before."

Rooted to her seat, Leesl turns her head and watches Noah's wife disappear through the lobby. A moment later the front door eases shut and Leesl can see the outline of a figure receding through the lower stained-glass windows. She runs her fingers along the keys, plays a few more notes, and then inches off the bench. The zookeeper said that he would be bringing the cheetah to her sometime late this morning, and so she ought to return home to open up the garage.

It is as she steps lightly around the back of the altar to the office, where she intends to leave her books until next week, that she hears the murmuring of a familiar voice. As she approaches she recognizes the verses: the story of Daniel in the lions' den, saved from claws and fangs by the grace of God. She rounds the corner and finds Noah sitting on the floor, the Bible beside him and a small, leather-bound journal in his lap. Walled in by stacks of papers, he glances up when she enters and does his best to beam.

"Lovely work today, Leesl!" he says with forcible optimism. Leesl winces. Earlier this week when she asked him what he thought of her selections, he sang a few lines in an off-key, desperate sort of bellow. He does the same thing now, butchering a phrase of "Eternal Father, Strong to Save," and she winces again without meaning to.

"Please don't do that," she whispers. She hesitates, and then asks: "Are you all right? You didn't come out for the service."

"I'm fine!" Noah replies. "Just got caught up reading!"

"But there were people there," Leesl informs him.

"Not many," retorts Noah.

His tone is curt, so Leesl drops the subject. Instead she tilts her head and indicates the papers. "Let me take those. I'll throw them away."

"Why?" asks Noah, peering up at her with renewed interest. "Are they private?"

Leesl shakes her head. "They belonged to the old minister," she says. "They're Reverend Matthews's things."

She must be the only person in town, she reflects, who knew anything at all about the old minister as a human being, the only person who kept coming up to the church after the failure of the services in which they bowed their heads and prayed for the rain to end. In the months before he died, he stopped writing sermons and puttering around the church. Mostly he sat at the stained-glass window with his notebook on his lap, telling Leesl that as long as he looked at the world through these colored panes, the sky would never be gray.

"What are you writing?" she had asked.

"Poetry," the old minister said. He had a theory that poetry was a lot like prayer: a signal flare shot off into the darkness, a call without any hope of a response.

She sits down cross-legged in front of Noah, the moisture in the cold stone floor seeping through her cotton skirt. "Here," she says, beginning to gather the papers to put them away. "Let me help you with those."

Noah remains where he is, his fingers gripping the edges of the notebook. Leesl glances at the pages, sees something that looks like a sonnet.

"What happened to him, Leesl?" Noah asks, plaintively. "Was it an accident or not?"

Leesl stops riffling through the papers and considers him, her blue eyes calm behind her glasses. "Of course it was an accident," she says. "What makes you think it would have been anything else?"

"Well," he replies, stretching out his legs with a groan. "I'll tell you something. I didn't always feel this way—but truthfully, Leesl, it is a very sad business being a minister. If I've come to see that, I wouldn't be surprised if other ministers before me had come to see it, too."

Leesl rests her knobby elbows on her knees. "It can't all be sad," she says severely.

Noah nods, looking past her. "There used to be a lot of things I loved about it," he admits. He tells her that the work had always come easily to him; that even as a child he had a talent for public speaking and a gift for reassuring people. His friends and siblings were in the habit of seeking him out when they were anxious or unhappy because with a few carefully chosen sentences he could ease the weight of all their worry. Noah had assumed, upon entering the ministry, that this transformation would be the most significant aspect of his work. He had imagined a steady stream of congregants lining up to seek him out, one after one, day after day, bringing their troubles to him so that he might share in their burden and teach them to lift their eyes toward heaven. "Raise your voices!" he would tell them. "Sing songs of praise to the Lord!" He had become a minister because he wanted to lessen the sorrow of the world, and increase its joy.

And during the first few years of his work, he says, he still thought that this would be possible; he still entered the nave with a hopeful step and a high heart. It was only later that he learned how little his vision of his work corresponded with the reality of it, only recently that he realized that nearly all prayer is lamentation: complaints, grumblings, grievances. Most of the congregants who filed into his church at ten o'clock on Sunday morning were not coming to offer thanks or praise. When their family members were sick or injured, when they lost jobs and were in debt, when they lost friends and were in mourning—this was when they came to pray. They prayed for help and for mercy and for healing, and when the Lord did not heed their prayers, they gave up hope and turned away again.

Leesl remains perfectly still while Noah tells her that over the past few months, he has found himself stumbling. The tales of woe that he hears make him woeful, in turn, and although he prays with his flock, he fears that the act provides little comfort to either party. When the prayers are not answered—when the family member becomes sicker and dies, when the couple remains barren, when the sorrow is not lifted—Noah feels himself to be personally responsible. He wishes that he could offer the peace that these people are seeking, but instead he is beginning to lose his own sense of peace. If he has succeeded in lightening anyone's burden, it is only because he has taken on that burden as his own. He has been going through the motions of the rituals with a growing sense of panic, the spirit draining out of him.

"Does anyone else know about this?" asks Leesl, startled by the frankness of this confession.

"No," he says. "I told myself that doubt is only natural, that this, too, would pass."

"What about your wife?" Leesl asks. "What does she say?"

Noah shakes his head. "It's not her problem, it's mine." He pauses, clears his throat. "Anyway," he says, "I waited for things to improve, but the doubt only grew worse. That's when it seemed like a good idea to look for a change of scenery. I figured that if I could succeed here, in a place like this that's been written off for years, if I could manage to turn things around—well, that ought to be enough of a miracle to turn my heart around, too. That ought to be reason enough to believe."

"So it's a test," murmurs Leesl. She has not been tested since her school days, but she remembers the experience as being petrifying.

He pauses, his forehead creased in thought. "It is, Leesl, it is. But perhaps every man's story is a sort of test: a series of obstacles, challenges to overcome. How else do we gain faith and wisdom? How else do we grow into the people that others believe us to be?" He shakes his head, sets the journal aside, rises to his feet, and extends a hand to help Leesl to hers. "The only problem is that these days I don't quite feel as though I'm up to the challenge."

Leesl allows him to lift her to her feet, his hand wide and dry. She doesn't know what to say to him. Before she leaves, Noah says: "I'm sorry for carrying on so, Leesl. I didn't mean to burden you with my personal troubles."

She only nods. As she walks back home, picking her way between the raindrops, she gazes out over downtown and sees the light boxes glowing in her neighbors' windows. She goes home to wait for the arrival of her cheetah, and while she waits she pours herself a glass of milk and tries to sweep Noah's melancholy words from the corners of her mind.

Leesl refuses to believe that her town is as taxing as it seems. If there were nothing here but the incessant rain, the vacant shops, the failed relationships, the abandoned homes, the fading zoo, the so-called broken dreams—if it were true that *that* was all there was, then no one would remain. The townspeople would have been gone long ago. Leesl is convinced that there must be something more here than that—something intangible, unseen.

seventeen

After three full days spent doing rounds with him, Noah's wife informs the zookeeper that she cannot help him anymore.

"This was supposed to be temporary," she says, when he suggests that they stop in at the diner to dry off and grab a quick lunch. "I only agreed to help you for that first afternoon, while you were still getting the animals settled. They're settled now. I should be spending more time at home—taking care of my own."

Although she tries to make her voice as stern as possible, the zookeeper's hard gaze wears her down. She looks into her soup and feels the heat flooding her cheeks.

"Is that so?" the zookeeper counters. "You think they're settled?"

She wants to say yes. But then someone slides through her

peripheral vision, and she turns to see the sheriff taking a seat on the stool beside her. As the man reaches for a menu, Noah's wife catches a glimpse of his hands: two fingers wrapped in bandages, and the rest of the skin crosshatched in tiny cuts.

The sheriff notices her looking. "The red panda," he says. "I've got worse ones on my calves from the raccoon."

Noah's wife tries not to feel sorry for him. Didn't she and the zookeeper show him how to put the portable pens together? Whose fault is it that he didn't pay attention? She doesn't like feeling responsible for people who are still strangers to her, and yet she cannot help but worry over the townspeople she has seen over the past few days with dark rings under their eyes, bandages on their limbs, claw marks on their arms. It has not been an easy adjustment for anyone, taking these animals under their wings. Earlier this morning even Mauro—bubbly, bumbling Mauro—swore at her and the zookeeper as they stepped through the entrance to the general store. He is tired of waiting for things here to change, he told them, deeply perturbed. He is sick of the rain, of the way that it teases him and toys with his emotions—letting up for a few days here and there so that he begins to think the worst is over, only to come ripping out of the sky with a vengeance some afternoon while he is walking back to his store from the diner. Worst of all are the bugs: the little black and gold beetles that have begun creeping in under the windowsill and scuttling up and down the walls at night. Mauro can hear them in the dark as he lies awake below his blankets, his lips clamped shut and his hands over his ears because he once read a story about insects that crawled into people's orifices, laid their eggs, and died. The zookeeper assured him that the beetles have no intention of doing such a thing, that they are only coming inside in the first place because the ground is too saturated for them to survive.

"Well, what do *you* know?" Mauro muttered to himself, audibly enough for them to hear him. "Bringing the animals into the people's houses? How can that idea be making sense? This town is not a fairy tale!"

While none of the townspeople are particularly happy about the development, Mauro has turned out to be one of the most distressed. When Mrs. McGinn saw him sneaking away from the town meeting the other day, she brought him right back and promptly assigned him several large birds. His store is now home to three wild turkeys, two blue herons, an emu, and an ostrich. Not one of these has Mauro been able to bring himself to love, despite Mrs. McGinn's assurances. The herons are the most inoffensive—they roost on the shelves of the lumber department and fish for minnows in the kiddie pool Mauro set up for them in aisle six. And Mauro rather likes the two-toed gait of the ostrich, her hairless neck and the black and white feathers that look so soft to the touch. Sometimes he leans on his elbows over the counter for minutes at a time, watching her raise and lower her wings in an odd and delicate movement reminiscent of a lady lifting and rustling her petticoats.

It is the turkeys he hates. They are a gang, the three of them, a bullying gang. They lurk, watching him from behind stacks of canned goods. Sometimes they drive him back behind the counter when he tries to come out to greet a customer, charging at him as he leaves what they must regard as his cage. He sees them picking and eating the beetles from the walls but even that doesn't change his opinion of them. They make him feel unwelcome in his own home.

"And anyway, this is not my home," he grumbled. "Rolling stones are too mossy. I should have been going back to Italy all the many years ago."

It troubles Noah's wife to hear Mauro so unhappy, just as it troubles her to see the sheriff with his hands torn up. She only agreed to help the zookeeper in the first place because he said that no one else possessed her talent with the animals; he did not warn her about having to deal with the people, as well. Animals are much easier, reflects Noah's wife. Their wants and their needs are obvious, open, straightforward: they are hungry, tired, satisfied, afraid. The townspeople, on the other hand, with their emotions in knots and their hopes and dreams and fears all tangled up in themselves and in their neighbors—well, what would make her think that she could handle all of that? That is Noah's job; not hers.

But these days Noah seems to have little interest in communicating with his congregants. He barely eats and he no longer sleeps through the night. He leaves the house before she wakes, and she doesn't know where he goes. Every time she has tried checking in the church, he isn't there. The two of them have not made love since before the first service; last night she leaned in to press her lips to the warm skin of his throat, and he turned his head away. She lay awake in the dark for many cold minutes afterward, the muscles in her stomach tense with unease.

And so she busies herself with the beasts that Noah brought into their house: the woodchuck burrowing beneath the quilts in the guest bedroom, the badger snoring in his crate. One of the bathrooms has been transformed into a reptile house, with an orphaned baby alligator half submerged in the bathtub and a tank of lizards sunning by the glow of a light box on the back of the toilet. The one-winged golden eagle surveys the backyard from her perch in the dining room, keeping her eye on the pens with the wild boars, the zebra, and the sheep. In the morning before Noah's wife leaves and at night when she returns, she makes the rounds around the house and yard with buckets of feed hanging from her wrists, the slender red fox trotting at her heels, and her husband nowhere to be seen.

Perhaps it is better, she tries to convince herself, that she is doing this on her own. How terrible Noah is with the animals! He draws too close to them; he reaches out too quickly when he tries to touch them, and it seems as though every evening she is patching up some new wound. The barricades that he arranges while she is away—chairs, tables, lamps—have not proven successful in keeping the species contained in their assigned spaces. The animals simply do not like him. Within their first few hours with the flamingo, the bird attacked Noah twice and would have done so again if they had not given her up to Leesl. Just yesterday Noah's wife found Noah in a confrontation with the saddle-billed stork (five feet high, sharp-beaked, bad-tempered), her husband trying to scare the bird away by pressing a spatula to its feathered chest. The stork didn't budge. When Noah's wife saw the patches around his beak turning red with anger, something the zookeeper had advised her to watch for, she swiftly stepped between them, took the spatula from Noah, and ushered the bird into the basement. They have heard him cackling through the heating ducts ever since.

She might have tried rehoming the stork, too, but she knows better than anyone that the townspeople have animals enough of their own. Every time she enters a house or a shop with the zookeeper, the occupant looks as skittish and as drained as she feels. No one is happy.

"That animal doesn't do a damn thing," complains Mrs. McGinn's husband when the zookeeper stops by after lunch to check on the sloth and say hello to his fiancée.

"Those monkeys? The little hanging ones?" says one of the firemen later that afternoon. "They eat all the food they can get their thumbs on the second it passes through this kitchen. We haven't had a piece of fruit for days!"

"I don't see why I have to have the seals, too," whimpers the postmistress. "Aren't they strong swimmers? Can't they survive outside?"

"The snakes, *really*?" demands the weatherman, whose bookshelves have been stripped of weather tools and are now stocked with fifteen glass terrariums. "I don't even live in this town. Was it really necessary to give me *all* of them?"

"They're social creatures. We needed to keep them all together," lies the zookeeper, his face blank. He shoves a sack of live white mice into the weatherman's empty hands and then he spins heavily on his heel. Noah's wife knows that he intends for her to follow him, but instead she drops into a wicker chair by the weatherman's window and turns her face to the glass. The weatherman watches her, suspiciously—at this point he is wary of all the townspeople, who scowl when they see him and reject his attempts to drive them out of here. And can he blame them? Noah's wife asks herself, gazing out into the street. No one likes being told by a complete stranger that the time has come to abandon ship—especially when they are so desperate to stay afloat that they are grasping at feathers, sharing their beds with marsupials and their bathrooms with amphibians.

"So whose side are you on?" the weatherman demands, interrupting her reflection.

"Excuse me?" she says.

The weatherman heaves a sigh of impatience. "Don't play dumb," he says. "I know what people are saying. They think I've holed myself up in this apartment because I'm up to no good, that I've come here only to torture them with my threats and my predictions. They don't think there's any truth to what I say: that this town is in danger of going under."

He grimaces and leans back in his chair, away from her. His feet are propped up on his desk and his arms are crossed over the buttons of his plaid shirt, his slicker draped behind him. The desk is lined with tools: hygrometers, barometers, and others she doesn't recognize. The walls are tacked with maps of the region, topographical charts of the river and the hills. Beside the door hangs a lunar calendar, its pages warped with water damage.

"I'm not sure," she says. "I haven't been here long enough to say." How should she know if they should stay or go? Noah was called here, and so she came. She will stay here until he is called away again. Her path is as clear and as simple as that.

The weatherman raises his eyebrows. "You're not sure," he repeats. "But you're the minister's wife. Shouldn't your husband be providing some kind of leadership right now? Don't you think that it's your job to know what's going on with his little flock?"

Noah's wife hears the contempt in his voice. "It's my job to help Noah," she says, bristling. "It's not my place to make decisions for him or for his congregation."

The boa constrictor lifts a gleaming head from its basket in the far corner of the room and pours itself in a rush of copper coils from the wicker to the floor. It slides across the room to the weatherman's desk and slips into the shadows. The weatherman shudders.

"Right you are," he says. "That's the only intelligent remark I've heard since I arrived in this place. People make choices. They're the ones who get themselves into messes like this one, so let them try to get themselves right out again. Your neighbors aren't anyone's responsibility but their own. Isn't that so?"

Noah's wife recalls the first service, remembers her husband's despair. The people he tried to help only turned against him. Is it their fault that he is not himself? Would everything have turned out better if he had left well enough alone?

The weatherman clasps his hands together, continues. "You know, they told me how strange this place was. They told me that its economy was built on a goddamn zoo, of all things, and then when the rain started, tourists stopped coming and the money stopped flowing." He narrows his eyes, glancing quickly at a forked tongue flicking inside the glass tank to his right. "I was warned that the people who were left here are stubborn and tactless and set in their ways. But I was also told that in spite of all that it is my job to get them out. They haven't listened to me yet, but I've got to give them one more shot. That's why I'm calling a town meeting—whether that McGinn woman likes it or not. Last night I combed through all the town statutes: if she tries to oppose a meeting for emergency measures, she hasn't got a leg to stand on."

Noah's wife shakes her head. "You don't understand how invested they are in this place," she says. "To be honest, I think you're wasting your time here."

He stares at her for so long that she begins to feel uncomfortable. "What choice do I have?" he finally says. "My career depends on this. I used to chase storms. I used to love it. No people, no problems. Just the four winds and me. Then I made one or two poor calculations, and all of a sudden they've got me on the evacuation circuit, running around to the towns nobody else will touch. If I don't get this right, I'll be out of work."

He pauses. For a minute the room is silent, but for the rain against the windows and the snakes shifting in their tanks. When the weatherman speaks again, his tone sounds less callous. "This is all I've got," he says flatly. "Didn't you ever have something like that? Something you were good at, that you would be sorry to lose?"

Noah's wife looks back to the window. "I used to take pictures," she says after a moment. "In the city. I used to work for a studio. I suppose I miss photography, sometimes." She checks herself. "But Noah needs me here."

The weatherman jolts upright. "You're a photographer?" He reaches for a small leather bag resting on the corner of his desk, opens it and draws out a plastic canister with a roll of film. "I've been taking pictures, too, for proof. I've got shots that show the river is rising, shots of the trees hanging over telephone poles and all the rotting, abandoned houses. The ruin, the devastation. If they insist on being blind to the situation at hand, well, I'll just show them these photographs in order to *make them see*."

Noah's wife looks uncertainly at him.

"You're a photographer," he repeats. "You've got the supplies for making prints, don't you? The only camera store in this town closed a year ago, and now there's no place for me to get these developed. Can you help me out?"

When he extends his arm toward her and releases the canister, she instinctively cups her hands to catch it. The weatherman grins. It is the first smile she has seen from him; the first real smile she has seen from anyone, she realizes, in days.

"So you'll do it," he declares. It is a statement, not a question.

The zookeeper calls to her impatiently from below, and she shoves the film into her pocket as she rises. She leaves the weatherman's apartment, feeling pulled in more directions than she knew existed. How did Noah ever manage it—the weight of all these requests and expectations? By the time she arrives downstairs she has made up her mind to tell the zookeeper that she is serious, she is finished with all of this, that she simply cannot do any more for anyone except her husband—but before she can speak, a battered blue car speeds through the crosswalk right in front of them and then, a moment later, there is the screech of brakes and the scream of an animal in pain.

And how could she have walked away then? When she saw Mauro's car stalled in the street, one peacock dead at the curb and two more struggling out from underneath the bumper with broken wings and mangled tail feathers dragging along behind—how could she have left him? With the exhaustion weighing down her limbs, she helps the zookeeper bundle the remaining birds into the van while they are too dazed to fight back. She places her hand on Mauro's shoulder when he wails and wrings his hands. She nudges him into his own passenger seat and then slides behind the wheel to drive him back to his store.

In the car she listens to his confession—he was driving too fast because he was distraught. He tells her that he had gone to search for the savings he had hidden in an old fishing dory along the banks of the river, only to find that the water had risen and swept the little boat away with the bills wrapped up and tucked under the seat. His dream of going home went with it. He contorts his face like a child and says that he is sorry for trying to leave but sorrier still that now he cannot. His eyes well up with salty tears and he covers his face with his gnarled hands.

"I was so wanting to be going home," he says.

And how could she have left him afterward, when the zoo-keeper arrived with the two peacocks in tow, their wings set and their broken tail feathers clipped? Mauro is appalled at the sight of them, and appalled further still when the zookeeper tells him that there is no place for the peacocks but here, in Mauro's store.

"They can't go back outside," he insists when the Italian tries to argue with him. "And who is responsible for them but you?"

But Mauro seems to cheer up a little after Noah's wife pours him a glass of his own wine from a bottle she finds below the register. The peacocks rustle their good wings and crane their iridescent necks, cooing as gently as mourning doves. In between his first glass and his second, Mauro builds a nest for them by pulling towels from the shelves of the outdoor aquatics aisle and arranging them in cottony folds on the bottom of one of the standing bathtubs for sale in the plumbing department. After some thought he drags over several of the tall potted plants from home-and-garden to make the birds feel more comfortable. He admires them there, their masses of feathers shimmering like precious jewels. They consider him with shining eyes and as soon as he returns to the front of the store they climb out and follow him, leaving long four-toed footprints on the concrete floor. They flutter up to the counter and dig their beaks into their pinfeathers, preening, before finally settling themselves down beside the cash register. Mauro beams: the second smile Noah's wife has seen that day. She does her best to smile back. She doesn't ask him why he would choose to hide his life savings in such an irrational place; she understands that there can be no good answer. Instead she keeps the question to herself and stores it away with all the others that she has been burying in a dark place in her heart.

"This is all temporary, right?" she asks her husband when she finally returns home, physically and emotionally drained. She pictures the river rising in its banks, sees Mauro's homecoming being swept right out from underneath him. "Do you really believe that the rain will end and the water will go down?"

"I do and it will," he says more loudly than he should, looking up in surprise from the stack of papers he is reading. He rises and comes to stand behind her, resting his broad hands on her narrow shoulders. "Try not to worry so much, love. Try to have some faith."

I do, she wants to tell him, and she thinks she really does. He drops a kiss into her hair and she slowly climbs the stairway toward the bedroom. It is true that she doesn't have much faith in this plan, or this town, or this God to whom Noah swears he is praying daily for strong winds and clear skies. But she has always had faith in Noah—and for as long as she has known him, that has always been enough.

eighteen

When Mrs. McGinn's husband spots a dark figure shuffling down the muddy road ahead of him, he mistakes the shape for yet another lost or wounded animal.

He has become accustomed to braking for runaway mountain goats and reindeer, and he keeps his eyes peeled for other strays. Just last week he spotted a seal splashing in the ditch; and while he was climbing out to deal with that, a zebra went galloping by on the other side of the truck. Mrs. McGinn's husband simply stood and watched it go. There are only so many animals that one man can handle on his own.

The only creature he is glad to have found is the smaller of the two giant tortoises. He doesn't know why he stopped when he saw her paddling in the gravel at the end of someone's driveway, but he did. After a few minutes of watching the rain cascading down the sides of her shell, he stretched his arms into the mud and heaved her up into the bus. He calls her George, feeds her canned fruit, and slaps the gnarled plates of her shell when he is irritated or amused. He feels more satisfied in the presence of this silent, sullen companion than he does with anyone else these days, and so when he runs his errands, George goes with him.

It is only when he and George draw closer to the figure on the road that he recognizes the minister: the black hood pulled low over his forehead, shoulders hunched, steps sluggish. He is at least two miles outside town; did he walk in the rain all this way alone?

"Hey," grunts Mrs. McGinn's husband, throwing open the door and swinging the bus to the side of the road. He doesn't bother to ask whether the minister wants a ride or not; he simply stares the man down until Noah gives up and climbs in.

"Thanks," says the minister. He glances with some trepidation at the tortoise on the seat behind Mrs. McGinn's husband before sliding gingerly past it, dropping down across the aisle. Mrs. McGinn's husband reaches back to pat the tortoise's shell, then shifts the bus into gear and lurches toward downtown.

He has never liked the feeling of being in motion. He hates the smell of the exhaust, the vibration of the rubber wheel beneath his fingertips. He hates the music on the radio and the sound of the windshield wipers squealing like pigs. Usually he drives with the radio tuned to static and with the windshield wipers off. The rain smashes into the glass and makes it difficult for him to see, but he prefers to have his vision obstructed. The world seems less real.

On Wednesdays Mrs. McGinn's husband drives the garbage truck, on Thursdays the recycling truck. On other days he drives delivery vans or the town taxi. Nine months of the year he carts the children of the town to a schoolhouse several hills over. The final day of the school year was last week, thank God. The roads were getting worse every day. Sometimes it took him a full two hours to bus the kids there, all of them loud and rowdy the whole way back. These days the bus is empty of children, but packed instead with folding pens, bales of hay, and buckets of feed. When the zoo flooded the zookeeper transferred all the animals' supplies to a row of storage units downtown, and now it is Mrs. McGinn's husband who must load up the bus every morning and haul the day's supplies around to his neighbors' houses. His skin has begun to stink to high heaven, and when he showers he scours himself with extra-hard brushes and lemon soap. The regularity, the circularity. The driving, the rain, the route. This is it, over and over again: his life.

"So," he says, his gaze flicking into the rearview mirror. "Nice day for a walk."

Noah nods.

"What were you doing out there, anyway?"

"Nothing," says Noah, his gaze hollow. "Walking."

Mrs. McGinn's husband grunts. In the mirror he considers Noah's face—his skin corrugated and sallow; his beard much shaggier than it was when he arrived, his curly hair wild and unkempt. Mrs. McGinn's husband tries to remember the man as he was only five or six weeks ago, when he appeared with his wife and spoke at the cemetery. He wasn't like this, anyway; his face was not ravaged with lines of weather and worry. His tone was resonant, his stance secure. He seemed certain of his purpose in this place—and now he goes out wandering for miles with no sense of direction? Mrs. McGinn's husband shakes his head, unsurprised. Well, well, what do you know—this town has ruined yet another one.

"If I were you, Minister," he says, feeling good-humored with George by his side and thus more talkative than usual, "I'd walk right on out of this town. Your plans for the church don't seem to be working out. What the heck is keeping you here?"

Noah remains facing the window, his expression as smooth as stone. "The situation isn't that simple," he says.

"For you? Sure it is," declares Mrs. McGinn's husband. "You just got here—that means that you've got a life somewhere else. Hell, I'd leave in a second if I had a chance. I've been itching to get out of here since I was a kid."

In truth Mrs. McGinn's husband does not often think of his childhood. And when he does, he rarely remembers his parents' home, which was full of broken glass and hateful words and hands lifted high, preparing to strike. Those years are a symphony of screams and slamming doors. Instead he remembers the weeks he spent at his grandmother's house, the summer wind pulling waves over his toes, the cries of gulls as he pelted them with bread crumbs. On the clearest of days he had stayed out on the beach for hours, watching the way that the boats slid over the edge of the horizon and disappeared. He imagined standing on one himself, looking over his shoulder and watching as the shore grew smaller and smaller until the world, now, finally fell over the horizon and vanished beneath the sea.

He never left, of course. Once his brothers grew old enough they were gone, peeling out of the driveway without a single glance in the rearview mirror. He had wanted to leave, too, but if he had taken off, then there would have been no one left to stand between his father and his mother. He was middle-aged when she died—too old to take up sailing, he decided—and so after he helped carry her coffin to the overcrowded cemetery he took a job as a driver. And here he is.

Sometimes when he thinks about the life he had imagined for himself, the universe feels so maddening and unjust that there is nothing for him to do but to lift up an empty bottle from someone else's trash bin and smash it against the side of his truck. There are moments when he sees his reflection in the window of the recycling truck—short and squat, red-faced, losing hair by the handful—and he thinks about clambering back inside and taking off, never looking back, but then he comes to his senses and tells himself what he already knows: Anytime you try to flee, you will only end up running into yourself. As the poet once wrote: *Caelum non animum mutant qui trans mare currunt.*

"You know Latin?" the minister asks, hearing him mutter the motto to himself over the rumbling of the bus engine.

Damn right, he does. There's a lot that people don't know about him. He likes to write stories, for one thing—tall tales and mysteries. He used to be a runner, but he won't run in the rain. Now when he has finished up his driving for the day, he goes down to the basement and slips ships into bottles. He paints the tiny hulls and assembles the tiny masts with a kind of furious patience that his neighbors would not understand, if they ever saw it. This is the closest he will ever come to the ocean.

"What does that phrase mean?" asks Noah. He tries to repeat it. *"Caelum—"*

Mrs. McGinn's husband interrupts the minister before the man can butcher it. "It means that men are trapped," he says. "It means that no matter how far you go, you'll always be stuck with yourself."

The truck rumbles through a pothole and both men grab at the dashboard while water sprays in waves outside the windows. Mrs. McGinn's husband swears and heaves the steering wheel to the right. He had never wanted to be a truck driver or—for that matter—any other sort of driver. He had never wanted to be the kind of person who knocks over mailboxes on purpose, the kind of person who throws cereal at people he loves or smashes plates against kitchen walls. He had vowed that this was exactly who he would not become.

"Is that why you stay?" asks Noah, his voice so deep that Mrs. McGinn's husband must strain to hear the question.

He shakes his head. "No," he says. "I stay because of Evelyn.

That's what sets me apart from all those jackasses she married before: I wouldn't leave her. Not for anything. Every man needs something to set himself apart, doesn't he, Minister?" He chuckles bitterly, guiding the bus through downtown to the parsonage, ignoring the elk that stands between the pillars of the old post office and the toucans winging through the drowning trees. "But I'll tell you, it's not an easy life in this place. Every day is a battle."

"And leaving," says Noah, "is an admission of defeat." For a minute or two they ride in silence. Then Noah asks, slowly: "What if you told your wife how you really felt?"

Mrs. McGinn's husband can see the minister's house now, and the lights that his wife has lit in every window. "She'd see it as a betrayal," he states. "And within ten minutes, she'd be out the door. She's fallen out of love plenty of times before."

He pulls up to the front door, tires crackling on the driveway gravel. The house looks crumbling and forlorn, the paint peeling from its siding, the white shades in the windows yellowed with age, the rain falling in curtains from the eaves. The minister's wife appears at the front door, a red fox cradled in her arms with its white-tipped tail hanging down to her waist.

For half a minute Noah remains seated where he is, gazing at his wife. "Jackson," he says quietly. He stands up and stumbles toward the driver's seat, pausing on the stair before descending to the ground. "Do you ever wish that you were not yourself?"

"Hell, yes," says Mrs. McGinn's husband. "Every minute of every goddamned day."

His life is like a ship in a bottle: the promise of movement, the dream of wind. All the journeys that could have been, lined up one after another on the plywood boards of his homemade bookshelves.

When all is said and done, he is not a bad man. He could be a better husband, a better father. But no one else here knows how it is to be confined within the invisible walls of an unhappy family history. The philosopher in Mrs. McGinn's husband believes that we are born into a certain temperament the way we are born into a certain place or time.

When he finally returns home, he settles George into the garage before he walks into the house. Mrs. McGinn sticks her head out of the kitchen and asks him something, but he ignores her and heads straight for the stairs. Once he reaches the workbench, he hears the slam of cupboard doors in the kitchen, the clatter of copper measuring cups. A few minutes later the thud of his wife's fists in the dough sends vibrations through the legs of the kitchen table to the floor.

Can a man fight his fate? he asks himself, lifting down his box of tools. He shakes his head. No, it isn't possible.

All he can do is build another ship, slip it into another bottle, and set it on the shelf in the place that has been left for it.

nineteen

The weatherman has never possessed much of a talent for prediction.

He has, in fact, never been one to place much stock in the whole idea of prediction, or of expectation in general. Why expect, and be disappointed? he would ask himself. Why try to determine today where you will be tomorrow, who will be with you, where you will go? Where is the adventure in that?

He has spent most of his adult life on the road. He makes no promises, establishes no ties. The job with the weather service is one he has held for over a decade now, and most of the time he loves it. He likes flitting from one city to the next, monitoring winds and tracking severe weather patterns, pursuing storms with the same passion and dedication that other men display in pursuit of women or wealth. The weatherman, for the record, has never needed to pursue women. He is persuasive, charming. Impossible to resist.

Or at least that is what he has been in the past. He has never encountered a town as defiant or as pigheaded as this one.

He believes that if he can only gather the citizens together to hear his warnings, he will have no trouble convincing them to evacuate. And once that is done, he can return to the city in triumph, his job secure and his name cleared of disgrace. He is growing tired of this particular task: tired of the rain, of the citizens' despair. He hardens his heart and grits his teeth and does his job, but the truth is that he does not relish commanding people to box up their lives and leave all they've ever known behind them. No one is ever pleased to see him coming.

Even today, the townspeople scowl at him when he enters the general store. They congregate near the mops and the sponges, most of them nursing some kind of bruise or bite, and all of them eyeing Mauro's birds with trepidation. Mauro, unaware of their baleful stares, whistles while he arranges olives and cheese slices on a plate and sets it on a makeshift table he has constructed out of cardboard boxes and packing crates. He has been in a markedly better mood since taking in the peacocks, who follow him around the store with their broken wings pinned to their sides. The wary eyes of the storks and the cranes peer between the shelves.

The weatherman presides over the proceedings with an air of mingled incredulity and condescension. He towers above the townspeople on a sturdy metal step stool. In the second row a man is sitting opposite a birdcage. A few seats down from him, a woman perches on a folding chair with a box beside her, and the weatherman starts when he sees a paw poking out from the holes she has punched into the cardboard. He watches her stuff pieces of her sandwich into the box and then he hears the sound of animal teeth ripping through the bread.

He tries to catch the eye of the minister's wife as she enters, but she avoids his gaze and herds her husband to an empty row near the back. Noah settles down among his neighbors and sits stiffly in place, one eye on the flamingo where she stalks among the lawn ornaments in the corner. His wife is pale and cool beside him.

"Listen," says the weatherman, once everyone has gathered. A peacock shrieks and Mauro hums a lullaby. "We need to talk about what's going on in this place." He flings his hand toward the window, directing their attention outside, where the sky is churning violet and the rain is pelting down into the streets.

"It pours when it rains!" exclaims Mauro with disconcerting alacrity. He eats two olives and smiles at the group arranged around him in an attempt at camaraderie. "Isn't it nice when we are all together like this? We should be doing this more often."

The weatherman ignores the interruption. "I've *been* to the other towns in the hills," he continues. "It's even worse here than it was there, and most of them have already left. You're no safer than they are. You need an evacuation plan. Let's talk facts: dates, times, locations. How early can you leave? Where will you go?"

"Rabble-rouser," mutters Mrs. McGinn.

"We're not evacuating," declares the zookeeper. He stands up, turns around to speak directly to his neighbors. "What would you do with the animals? We've got a responsibility to them. We made a promise. We've got to stay put until the water recedes in the zoo."

"Don't be so daft," says the weatherman with a short laugh. "You mean those tigers you've got displayed in the windows? The penguins in the diner? That certainly can't be a reason to stay. It was a stupid idea to begin with, and it's a stupid idea now."

"Adam," says Mrs. McGinn's daughter, tugging at his sleeve. "Please sit down."

"Angela Rose!" exclaims Mrs. McGinn. "You can't honestly be siding with this man."

"You know," says Mauro, "where I come from there is a whole town that is living on the water, with bridges and boats and the people there are not so worried as all of you. The people there are not always talking about staying or going. They are just staying. They are enjoying riding on the ferry. People are coming from all over the world to ride on their ferry!"

"Mauro, we don't have a ferry," someone snaps.

"That's no problem!" exclaims Mauro. "We build one!"

There is a sudden roar of indignation, and the weatherman spends several minutes trying to restore order by pounding his hammer on a crate and grimacing at his audience. "Settle down!" he shouts. "Settle down!"

But they will not settle down, and the sound of his voice in their fray only incenses them further. What does he know of their town, he who only arrived with the rain? He can have no idea of what it was like before, when blue skies slid between the mountains and the trees bloomed silky and full. He has not fallen asleep on the warm and grassy banks of the river, as they have; he has not stayed until the golden light of dusk to see the sun topple over the far side of the western hills. This was once a beautiful place. Wildflowers sprouted between cracks in the sidewalk and people grew tomatoes and basil in their gardens. They raised their children here; they buried their dead. How can he expect them to turn their backs on all that, to give up on this town the way the rest of the world has given up on them?

"Listen!" bellows Noah, taking advantage of a sudden lull. His neighbors turn to stare. He clears his throat and rises slowly to his feet while his wife looks up in astonishment. "There comes a time in all of our lives when we must be *tested*," the minister declares. He strides out into the aisle and paces up and down the rows of chairs, warming now to his speech, seeming to enjoy the fact of so many pairs of eyes upon him. It has been a long time. "A time when we are forced to ask ourselves whether the beliefs we have always cherished are true, in fact, or false; when for no apparent reason, through no fault of our own, we realize that suddenly we stand to lose everything that we once held so dear.

"The question, my friends, at a crossroad like this one, is the following: are we to cling to the lives we have always known, fighting to regain the ground we have lost? Or do we leave those former lives behind, abandon the selves and the world we once knew, and start all over again?" He pauses, his jaw hanging slack, his expression suddenly blank. "We keep moving on, hoping that there is something better out there in the next town, or tomorrow. But maybe there isn't. What if the next town is just as gray, in its own way?"

There is a brief silence after he has finished speaking, when he stops pacing and freezes in place. Once again, the townspeople erupt.

"Are you *kidding*?" several voices demand at once. "What does that even *mean*?"

"Pretty words," grunts Mrs. McGinn's husband. "How the hell does that help us?"

The librarian scoffs and points. "How are we supposed to take this man seriously when he's got dirt on his face and twigs in his beard?"

The weatherman looks at the minister more closely. Indeed—what she says about him is true. Noah's cheeks turn crimson and he quickly combs at the sticks and the leaves in his hair, but it is too late. The rest of his neighbors are rising now, and he ducks into a different aisle. The weatherman looks at Noah's wife, who has been sitting throughout this scene with her gray gaze fixed upon her husband. When he disappears behind the canned goods, a peculiar expression flits across her face—there and gone before the weatherman has a chance to decipher it.

Mrs. McGinn stands. "The rain is lightening," she declares. "The weather is already better than it was."

"Is that right?" retorts the weatherman, gearing up for his final grenade. "I don't think so. Your zoo is already underwater. The river is rising. The puddles are growing wider and deeper. The trees are losing their leaves, and the plants that were alive two weeks ago are dead."

"That's not true," mutter the townspeople. "You're making it sound worse than it is."

"It *is* true!" he exclaims. "And I've got the evidence to prove it." He throws out an extravagant arm to turn their attention to Noah's wife, the evidence packed into a handbag at her feet. He will show them how, in the lower parts of town and the areas that have already been abandoned, the pools in front yards have begun creeping up mossy porches. He took pictures of the water coursing through gutters, of the buckets set out to collect leaks in shops and storefronts. He will show them the places where the telephone wires are leaning dangerously close to houses, where the force of the wind and the rain has broken windows, tossed mailboxes to the ground. She should have his print of the town cemetery, the headstones crooked and loose as if the water table has risen so high that it is beginning to push them up and out of the ground. The images will frighten them, and they *should* be frightened. By forcing them to face the reality of their situation, the weatherman will ensure that they are gone by tomorrow morning.

He waits for Noah's wife to reach into the bag, to pull out the prints and pass them through the crowd; but she only sits more tensely with her hands pressed together in her lap and her face angled toward her knees.

"I don't know what you're talking about," she murmurs.

The color drains from the weatherman's face. "What did you say?" he mutters.

She raises her chin and looks him in the eye. Her jaw is square, her gaze like granite. "There isn't anything in this town that the people here can't handle."

Mrs. McGinn emits an audible, delighted gasp. The weatherman stares at her while the voices of her neighbors explode once more. For the next several minutes, they argue among themselves: some have been swayed by the weatherman's warnings and the fear of the rising river, while others insist that the worst of the rain has come and gone and that the river has never flooded before. Already it is clear that they are becoming irrevocably divided: those who will stay and those who will go. They turn in their seats to quarrel with the people sitting next to them and behind them, proclaiming the point one way or the other.

Meanwhile the weatherman buttons up his slicker, steps off his stool, and storms over to the minister's wife. "What the hell was that?" he demands, leaning ominously over her chair. "Some misplaced attempt at solidarity?"

She looks up at him, her eyes like mirrors. "Noah was called here," she says. "He was called to rebuild the congregation and to save this town. We can't leave until he's done it."

"Save the town?" repeats the weatherman with a quick, sardonic smile. "I'm sorry. My mistake. I thought that's what *I* was trying to do here."

"No," she says, suddenly as stubborn as the rest of them. "You're just out to save your own skin, not theirs. That's why you want them to give up."

He glares at her. He had expected the rest of this town to be foolish, but he had not expected it of her. Indeed, from the look of her—that delicate face, that colorless expression—and from the way she so passively accepted the favor that he asked of her, he was under the impression that she was the sort of woman who always did as she was told.

He soars toward the exit, his raincoat flapping in his wake. After the door slams shut behind him he pauses for a moment in the middle of the street, staring at the road that brought him into this silent, murky town—the same road that will take him out again this afternoon, as soon as he has packed up his car. The rain thuds against his shoulders and a mountain goat wanders past him, braying.

He is finished with this place. He is done with these strange people, and their strange little faith that all will be well if only they believe in it, if only they turn their backs on the facts. The world can only be the way that it is, the weatherman knows. It is rarely the way that one wants it to be.

twenty

Stan is afraid to go out beyond the breakwater.

"Look at those waves!" he says to Nancy. He stands with his feet spread wide on the rickety pier beside their boat, clutching his orange life preserver in two fleshy hands. His eyelids twitch, as they always do in direct sunlight. "Just look at them! I don't think we'd survive out there, I really don't—not for five minutes, even."

Nancy looks. The sea is full of soft white peaks that arc against an indigo sky. The wind is high and she can see sailboats leaning to one side, all bowed in the same direction. The sun is pink and growing pinker, dropping like a stone toward the surface of the water.

"We don't have much time, Stan!" she says. "Didn't you say you'd go with me for a sunset cruise? The sun is almost setting! Now, come on—we have cocktails on the boat. A stiff drink is all you need. When we go on our trip we're going to have to keep you drunk, that's all."

She laughs. Stan laughs, too, but less convincingly. This was not his idea.

In the beginning, when he was nervous about setting foot on the pier (as if those boards could hold a person's weight above the water! he said to himself), it was Nancy who coaxed him out, day by day and inch by inch, until they were finally able to sit on the end of it—their toes dipping into the water, tempting the fish—and have a picnic. Nancy made cream cheese and tomato sandwiches (Stan's favorite) for the occasion.

"Hurray!" she said to him, with a loud kiss on the lips. "We made it!"

It was kind of her, Stan thought at the time, to say "we" instead of "you." It was kind of her to pretend that this was *their* obstacle, and not *his* obstacle alone. He is her husband, after all; he wants to be her protector and her provider (though he knows full well that Nancy would say she can both provide for and protect herself, thank you very much), but how is he supposed to do either of those things, how is he supposed to fulfill any of his roles if he continues to let his fear dominate him in this vexing manner? He can't help it. He is an anxious man.

But Nancy loves him anyway.

After they made it to the end of the dock, the next step was to set foot on the boat. This took him several days—several days of pacing nervously on the dock just beyond the ladder to the boat while Nancy climbed aboard and worked at cleaning and sprucing, as she called it. From time to time she hailed him from the boat as she washed the portholes with warm soapy water or as she sat on the wooden benches near the helm, soaking up the sun and sewing white eyelet curtains for the cabin.

"How are you doing, my dear?" she would say, casting a loving look in his direction.

"Oh I'm just fine, Nancy, I'm fine!" he would say. He would continue to pace. "Any day now I'll be right up there with you, I promise. I'll help with the cleaning and everything."

"There's no rush, Stan," she would respond. "We've got all the time in the world."

Sometimes it seemed to them that their days were as long and empty as the ocean. Stan's great-aunt had recently passed away and left them several very full bank accounts to be spent however they pleased. The day they heard the news, they quit their jobs and sat down together at the kitchen table to decide how best to use the money.

"Is there anything you've always wanted to do, Stan?" asked Nancy. She poured lemonade into a tumbler and reached for a wafer cookie.

Stan was surprised by the question. "No," he said finally. "I can't think of anything. I have everything I need right here."

He patted her hand thoughtfully and then said, in a rather absentminded way, "What about you? Is there anything you've always wanted to do, Nancy?"

"Well—" she said. She pursed her lips and hesitated. Her tone was at once hopeful and concerned. "Well—this may sound crazy, Stan. And I know that you're not a big fan of boats and so I suppose it could be a little bit of a problem—but to be perfectly honest with you, what I've always wanted to do is sail around the world."

"Sail around the world?" repeated Stan, stunned. "You never told me that."

"Well, we could never do it before!" she said. "But that's what I'm saying—now we could! Think about it . . . the open seas, the wind at our backs, only you and me in the middle of the ocean, miles away from everything, stopping at exotic ports whenever we felt like it . . . wouldn't that be *amazing*?"

"Amazing" would not be the word Stan ever would have chosen to describe such a venture. He finds the whole notion completely terrifying. He doesn't like the water but he does love Nancy, and so after a few minutes of thinking about it silently (Nancy ate another wafer and considerately looked away while she waited for him to reach his conclusion), he heard a voice—that sounded suspiciously like his own—agreeing.

In the end, he was glad he did. He had not seen Nancy so delighted in years. She clapped her hands, childlike, and parted her lips in a girlish grin. Her teeth were even and gleaming.

And so this is what they have been doing, every day for the past two months. Taking small steps—*very* small steps—from the shore to the sea. Once Stan made it onto the boat, Nancy persuaded him to allow her to lift the anchor and drift for a few minutes unmoored beside their pier. After this they began to take short cruises in the harbor, during which Nancy practiced zigzagging around other boats as if they were orange cones on an obstacle course, while Stan gripped the railing with aching fists and stared intently at the muddy green water, trying to calculate precisely how many feet he would have to fall before he hit bottom.

"Five feet," he muttered to himself, glancing at the depth meter. "No, six. Seven. Six."

The numbers fluctuated with the waves.

The other sailors in the harbor cast uncertain glances in their direction. In the beginning Stan found this embarrassing, but Nancy has done her best to reassure him.

"They're not *judging* us, Stan," she says. "They've all got their own problems to work through."

She ties a violet cardigan across her shoulders and then lifts her arm to wave to the harbor magician, as she so often likes to do. She has a ring on every finger and her whole hand glitters in the sun.

"Hellloooo!" she calls. "Hellllooo there!"

Ever since meeting the unusual magician, Nancy has made it a point to invite the man in for dinner every few days. She will watch for the breaks in the afternoon when he finds himself without an audience, and then she will climb down from the boat with a swish of her white silk skirt and march over to speak with him. In general she tends to worry about people who stand alone for too long. Everyone needs a little company.

"Now, what do you think about tonight?" she will ask him. "Would you prefer the moussaka or the roast lamb?"

Nancy is a gracious hostess, as she loves having company, and she is conscious that she must get her fill now before taking off for the empty ocean. She has begun to serve all of their meals on the boat, and while the plastic folding table can be somewhat of a problem when it buckles or leans, she says that it is worth the trouble to be able to eat in the open air. The three of them shuffle feta and olives onto their forks as they watch thin white clouds waltz through blue skies. Seagulls cry, looping in great pinwheels above their heads.

The magician remarks on the beauty of the ocean and politely inquires how much time the two of them spend on the water. His uncovered forehead is growing pink in the sun.

"Well," says Nancy, reaching back to adjust the tortoiseshell clip in frizzy hair that—despite her best efforts—has blown wild again in the wind. "We're taking small steps from shore to sea. In a few months we're leaving to sail around the world."

"Really?" says the magician. "That's unbelievable!"

"Yes," says Stan with a profound sigh, his eyelids twitching again. "It is, isn't it?"

Nancy shoots him a look. "We were fortunate enough to come into a little money," she explains. "And then we thought—why not! Life is short! You never know what might happen to you tomorrow—so you've got to do everything now. Live to the fullest!"

Nancy's cheeks are flushed with excitement. The magician glances toward Stan, but Stan is staring at Nancy, seemingly transfixed. His gaze is always steady when he looks at her.

"So far," continues Nancy. "So far we've been scuba diving, we've gone swimming with sharks, we tried hang gliding, we jumped from a plane—"

"Your hands cuffed or no?" the magician wants to know.

"Our hands weren't cuffed," Stan assures him.

"And you've done all of this recently?"

"All of this in the past four and a half years," says Stan.

Nancy nods. "Four and a half years," she repeats. She stands abruptly and picks up the plates, carries them from the deck to the galley. Stan and their guest rise and begin to help her—collecting the silverware, the cloth napkins, the serving dishes—and once everything is cleared the magician thanks them and excuses himself so that he can practice some of his newer tricks of light and fire at the other end of the pier before the night grows too cold.

Nancy waves at his diminishing back until the magician has disappeared from sight, and then she turns to the sink. As she reaches for a sponge she bumps a ceramic vase on the ledge and it plummets to the floor, cracking in half and spilling a spray of lilies. Stan bends and reaches for them, a dish towel slung over his shoulder, and when he rises again he finds that Nancy is watching him with damp eyes.

"Everything breaks," she says, suddenly seeming very, very small.

"Nancy," says Stan. "You know that if you want to, I'll sail around the whole world. And I'll jump out of whatever you want to and scuba dive on down as far as you want to because

I love you. We can keep on running and diving and hang gliding, but when it's all over we'll always end up right back here, right where we are now, and you know as well as I do that the weeks and weeks of sailing won't have changed a thing."

Yes—Nancy knows. She moves toward Stan and before he is prepared for it she has tumbled against him, her hair crumpled against his chest, her body heaving with her grief, her soapy fists pounding weakly on his shoulders. Stan wraps his arms around her while she cries.

twenty-one

Mrs. McGinn's daughter has dreamed of getting married and leaving this town, of buying her own house with a breakfast nook and a laundry chute and a huge backyard—but she has never dreamed of having children.

She has seen firsthand what having a mother will do to people.

Of course she loves her mother, as everyone must, but sometimes she finds herself wishing that someone else had given birth to her—someone who was quieter and more discreet. Mrs. McGinn has the tendency to overpower the people she loves, pulling them into her orbit like small moons that have no choice but to reflect the radiance of her, their most significant star. Mrs. McGinn's daughter has certainly tried to carve out her own path, to distinguish herself from her mother. Why else would she have gone to the trouble of piercing her own ears or painting her fingernails black? She desperately craves the disapproval of her mother, feels secretly thrilled at the fights they have after these slight physical adjustments. She loves it when Mrs. McGinn informs her that she looks like a gypsy.

"Angela Rose," her mother had declared after the piercing. "Take that metal out of your head."

"No," retorted Mrs. McGinn's daughter. "Never. Not a chance."

She wonders why this is the first conversation that comes to her mind when she realizes that she has missed her period. She is seated on the edge of the tub, her thighs cold beneath her skirt, and her stomach still queasy. The floral-printed towels are frayed at the edges, the bathmat plush but faded pink. She has lived longer in this house than in any other; this has been her bedroom since her late adolescence. When she was younger the father figures rotated through her life like carousel horses, and her mother tried to make a game of moving in and out of houses. One set of framed wedding photographs came down, and eventually another went up. The furniture shifted, the wallpaper changed. The husband would leave his mark on the house and then he would be gone. Soon after, she and her mother would pack up for a new place, exchange their keys and move on. But try as she might, her mother never managed to leave her memories behind.

Mrs. McGinn's daughter is determined that her own marriage will be different. Hers will be the kind that lasts.

If she ever gets to that point, that is.

When she is well enough to stand without feeling nauseated again, she stumbles over to the mirror and drags a brush of navy blue eye shadow over her lids before heading downstairs to the kitchen. As she enters the room with her heavy step, her ankle-high boots unlaced, Mrs. McGinn turns away from the stove to look at her.

"You're pregnant," says Mrs. McGinn.

Her daughter heaves a sigh of the long-suffering. There isn't any point in asking how her mother could tell. That woman has the nose of an albatross—a bird that can smell a person's lunch from a mile down the road and then come flying into windowpanes to get at it. Most of the townspeople have had to learn about the albatross the hard way.

"Are you out of your *mind*, Angie?" demands Mrs. McGinn. "You couldn't wait until after the ceremony? My Lord, you two are like animals!"

"Just don't tell anyone, all right?" snaps Mrs. McGinn's daughter. She would prefer that Adam hear the news from her—but how will she break it to him? They have not been speaking. Although he sleeps above the diner, he spends most of his time out doing rounds without her, and when they pass each other in the diner or on the staircase, they avert their eyes and carry on in silence. She supposes that he is waiting for her to apologize, or waiting for her to say that she's come around, that she will be happy to stay here, no problem. Well, tough luck. She isn't happy, and she won't stay here. She has been up-front about that since the beginning.

She turns her head away and her braid sails sideways. Her already rosy cheeks grow ruddier under the intensity of her mother's examination.

Mrs. McGinn slowly exhales and removes the skillet from the stove. She marches over to her daughter, places her hands on the girl's shoulders, and looks her in the eye. "This isn't the way I would have liked to find out about my first grandchild," she says. "But you know I love you. Jackson and I will support you until you and Adam can get a little more organized. These things happen for a reason, I suppose. Everything will be fine. You both can stay here with us until the rain dies down and things get back to normal around here."

Mrs. McGinn's daughter thinks of the koi in the bathtub upstairs. When she went into the bathroom to feed them this morning, she found one of them dead, his gold belly facing the ceiling, and she had to spend several long minutes trying to fish him out with a pasta strainer. Nothing about her life is normal.

"The rain isn't dying down anytime soon," she says with a scowl that looks much like her mother's. "You know that, don't you? Just take a look out there! Things are going from bad to worse! Soon it will be impossible to get through the streets—that's what Mauro said. And did anyone here even listen to the weatherman, or were all your heads in the sand? What the heck are we going to do when the river flows over?"

"Ever the contrarian!" replies her mother, unfazed. "We've got to make the best of a bad situation, my dear. That's what gives a person character."

Mrs. McGinn's daughter would prefer that her mother had a little less character, and that she herself had a little more. As it is, she has no income, no job. She has nowhere else to go. "Whatever," she says. "Just remember what I said about Adam."

Mrs. McGinn nods, distractedly, but the next day Mrs. McGinn's daughter realizes that her mother has turned a deaf ear to her request for privacy. All morning the townspeople come flocking to the diner to express their satisfaction and delight over the news. Mauro drops by first to let her know that he will be returning later with champagne.

"Of course we will be having the champagne!" he says. "The champagne is the happiest drink! But maybe it is not for you. I will be bringing, too, the juice, also."

Mrs. McGinn's daughter isn't certain why champagne is the happiest drink, but when she pictures it she thinks she understands: the good cheer, the optimism conveyed by a glass of liquid gold with bubbles rising ever upward. In general, the people in this town tend to find great comfort in elements that rise up toward the sky rather than fall down from it. They are particularly fond of balloons.

"Blue and pink!" says Leesl. "I brought both!"

"Please keep it down," says Mrs. McGinn's daughter to her visitors. "I'd like to be the one to tell my fiancé."

"Well, yes!" they say. "Why wouldn't you? Mum's the word!"

The penguins, curious about all the commotion in the main dining area, come wandering out of the walk-in refrigerator every time the bell chimes above the front door. When Mrs. McGinn's daughter sees them, she scolds them and takes them back to the cooler, settling them among the plastic tubs of butter and vats of heavy cream with ten open cans of tuna fish. She drops down onto a low stool beside them, hides her forehead in her hands, feeling sick to her stomach and wishing she could hide in here all day.

She is overwhelmed by the outpouring of emotion from her neighbors, particularly because she feels that theirs is an enthusiasm she does not share. For the townspeople, however, this news is exactly what they need after the weatherman's disastrous meeting and the subsequent exodus of approximately one-half of their number. Mrs. McGinn's daughter is surprised to find how relieved they seem to be; how ready they are to accept this unborn child—the first infant this town has seen in at least four or five years—as a sign that they have not been forgotten, that although some of their neighbors have been swept from their midst, they have gained one in return.

"Providence," says Leesl, somewhat cryptically.

"Remember," remark some of the middle-aged couples, waxing nostalgic, "when you used to babysit for us? Now our children can babysit for you!" One of them hands her a stuffed giraffe.

Mrs. McGinn's daughter clasps it to her chest in the cooler and considers the summers she used to spend with her neighbors' infants when she was in high school, pacing with one or the other of them from oven to refrigerator across the white stone floor of the kitchen, trying to lull them to sleep by crooning off-key versions of "Oh My Darling Clementine" and "A Bicycle Built for Two." Her arm had been molded around those babies for so many hours at a time that by autumn, the nerves in her hand would feel knotted and tangled. Every once in a while she is woken still by a pulsing ache in her wrists, recalling a phantom child the way that soldiers speak of the dull pain of phantom limbs.

Is this what motherhood means? Mrs. McGinn's daughter would like to know. She has always lamented the way that her life has been so forcibly stamped by her mother, but she wonders if she might have had it wrong. Who molded whom? Which of them is living a life shaped by the other?

She recalls a conversation she had with the townspeople earlier this morning while her mother was bringing breakfast platters out to the tables. Her daughter watched her set the plates down with a flourish. Mrs. McGinn was loving all of this attention, she knew. She was loving the flowers and the gifts. She was eating this up.

"The real question," called her mother from across the room, "is what you're going to name the baby. That's the best part of being pregnant. Coming up with possibilities!"

"It seems a little soon for that," said her daughter, leaning over the counter.

"Nonsense," replied Mrs. McGinn. "Have you considered Evelyn?"

"Are you serious?"

"Yes." Her tone was regal. "It's a name that's served me perfectly well over the years."

The townspeople who heard this hurriedly swallowed bites of their waffles so that they could chime in. Mrs. McGinn's daughter half listened to their suggestions, both irritated and amused. All of her neighbors wanted the baby to be named after themselves.

"I wonder why that is," she wondered aloud. Mauro heard her.

"I tell you why!" he said, brandishing his bottle of champagne. He had already offered "Mario," "Marco," or "Maurice" as English alternatives. "Because it is as the Romans say! *Nomen est omen.*"

"The name is a sign," translated Mrs. McGinn's husband, barreling through with a bag full of recyclables. He nodded at his wife and disappeared into the back.

"The name is a sign?" repeated Mrs. McGinn's daughter.

"That is what the Romans are saying," confirmed Mauro, riffling through the pages of an empty baby photo album that one of the neighbors had brought as a gift. "The name is a sign. The name is the fate. This is why it is important to be choosing the right one. It is determining who you are, and what you are doing, and how the world is seeing you."

"I don't know if I believe all that," retorted Mrs. McGinn's daughter. "I'd like to think that we have more of a say in who we are than that."

Mauro shrugged. "You don't have to be believing in it," he said. "That is not making it any the less true."

Recalling this now in the cooler she shivers, draws her knees to her chest and hugs them close. The hair is rising on her arms. That is exactly why she never wanted to be a mother, she reminds herself. It is too much pressure. It is too much for one person—or even two—to bear. What if she does something to ruin the child? What if he grows up to hate her? How can she know if she will be a better mother than she is a daughter? She can be sullen, she knows; she can be sharp and ungrateful. But it is hard to be happy in this town, in this family. More than anything else, the pregnancy underscores the sense she has of being snared.

It is here that the zookeeper finds her: alone in the cooler, her chin in her hands, her expression withdrawn. One of the penguins, waiting by the entrance, manages to escape as the door is slowly swinging shut behind him. The zookeeper, no small man, covers the distance to his fiancée in four long strides. She has time only to rise to her feet before he has enveloped her in a burly arm and has crushed her against his chest and is telling her in a voice thick with emotion that he has already heard the news, that he couldn't be more pleased, that she shouldn't worry at all because she should know by now that he's in this for the long haul. She can feel his heart hammering against her cheek.

"Don't worry," he murmurs. "Don't worry about a thing, Angie. I'm right here with you, and I'm not going anywhere."

He keeps soothing her, keeps holding her close, but what he

means to be a reassurance comes as a painful blow. Not going anywhere?

The panic rises in her chest and presses at her lungs, leaves her feeling dizzy and faint. Her blood thrums through her ears and she sways a little on her feet. With her head buried in her fiancé's shoulder, she can see the bars of her cage materializing before her: day after gray day in a town that is going under, a future no brighter than the tarnished silverware she wipes clean before the lunchtime rush.

After a moment she frees herself from his embrace, and she follows him out of the cooler and back into the diner. He holds her hand and talks to their neighbors, thanks them for the gifts and chuckles with them over competing pieces of parental advice. Later on, when he leaves for his rounds, she kisses him good-bye and watches him walk out into the rain with an unusually buoyant step. She is surprised that he is so pleased about the news; she had not known that he would feel so strongly about fatherhood.

Once she is certain that he is safely on his way and that her mother is not watching, she returns to her room and pulls her suitcase out from underneath her bed.

twenty-two

Ever since the weatherman abandoned this town, the place has been plagued with nightmares.

"It's not a curse," says Mrs. McGinn wearily, when someone asks her what she thinks about it. Dark crescents pulse below her eyes, and her tone lacks its usual vitality. "It's strain. It'll pass. In the meantime, you should go sit beside your light boxes. Didn't I tell you that they were designed to lift low spirits?"

And because the townspeople do not have another option, that is what they do. Noah's wife can see the lights winking from a handful of windows as she slogs through the streets in search of Noah, the rain twisting down in strings. She thinks of the dreams she has overheard her neighbors sharing with one another every time they congregate, each person trying to out-terrify his neighbor: monsters and wild dogs, car accidents and plane crashes, skydives gone wrong, final exams they have not prepared for. They spend so many hours comparing notes on the fires and earthquakes of their subconscious that they do not have time to reflect upon the reality in which they find themselves: a town beset by darkness, a rain that will not end. As far as Noah's wife can tell, none of her neighbors dream of floods.

The town itself is more deserted than she has ever seen it: front yards are rutted with tire tracks, littered with trash and tattered furniture. Frightened by the weatherman's dire warnings, half of the town returned home after the meeting to start packing suitcases. The next morning they loaded their cars and pickup trucks, jogging back and forth to the front door with their hoods pulled low over their eyes, their animals watching anxiously from the windows. By the time night fell, most of them were already on their way. Their vehicles were crammed full of suitcases and books, boxes full of cooking supplies, end tables, lawn chairs—everything that they could fit. As they drove slowly past the neighbors who were watching them from behind half-drawn curtains, they felt relieved that they were moving, glad to be leaving this watery world behind. They asked themselves why it took them so long to make the decision, and they pitied the people who were still here.

Noah's wife can still hear a few car engines in the distance and through the rain she can see the headlights of the stragglers streaming out into the hills, the sad and luminous parade rolling onto the two-lane highway that links the town to the rest of the world. For a moment she imagines herself to be leaving with them, pictures the highway through the mountains: softly sloping, swift and dark. She cannot blame them for going. Remembering the weatherman's warnings, she, too, feels a cold rush of panic sliding through her limbs. When she crosses the creaking wooden bridge over the river she hears the water roaring underfoot, sees it clawing at the banks. She steps watchfully over the planks, the ghost of the old minister looming before her.

She has suffered loss before, as everyone has. Her sister packed her bags and left home the minute she turned sixteen, and, a few months later her mother, driving home from a night out after a gallery opening, wrapped her car around a tree in a fatal embrace. In the weeks that followed, Noah's wife floated unmoored. She suffered terrible insomnia, and when she did sleep, she was restless. She went days without speaking to another soul. After barely surviving a year of college, she quit school and left her childhood home to move in with the soon-to-be Dr. Yu, to whom she attached herself with all the force and devotion she possessed. She learned to make herself indispensable—first to Dr. Yu, and later on to Noah. She never felt secure when she was on her own; somewhere deep in her subconscious she harbored the fear that if she did not have someone there to really see her, to speak to her, to need her—then she would simply disappear. Her own nightmares have always been variations on this theme.

The past two nights her dreams have been flooded with gray landscapes and unfamiliar streets that she wanders alone, looking for Noah. She walks into stores to ask strangers for help, the bell chiming above her, but no one answers. She approaches shadowed figures in brightly colored coats, but when she tries to speak to them, they seem to look right through her. The dreams feel so real to her that she is almost startled, during the daylight hours, when her neighbors stop her on the sidewalk to request her presence in their homes. Although the animals have been settled in most of their houses for over a week already, the worries of the townspeople have not subsided. Every time one of the animals does something unusual—eats more or less than its caretaker thinks it should, makes a noise it has never made before, sheds a skin or molts its feathers—Noah's wife is sought and called. Her neighbors are stubborn in their insistence that she is a better helper than the zookeeper: calmer, kinder. Leesl's cheetah rubs its tufted chin against the garage fence when Noah's wife approaches; Mauro's peacocks flare their feathers in delight at the sight of her. Although she is usually reluctant when the townspeople first accost her, after a few minutes with the animals she always warms to the task, and by the time she leaves she is genuinely sorry to leave the beasts behind.

Today, however, she refuses to be distracted. "I'll stop by later if I can," she promises, shifting her umbrella to her other hand. "By the way, have you seen Noah?"

Her neighbors shake their heads, their brows furrowed as if in sympathy, but she can tell that they are feigning concern they do not feel. Although her instinct is to defend her husband, Noah's wife isn't certain what to say. It is true, she must admit, that Noah has been of little help with the animals or the townspeople since coming up with this plan in the first place. But then, her husband's calling is to walk with God. How could he focus on the divine if he were down here in the trenches with the rest of them, cleaning cages and transporting feed? He has always been a man who is set apart from other men—something that has never bothered Noah's wife before. The only difference now is that he has also set himself apart from *her.*

Why has he begun to spend his days wandering? What is it that he is looking for? Twice now Mrs. McGinn's husband has passed him out on the road and given him a lift back; and this morning when Leesl found him pacing through the marshes, she took his arm and brought him gently home. His wife, preoccupied with the care of extra animals, looked up in surprise when he entered, not having realized he was gone. An egg carton fell from her hands and an orchestra of crickets spilled out across the carpet. They leaped behind the furniture and sang their praises from the corners, thankful not to be breakfast for the bearded dragon. Noah strode toward her, apologized profusely for his absence, and continued forward into his office. When she stopped in to ask him something two hours later, he was gone again.

Outside the diner now she closes her umbrella and pulls open the door, shaking the water off her hood before she enters. Inside, she finds Mrs. McGinn wiping down the tables with her apron askew and her hair completely wild. The hairdresser is among those who have recently left town, and although Mrs. McGinn has tried to tame and twist her curls on her own, she has had little success. She looks frazzled, unkempt, and Noah's wife tries to quell the stirrings of alarm. If Mrs. McGinn cannot keep herself together, what hope is there for the rest of them?

"Evelyn," she says. "Have you seen my husband?"

Mrs. McGinn frowns and jabs her hands into her hips. She always likes to know where people's husbands are. "No," she says. "I thought Jackson dropped him off last night." She scrutinizes Noah's wife. "Is there something you haven't told me? Are you two leaving, too?"

"Of course not," says Noah's wife. What monsters she and her husband would have to be, to desert this town after all that has happened! Wasn't it Noah, after all, who saddled his neighbors with the wild animals? Wasn't it she herself who refuted the weatherman's counsel? If they were not tied up in the fate of this place before, then they are certainly caught up in it now.

"Good," says Mrs. McGinn. Her face turns hard. "Because the people who left here are cowards. They are afraid of something that will never happen."

Noah's wife does not respond. She remembers developing the weatherman's photos at home last week, everything in her bathroom bathed in a soft amber glow from the filter she placed over her light box. The baby alligator splashed in the tub behind her while she stood at the sink and watched the shapes materialize on paper, the images appearing faintly at first and then darkening the longer she left them soaking in the developer. It had always thrilled her to see the change occur—to watch the world coming into being on her paper where nothing had been before—but something about these images stamped out her enchantment with the process and left her feeling cold instead. There was water creeping up the steps of the town hall; there were tropical birds shivering on caving roofs, and two drowned raccoon carcasses bumping up against a curb. It was clear from the series that the river was indeed rising ever higher, that the trees were losing more leaves by the day and the telephone and power lines were all in danger. She stopped developing after she rinsed the print of the town cemetery and clipped it up to dry. She felt too disturbed to carry on.

The fact was that Noah's wife did not like what she saw. Indeed: what had drawn her to photography in the first place was not a passion for realism, but her desire to portray the world as something other than what it was. She had a talent for making the couples and families who came into her studio look happier than they were; she had a knack for bringing out beauty where others couldn't find it, a skill for flooding a dark room with light.

She refuses to believe that Noah has changed and will not change back. All of that former confidence, his old faith and joy—those are all still a part of him. She glances through the rain-streaked glass, sees light boxes winking from second-story windows across the way. If they leave now, before Noah has achieved what he set out to do for this town, what if he never recovers from the disappointment? What if he never returns to the man he was before? They cannot leave until he has accomplished what he came here for; and as she realized suddenly at the town meeting, there would be no way for him to turn this town around, no way for him to save these souls, if the weatherman convinced them all to evacuate before Noah had his chance.

"Listen," says Mrs. McGinn, who can see that Noah's wife is troubled. "Why don't I bring you a slice of cake? That always makes Angela Rose feel better. It'll be on the house." As she rises, she turns and adds, as if this should be obvious: "You know, things here are not as grave as they appear."

Noah's wife watches Mrs. McGinn's retreating back until the woman vanishes into the kitchen. Although she appreciates the sentiment, Noah's wife understands that the appearance of things in this town depends on where one looks. Mrs. McGinn has not seen the evidence that Noah's wife has tucked away within her nightstand. Indeed, even if Noah's wife set the stack of photographs directly in her hands, Mrs. McGinn *still* might not recognize the danger before her. It is likely that, if she flipped through the images, she would only see her town as it was and as it could be once again. The strength of her hope, of her belief in the world as she wants it to be, is simply too powerful.

"So what is going on with Noah?" asks Mrs. McGinn when

she returns. She sets down a thick slice of angel food and slides a fork across the table.

"Nothing," Noah's wife says forcefully, as if the volume of the words could make them true. "He's fine."

She looks away from the window and pulls the cake close. Perhaps she and Mrs. McGinn are not as different as she thought.

twenty-three

Leesl plays the organ because the organ—much like Leesl herself—is not expressive.

Leesl doesn't like the phrase "not expressive," and also she doesn't think that it is entirely fair to use it with respect either to her or to her instrument. It offends her on behalf of them both. It is true, she concedes, that it is not possible to make a note louder or softer by touching the key with her fingers, but then, this is not a piano and if Noah had wanted a pianist he would have found someone else, someone who was not Leesl; and then again, what the instrument lacks in its dull white keys it makes up for in its pedals—its tarnished pedals that she plays with her bare feet, her toes curled along the cold metal—and in its pipes, regal and gleaming.

Even though it is clear to her that no one has any intention of attending services, Leesl continues to play the organ as often as she can. She has not seen Noah in the church since the town meeting last week, but she is not worried. She lets herself in and sits down at her instrument, certain that sooner or later he will turn up. In her experience, ministers always do.

As she plays, she remembers the way that the former town minister used to disappear for days at a time, only to resurface with grass in his hair and his face lined with deeper grooves than were there before he left. When she asked him where he had gone, he merely sat down with his journal and told her that he had come to believe that a man's religion was a very personal thing; too personal to explain.

"We've got to look for it everywhere, Leesl," he said cryptically. "In the woods, in the hills. It's a bit of a trick, is what it is. We've got to learn to fool ourselves."

Leesl wondered over what he meant, but she did not bother asking him to clarify. He seemed to grow more arcane with every day of bad weather. When his congregants stopped coming to church, he ceased writing sermons and began sending out his poetry instead. Most mysteriously, he began walking: strolling for hours in the woods beyond the church or marching through the abandoned neighborhoods on the outskirts of town in rectangles with ever-widening perimeters. He began to eat more, Leesl noticed, although the foods were more unusual and his gaze was vacant as he chewed. Once he told her that he was also sleeping more soundly. In general he seemed to be of good health; what was there to worry over?

"Leesl," he once asked her, "do you believe that being unable to touch or hear or see a God means that He is everywhere at once?"

"Yes," said Leesl simply. It is what she had been taught. "I do."

The old minister sighed. "I've always thought so, too," he said. "But I tell you, Leesl, lately it's been lonely up here. There have been times when a man can't help but ask himself whether a God he cannot touch is a God who isn't anywhere at all."

The sound of the old man's voice in her mind causes her to miss a line of music, her fingers stumbling to a stop. Leesl rests her hands at her sides, her knuckles growing white around the edge of her bench. She is tired of asking herself what happened to the old minister; she is tired of the townspeople asking her, too. What are they implying, after all, when they ask her what she knew of him? Are they suggesting that she could have done something to prevent the accident? When they stop her in the street, she merely blinks at them from behind her bottle cap glasses. She refuses to admit to anyone the number of nights she has lain awake in the dark of her creaking house, imagining what she might have done differently. Once he started acting strangely, should she have followed him? And if so, does that mean that she is supposed to be following Noah now, too?

She pictures the ancient cheetah she has penned up in her garage. The cat is sixteen years old, toothless, nearly blind, with fading spots and a milder temperament than even Leesl herself.

The zookeeper showed Leesl how to mix the cat's medication into shredded meat and pass it through the garage window on the end of a shovel. For the first few days, Leesl kept her distance, but lately she has taken to opening the garage door and sitting herself down just beyond the chicken-wire fence that she constructed, watching the giant cat snooze on a bed of threadbare throw pillows, her claws dug deeply into one of Leesl's old stuffed animals. Sometimes when Leesl sings to herself she believes she hears the cheetah purr.

She slides off her bench and lifts her raincoat from the pew in which she tossed it, moves with reticence toward the door. Unlike the rest of her neighbors, she has never liked to involve herself in others' affairs; since she prefers to be left to her own devices, she assumes that others deserve the same. Live and let live, her grandmother used to say. And then, in poorly accented but musical French: *Laissez-faire, ma petite. Laissez-faire.*

But how is one supposed to live and let live in a town like this one? How is one supposed to mind her own affairs when her neighbors are so adamantly *present*, so vulnerable, so overwhelmed? With a fresh resolution in mind, she strides the last few steps of the nave and heaves the great door open. To her astonishment, she does not need to track down Noah: he is standing on the other side, his raincoat plastered to him, water streaming from his shoulders to the steps. At the sight of her, he startles.

"Oh," he says, in some confusion. "Hello, Leesl." The skin below his eyes is swollen.

"Noah!" says Leesl. "Where on earth have you been?"

He follows her into the nave, allows her to remove his coat. "Leesl," he says musingly, as she peels the fabric from his skin, "if you knew that tomorrow the world would go to pieces, would you still plant your apple tree?"

"Excuse me?" says Leesl.

Noah shakes his head. "Never mind," he murmurs.

Leesl takes his elbow and leads him gently back to his office, sits him down in his armchair, and pulls a stack of wool blankets from the closet.

"Here," she says, dropping one of them onto his lap and wrapping another around his shoulders. "Take these. Why don't you stay right here for a while until you warm up? I'll run down the hill to find your wife. Should I brew some tea for you before I go?"

"Leesl," he says again. "If you were to find out that all the voices you'd ever heard had been fantasies, that what you'd believed to be visions had been dreams, that all the breath and the spirit you'd felt in the world had been nothing but a cold wind blowing upon rocks and that your life up to this point had been one debilitating lie—if that was what you awoke to discover, then wouldn't *you* be frightened, too?"

His voice is small, his posture meek. His shaggy hair is falling over his forehead. He closes his eyes while the silence expands between them.

"Noah?" she says at last.

He doesn't respond. From the slow rise and fall of his chest, it would appear as though he has fallen asleep. She brushes her fingers lightly across his forehead, finds that his skin is warm to the touch. He is feverish, she decides. Who knows how long he was out there on his own? She backs out of the room on the balls of her feet, pulls the door quietly shut behind her, and goes looking for a kettle in the kitchenette downstairs.

When he comes out of his office, looking worn and frail, Leesl is waiting for him. She steps forward to meet him and places the mug in his hands. She does not comment on his ragged hair or his shoulders splashed with mud. She hopes he hasn't noticed that his beard is growing grayer by the day. She doesn't mention their conversation and neither does he; she assumes that he would prefer to bury it.

Perhaps it is because Leesl herself is not expressive that she is better able to appreciate the expressions of others. Perhaps it is because she has been so often in the church with him, the battered brown hymnal yawning wide and open before her, her fingers tripping along the cracked keys of the organ, while he works at writing sermons or dusting candleholders or placing wafers onto a gleaming silver tray, arranging them in spirals that curve inward and tumble forward into the empty center of the plate.

She plays more often and she plays more loudly because she doesn't like how silent the church has become, or how lonely she feels beneath the vaulted white ceiling even when the minister is right there with her. She doesn't like the way that Noah stands so still on one side of the church, staring for long minutes into the navy blue sky of the stained-glass windows. She doesn't like the way he drifts so noiselessly across the soft carpet of the altar, he who used to hum off-key hymns to himself as he went. She doesn't know what to do, she doesn't know what to say, and so she continues to play, lifting her bare foot from the pedal so that the sound is unmuffled, pure and loud, so that the church is filled with songs that rise skyward to meet the rain that drums down on the dark shingles of the roof.

twenty-four

Ever since taking in the peacocks, Mauro has adopted a more stately way of walking.

Sometimes when the townspeople step outside to glare at the sky or empty their rain gauges, they see him following the birds through the streets. The peacocks move slowly forward, tails closed tight as clasped fans, and Mauro struts behind them with his stubbled chin up, his chest out, and one of their feathers tucked with a handkerchief into the front pocket of his button-down shirt. If he stops to say hello to a neighbor and the birds lose sight of him, they take great bustling strides around corners until they find him again, flaring their tails in an explosion of turquoise passion. The sudden appearance of so many feathered eyes used to startle Mauro as much as it still startles his neighbors, but he has since become accustomed to these brilliant displays of affection.

The townspeople frown. "Mauro, where is your raincoat?" they demand. "Where is your umbrella? We've told you this a thousand times—you're going to catch your death out there."

Mauro shrugs, grins. The peacock feather in his pocket is already soaked through and drooping, but he doesn't mind. There are plenty more where that came from.

To be honest, he is not too concerned these days about his death. If it will come, let it come! Since his savings and his homecoming have been washed away, part of him feels that there is not much left to live for. Part of him is determined to survive in this town. And yet another part—the strongest, perhaps—loves the peacocks so dearly that he does not care if keeping their feathers in the house portends death.

In any case, he has already dropped so many umbrellas on the floor and looked so many owls in the eye that a few feathers here or there will not change his fate now. The librarian keeps the owls caged on the shelves in the dusty biology section, and no matter how hard Mauro tries, he cannot escape their yellow gazes. It must be something about the way they turn their heads, he decides as he pages through tips on bird ownership. What is the use in fighting it?

The truth is that Mauro is tired of trying to navigate the cosmos, tired of looking for signs. His hope for a happier future is gone, and so why not simply make the best of the present? What is wrong with cheerful acceptance of the inevitable? As he walks down the streets with his peacocks, he feels oddly elevated and elated, as if he exists on a higher plane than do his neighbors.

He believes that he can see these things more clearly. He watches the townspeople come out of their houses and peer at the sky as if trying to read the clouds. Leesl leans down to check the level in her rain gauge; Mrs. McGinn's husband climbs out of his truck to determine the speed of the water rushing through the streets.

Mauro smiles to himself, shakes his head. He has a theory that everyone these days is looking for some kind of sign: some visible, tangible proof that their faith in this town has not been misplaced. Granted, he also has a theory that if a person spends a certain number of minutes walking in the rain without his slicker or umbrella, this person need not shower as often as he would in a place where it does not rain like this. He believes that carbonated beverages make a person smarter and that horses have a certain sense about the future. In recent days he has looked into the blank brown eyes of the elk and the zebra and the bongo, and he has decided that the same theory does not apply to them. They are only hungry, and stupid, and sometimes mean.

What his friends and neighbors do not understand as well as he does (and yes, he calls them his friends, even if they might not think of themselves in such terms) is that there are no signs except the ones we choose to read. The stop sign is not a stop sign if Mauro does not brake for it; the weatherman's warning is not an omen if no one here will heed it. A man chooses what he will see, what he will follow, and right now Mauro is perfectly happy to walk in the rain and follow his peacocks. Their tails drag a little in the mud as they look for bugs along the riverbank, and Mauro ambles happily behind, making up his mind to bathe them later.

Near the river, Mauro notices that they are not alone. It is easy enough for Mauro to recognize the figure down by the water, since the minister is the only person in town who dresses all in black, from his slacks to his slicker to his boots. Mauro pauses with the peacocks beneath the makeshift shelter of a willow tree whose branches whip and quiver like ribbons in the wind. From there he watches the minister trudge down the bank to the water, sees him crouch low to the ground and stretch out a hand to feel the river coursing through his fingers. Mauro himself has done this many a time before. When money still flowed into town, the city council hired a young architect to design a series of pedestrian bridges spanning the water at measured intervals from one end of town to the other. Mauro remembers many sweltering summer afternoons spent drifting slowly downstream in his rowboat, a fishing line hanging over the side. The little craft would slide from sunlight to shade, flowing into the long shadows cast by one bridge, and then another. After he had wrestled the fish into the boat, he would watch them take great gasping breaths, their curved sides heaving, clouds floating through their mirrored eyes. Mauro used to love those summer hours. He remembers feeling content and at peace every time he set foot in that boat, happy in a way he rarely felt on land.

Why else would he have hidden his money there? He

shakes his head in consternation, still cannot believe the boat is gone.

He peers down the bank, tries to determine what exactly Noah is doing. Do all ministers share this strange affinity to water? Does Noah not remember that the last minister who went down there did not make it up the banks again?

Mauro knows that lately Noah has been acting strangely: he has seen the minister wandering at odd times through odd places in town. This must be how Noah came to be at the river on his own, staring with great concentration at a rotten log extending out into the water. Mauro watches him rise to his feet and take one cautious step out onto the log. When it holds, he takes another, his arms stretched wide for balance. He sways a little in the wind, looking like a great black bird trembling in the rain above the water. Noah takes a third step, and a fourth. A few more and he will have reached the end of the log.

As a child Mauro had once attended a circus, and the sight of Noah now reminds him of the performers he saw walking on tightropes and swinging on trapezes as if they were born to live in air instead of on land. For weeks afterward he spent several hours a day constructing his own gymnasium in his mother's garden. He balanced on fences and hung from trees, but he was no good at it—and although his mother did not scold him when he came inside with scrapes and bruises, by the time he broke his arm she lost her patience. *Basta,* she told him, enough was enough. Of course we all must test our limits, she said, but the wise man will recognize when he can go no further.

With an unfamiliar sense of foreboding, Mauro tenses beneath the willow tree, feels the tufts of coarse white hair rising on his arms. The man is a minister—not an acrobat. What is he trying to prove?

Because the log slopes down into the water, Mauro cannot tell exactly where it ends. Two steps farther and the current is washing over Noah's feet, so that although Mauro knows the minister is still standing on the rotten wood, he can no longer see it. Indeed, there is a fraction of a second before Mauro tears himself free of the tree branches and goes barreling down the bank, the peacocks shrieking at his back, when he believes that the minister *is* walking on the water, that unlike Mauro himself he has succeeded in going several steps beyond his human boundaries, that the God he has been looking for is right there hanging on to him, keeping his feet suspended just a hairsbreadth above the grasping silver waves. From the expression on Noah's face—the sudden illumination, the flare of unsullied joy—Mauro is convinced that in that instant, he believes it, too.

And then he falls. He falls like a bird shot from the sky, like the rain in a town that he will have to leave behind. He falls like Mauro's heart when the illusion crumbles to pieces before him, when the world reminds him once again—brutally, ruthlessly—that there is no one guiding his steps or holding him up; that when his foot strikes against a rock or his fingers slip one by one from his homemade trapeze, the only thing reaching out to catch him will be the earth itself, cold and hard and merciless.

twenty-five

Although Dr. Yu has been trained in the art of empathy, she does not find it very useful.

Once when she was in medical school, she was made to wear a pair of garden gloves and told to open a bottle of pills in order to simulate the trials of patients with arthritis. In the same class, she had to listen to her instructor while wearing earplugs (partial deafness), read magazines through goggles smeared in honey (deteriorating vision), and walk for half a day with handfuls of small stones in her shoes (diabetic neuropathy). She and her classmates rolled down hallways in wheelchairs and limped through stairwells with canes.

Dr. Yu found the whole experience to be highly ridiculous. How can anyone expect her to help patients if her hands are gloved and she cannot write out prescriptions? If she cannot see, cannot hear, cannot walk down the hallway from one waiting area to the next—how is she supposed to do her job? "This is not a literature class," she was tempted to say to her professors. "This is medical school. If I wanted to learn how to feel pain, I would have gone someplace else. The reason why I'm here is because I'd rather learn to cure it."

By the time she graduated from medical school, she was one of the top students in her class. She learned how to perform both the classic and the cutting-edge surgeries, and by the end of her training she was wielding the tools of the operating room with the same familiarity and aplomb with which she held her own toothbrush. With several years of practice now behind her, she feels that she has seen every possible kind of heart, every failure and weakness, and she knows how to deal with each one. She is an excellent doctor. There should be no doubt about that.

It is, in part, *because* she is an excellent doctor that she is not surprised to be woken an hour before dawn by an insistent pounding on her front door. Accustomed to late-night calls from the hospital, she is completely alert and on her feet within six seconds, and by the time six more have passed she is shrugging into her cotton robe and jogging down the stairs. This would not be the first time that one of her neighbors has come to the door in the middle of the night to complain of a slightly racing heartbeat or a touch of fever. Dr. Yu always brings them inside, sits them down, and dutifully checks them over. She is familiar with the sense of being needed.

But when she yanks open the door she does not find a

neighbor; only a newer version of her best friend, with coal-black hair and half-moons carved out below her eyes, supporting an old man who is shivering uncontrollably. Under the slim beams of the porch light, the minister appears so much gaunter than he was when Dr. Yu last saw him, his face so sharp and so ashen that in the seconds before someone speaks, Dr. Yu does not recognize him.

"April," says her best friend, her voice thick with exhaustion. "I didn't have time to try and reach you before we left. Can we stay with you tonight?"

Tonight, Dr. Yu reflects, is nearly over. The sky in the east is already glowing pale and yellow, and the birds nesting below her mailbox are awake and singing in the dark.

"Of course you can," she says brusquely, stepping out of the way. She is aware that now is not the time for questions. "Come on, then—let's get the two of you inside."

They follow her into the hallway, clinging to one another like survivors of a shipwreck, water dripping to the floor. Their clothes are so soaked through that it looks as though they have been wet for days, even though her best friend must have driven hours through a dry and cloudless night to get them here. Although Dr. Yu will toss everything in the dryer before going back to bed, after several rounds through it she will find that the clothes are still damp. She will examine them in the morning before she makes the coffee, holding them up to the light in irritated disbelief. It will be as if the cloth itself is demonstrating a kind of willful resistance; as if the fabric had forgotten how to be anything but wet.

For now she simply helps them peel their slickers from their skin, wondering how long it has been since she herself has worn a raincoat. Noah has so many goose bumps rising on his arms that his skin looks pockmarked, diseased. She wraps him tightly in a blanket and leads them both down to her best friend's old room, which has not been touched by anyone but Dr. Yu's cleaning woman in the years since her best friend moved out.

"Could you check him over?" her best friend asks, once Noah is sitting on the bed. "Just to make sure nothing is broken, and everything is normal?"

Dr. Yu obediently reaches for Noah's clammy wrist in order to read his pulse. Her examination is brief but thorough, and she assures her best friend once they are back out in the hallway that his vital signs are all fine. She would not say, however, that everything is *normal*; the minister has the air of someone suffering a kind of posttraumatic shock. Dr. Yu has only ever witnessed Noah as being cheerful, passionate, aggressively attentive. When she spent time with her best friend after the marriage she would become cross with the way he intruded on their conversations, positioning himself in the center of the room, on his imagined soapbox, to offer up his unsolicited advice. She was most irritated when he critiqued her on her bedside manner, on the way in which she spoke about and interacted with her patients. She would never have expected him to offer his wrist, his ear, his bare chest to be examined with as little cognizance as he did just now. He did not even look to the door when she and her best friend retreated from the room.

In the kitchen, Dr. Yu puts a pot of milk on the stove, remembering her best friend's routine indulgence of drinking milk steamed with honey before bedtime. Her best friend drops into a chair, and when the drink is prepared, Dr. Yu sends a mug skating across the table toward her. It is strange to have her best friend here, in this kitchen, after living apart for so long. The painted walls, the framed photographs, the colors of the towels and the dishes—none of these were Dr. Yu's doing. Her best friend always possessed an instinctive, enviable sense of light and balance.

"All right," says Dr. Yu, her tone clinical and probing. "What happened?"

Her best friend twines her fingers through the handle of her mug. "There was an accident," she finally replies. Her words are heavy and slow. "Noah went down to the river, and he slipped and fell in."

"Were you there, too?" asks Dr. Yu.

"No," says her best friend. "Mauro was there. He pulled Noah out."

"Mauro?"

"A friend of ours. He owns the general store," she explains. "He's been keeping some of the larger birds, like the wild turkeys and the peacocks."

The larger birds? Dr. Yu's face registers her bafflement,

which only increases as her best friend describes a situation that sounds like something out of a fable—a murky little town bedded down among the hills, beset by bad weather and capricious personalities. As her best friend speaks, Dr. Yu tries to imagine the vivid hues of the umbrellas, the puddles gleaming in the streets, the river rising up between the banks. Fine, fine. All of that, she can understand. It is when her best friend launches into the story of the zoo that Dr. Yu narrows her eyes, her forehead creasing in skepticism. Wild animals roaming free in the town? Pacing through empty storefronts, grazing in people's backyards, swimming in bathtubs? She finds the whole thing as ridiculous as it is dangerous. It simply doesn't make sense. If there was a problem with the rain, why didn't they send the animals away much earlier? And if the situation now is truly so severe, why haven't all of the townspeople evacuated?

Her best friend raises and lowers a shoulder when Dr. Yu demands a real explanation. "It's complicated," she says, as if that ought to answer every question.

Dr. Yu frowns. "I don't understand."

"Not everything can be explained." Her best friend's gaze is as solemn and reflective as Dr. Yu remembers it. "Anyway, it's hard to describe it to someone who hasn't seen it."

Is it Dr. Yu's imagination, or is there an edge to her best friend's tone? She understands that she has been unavailable, that there were phone calls that went unanswered and a promise to come visit on which she never followed through. She is sorry to hear, of course, that things were so strange and so hard—and yet from hundreds of miles away, what help or solace could Dr. Yu have offered? It is difficult to heal a person one cannot touch and to fix a life one cannot witness. Besides: Doesn't Dr. Yu have enough trouble of her own?

"Well, you're here now," she says with all the affirmation she can muster. She pats her best friend's hand. "You made the right decision."

Her best friend glances down the hallway. "I didn't have much choice," she replies. "He hasn't been himself for weeks. If Mauro hadn't been there—" She shudders. "I don't want to think about what could have happened." She pauses, then adds: "April, do you think that you could talk to him?"

"Talk to him?" Dr. Yu repeats. She shakes her head. "I'm a heart surgeon, not a psychiatrist. This is not my area of expertise."

"Please," her best friend persists. "There must be something you can do."

Dr. Yu considers her best friend, whose hair is so black that it gleams almost blue in the strong white light of Dr. Yu's kitchen. *Is* there something she can do? Dr. Yu asks herself. She treats the body, not the soul. What good would it do to take Noah in for a real examination? What use would she be if she tried to speak with him, she who—according to her father—so often fails in understanding the affairs of the heart?

The truth is that after her abysmal performance with her father, she does not trust herself with another man's despair. She is tired—so tired. She does not mind that people come to her door day and night in the hope that she will cure what ails them—she only wishes that once in a while someone would ask what is ailing *her*, Dr. Yu, instead of assuming that a doctor would not need someone else to ease her pain. And how to explain that to her best friend, who has always been convinced that Dr. Yu has all the answers? That kind of blind adoration was something Dr. Yu once thrived on, but it is no longer what she needs.

Dr. Yu deliberates. "It sounds to me," she says slowly, "as though there is something unfortunate about that place. Who stays in a town where it rains every day, especially after they have been warned that the weather will only get worse? What kind of people live with parrots and alligators and cheetahs in their houses, or with bongos in the backyard? No wonder Noah was losing his mind back there. He cannot be expected to reach people who are deliberately making themselves unreachable. Give him a few days here—back in his old city, his old routine. Soon he'll be just fine."

For a moment her best friend doesn't answer. Finally she rises from her chair and sets her mug down in the sink. Dr. Yu hopes this is a good sign. A few hours' sleep, she is convinced, will do all of them a world of good.

"Honestly, April," says her best friend, pausing at the threshold of the hallway. From this angle Dr. Yu can see the slump of her shoulders, the disappointment coloring her face. "I think that you could try to be more understanding."

The accusation, an echo of her father, strikes Dr. Yu harder than her best friend intended. She *is* trying to understand. The fact is, Dr. Yu would like to say to her best friend's retreating shadow—the fact is that there is only so much suffering a person can reflect upon while still managing to function in the world every day. Compassion is all right in moderation, but an excess can knock you flat, leave you mournful and paralyzed, strip you of your usefulness. Perhaps it is true that she could be more empathetic, and less detached. Perhaps she ought to express more emotion and encourage her father, her patients, to express theirs.

Like everyone else in the world, she, too, has had her heart broken; she, too, has suffered grief. There have been days when the silence in her house has nearly bowled her over with sadness, and there have been mornings when she wakes to find that she does not have the will to rise, the energy to shower or to eat or to dress. This is the truth about sadness: sometimes the clouds can descend without warning.

twenty-six

In the hours following Noah's fall into the river and his subsequent departure with his wife, the diner explodes with activity.

Granted, the town is a small one. But although busy days in the diner might not measure up to the kind of packed lunch crowds one would expect to find in a restaurant in the city, the McGinns are running low on both servers and supplies and so the rush is causing Mrs. McGinn, for one, to break out in hives. The zookeeper, noticing this as soon as he comes down the stairs into the dining room, offers her an ointment that he has been using on the wolves. He has told the townspeople time and again about the reaction the wolves will have to poultry, but some idiot or another persists in wedging chicken bones through a crack in the door to the storefront where they are kept. The zookeeper cannot tell if the action is benevolent or cruel: Does the anonymous chicken-donor only mean to feed them because they are looking lean and hungry, or is he (or she) hoping that in eating the bones, the wolves will die?

This was what he was pondering while brushing his teeth this morning. Then, after he had spat into the sink and turned off the faucet, he stared at his reflection in the mirror and he asked himself: When did my thoughts become so dark?

He will need to pull himself together over the next few months. This is not the kind of father (cynical, critical, impatient) that he had ever expected himself to be. As he informed his reflection this morning, he had better shape up. He had better make a concerted effort from now on to be more generous, more tolerant, slower to chastise and to judge.

And yet the townspeople are not making his resolution very easy. After he hands Mrs. McGinn the ointment, she grasps and pockets it. When the zookeeper tells her that he will be needing it back (unless the walking chicken-bone dispenser discontinues those toxic nightly visits), she only frowns and shoves it deeper into the front of her apron with the air of a magpie hoarding a gleaming shard of glass.

"We'll see," she snaps. "Are you going to help out down here or not?"

The zookeeper stares at her. No, he wants to say. Most likely not. Does she have any sense of how he is forced to spend his time? He is not sitting up there admiring the ugly beige walls of her guest bedroom, lounging on the threadbare sheets and reading fat Russian novels (his favorite kind of fiction, if anyone ever cared to know), while she sweats over platters of grilled cheese and five-gallon vats of tomato soup. No. He is marching the streets of this town at all hours of the day and night, tracking down tropical birds and snakes that have gone missing. He is treating the bites and scratches that the townspeople acquire when they cuddle up too close to their charges. He is burying reptile carcasses and treating mammals for anxiety and he is doing it all on his own, now that the minister's wife has abandoned the project and deserted *her* animals, as well. That red fox has been trotting up and down driveways for hours, peering into doorways and climbing onto windowsills in search of her.

Meanwhile the zookeeper is eating infrequently and sleeping fitfully and worrying about his wife-to-be and his unborn child on top of it all. He exhales and tries to calm himself, the thought of his fiancée reminding him of his resolution.

"I can give you an hour," he tells Mrs. McGinn, making a concerted effort not to snarl. "What do you need me to do?"

She instructs him to take orders and bring out drinks while she goes back into the kitchen to see what kind of meals she can concoct out of the supplies in her dwindling stockroom. Deliveries have become more sporadic as the rain has worsened, and it has been several days now since anyone has seen a fresh fruit or vegetable. The zookeeper does not need to be reminded of the problem; he is already mulling over what sorts of canned foods he might be able to feed the primates if they run out of produce. The hoofstock still have plenty of tall grass and leaves and hay to go through, and right after the flood the zookeeper stocked the extra freezers in back of the diner with pounds upon pounds of meat for the carnivores. He is grateful now that he was able to do so, and that he did not have to resort to distributing the frozen meat for safekeeping among the townspeople. From what he has observed of their behavior lately, he doubts whether they would have been willing to return it to him.

Overnight, his neighbors have turned into hoarders. As he scratches their orders down on his fiancée's notepad, he can see them shoveling sugar packets and ketchup and creamers into their purses, their trouser pockets, the folds of their slickers and the tops of their rain boots. Unaware that over so many years living among animals the zookeeper has honed his peripheral vision, they think that they are caching on the sly.

"Can you believe this?" the zookeeper says to Mauro when he pauses to refill someone's lemonade. The Italian is leaning against the counter and gazing over the diner like a lion surveying his pride. Since the word of his impromptu rescue has spread, Mauro has become something of a town celebrity, his air more pompous and all-knowing than normal.

"Yes," he says now in a tone that is self-consciously solemn and wise. "The people are buying up all the things in my store, too. All the lightbulbs, the batteries. All the water, all the cereal, and also cans. They are buying so many things that they cannot be fitting them all in their cars. They are wanting me to come also with them in my truck." He shakes his head. "The worst is the fighting. When they are taking the cans from the other people's shopping cart, when they are stealing the juices from the other people's car. I am seeing it happen in the parking lot. I am not surprised if soon we are having thieves in the night!"

"Do you mean that?" asks the zookeeper. "It can't be everyone."

"Everyone," insists Mauro. "Even the ones you are not expecting! The little Leesl is buying up much more than one person could be needing. She is coming to my store four, five times every day. What are you making of that?"

"It's pandemonium," mutters the zookeeper. He glares at the crowd in the diner. How is he supposed to remain patient with them when they are behaving so badly? All of this hoarding, this hiding, this sneaking around and stealing from their neighbors' caches—why, they are no better than a conspiracy of ravens.

While he is working to become the best person that he can possibly be for his future child, the townspeople are devolving into the worst versions of themselves. The zookeeper almost died twice while crossing the street this morning, so reckless and impatient have his neighbors become while driving. Then, on the streets and in the stores, he saw them stealing one another's umbrellas—which could only be done out of spite, not necessity, since each townsperson owns more umbrellas of different shapes and sizes than there are days of the week.

What vexes him the most about this is his own reaction, his feeling of *surprise.* He knows better than that. He knows that people are selfish, petty, covetous, stubborn, mean-spirited creatures, which is why he has always preferred to spend his time in the animal kingdom. The animals, at least, are what they are. They present no pretense of aspiring to anything higher, of possessing any driving force other than simple, unadulterated instinct. He trusts them in a way he cannot trust his neighbors—not now, not like this. He slams his notepad down on the counter and stomps into the kitchen to inform Mrs. McGinn that he will no longer be waiting on her customers. Let them get their own damn soup, if they want it so badly. Let them take it from their neighbors.

When Mrs. McGinn's daughter eventually appears in the dining room, her face a little green around the edges, she finds him sitting alone in a corner booth, nursing an oversized bowl of oatmeal. She greets him and sits down. For a few minutes she watches him mope.

"You've got to give them a break," she says.

"What are you talking about?"

She shrugs. "They're not themselves right now. Everyone's frightened, confused. This is the second minister that's gone into the river and the second one they've lost, whether they wanted him here or not. Haven't you listened to the conversations at the tables? It's all that anyone can talk about."

The zookeeper raises his shaggy head. It was a shock to wake up to the news that Noah and his wife had departed—that much was true. Although the zookeeper never cared much for the minister, he had grown more dependent on the minister's wife than he cared to admit. The fact that she left without any notice, that she did not stop to bring him her animals or say a proper good-bye—well, it is enough to make even a person like the zookeeper (with his prickly soul and his deeply rooted disdain for others) feel somewhat forsaken. Perhaps this is a natural reaction; perhaps, after being so many times abandoned, the townspeople cannot stop themselves from grabbing at things, from holding them close.

"Do you think we drove him to it?" the zookeeper asks, the words rising to his lips unbidden.

He hates himself for asking it, hates that the question is as impossible to answer for this minister as it was for the last one. Why do you think he did it? the townspeople are asking one another across their lukewarm lunches on the day of Noah's departure—the same question they were asking themselves on the day of his arrival.

"Maybe he just needed to get away," says Mrs. McGinn's daughter. The zookeeper's attention snaps back to her, drawn by the peculiarity of her tone. "Look at this place." She indicates in the cramped diner, the charcoal skies, the muttered complaints of their neighbors. "Can you blame him?"

"No," the zookeeper admits. "I suppose not."

"But you still refuse to go?"

The zookeeper stares at her, his patience evaporating. "Not now, Angie," he declares. "We've been over this about a thousand times. We've got responsibilities here!" He stops, steadies himself. "This is my job," he reminds her, more calmly. "If I'm not a zookeeper, I'm not anything."

"And what about me?" she demands. "What am I?"

"Right now? You're a citizen of this town. You're a daughter and a fiancée and soon you'll be a mother. You need to focus on the big picture, Angie. You need to get some perspective." He reaches for her hands and lowers his voice. "We've talked about this enough. I don't want to fight anymore."

She nods, her expression tight. To the zookeeper, it seems that her face is rounder, softer than it used to be. "You're right," she says. "I won't bring this up again."

She rises and moves toward the kitchen, her steps heavier than usual. The zookeeper sighs and pushes his half-empty bowl away from him.

What does it matter why Noah walked into the river, why the last minister died, why anyone does anything at all? People are impossible to predict. Look at his neighbors: one day so helpful with the animals, so attentive to their needs; and the next day cramming pepper packets down their pants. He knows that they are frightened, but isn't it too late for fear? Those who wanted to go, who were able to go, have left. These are the people who remain, the hearty souls who cling to their houses and their memories and their hope for something better while they are waiting for the rain to end and praying that the river does not rise up any higher.

And what if, he asks himself, this little town is washed away? Would the world be so much worse without it?

In reality, he doubts that anyone would notice they were gone.

twenty-seven

Noah wishes that his wife had not come with him to the church.

He doesn't want her to see him like this: shaky, uncertain. He stumbled over the threshold on the way out of Dr. Yu's house this morning and suddenly she was right there beside him, lifting up his elbow and guiding him out to the car. I'm not an invalid, he nearly snapped at her—but then again, how could he be certain? The memory of their flight two nights before left him feeling tentative and cowed. He recalled the sound of their tires splashing through puddles the size of small ponds and the image of the headlights beaming weakly through water while he shivered in the passenger seat and his wife tried not to look unnerved. The rain cleared once they were out of the hills, and for the remaining hours of their drive he leaned back against the headrest and peered mutely at the stars.

What the hell had he been thinking?

"There is something strange about that place," the head elder says now, shaking his silver head with something between compassion and disdain. "You did your best, Noah," he continues gravely. "Lord knows you tried. It simply wasn't meant to be."

Around the table the other elders murmur their assent, their clasped hands reflected in the sheen of the great mahogany table. Noah stares at their familiar faces with a flood of deep relief, the tension of the past two days finally easing from his muscles. They are right, of course—it was the town! How can any man be expected to stay sane in a place like that?

The head elder clears his throat and then continues. "Unfortunately we cannot offer you a position back here at the present time," he says. His eyes are deep-set and unblinking. "In your absence, of course, we called someone else to take your place. But if you are willing to wait a few days—a few weeks at most—I am sure we will have no trouble identifying a new assignment for you in a different church. As you well know, any congregation would count itself fortunate to have you." The elder pauses and shuffles through the stack of papers before him. "In the meantime, I'm afraid that we cannot return you to your former house, as the new minister and his young family are quite settled in it by now. Do you have a place to stay?"

Noah nods, unthinkingly. It is only when he and his wife have left the committee room and are stepping softly through the nave that he realizes he should have checked with her before responding.

"April won't mind?" he asks her, and she shakes her head, her dark hair swinging across her shoulders.

"No," she says. "I think it will be fine." She glances sidewise at Noah, something odd in her expression. "I'm sure that we can stay as long as you like," she adds, "if you're certain that this is what you want."

He halts at the back of the church, troubled by her statement. The vaulted ceiling soars above him, the candles blaze upon the altar. This church is twice the size of the one he has just left behind. In comparison, this one is opulent, grandiose, miraculously intact.

"What do you mean?" he asks.

She shrugs, fiddles with the cuffs of her checkered blouse. "Nothing," she says. "I only meant—" Then she stops herself, shaking her head. "Nothing. I guess I thought that once you were feeling better, we would be going back."

"Back?" The idea appalls him.

"Most of our things are still there. We left in a hurry," she reminds him gently. She hesitates, and then she adds: "Besides—we took in so many of those animals. Who will look after them if we're not there?"

Noah pictures the town. He imagines the rain pouring into the streets, the townspeople sealed within their houses, watching from behind closed windows. He can almost hear the howling of the wind, can almost feel the rain slamming against the walls. His hands tremble and sweat soaks the back of his shirt. For a moment his vision tunnels into darkness, and when his head clears he is unsteady on his feet, supported once again by his wife. He tries to pull away to prove that he can stand just fine on his own, but the earth sways beneath him and he cannot stop himself from leaning on her shoulder.

"Let's get you home," she says, and he doesn't protest.

He wouldn't have leaned on her so fully had he thought that anyone was watching them; he would have tried to manage on his own. But it is only when they approach the curb that he notices a figure leaning on the hood of their car, considering Noah and his wife from beneath a dark, sardonic brow, and so there is no time for him to straighten up. Noah does not recognize the man at first—the sun makes his head ache, makes the entire day feel like a dream.

"Well," says the man, striding forward to offer his assistance. "What a coincidence."

His face strikes an ominous chord, but still Noah fails to place him. It is his wife who speaks first. "The weatherman?" she says.

The man smirks, slick-haired and red-faced, a patch of dry skin peeling from his sunburned nose. "That's what I used to be, sure," he says with a fake and brilliant grin. He extends his hand. "But not anymore. I've been fired, so you might as well call me Jonas."

"Excuse me, Jonas," says Noah's wife while Noah removes his arm from hers and grasps the man's hand. "I didn't expect to see you here. I'm sorry to hear about your job."

"Me?" he scoffs. "I didn't expect to see *you* here! I had you pegged for a true believer—I thought you were determined to stick it out in that ghost town until the bitter end." He shrugs. "Anyway, I saw your car out here—recognized it as I was heading down the street for lunch. I haven't seen that much mud and rust on a car since I hightailed it out of those hills two weeks ago. The feathers and claw marks in the upholstery were a dead giveaway, too. God, I'm glad to be out of there."

Noah's wife smiles at him in sympathy, the skin crinkling at the corners of her eyes. She responds but Noah does not hear what she is saying; he only lets his eyes rest upon her face. Her skin is still pale from weeks without sun, and when she smiles at Jonas her soul seems to shine right through it. She is clever and calm, generous and lovely. Noah warms at the sight of her and wonders, as he has wondered before, how she came to be so good.

Their relationship has always worked because the balance is just so: he is the one who guides them, dreaming of a distant point, while she steadies them and keeps them on course. He has never found someone as utterly *devoted* as she is—to her friends, to her work, to her clients, to him. Whenever he forgot his books at home, she would bring them to him. While he composed prayers to say at dinner, she made sure the meal was on the table. And yet although he loves how she supports him, he has not been able to ignore the fact that lately she seems driven to support many people in a similar fashion. He tries to ignore the doubt that tugs at the corners of his mind, but what if the truth is that he and she are not the perfect complements they appear to be? What if his wife is simply very good at being complementary?

"So," Jonas is saying, his tone as conversational as if the three of them had been friends for years. "How many people came out with you? Is there anyone left back there?"

"About half the town left after your meeting," replies Noah's wife.

"The other half is still there?" he exclaims. His eyebrows rise halfway up his forehead. "Two full weeks later, and it hadn't stopped raining?"

She shakes her head. "Not when we left."

He exhales in a whistle, low and flat. "Damn it," he says. He squints at her. "Tell me—why aren't you with them? What finally changed your mind?"

Noah's wife glances briefly at her husband. "Things took a turn for the worse," she says.

Jonas nods. "Listen," he says after a moment, his tone thick with rancor. "You've got to take care of yourself first, before you try to take care of anyone else. Look out for number one." He pauses, shoots Noah a look whose significance Noah does not understand. "As for the rest of them, don't give them another thought. They're a bunch of misfits, and they made their choice. How can they expect anyone to help them if they won't help themselves?"

Yes, Noah wants to say—that town, that church, those people. He wants to be able to say that they have ruined him. And yet . . . ? The church towers in the background behind his wife, its brick walls hard and unyielding, its steeple gleaming as if freshly sharpened. He shivers in the sun. The building that should provide him with that old sense of inspiration and purpose only leaves him with a gut full of dread. He felt this way before he left, he suddenly remembers. The feeling is familiar; it is the reason why he sought a change.

"Stubborn as pack mules, they are," Jonas continues. "Stupid. Self-involved. Hopeless. If they hadn't been so pigheaded, I could have convinced them to evacuate. Then I'd still have my job." He shrugs, kicks at a yellow weed spiking out of the sidewalk. "The point is: it's a beautiful day out here. The sun is shining. Might as well sit back and enjoy unemployment while it lasts—isn't that right, Minister?"

Noah cannot listen anymore. "It was a foolish project to begin with," he interjects, his tone uncharacteristically sour. "We were bound to fail. I couldn't save that town any more than you could."

Jonas does not seem to appreciate the comparison. "I didn't *fail*," he insists, his face glistening with sweat. He glances at Noah's wife. "I simply stopped trying. If I'd wanted them out, I could have gotten them out, no problem. The fact is that it wasn't worth the hassle. There was nothing worth saving there."

"You lost your job over it," Noah reminds him.

"My peace of mind was more important than my job."

Noah shakes his head. "The truth is you couldn't have done it. It's fine. I couldn't do it, either." He keeps his gaze fixed on Jonas even though he feels the shadow of the church looming over him. He is desperate to explain his revelation, but he cannot find the words to share it. The idea that we can change the people around us, that we can help them or save them or make them something other than what they are—it's a delusion. It's the illusion of control. Noah did not see that before, but he certainly sees it now.

"I could have gotten them out," Jonas repeats. His face remains placid but his grin is sharper than it was. "I could *still* get them out. Sounds like a challenge."

Noah's wife stands between them, looking from one to the other, all the light gone now from her face. Noah turns away from her and shrugs.

"Life is not a challenge," he murmurs, as if to himself. "It's not a test, or a choice. It's simply something you're born into."

His wife is saying something, but he cannot hear her. Before he knows what he is doing he has taken off again, striding through the dappled light that the branches have thrown across the sidewalk, gliding smoothly over pools of shade. His legs are long and he has already gone two blocks before his wife catches up to him, breathless, calling his name. If she had not snagged his sleeve when she did, if he had not looked down into her face and been struck right there on the pavement with all the force of her devotion and all the weight of how he loved her, he might have gone on walking for miles, the church at his back, putting as much distance between himself and that steeple as any man could.

twenty-eight

Someone must take action to save this sinking town.

And if not Mrs. McGinn, then who? Mauro? He might have pulled the minister out of the river, but he did no more than any lifeguard would have done. Her own daughter worked as a lifeguard at the outdoor pool in the years before it closed, and then the indoor one after that. If she had been at the river, she could have saved Noah's life as well as anyone.

Heroism is all about timing.

"Isn't that right, Angela Rose?" she would like to ask her daughter. Still in her pajamas, she pads down the hallway to her daughter's room and opens the door, but the girl isn't there. Mrs. McGinn pauses, examines the room. Everything is in its place: the shelves of stuffed animals, the plush pink carpet, the canopy bed and the quilt that Mrs. McGinn made herself, sewed with her own two hands by the light of the living room lamp. And yet something about the room does not seem right.

"Angela Rose?" calls Mrs. McGinn, but again there is no answer.

Mrs. McGinn's mind flashes back to last night, to the dream she had of empty streets and empty houses. The entire town had been abandoned and she was left as its only occupant, bailing water from her diner with a white plastic pail in preparation for the customers who never came. The dream seemed so real that when she woke this morning her arms felt as though they were aching, muscles sorely tried by the task she had imagined for herself.

She wanders back down the hallway to her own room, where she dresses and arranges her hair as best she can. Her husband is already gone, transporting the day's animal supplies from the town hall to the houses. He had woken her with the sound of breaking glass in the kitchen, but she had not ventured downstairs to find out if the crash was accidental or deliberate. Now when she walks through to reach the front door, she sees no sign that anything occurred at all. Say what people will about her husband and his temper—at least he does his best to keep his messes to himself.

Out on the main drag she wades through several inches of water, lifting her boots extra high in a futile attempt to avoid the fallen leaves and twigs that are bobbing around her ankles. The streets are flowing. She sees a lopsided bench, sinking into the mud, and a herd of elk examining her from the highest point in the park. A small child paddles by in a kayak. When she opens the door of the diner she finds that the water in the streets has begun to seep below the door, coating the main floor in a murky layer. She stabs at it with the toe of her boot and watches the ripples run over the tiles. A quick surge of fear rises in her chest, and she instantly quells it. Who ever heard of a rain that lasts forever?

She feeds the penguins and hangs a sign on the door (CLOSED TODAY, REGRETFULLY) and steps back outside while she mulls over what to do next. Where is her husband? Where is her daughter? Who can she find to help her clear out the water? From her position on the side porch, she can see past the wooden rocking chairs (rotting and sprouting moss) to the back of the diner, where the river is rising and slamming against the building's foundations. No wonder her business is crumbling. How can anything withstand a force like this, day after day after day?

The fear rises and again she presses it back, tries to remind herself of what her mother used to tell her about being scared. Her mother's theory was that anytime she felt frightened, she ought to channel that emotion into something else: she ought to get angry or passionate instead. This is why, even from an early age, Mrs. McGinn has always been a fighter.

She knows that she will find her troops in the general store. Mauro says that people have been storming in from dawn until dusk to complain of the slow leaks in their roofs and the water seeping through the cracks of their basement windows. When she marches in, he is in the middle of a tutorial. She stops and pulls up short inside the door, watching as he shows a group of his neighbors how to apply caulk around the windowsills and patch up fissures in the walls. Seeing that the townspeople still seem uneasy, he brings out the shoebox that he keeps on a shelf below the cash register and begins passing out his lucky coins, his lucky stones, and his ball-chain necklaces from which hang medallions with the tarnished images of saints.

"Here," he tells his audience. "Take these. For the good fortune!"

Although the townspeople have always regarded Mauro's superstitions as old-world and quaint, they take the objects from his oversized palms with ginger fingers and no complaints. Mauro's turkeys glower at them from behind stacks of canned paint.

For Mrs. McGinn, this is as good a time as any. "Desperate times call for desperate measures," she announces dryly, and the townspeople turn toward her. She sees Mauro wrinkle his forehead, trying to commit the phrase to memory.

"We need more than luck, people," declares Mrs. McGinn. "We need to take a stand. We need to fight back."

"Who are we fighting?" asks Leesl, who had been attending Mauro's tutorial with a spiral notebook and a ballpoint pen. Mrs. McGinn glares at her, as fierce as she has always been.

"The elements!" says Mrs. McGinn. "The river! The rain! This is our town, these are our stores and our houses. Don't you want to take it all back?"

"The house is where a heart is, of course," exclaims Mauro, smiling wildly. He, too, is afraid that this town is on the verge of collapse; he is terrified that his neighbors will all jump ship. And if they leave, what will he do, how will he live? His savings are gone.

The townspeople do not consider themselves to be fighters by nature; usually they leave the fighting to Mrs. McGinn. They are as tired of her as they are of the rain. They do not like each other anymore. They are here because they need to patch the leaks in their roofs, but they would rather be at home, shut up in their own dark houses with their own wild animals wandering through the living room. The animals do not bother them, do not ask them all these questions about the philosophy of staying or going, giving up or fighting. Unlike their human neighbors, the animals leave them alone.

"Do we have a choice?" asks someone in the back, once Mrs. McGinn has finished.

She stares at him. "No," she says after a brief pause. "No, not really. Do you want the rain to win? Sound the alarm—tell everyone you can find. Mauro, you've got sand in the back?"

"Yes," he says. "For the bagging!"

"Great. We'll do that, load up your truck. Everyone else will meet us at the river."

The townspeople go, grumbling and grudgingly. Mrs. McGinn

and Mauro pour sand into canvas sacks and garbage bags and sling them into the back of his truck. Mrs. McGinn is already sweating only twenty minutes in, but Mauro works cheerfully, without tiring. On the way to the river, he turns on the radio and whistles along. He is glad for any chance to buy himself some time, to keep his neighbors in town so that he will not be left here on his own.

The trees near the bank are bent backward in the wind, the rain shuffling through their leaves. There is no sign of the cattle, the goats, or the caribou, all of whom have distanced themselves from the powerful rush of the river to seek food and shelter on higher ground in the town. The houses along the bank stand sober and gray, their windows shuttered, the water pouring from their roofs. Mrs. McGinn swivels her head as she climbs out of Mauro's truck, searching for the flash of a colored umbrella in the streets, but in that moment she sees no one. From here, the whole town looks as though it has already been deserted.

Near the river she is struck by a chill so sudden that it takes her a second to realize that it isn't the wind at all—only her own sense of dread. The rain falls into her eyes and runs down her cheeks and she looks up, glowering at the sky. It is drizzling again today, the clouds lightening in a way that suggests an end may be in sight, but for the first time since the rain began Mrs. McGinn feels as though she cannot trust that kind of sign. The clouds have lightened before, only to twist harder and darker for many days after. She has tried to be so positive about the situation in this town—she has tried to hold this place together—but things are getting bad enough now to deflate even an optimist's faith in sunny days and happy endings.

And is she not an optimist? Mauro may be singing as he slings the sandbags down the bank, but why should he be happier than she? (Although this is not—she must remind herself—a competition.) She has always considered herself to be a cheerful person. Why else would she have kept getting married, for goodness' sake? Once or twice really should have been enough. And yet she wants to believe that the darkness will always give way to the light, that a person is not handed more sorrow than she can bear, that the universe would not wash away her home and her history without due cause. She has done nothing to deserve this.

When the headlights of her neighbors begin appearing at the top of the bank, she tries to shake off her sudden melancholy, tries to pull herself together. As they come trickling through the grass in their boots and their brightly colored slickers, she grabs another sandbag and hauls it down the hill, slipping a little in the slick and bending cattails.

Mauro shows his neighbors how best to construct the wall—a survival skill he once picked up from an independent, woodsy uncle. He staggers the rows and steps on the bags to compress the sand and seal them more securely together. It is difficult in the rain and the wind, but the pounding of the river against the bank and the perilous rush of the current keep the townspeople where they are, wiping earth and water from their eyes as they work doggedly and silently at their task. If any of them feel as though they are fighting a losing battle, they do not say so. The wall begins to climb, row by row, sack by sack, leaning into the sky. After only an hour Mrs. McGinn is already so weary, so sore, that she does not even have the energy to notice or admire the way that her neighbors have come together to wrestle with the forces of nature, to take the stand she recommended against the weather and the river and their own unhappy fate. Instead she keeps her head down in the rain, slogs slowly up and down the bank, listens to Mauro's shouted words of affirmation with a mix of misery and detachment.

"If we are doing this so well together," Mauro yells, "we can be doing anything! There isn't anybody who can be stopping us!"

He makes a second run (and then a third, and a fourth) back to the store to pick up more bags. The wall continues to rise. When the river crashes against it the townspeople stop in their tracks and shield their eyes from the rain and look on, anxiously. So far, it holds. They work all day into the afternoon, long after they are soaked through to the skin and their fingers are numbed by cold.

Mrs. McGinn is taking a quick break, leaning against one of the cars and blowing on her hands to warm them, when the zookeeper comes to find her.

"Evelyn," he says. His face is drawn tight, his tone strained with worry. "I think that Angela Rose is gone."

"Gone?" repeats Mrs. McGinn, the word muffled by the rain.

He nods, pulls a sopping sheet of paper from his coat pocket. "She left a note."

He hands it to her. Although she takes it from him, she cannot read it. Her daughter's familiar script blurs before her eyes while the river rushes past in the background. How did they get here? There is not a particular moment that she can pinpoint; there was never a torrential downpour. There was just the slow accumulation of many days of rain—little by little, drop by drop, so that now it is too late for her to change her course.

If her daughter is gone, what is the point? It is all well and good to save this town, but the heroism feels empty in a way it did not feel before.

When the townspeople see Mrs. McGinn crumple to her knees, when they see her cover her face with her hands and hear her wail, their blood runs cold and their hearts plummet like stones. If *she* cannot hold herself together, what hope is there for the rest of them?

Perhaps it is time, they murmur to one another, watching one of the sandbags slide off the top of the wall and into the water. There is a splash, and then the river swallows it whole. Perhaps we have done all we can, and it is finally time to pack our bags and leave this place behind.

twenty-nine

Was it wrong of Noah's wife to leave that town the way she did?

In the moment, she felt she had no choice. When Mauro surged into her living room, when he seized her elbow and brought her running out into the night to find Noah unconscious in the passenger seat of the truck, his head falling limply against the window, his clothing soaked, the skin on his face sagging and gray—well, her heart sank to her toes and ever since then her chest has felt so empty that she has found herself believing that she must have left it there, glistening on the gravel driveway in the rain.

Her husband needed help, and so she sought the only help she knew. But Dr. Yu insists that there is nothing she can do, her tone growing terser and more distant every time Noah's wife asks for her advice. Noah, meanwhile, has not left the living room since she brought him home from church the afternoon before. He alternates between napping in front of the television and paging through Dr. Yu's old textbooks, marveling over the intricacy of the organs and telling his wife that there is nothing he can do but wait for his next call. The elders will find a place for him, he is convinced; until then, he and she must bide their time.

"Please don't worry so, my love," he tells her when she wakes at dawn, his gaze unnaturally bright and his beard wild and unkempt. "This, too, shall pass."

For the first time since she's known him, his words ring hollow in her ears. She pauses, waiting for him to say something more meaningful, but he doesn't look up again. That's it? she wants to know, her exasperation increasing. She is tired of listening for calls, tired of waiting for a voice from on high to declare where they will go and what they will do. What if there *is* no voice on high? What if they are waiting for a call that will never come? Who will make the decisions then?

She cannot help but wonder what Mrs. McGinn would do.

Before the thought has fully formed in her mind, she is already out the door, across the yard, and turning her key in the ignition of their car. If Noah won't take action, someone else should, she mutters, her knuckles white around the steering wheel. She will demand some answers—that's what she will do. If the problem is that God is no longer speaking to Noah, then

Noah's wife will simply have to go and speak to Noah's God on his behalf.

Once she arrives at the church, she parks at the same curb where she parked yesterday. She cuts over the lawn and holds her breath as she crosses the threshold. It is still early morning, and inside the building is empty and cool. Her footsteps resound against the stone as she hurries down the aisle to the altar and slides into her old familiar pew, setting down her handbag and bowing her dark head in prayer.

At first, when nothing comes to her, she worries that she must not be doing it correctly; the truth is that she has never tried to pray on her own. She had always assumed that it would be enough to follow Noah, that she could absorb his light and faith simply by being near him. She loved the ritual, liked knowing exactly what would come next. She felt reassured by the fact that in the church her path was predetermined, that everything she said and did fulfilled a certain purpose—even if she didn't fully understand what that purpose was. But now when she knits her brow and tries to picture God, she can see nothing but human portraits: Mauro's loose brown jowls, Leesl's pinched expression. The faces of the townspeople tick through her mind like snapshots, each one of their gazes more piercing than the last.

"Excuse me," says a voice beside her, banishing the procession from her thoughts. "Aren't you Noah's wife?"

Her head jerks up with a start. "I am," she says. If for half a second (despite her better judgment) she mistook the voice to be the voice of God, the thought evaporates when she sees the warm human form beside her. She widens her eyes, recognizing the head elder. "Yes, I'm Noah's wife."

"I thought so." The elder leans back into her pew, his robes draping full over his clothes and his hands clasped in his lap. For a few minutes the two of them sit side by side in silence. Finally the elder says: "I don't think I've ever seen you here without your husband."

Noah's wife nods. "This is the first time."

"Ah," he says, and nothing more.

She tries to interpret his silence. Is he waiting for her to say something else? If she confided in him, would he know how to help her husband? But the elder interrupts her thoughts before she can compose a question.

"Would you consider yourself a believer?" he says abruptly.

She is taken aback. To believe or not to believe—that has never been her role.

"My husband believes," she says automatically, and at this the elder raises his eyebrows.

"Does he?" he says. He smiles without showing his teeth. "Come now. You must know as well as I do that he's not the man he was. I don't think I've ever seen a person so changed as he is, in such a brief span of time. Something happened to him in that town: he lost the grace of God. Anyone can see that."

She stiffens. "No, he didn't."

"Yes, he did. Although—" Here the elder pauses, as if deep in thought. "He might have been lost before he went. Why else would he have left here in the first place, when we counseled him against it?"

"Counseled him against it?" she repeats.

The elder shakes his head. "We asked about you," he tells her. "We told Noah—think of your wife, think of your family. But he insisted that this was the right decision." The elder lets this sink in. "Listen," he says after another minute has passed. "We can't in good conscience send him to another church, given his condition. He needs to spend some time away."

"There's nothing wrong with him," insists Noah's wife, weakly. She thinks of her husband where she left him on the sofa, his clothes disheveled and his hair unwashed, and knows that this is not the truth. "Maybe he's not as confident as he used to be, but—"

"That's the crux of it exactly," agrees the elder, rising to his feet. "It is only natural to doubt, but Noah needs to learn to conquer it. Right now, he's simply giving in to it."

The elder inclines his head and then he leaves her there, reeling. There can be no praying after this. Once he has gone, she stands, too, and stumbles up the aisle. In her agitation she reaches for the first door she sees, which is not the one she entered by. Instead of stepping out onto the front lawn, she emerges into the light at the far end of a cemetery, one that begins at the church and sprawls a mile or two down in the direction of the ocean. Noah told her the first time he brought her to the church that this cemetery was one of the largest in the area; this is where most of the city comes to bury their dead.

Copper-colored sunbeams lean against headstones. The grass is soft and spiked, and here and there a tree sends gnarled, branching shadows toward the tombs. The sun is only partly up the sky but already it promises to be a warm and heavy day, the air thick with the heat and humidity of the bay. Noah's wife wanders among the rows of stones with no sense of where she is headed. She does not want to go home to Noah; she cannot go back into the church. She remembers the last cemetery she was in, the one on the hill in the rain when she stood beside Noah and heard him promise that everything would be all right. How appalled she had been when the townspeople had not believed him! Can she blame them now for their doubt?

There are other mourners, here and there. A woman with a hawklike face hurries down one row with a parasol to shield herself from the sun; three aisles over, two men with canes and bowler hats murmur in low voices. As Noah's wife passes a mother and a little girl, the child throws her hands over her eyes and suddenly bursts out crying. Noah's wife looks for what it was that could have scared her, but there is nothing frightening in sight.

"Some people are afraid of cemeteries," says a squat and mustached man standing a few feet away from her. He indicates the girl and shrugs. "But what is there to be afraid of here? The worst has already happened. You've already lost someone."

Noah's wife glances at the stone that he is standing in front of. The man sees her read the dates, watches the numbers tick across her face. He is already prepared with his answer when her head snaps back in surprise.

"Our son," he says. "Sixteen. Car accident."

Noah's wife is shaken. She remembers the night the police cars appeared at her front door, blue lights flashing through the living room windows, bearing the news that her mother had been killed. "I'm so sorry," she says, the words feeling painfully inadequate.

But what else is there to say? She thinks of those first few weeks after her mother was gone, remembers the shower of cards and phone calls, the warbling cry of the doorbell and the front porch crowded—or so it seemed—with sympathetic faces drifting above black coats. It unsettled her then, as it also did when her sister disappeared, to realize that someone could slip from her life so quickly, so fully. Since then, she has made a point of holding on more tightly to the people she loves.

The man bends over the grave, ducking his head so that his expression is hidden. "Yes," his voice husky. He lays a spray of drooping lilies over the tomb. "Well. What can you do? I come and see him every morning."

Noah's wife hesitates. "My mother," she says after a moment, "died in a crash when I was young. But after she was gone, I couldn't bear to go to the cemetery to see her. I know I should have. But the reminder was too much."

"Not everyone grieves the same way," says the man with a shrug. "My wife doesn't come here either. We've got a friend who recently lost his wife, maybe a few months ago—I've thought about asking if he wants to join me here, but I don't think he has it in him. Instead he seems to cope in his own peculiar way—by doing magic, of all things." The man laughs, low and kind.

"How does your wife grieve?" asks Noah's wife.

"Nancy?" says the man. For a moment he considers. "She grieves by trying to live more loudly, more boldly than before. She doesn't know how else to do it. I think that if you asked her, she'd tell you that this is what it means to make the best of things. Or she'd tell you to mind your own damn business. It's hard to say."

He grins, weakly, his eyelids twitching. Noah's wife attempts a smile in return.

"What about you?" she asks, hoping she is not out of line. She is so grateful to have someone to talk to. "Do you think she's making the best of things?"

The man tilts his head toward the grave. "Sometimes there isn't any way to make the best of things," he says. "And I think that to insist that there is—that everything happens for a reason, et cetera—well, oftentimes that's nothing but a good-looking lie."

His expression is pained. He pauses and glances in the direction of another mourner, her blond head bowed over a plot near the corner. "But that makes me sound as if I'm criticizing Nancy," he says, "which is absolutely the last thing I want to do. I believe in Nancy, and I even believe in those good-looking lies. Sometimes that's what we need to tell ourselves in order to get by. If some people want to believe that this is all part of some great plan that's meant to make us stronger, well, I won't stop them. I'm not going to stand here and say I know best just because I think I see all the bad that could and does happen, just because I recognize the imminence of death and darkness and I'm afraid. It's not like I've got it all figured out, either."

Something about his tone—the sympathy, the intelligence, the tranquillity—reminds Noah's wife of her husband as he used to be, before they went into the hills to that sad little town. And yet how can this man be so calm in his uncertainty? How can he stand in front of her and tell her that he has no idea why things like this happen without admitting that this perspective has no hope?

"But if you don't believe in a greater plan," she says carefully, "and if you don't believe that everything happens for a reason—then what keeps you going?"

The man stares at her. Perhaps she should not have asked the question; maybe the subject is too serious to discuss with a stranger. Then again, when one makes an acquaintance in the cemetery, what else would one talk about besides death?

"What do you mean, what keeps me going?" he asks.

She shrugs. She thinks of Noah, remembering the dead weight of him on her arm as she led him out of the church two days before. "If you don't believe that there's some purpose behind all this," she says slowly, "and if you don't believe that there is some force for good at work, even in times of hardship or sorrow—then how can you not feel despair?"

"Well, I suppose it's because I believe in Nancy," the man says simply. "With Joseph gone, I believe that she and I have got to take care of each other."

"So it's an obligation," says Noah's wife, her tone as hollow as her husband's. "That's what keeps you going."

The man raises his eyebrows. "It's love," he replies. "But if you want to call it that, sure. A reciprocal obligation. Fine. But I don't resent her for it. To tell you the truth, I'm glad about it, I'm glad I've got her as my responsibility. What would I do without her? If there's one thing I've come to learn after thirty-odd years of marriage, it's that a man's life is not his own. We all belong to someone else, in one way or another. There's all kinds of people who have shaped us, made us who we are—not just the people we keep close to us, but also tens and hundreds of other people we don't even remember, strangers we stood behind in line and talked to for a minute. Do you know what I'm saying? I'm saying that if I didn't crawl into a hole and die on the day of Joseph's funeral, it's because I believe that I owe something to each of those people, to all of them, and to Nancy most of all."

The morning sun is growing more formidable by the minute. Noah's wife closes her eyes against the glare, sees once again a host of colored umbrellas. Her soul aches for the old faith she had in Noah, the certainty that he could not lead her astray.

"You know," says the man, still musing, "for a long time after the accident I asked myself something similar to what you've been getting at just now. How is it that a man can carry on after something like this? A father's duty is to protect his family from criminals and thugs and truck drivers who fall asleep at the wheel." His voice is soft and musing, his expression introspective. Noah's wife feels as though he has forgotten she is there. "For those first few months, I was a little ashamed of myself—ashamed that I was able to roll out of bed and stand up every morning, to carry on with the business of living when my only son had descended among the dead. The grief struck me hard, but I used to wish that it had struck even harder. I wanted it to knock me out, flat unconscious, so that I wouldn't have to think about it anymore." He sighs, shakes his head, seems to come back to himself. "But there was Nancy to consider. Always Nancy."

She nods in perfect comprehension. How astonished she had been to discover that Noah loved her—how thankful to know that she would never have to be alone again. She chastises herself for doubting him. Her first love and her first duty are to her husband. Is that not what marriage means?

The man smiles at her and turns away from the grave. "I'm sorry," he says. "You don't even know me, and here I am pouring out my soul to you." He sighs. "This place tends to have that effect on me. I don't like the quiet here, and so I can't stop talking."

Noah's wife looks down at the stone, wonders where in this sprawling field lies Dr. Yu's mother. Would Dr. Yu come here, if Noah's wife asked her to? Noah's wife misses her friend as much as she misses her husband—but then, this is the difficulty of loving people who are so much greater than she is, she reminds herself severely. This is what comes of loving people who dream bigger than she herself has ever dared to, who are determined to save lives and souls and bear the weight of so many earthly troubles on their shoulders.

"My friend," says Noah's wife, "who lost her mother—I think she doesn't come because she blames herself." Her eyes fill quickly, unexpectedly, and the stone blurs at her feet. "It's not her fault. She always thought she could take care of the whole world."

The man nods, his expression grim. "No one ought to try and take that on," he says. "I don't think it's anybody's job to battle against sadness and death and grief—all the forces of darkness, if you will. Everyone who comes to this place, we come because we've lost what we loved. The darkness is already here. After a while you stop running from it. You find something else to love, something worth holding on to, and you don't let go of it."

Noah's wife considers him, searching desperately for something to say. "This, too, shall pass," she finally murmurs, echoing her husband. She wanted words of consolation, and to her surprise these seem to do the trick. The man has already turned to go, but when she speaks he pauses to gaze at her over his shoulder. "Indeed it will," he promises. "Somehow it always does."

thirty

Mrs. McGinn's daughter says farewell to the penguins before she goes.

Her suitcase safely stowed in the trunk, she eases the family's old station wagon out of the garage and onto the street. Her mother walks everywhere, and her stepfather drives anything and everything but this. She doesn't think they'll miss it.

The rain falls fast and black to the windshield and she flicks on the wipers and the low beams as she splashes through the sleeping town. The lights are off in most houses and the car passes unnoticed from lamppost to lamppost, sliding through the water that rushes hushed and jeweled through the streets. She pulls to the curb outside the diner, hurries around to the back with her keys in her hand. Her feet are snug in her boots but she can hear the water on the floor as she walks through the darkened kitchen to the cooler. For a moment she feels a pang of alarm, followed by a hard roar of guilt. But what would she do if she stayed here? she asks herself angrily. Whatever the fate of their relationship will be after she leaves, she maintains a dogged faith in her mother's intelligence and her strength, in her ability to overcome any obstacle in her path. She is certain that her mother will know how to deal with the flood in the diner.

As for herself, she steps gingerly until she reaches the door to the cooler, and then she yanks it open and swings herself inside. The light goes on automatically and she pauses for a moment in its fluorescent glare, looking down at the penguins who come waddling out from their nesting places in the shadows. They blink in the light, peering up at her in pairs. That is what she has always loved about the penguins: their fairy-tale monogamy. To her, they stand for loyalty.

"Don't look at me like that," she tells them in the stern tone she learned from her mother. "You don't understand. I don't have a choice."

She can hear the voice of her mother in her mind as clearly as if the woman were standing right beside her. "You always have a choice, Angela Rose. We're not animals."

But aren't we? her daughter would like to know. What makes us so different from them? She remembers something her fiancé once told her about the penguins in the wild, something about their long and arduous trek across the snowy Antarctic to lay their eggs and feed their chicks. She would like to think that she is doing exactly the same thing, in human terms: going elsewhere to have her child, since she certainly will not raise it here in the eternal rain, where there is no sun and no hope but only the miles and miles of mud. What kind of mother do these penguins take her for?

"Besides—there was a plan," she informs them. "We had a plan. I told Adam that I wouldn't stay in this town, and he promised that he would get out of here with me. I'm not the one who changed my mind about our life together—it was him." She pictures her fiancé as she last saw him, lounging in one of the booths of the diner late last night with the red fox nestled on the cracked vinyl seat beside him. The zookeeper was trying to feed the fox frozen berries and earthworms from his fingers. He had glanced up at Angela Rose as she passed, his face coarse and handsome in the shadows. His expression was concerned, although when he looked at her the taut lines softened. "The little guy won't eat," he told her. "Not a bite since the minister's wife has been gone. She should have thought of that before she left him."

She twists the ring around her finger—his grandmother's. He had proposed to her outside the abandoned movie theater where they had been on their first date, had gotten down on one knee and promised never to leave her. He knew that was important to her, knew she craved stability just as much as she craved culture and adventure and escape. It was paradoxical, yes, but he understood without her having to explain it.

The penguins coo at her, softly but insistently. "Of course I still love him," she says. "Lay off already, will you? It's more complicated for us than for you. You can't always be near the people you love, you can't always live in the same cooler, or on the ice floe next door. The world doesn't work like that. If a person isn't happy where she is, maybe she shouldn't stay."

She opens a couple of cans of crabmeat, strokes the penguins three times each on their heads and down their soft black backs, and then when she is sufficiently saddened, she turns away. The car is waiting where she left it.

The road out of town feels familiar, although it has been months since the last time she left. In high school she took jobs in the city for the summers, lived in tiny high-rise apartments where the heat was damp and thick. She ordered cheap burgers from chains along the harbor, ate dinner while walking between downtown and the water. She adored the crowds, loved living as a stranger among strangers. They didn't know her mother there. She could have been anyone.

At one end of town, the main road slopes down to the river and the zoo, which by now must be completely underwater. At the other end it loops up and out toward the mountains and the coast, the pavement rising and falling over the hills. It is the only way in or out of town. For a moment Mrs. McGinn's daughter imagines the stars spinning behind clouds that are darker than she's ever seen them before, draped black and full across the pointed tops of pine trees. Once she's on the road she pays little attention to where she is going, driving almost by instinct, the car pulling her forward. The wind whistles past the windows and the rain drums against the glass. She turns up the volume on the radio, but finds her old station drowned in static. She tries another station, and another, but there is only white noise.

The zookeeper used to take her on weekends away to the city once every few months to see concerts. They stayed out until dawn and ate lunchtime breakfasts at crowded cafes and she knew that he tried to like it, for her, but couldn't. The city lights as seen from their hotel room simply did not capture his imagination the way they did hers; he did not thrill at the idea of a million other lives blazing just beyond their reach. She could watch the headlights on the highway for hours, entranced by the glowing splendor of the city, but he could not find in it the same beauty he found in campfires or fireflies or the gleam of a wild beast's eye in the beam of his flashlight. When the situation at the zoo went downhill, when he had to lay off his workers and cut down on the animals, he could no longer take the time to spend the weekends away with her, and although she understood, she hated to think that (at least in part) he was relieved.

What will he think of her when he discovers that she's gone?

When she sees the road vanish before her, she slams on the brakes and the car shudders into a long skid, sending her vaulting forward as a spray of water whooshes past the windows. There is a long moment afterward when she tries to calm her nerves, to stop the trembling of her fingers on the wheel, and to catch her ragged breath. Finally she shifts the car into park and opens the door.

Once she has climbed out and is standing on the ground

beside her car, it becomes clear where the missing road has gone. The front of the car is partly submerged in one end of a long blank lake whose surface is as sinister and as void as the sky. The rain continues to fall into it and the drops disturb the surface in a steady cascade that sends ripples running headlong into one another in their attempt to spread. The night is deep and the clouds are dense, and although Mrs. McGinn's daughter is certain that the other edge of the lake must exist somewhere, that the road has to rise right out of it again, she cannot see the far side. For all intents and purposes, the road is gone. She cannot pass.

For a long time she stands there in eerie calm, her shoulders hunched, staring out across an endless stretch of water. The rain beats against her brow and thrums in her ears, and for a brief moment this is all that exists, all that is left of her world: the water pouring headlong from the heavens, the white beams of her headlights slowly dying in the night, the treetops hidden behind the hills, and her growing sense of foreboding, the fear that it is no longer possible to move forward. They have waited too long.

Was it true that Noah had tried to walk upon water? She places one foot lightly forward, feels it immediately sink. She hurriedly backs up, retraces her steps, returns to the car.

She slides back into the driver's seat and pulls the door shut after her, and she would have swung the car right around and chugged resolutely home (humiliated, of course; but perhaps she could find the note before anyone else did), had the engine not been killed by its partial submersion in the lake. When she turns the key in the ignition the engine grumbles and sputters and ultimately rejects her plea to start. She might have been angry but all her emotions are spent, and so she leans back against the headrest and closes her eyes.

"And now what?" she says aloud. Of course there is no answer.

Someone will come for her, she says to herself. Once the day begins, a delivery truck will approach from the opposite side or a townsperson will attempt to flee. She knows she won't be stuck out here for long; she has too much faith in the world for that.

She is like her mother that way, she supposes, drifting off to sleep, her arms crossed over her abdomen. She clings to the belief that she deserves something more than the small life that she has been leading, to the hope that there is something grander and better out there for her and for her child. She cannot give up on her hope because, like her mother, she simply loves too much. She loves with too much force.

thirty-one

Dr. Yu's father does not believe in self-pity.

He has lost as much as anyone else, but that does not mean that he will hole up in his house and sandwich himself between the cushions of his couch, eating bowl after bowl of cold cereal and staring at the flickering television screen as if that is the only light left in the world. He may be in mourning, but at least he has more sense than that.

"It is a beautiful day out there!" he shouts at the minister upon entering his daughter's living room. He throws open the blinds with a magician's flair and stands directly in the sunlight as it pours through the windows.

Noah blinks several times, raises an arm to shield his eyes. He stares with a vague sense of recognition at the leathered face before him, tucked within the hood of an oversized forest-green sweatshirt. Dr. Yu's father wears thick spectacles, and the eyes glinting through them are clever and brown. He is shorter than Noah by a foot, and at least thirty years his senior.

"We've met before, haven't we?" asks Noah.

"Several times, Minister," says Dr. Yu's father, extending his hand in greeting. His feet are planted far apart and his head is tilted slightly back, his stance as poised as an athlete's. "I'm Ezra. April's father."

Dr. Yu told her father of the arrival of her unexpected houseguests when she stopped by to bring him breakfast several days before. She comes nearly every morning—insisting on it, despite his protests that he does not always need her there—as if he cannot fry an egg himself. He was eager to see her today, however, because he was curious to know how the minister and his wife were faring.

"I heard," continues Dr. Yu's father, "that you were feeling rather down."

The minister doesn't move. "I'm fine," he says. "I'm waiting for my next assignment."

Noah's tone is stoic, but his posture suggests defeat. Dr. Yu's father considers the man as if he were a piece of flotsam washed up on the shore. "You've been here a week already," he announces frankly. "How long do you intend to wait?"

Noah shrugs. "As long as it takes, I suppose."

For a long while Dr. Yu's father peers at the minister without saying anything. He is surprised to find that he recognizes something of himself in this man; surprised at the swiftness and the certainty of his realization that the minister, too, has suffered loss. And yet what has he lost besides his job? And why must he wait to be given another?

"You know," says Dr. Yu's father, helpfully, "those times I saw you before, you had so much energy. You were active. You seemed to be the kind of man who went after things, rather than waiting around to follow instructions. Couldn't you go after your next assignment that way, the way you used to?"

"I can't do what I used to do," Noah replies, with a strange, indulgent smile. "I used to walk with God."

Dr. Yu's father waits for more of an explanation, and when none is forthcoming, he says: "And now?"

Noah's gaze flicks up from the television again and settles on him. Dr. Yu's father is so overwhelmed by the anguish of the man's expression that he takes a step back.

"And now I don't," says the minister.

Dr. Yu's father shakes his head. His daughter is overworked and overwhelmed enough without having to deal with houseguests who need as much care as her patients. He will not have her go to pieces—not on his watch. Last night, as he struggled to free himself from a new set of handcuffs, he made up his mind to come to her rescue. He did not know then that the minister would need rescuing, too.

"Tell you what," he says, trying to keep his voice brisk. "I'm alone myself, most of the time. I'd be glad to have you—well—'walk' with me."

"Excuse me?" says Noah, looking puzzled.

"My shows down at the harbor are getting more popular every day," says Dr. Yu's father, inventing the plan as he goes. "April doesn't like me going down there on my own, and the truth is that the work is getting to be a little more than I can handle. I could use the help. And I wouldn't mind the company, either."

He can see the minister struggling to come up with a response. Dr. Yu's father knows that Noah doesn't really want to leave the safety of his sofa—but he also knows that a man who has spent a lifetime helping others is unlikely to refuse to do so now. As soon as Noah nods his head in acquiescence, Dr. Yu's father directs him toward the bathroom.

"Take a shower, you'll feel better," commands the magician. "Then get dressed. You're coming with me."

THE HARBOR IS nearly deserted at this hour, gulls wheeling and crying over the docks. The boats rock on soft golden waves, the flags on their masts wilting without wind. Dr. Yu's father hauls a duffel bag out of his trunk and leads Noah to a gazebo set back from the water. He assures Noah that the crowds will come later.

"The families stroll through in the afternoon," he says, ascending the steps of a creaking wooden stage and dropping the bag down on the floorboards beside him. He stands sheltered by the slats of the gazebo roof, looking over his imagined audience and thrilling at the atmosphere of expectancy that pervades the sea of folding chairs and picnic tables. "This is the calm before the storm," he adds.

As he transfers items from the bag to a card table he has set up in the middle of the gazebo, Dr. Yu's father explains to Noah that he has been coming to the harbor every day for several weeks now. At first his intention was only to practice his tricks with fire away from his house and his neighbors, but once he noticed that passersby were stopping to watch him, that children were asking for rabbits and flames, he settled into a routine and began putting on three performances a day. His presence at the harbor has become important to his fans.

But what a godsend it will be, he reflects, to have Noah here for a few days: a pliant, unemployed houseguest who should feel guilty enough about imposing on his daughter that he will have to agree to a favor. If he remains as mute, as shadowy onstage as he is wandering through the chairs right now, the audience will hardly see that he is there. Perhaps he could help Dr. Yu's father rig up a better curtain than the ragged quilt he has hanging off the front of the gazebo now—but for the moment he pushes it aside to reveal the collection of objects he has finished arranging on the card table before him.

"Pay attention, Minister! Here is the secret of the coffin escape," he calls across the empty rows, pointing to an oversized rectangular box he has leaning against one of the wooden posts. Maybe he could set Noah to the task of locating a more realistic coffin, as well. "It's the way that all the great magicians used to do it. You simply remove these long screws, here, that hold the bottom of the coffin to the sides. You replace them with this shorter kind of screw so that all you need to do when you're inside is to push as hard as you can against the top. The sides and the lid should lift up and away from the bottom, since they're no longer well secured. And that's it! Voilà! You're out."

Noah considers the box. "You don't think it's a little macabre, to have a coffin trick at all?" he says. "Couldn't you escape from something else?"

"Minister!" says Dr. Yu's father with a chuckle. "I wouldn't have expected you, of all people, to be susceptible to superstition. I suppose you're not going to like it when I tell you about the dirt I plan to scatter alongside it, either."

"Why would you do that?" asks Noah, resignedly.

"For effect! A successful magic show is like a good dinner party: it's all in the presentation. Speaking of which, I'm going to need your help with some of this. Perhaps I could send you out later to pick up the rabbits?"

Noah remains silent, which Dr. Yu's father takes as an affirmation. He will tell the minister later about the assortment of other animals to be collected: a crateful of birds, a chicken, seven white mice, two snakes, and two kittens.

"You will make a wonderful assistant!" exclaims Dr. Yu's father encouragingly. "I can tell already."

"An assistant?" repeats Noah.

"Of course! Why do you think I brought you all the way out here?"

"I don't know," says Noah. He blinks into the light. "I don't think my wife—"

"She wants what's best for you," insists Dr. Yu's father, remembering what his daughter has told him about her best friend's unswerving commitment to her husband. "We all do. And right now, you need something to keep you busy while you're waiting. You need a little fresh air. Why don't you come join me here in the gazebo, and I'll show you some of the tricks I've got up my sleeve for the show."

Noah seems disconcerted, but he obeys. What excuse does he have not to? He rises from his picnic table and then climbs the steps onto the battered wooden planks. As he walks over to join Dr. Yu's father, one of his footsteps rings hollow.

"Be careful," says Dr. Yu's father. "Not every board is as sound as it should be. All right, here is one of the tricks that—as my assistant—you'll need to know very well. I'll ask for a white handkerchief from someone in the audience, and as I'm coming back up on the stage, I'll exchange it for this other handkerchief I'll have in my coat pocket. I'll call for you to bring a candle, but I don't want you to come. That way I'll have to come looking for you, which allows me a moment away from the stage to secretly hand you the first handkerchief. The audience will hear me instruct you again to bring a candle, which you finally will do, after concealing that handkerchief in a hollow space in the candlestick specifically designed for this trick. When I cut up the substitute handkerchief, I'll stuff the pieces in my 'magic pistol' and shoot at the candle, telling everyone that this way the cloth will 'pass through' the flame to become whole again. When we break the stick, there it will be, completely restored. And voilà!"

While he speaks, Dr. Yu's father picks up the objects in question and places them in Noah's hands for examination. When the explanation of the trick is over, Noah sets them down again on the white tablecloth. One of its corners looks as though it has been seared.

"Oh, just a little accident," says Dr. Yu's father. "The flame got away from me while I was practicing. Occupational hazard, I suppose!"

Finding Noah to be insufficiently impressed by the handkerchief trick, Dr. Yu's father tries a different tactic. He holds up a classic black top hat (a little frayed around the edges) and, without explaining what he intends to do, he reaches inside and pulls out an egg. He tilts the hat forward over the stage, turning it upside down to prove that it is empty, and when he flips it back up he plunges his hand again inside and retrieves a second egg from the folds. On the third try he finds a quarter, which he places into Noah's hand with a flourish and a bow.

This time Noah shows more curiosity. Dr. Yu's father takes it as a good sign when the minister requests an explanation, and so he teaches Noah how to palm a coin, a card, an egg. To the audience it looks as though the object appears from nowhere, but in reality it is already in the magician's hand by the time he reaches into the hat. The success of the effect is in the act of concealment, not the revelation.

Noah has understood since he was a child that things like magic hats and vanishing tricks are only make-believe, and yet the explanation of the mechanics behind the illusion seems to deflate him once more. Dr. Yu's father sees the cloud return to the minister's face.

"Something wrong?" he asks.

"No," says Noah. "But I think I preferred magic when I didn't know the secrets."

Dr. Yu's father nods and takes a few steps to the right, gently rests his hand upon the coffin. For a moment he is silent, reflecting. "What people want from a magic show," he finally says aloud, "is the same thing they want from a movie, or a book. They want that suspension of disbelief. They want to believe that the world could be different from what it is, that ordinary objects could become extraordinary at the snap of their fingers if only they knew the right words. That's the whole point of the illusion."

Noah moves over to the table, picks up a coin and tries to palm it. It immediately falls from his hand and rolls beneath the table, a momentary flash in the shadows.

"I thought I knew the right words once," Noah says. "But either I've lost them somewhere along the way, or they never existed at all."

Dr. Yu's father studies him in silence, truly sympathetic for the first time today. "Oh, I don't know, Minister," he says softly.

"I think it's too soon to be giving up already. You'd be surprised at the kind of things that can be made to reappear. Perhaps the only thing you're missing is a little more practice."

He takes the black top hat and tosses it to the minister, who instinctively reaches out to catch it.

thirty-two

The basements fill first.

The water flows over concrete floors, slowly rising toward the stairs. Outside, the rain rushes down roofs, cascading through gutters and dripping through windows. The cattle stand stock-still with their heads bent in the downpour, unable to free their hoofs from the mud that rises to their knees. When the animals indoors sense the water rising beneath them, they panic. The birds fly against the windowpanes, the monkey screams for hours without ceasing, the penguins refuse to eat. Leesl's cats throw their weight against the door, over and over again, trying to escape, rubbing at their bruised faces with tufted paws.

Mauro cannot find his peacocks. They were in his bedroom when he fell asleep last night, he knows it; he remembers that they were there with him while he suffered through a nightmare of the creditors who drove him out of his hometown. In his dreams the men had crooked fangs and hungry eyes. They howled in pursuit of him and Mauro trembled in his sleep, reached out for the birds. When his hands brushed feathers he settled down again and reverted to his more habitual dreams of angels.

And yet when the first few beams of weak gray light come washing through his window blinds, the peacocks are gone. Mauro swings his feet to the floor, so worried over the birds that he does not notice the fact that when his toes touch the floorboards at the bottom of the stairwell they are instantly cold and wet. *"Pavoni!"* he calls, splashing toward the front door and wrenching it open. "Where are you? Where would you be going?"

He barrels in his striped pajamas out beneath the awning that extends along his stretch of sidewalk. While the water soaks into the cuffs, slowly seeping up toward his knees, he stands frozen in place, his unshaven jaw hanging low, staring at the commotion in the streets. His peacocks are not out there—he can see that at once—but all the rest of the townspeople are rushing out of their shops and their houses, bearing armloads of their belongings. If Mauro were in a better mood, he would be curious to see which objects his neighbors have chosen as the most important. The photo albums? The wedding china? The baby clothes? At the moment, however, everything is a soft, damp blur of colors and sounds: the colored raincoats, the cardboard boxes, the suitcases, the umbrellas. Cars are idling in the streets while their owners load up the trunks, and on any other day Mauro might have panicked at the sight of them, might have understood by his neighbors' frantic movements and their hysterical voices that they intended to leave this town, and leave Mauro behind with it—but all he can think about now are his peacocks. He does not reflect upon the water rushing through the streets, the puddles leaking through the cracks in doors and windows. He does not see anything but the absence of the two shimmering beings he has come to love so dearly.

He pulls his keys off the hook where they hang just inside the door to the general store and, yanking it shut behind him, he strides toward his truck. His pajamas are sopping by the time he climbs into the driver's seat, but he doesn't care.

"Mauro!" yells one of his neighbors, startling him by banging on his windshield. "My car has stalled! Are you leaving? Take me with you!"

Mauro whips his gray head from side to side, rolls down the window so that the man can hear him. "I am not leaving!" he yells. "I am looking for my peacocks!"

The man—an insurance salesman, remembers Mauro now—stares at him in disbelief. "What do you mean, you're not leaving? You've got to leave. The whole place is going under! Some of the sandbags have fallen in already, and the wall won't last much longer. What do you think we're all doing out here?" He steps back, a little unsteadily, and Mauro takes advantage of the moment to slam his bare foot on the gas and peel forward. Water sprays up from beneath the tires, flying through the open window before Mauro has a chance to close it. He purses his lips, swears a little, and careens around the corner.

On the next street over, the situation is much the same. The cars' engines are purring while the townspeople rush up and down their sidewalks and driveways, preparing for departure. The rain slams onto the hood of Mauro's car with more force than he has ever seen from it—excepting, perhaps, for the night when the zoo flooded. He remembers lugging tanks of reptiles through the mud, packing penguins into the cars. The animals had been fortunate, he reflects, to have had people willing to carry them out and settle them on safer ground. The townspeople are now the ones in trouble, but there is no one left to deliver them.

The wind is pulling at his car and he tries to return his attention to the road, guiding the sputtering vehicle up one street and down another, flicking his gaze out the window every few feet in the hope of finding his peacocks strutting through the streets. The penguins are out on the side porch of the bakery, waddling between the railings and squawking to one another in shrill tones. The toucans, accustomed to roosting in the trees, are shivering and cowering in bushes. Glancing up, Mauro sees why: the wind is too strong. Branches are cracking and falling, tumbling down onto telephone wires. As he drives, he must avoid debris in the streets—lost pieces of luggage, floating slickers. He startles at the sight of a large cat in the road, only to realize after he passes that it is already dead, its body limp, its fur matted with mud. At once Mauro feels both stricken and relieved: appalled, of course, that an animal has died, but glad at least that it is not one of his birds. His turkeys are still alive, he realizes, when he sees them scavenging through overturned trash cans with the red fox and the badger hovering behind them. And the ostrich—she is a survivor. It is only the peacocks he is worried about, delicate and otherworldly as they are.

Running on adrenaline, he weaves through the streets for an hour at least. He is so distracted that he does not even notice how far he has gone, does not see that he is on the highway that runs through hills out of town until he is already several miles down. The peacocks cannot be here, he says to himself, preparing to twist the wheel and swing his car back around. How would they have been able to walk so far on their own?

He tells himself that it is impossible, and yet he stops in his tracks, the car shuddering to a halt, when he sees a glimmer of turquoise a little ways up the road. He waits for a moment in his car, his pulse racing with the anticipation of reunion and success, watching the spot of color move toward him. The figure moves like a bird—awkwardly, abruptly, as if made for flight and unhappy to be earthbound—but when it draws closer the realization begins to dawn on Mauro that those are not wings, but jutting elbows and knees; not feathers, but an emerald-green umbrella and a shimmering blue raincoat. He does not want to admit it to himself, but he has no choice. That is not one of his birds. He opens the door to his car and steps out.

"Angela Rose?" he calls. "That is who?"

In the car on the way back to town, Mrs. McGinn's daughter lets her head fall back against the headrest and tells him the story of her intended departure. Her face is wan, with half-moon shadows pressed below her eyes. Even wrapped in the additional layer of Mauro's coat, her shoulders are shaking and her teeth are clattering together.

"You should not be walking so far in the rain," he says sternly. "Why are you not thinking more of the baby?"

Her expression grows even more haggard. "I *was* thinking of the baby, Mauro," she replies. "Why else do you think I was trying to leave?"

To Mauro, this does not make sense. The girl's family is here. The father is here. Why should the baby not be here with them?

"I would have made it, too," she says. "If the road hadn't been flooded. I waited for a while, but it was so cold. I figured I might as well begin to walk back. Better than freezing to death out there."

Ah yes, says Mauro to himself. The road. He is not looking forward to relaying the news to the townspeople. He would rather not be the one to tell them that no matter how tightly they have packed their lives into their cars, they are not going anywhere. With the road submerged, no one will be getting in or out. He thinks about his general store, tries to calculate the amount of canned goods he has left on his shelves. How many days will that buy him?

"We'll call for help when we get back," says Mrs. McGinn's

daughter, as if reading his mind. "Maybe someone can send a helicopter, or a few planes. There aren't all that many of us."

Mauro admires her practicality, her calmness, in the face of so much chaos. He would like to ask her what the zookeeper will say about this, but he decides against bringing it up.

"Mauro," Mrs. McGinn's daughter says to him, her gaze level and cold. "I don't intend to die here."

Neither does he! Mauro wants to retort. He would have said as much if they had not rounded the curb into downtown right at that moment, if they had not seen the telephone lines fallen with their wires tangled in what is left of the trees. The townspeople are screaming to one another over the sound of the rain, shielding their eyes from the water and heaving the last few loads into the trunks of their cars. Many of them have left their front doors open in their haste, and the animals are bounding down the driveways, paddling through the drowned lawns. Mauro hits the brakes just in time to avoid a kangaroo that is leaping past his front bumper and then yanks the wheel to the left when he sees one of the gray wolves paddling in his direction, aiming for a possum that is hanging from underneath a mailbox. The zookeeper sprints across the sidewalk in pursuit of an otter, and when Mrs. McGinn's daughter sees him she tenses and grips the door handle. Mauro pulls to the curb and the zookeeper catches sight of her through the window. He stops short and stares at her while she gazes mutely back, her eyes wide with an emotion Mauro cannot read.

Mauro pushes open the driver's-side door and leaps from his

seat. As much as he would like to witness it, this is no time for a passionate reunion.

"Adam!" he shouts, breathless. "The highway—it is underwater. If people are going that way, they will not be getting out!"

"What did you say?" demands the zookeeper in disbelief. Several of the townspeople pause with their car keys in hand, having caught snatches of Mauro's warnings even through the pounding rain. Those who are farther down ask their neighbors to repeat what they heard, and the news goes soaring down the street with the speed of the African swallow. For half a moment, they stop their running and their yelling and they wait, their skin clammy, their feet soaked and cold.

"I am saying, do not try to drive out," repeats Mauro. "There is no point. You will not be getting anywhere at all."

There is a quick murmuring as his words are passed once more from one end of the road to the other. In the distance they can hear another telephone line topple with a crash.

"But we can't stay here!" someone calls from across the road. "The sandbag wall is crumbling! Our houses are flooding! Where do we go?"

Another tree branch cracks above him and Mauro looks up. In the distance, serene against the roiling sky, is the church. Gold light flares from its windows and Mauro squints, wonders who could be up there lighting lamps and candles now that the minister and his wife are long gone. In the sudden stillness that has followed his neighbor's question he notices that the animals who have fled their houses are all moving, uniformly, in that direction; and although it takes him a moment to put two and two together, suddenly Mauro knows exactly where his peacocks are.

"We go," he says slowly, "to the high ground. Where else than that?"

His neighbors turn toward the hill to see what he sees: the steady parade of fur and scales, talons and claws, feathers and tails. There are the mountain goats, scaling rocks with ease, and the bats winging sleepily from tree to tree. There is the zebra, hurrying ahead of the coyote, and the penguins marching single file. There are the elk, the reindeer, the turkeys, the geese. There go the beasts that they have housed in their gardens and homes for all those long, gray, endless hours, ascending as if being pulled by something townspeople cannot hear—the call, perhaps, of something primitive and wild.

thirty-three

Today one of Dr. Yu's patients died on her operating table.

She should be there right now, filling out paperwork in her office or talking to his family members or doing *something*, at least, something other than sitting in her car like one of the living dead herself, her face drained of color and her fingers numb around the wheel while streetlights stream past her and voices murmur softly from the radio. It was her supervisors who sent her home. They told her how exhausted she looked, insisting that she get some rest.

"April," they said. "You know that it wasn't your fault."

Yes, she knew that it wasn't her fault, but the thought of it consumes her. She can't stop the burden from weighing down her steps or keep the memory from preying on her mind.

When she walks into the house, coming off twenty of the hardest hours she has ever spent at the hospital, she finds her father on the couch, his wrists clasped into a new pair of handcuffs. Noah is chasing down one of the magician's white mice in the kitchen, a mason jar in one hand and a flattened newspaper in the other. Dr. Yu has never seen him so harried, never seen him looking so unkempt as he does these days with his long hair flying and his rumpled clothing often damp with sweat. Before, he had made it a point to be always presentable, eternally composed.

Dr. Yu's best friend is home, too, watching the spectacle in the living room with visible distress. She corners Dr. Yu in the kitchen. "Do you see him out there?" she says in a whisper, yanking the door shut behind them. "He's been running after mice all day. Can't you try to do something for him? Give him something?"

Dr. Yu considers this, takes a bite of the pear that she had been about to slice up. She feels resentful, vexed. What does her best friend expect her to do?

"I like him better this way," Dr. Yu says belligerently, and she means it. With his beard ungroomed and his hair graying, with his shifting gaze and his sorrowful tone—Noah seems more human than she has ever seen him. "Before," she adds, "he was unreal. And anyway, he likes the magic. My father says he isn't bad at it. If this is what he needs to do in order to work out whatever he's working out, then I'd recommend you simply let him be, and let him have it."

Easier said than done, as Dr. Yu knows from experience. The truth is that she has no idea whether or not the magic is what

Noah needs. But she knows that what her father needs is a companion, someone to watch over him, to keep him out of jail and out of the salty harbor. Dr. Yu cannot always be there for him, and if the presence of the minister helps her father keep his feet on solid ground, then so much the better. Let Noah help him.

"Unreal?" repeats her best friend, bristling.

"You know what I mean," says Dr. Yu curtly. "Too righteous. Too perfect. No one is that way. Sometimes it seemed like it was all an act. If now he's a little bit damaged, that only means that he's just like everyone else."

So Noah is not the man he was, Dr. Yu thinks to herself. Neither is her father. In an unexpected flare of nostalgia, she remembers her father's penchant for nature walks during her elementary and middle school years. He used to pick her up after school and take her through the parks around their house. He carried a leather knapsack with sketch pads and bottles of water, and from time to time they would settle themselves down in the shade to share their trail mix and record their observations. She would trace tree leaves and flower petals while he hurled peanuts at the squirrels and explained where the butterflies flew when they migrated north for the summer. She wanted to learn to be exactly like him: curious, precise. He showed her the splendor of science, instructed her in the twin arts of observation and analysis. He was the one, in fact, who encouraged her to pursue medicine in the first place. Who would ever have expected him to trade his field guides for his magic books, his beetle collection for his skeleton keys?

"Noah has never been just like everyone else," replies her best friend stubbornly. "He believes in more, and hopes for more. That's why people follow him: his life is so much larger."

The kitchen is nearly dark, the only light flickering over the stove. Her best friend leans back against the sink, while Dr. Yu, completely fatigued, drops down onto a low stool beside the counter. From there, she regards her best friend with a mixture of pity and impatience. What makes Noah so different from the rest of them? she wants to know. What sets him apart from the millions of other people who live off groundless hope and grand ideals? The only difference is that when Noah's plans for that little town failed, he fell apart. Meanwhile the rest of the world must keep on spinning.

Dr. Yu narrows her eyes. "You're allowed to criticize him sometimes. You're allowed to say that he is making you unhappy."

"He's not," insists her best friend immediately.

Dr. Yu doesn't believe her—in truth, she doubts that her best friend believes herself—but she can understand the knee-jerk reaction. It is difficult for anyone to admit that something that should be making her happy isn't; that the life she waited so long for or worked so hard to achieve has not, in fact, turned out the way that it was supposed to. How does one reconcile the dream of how she imagined things would be with the reality of things as they are?

It is not her fault that her patient is dead. She knows this; her supervisors know this. She had done everything right. The man had survived the surgery, his chest had been closed back up and he had been sleeping soundly on the table when his heart simply stopped. There was no reason for it, no explanation. He was there and then he was gone.

"If we're not going back to that town," her best friend is saying, "then we should at least be moving forward." She squares her shoulders. "I know that your father is having a difficult time, and I'm very sorry for him, but I'm also worried—" She stumbles in her speech, takes a deep breath, and then barrels forward. "I'm worried that he'll only end up dragging my husband down, too."

Dr. Yu stares at her. Her best friend has never contradicted her so forcefully; she has only ever been supportive. She understands that her best friend's loyalty is to her husband, but to place Noah above Dr. Yu's father, to insist on her husband's well-being over everything else—Noah's wife has gone too far. What has Noah lost besides a congregation? What does he need consolation for? It is Dr. Yu's father who has a real foundation for his grief.

"My father isn't forcing Noah to do anything he doesn't want to do," Dr. Yu snaps back. Her nerves are frayed; her patience is running perilously low. It has been ten days now that her best friend and her husband have been guests in her house, and not once has Dr. Yu spoken her mind, not once has she said anything unkind about their prolonged stay, their moody indecision, their seeming inability to pull themselves together. "Am I glad that Papa has the help? Of course I am. Is it my responsibility to pull your husband away so he can go back to being a minister? Of course not! And it isn't yours, either." She stands, reaches past Noah's wife to the door, and wrenches it open. "Better a magician than a minister, if you ask me. At least *one* of them has the guts to acknowledge that the job is nothing but a lot of smoke and mirrors."

Her best friend pales at this, but Dr. Yu ignores her. "The world is a whole lot bigger than you and Noah," she flings over her shoulder as she strides into the hallway. "It's about time you figured that out."

As she enters the living room her legs are trembling and her heart is beating hard. She feels shaken, close to tears. Her father peers at her as she crosses the carpet to join him and slumps down on the sofa at his side. With his keen eye he can see that something is wrong, and when Dr. Yu's best friend goes hurrying through the hallway with her head down, refusing to make eye contact with either of them, he sighs and shakes his head.

"April," he says, "you're my only daughter and I love you. But God knows, if you insist on trying to fix everyone and everything all the time, you'll only wind up frustrated."

"I'm not trying to fix everyone, Papa," groans Dr. Yu, sliding down on her cushion.

"If you just made an effort to listen to people, to give them some space," he insists in his earnest way, "I think you'd be surprised to find that these sorts of things will usually heal themselves."

"What sorts of things?" she asks, leaning her head back, too tired to explain herself to him.

"Melancholy," says her father. "Grief. The stuff of broken hearts."

He draws close to her and with a quick, unexpected motion, he reaches behind her ear. When he pulls his hand back, he opens his fist to reveal a pair of glittering jewels—her mother's favorite earrings. Dr. Yu startles at the sight of them. The earrings are made of paste, but they shine. She had assumed that the set had been buried along with her mother.

"Where did you find these?"

Her father takes her hand, gently pries open her fingers, and drops the earrings into her palm. "It would be a sad world indeed, my dear," he says in the philosophical, mystical tone that he has taken up recently along with his magic books, "if the only things that existed in it were what we could see, and touch, and cut open. Come now, sweetheart. I hope you've got a little more faith in the human heart than all that."

thirty-four

Mrs. McGinn refuses to go.

What is the point, without her daughter?

She lies alone on her bed, her face pressed into her pillow, weeping. She has been in this position since she returned from the river several hours ago, her daughter's soggy note disintegrating under the pressure of her clenched fist.

A sloth watches her from the armchair in the corner, his long curved claws dug deep into the upholstery. While Mrs. McGinn's husband attempts to talk some sense into his wife, the zookeeper works at luring the sloth out of the room by waving potted houseplants under his nose. Neither of the men is having much luck.

"Where did that damn animal even come from?" demands Mrs. McGinn's husband. "I thought we were only in charge of the penguins. I thought that was all I agreed to."

"The sloth was reassigned," explains the zookeeper through gritted teeth. "After the first wave left, people had to double, triple up on animals. Evelyn volunteered to take him."

The zookeeper's jaw is set, his gaze black and resentful. He glares at the lumpy shape of Mrs. McGinn on top of her comforter. As he watches, she lifts her face and rests one cheek on the pillow so as to ease her breathing. Half of her makeup is caked to the pillowcase, and the little that is left on her face is pitted with tears. She has never looked more ugly, the zookeeper reflects. He feels a brief, warm rush of retribution. Good.

It is not a pretty scene out there, after all, and it is easier to blame her for it than to blame himself. When he takes the time to think about it, he is forced to acknowledge the fact that it was both of them—she and he in concert—who brought this town to its knees. She claimed all the while that staying here and enduring the rain until it ended was the only way to lift the town up, to raise it to its former glory, while he simply stuck it out because he had never known anything else. Which of them, he asks himself now in disgust, was the most selfish?

No wonder his fiancée didn't want him.

He can't bear the thought but he also can't stop thinking it, and so he distracts himself by hating Mrs. McGinn while he tries for what feels like the fortieth time to coax the sloth from the chair. There is a car full of primates waiting for them outside. Once he had realized that his peacocks were safe and dry, Mauro had volunteered to drive vanloads of animals up the hill to the church. Many of them are making the trek on their own, of course—the antelope marching single file, the wild boars lurching over rocks, the tortoise forcing a steady path up through a strong downward current with the water cutting in clear streams across his shell. It is the birds who tire halfway up the hill, retreating into bushes with sodden wings, who must be drawn out and collected and driven the rest of the way to the building, and it is the tanks full of reptiles that must be lifted from their windowsills and hurried down driveways in the rain. The zookeeper had assumed that they would have to leave some animals behind, but Mauro was insistent on getting them all out. He fished the koi out of an abandoned bathtub and dropped them into buckets. With the zookeeper's help, he tranquilized Leesl's cheetah and lugged the feline into the back of the van. Leesl's other cats twined around their ankles, and when they saw that the front door was standing open they slunk into the front yard and paddled through the lawn to the road. Once there they turned their squashed faces to the sky and joined the sluggish parade of paws and wings and wheels as the townspeople and their animals made their way to higher ground, to the church standing somber in the downpour.

"And once you've got all those animals there," says Mrs. McGinn's husband to the zookeeper with no small amount of scorn, "what exactly do you intend to do with them?"

The zookeeper does not appreciate the question, as it is one that he has been asking himself all morning. Will the wolves lie down with the lambs? No, most likely not. He can only hope that Leesl has some sort of plan; Leesl who, as Mauro informed him, had the church ready and waiting hours ago for her neighbors' arrival. The zookeeper has not had the opportunity yet to see the church himself. He has been too busy rounding up the last of his charges down here and cramming the remaining food and water supplies into the back of Mauro's truck.

There is the sound of a wet foot on the stairs, and before the zookeeper has time to react, Mrs. McGinn's daughter swings around the corner and into the bedroom. She avoids his gaze, stepping lightly to her mother's side.

Mrs. McGinn raises her head at the sight of her. "Angela Rose?" she cries. The zookeeper sees the relief flood her splotchy face. Half a second later, the expression is replaced with one of righteous indignation. "Where on *earth* did you think you were going?" she demands.

"Mama," she says, brushing Mrs. McGinn's curls away from her cheeks. "What are you still doing here? I don't think we've got much time."

At this, Mrs. McGinn drops her head back down to the pillow, once more in despair. The zookeeper has never seen someone run through so many emotions in such a short amount of time. "I thought we could outlast it," she groans. "I thought we would win."

Her daughter shakes her head. "The sandbag wall is halfway breached already," she says. "And the river's still rising. Come on, now." She tugs at her mother's elbow. "People are asking for you."

Mrs. McGinn moans again, shuddering. "The only reason people would be asking for me," she says, "is to demand some kind of justice. I doomed them, Angela Rose. I doomed them to a watery grave. It's better if I stay here."

Two spots of color appear high on her daughter's cheeks. "Stop it, Mama," she snaps. "If you say something like that again, we *will* leave you here. There's been enough of us feeling sorry for ourselves as it is these past few weeks, and it isn't doing anybody any good." She raises her chin and gazes swiftly, severely at the zookeeper, who leans back. The girl turns again to her mother. "This isn't anyone's fault. The whole lot of us could have left years ago if we'd wanted to, but we didn't, and now we're here. It is what it is."

The zookeeper has never seen the town matriarch looking so meek. For a moment there is silence, and when she finally speaks her voice is humble and small. "I'm tired, Angie," she says. "I'm so tired."

Mrs. McGinn's daughter glances again at the zookeeper, instinctively looking to him for support. Although he would like to help her, he cannot come up with any words of consolation, anything that would change Mrs. McGinn's mind. The truth is that he is tired, too. He is tired of worrying over his charges, tired of trying to improve the situation in this place only to find that his little world is spinning ever wildly out of his control. It is too hard, trying to take care of so much. There is a part of him that wants nothing more than to sit down in that velvet armchair and settle in forever, to wait with the sloth and Mrs. McGinn until the water rises up the stairwell, until the waves lap at his knees, his chest, his chin. For half a second he remembers the former town minister, believes that he could understand, now, the old man's desire to let everything go.

"Screw it, Angie," he says dully. "What's the point?"

The plea in her eyes flips to fear—he can see it happen, can see how surprised she is that he will not back her up on this. Well, what did she expect? Things changed after she took off. There's no changing them back.

For a long minute everyone in the room is silent. There is only the sound of the rain in the trees outside the window, and then—suddenly—a car horn.

"What is happening up in there?" comes Mauro's voice from down in the street.

"He's waiting for us," mutters the zookeeper.

"Let him wait, Adam," retorts Mrs. McGinn's daughter. "Or better yet, why don't you go down and join him? Take off, for all I care. I'm not going anywhere. If she's staying"—with a curt nod at her mother's prostrate form—"then I'm staying." She drops down on the foot of the bed with a gesture as dramatic as her mother's, one knee crossed over the other and her hands folded in her lap, at once stubborn and serene, looking for all the world as if she is waiting to be served a cup of tea at her own baby shower.

Mrs. McGinn's husband explodes. "Are you *kidding* me?" he shouts. "What the hell is *wrong* with you people?" He storms out of the bedroom and down the flight of stairs. From the kitchen, they can hear the sound of pots and pans being pulled out of cupboards and flung to the floor; the shattering ceramic of three or four china plates. Finally the front door opens and slams, and once more all is quiet.

The sloth, frightened by the noise, loosens his grip on the armchair, lifts himself up and over the back, and slides slowly down until he is huddled on the floor beneath it. From that position, the zookeeper knows, it will not be difficult to swoop down with a blanket, bundle the sloth into it, and transfer him into the van that is idling in the street. There is a quilt folded at the foot of the bed, but the zookeeper cannot bring himself to reach for it.

"Well?" says Mrs. McGinn's daughter. "Are you staying or going?"

That is the question, isn't it? reflects the zookeeper, crossing his burly arms over his chest and considering his fiancée with every last ounce of composure he possesses. This has always been a story of departures: who was leaving whom, and who was being left.

The zookeeper has half a mind to walk out that door, just to spite her. Isn't it his turn?

Outside one car door slams shut, and then another. The zookeeper waits to hear the sound of the engine roaring into gear and then growling away into the distance. He does not care that he is not in the car, that he is not heading up to the church to eat canned vegetables and stale Communion wafers along with the rest of them. He knows that the townspeople, accustomed to the long winters around here, have supplies stockpiled in storage units and basements—but even if they manage to get all those cans and boxes to the church, how much time will that buy them? Five, six days? If they get hungry enough, they will start clamoring to kill the animals. The zookeeper knows it, and he would rather not be there to watch it happen.

What he hears instead of the car is the sound, again, of footsteps on the stairs. This time there is not just one pair, but several, and the whole house shudders with their stomping. In a few seconds Mrs. McGinn's husband reappears in the room, this time with Mauro and another man close at his heels. The zookeeper recognizes the town tailor; he had planned on going to the man when it came time for his wedding.

"Evelyn," rumbles Mrs. McGinn's husband, "I brought reinforcements. I know you may not care whether you live or die, but I'm telling you that right now the choice isn't yours to make. Angela Rose won't leave without you and I won't either—but rather than hanging around in this bedroom like a goddamn fool, I'm taking you with me. Whether you like it or not."

Mrs. McGinn's daughter starts to say something, but her stepfather cuts her short. "Stop it, Angie," he snaps. "There's a lot of people counting on your mother. And on you, for that matter. You'd do well to think twice before you let them down again."

Mrs. McGinn's daughter rises halfway off the bed, the color draining from her face. Before she can respond, Mrs. McGinn's husband strides forward, lifts the edge of the comforter, and yanks it toward the end of the bed. Mrs. McGinn comes sliding down with it, her mouth gaping. Mauro and the tailor hurry around to opposite sides of the head of the bed, where, apologizing profusely to Mrs. McGinn all the while, they grab the other corners of the quilt and raise them high. The plan is absurd, but somehow it works: the three men heave the blanket off the bed and carry it down the stairs as they would carry a hammock, the center sinking inward with Mrs. McGinn's weight, her smeared face peeping over the patchwork in childlike confusion. She is too baffled to protest, and by the time she makes up her mind to try to struggle off, they have already arrived outside and pitched the entire load—Mrs. McGinn included—into the backseat of the van. Mrs. McGinn's daughter runs after them, howling, while the zookeeper brings up the rear with the sloth swaddled in his arms. There is a brief scuffle in the street, but before anyone fully realizes what has happened, they are all in the car, careening out of the town and up the hill.

How ridiculous, the zookeeper says to himself. In the van he finds himself seated next to Mrs. McGinn's daughter, the familiar scent of her lavender soap making him dizzy. When the tires sink into the mud and the van is stalled, momentarily, in the road, she buries her face in his sleeve and begins to cry.

They make it to the church just in time. The wall around the river does not hold. Within an hour of their departure, the remaining sandbags crumble and tumble into the river, displacing the water that rises in waves from the bottom of the banks to the top of the shore. And even now the rain continues to fall. The clouds break; the sky splits apart and pours down. The fountains of the great deep are broken up, and the windows of heaven are opened.

The water rushes up porches. Front doors buckle and fall inward, opening the way for the river to roll through the entryways, upending kitchen tables and chairs and leaving pots and pans bobbing on the surface. The furniture is splintered and submerged. The books are all buried; the insides of cars are flooded; cans of food and boxes of cereal are taken up and swept through the streets of the town. The water uproots the mailboxes and carries them away.

Leesl greets them at the church door and closes it behind them, lets them know in her glad and soft-spoken way that they are the last to arrive and that everyone is now accounted for. She hands them plastic bowls of soup and directs them into the nave, assuring them that there are stacks of blankets in the closets and plenty of non-perishable foods downstairs. Mrs. McGinn, supported on both sides by Mauro and her husband, makes it to the first row of pews before her knees give out and she folds down into it. Her neighbors watch her, disturbed. The zookeeper looks for anger in their faces, looks for blame, resentment, dislike. But he doesn't find it. They are only weary, and shocked. They do not have the energy to point fingers, nor the courage to ask what will come next.

thirty-five

When Dr. Yu's father attempts to pull a handkerchief from a candlestick, the whole thing goes up in flames.

Noah's wife had been half expecting it to happen. She is sitting stiffly, perched on one of the battered lawn chairs he and Noah have arranged for spectators on one side of the gazebo, holding her breath as he shouts his abracadabra. The audience gasps at the sight of the fire and she gasps with them, but unlike the people who clap and cheer as he leaps to put it out, she is certain that this effect was not intended. From her position near the aisle she can see Noah standing off to one side with a look of dismay. By the time he makes up his mind to take a few steps forward onto the makeshift stage, Dr. Yu's father has already doused the flaming handkerchief in a bucket of water that was meant to be turned into wine.

The show has been disastrous so far, and they are only thirty minutes in. During the first demonstration with the hat, Noah dropped one of the eggs that he palmed. Meanwhile the flowers that were made to disappear did not reappear when they should have, and when Dr. Yu's father attempted to show the audience that the rope they had seen him cut was still in one piece, the two ends fell apart in his hands. Even his quick-change went awry. He stepped into the cabinet in his tuxedo and should have emerged in his wizard's gear within seconds—but instead it took him six or seven minutes and when he finally stumbled out he was red-faced and panting and only partly successful. His hat and his shoes were in place but his bow tie and coattails poked out from underneath a skewed cape.

Fortunately, the audience members do not seem to mind. The children gape at the colors and the lights while their parents slap their knees and laugh at what is quickly devolving into a comedy routine. While a few of the spectators grow bored and wander away to other parts of the pier, new people amble in every few minutes.

Noah's wife is here because Noah asked her to come and because it did not occur to her to refuse. How familiar it is, she realizes with a deep ache in her chest, to sit within a rapt crowd and gaze up at her husband. She misses the old Noah: his charisma, his drive, his extraordinary certainty that his path had been chosen for him and that as long as he followed it, all would be well. This man whom she sees standing now on that makeshift stage, this man who looks and sounds like her husband but lacks all of his grace and power—he is a lesser version of himself. As she watches the colored scarves flying, she finds herself resenting her husband for being up on that platform, standing behind the curtain that he rigged up with a system of pulleys and ropes. What is she supposed to do when he has made himself a stranger to her? And if he is no longer the Noah that he was, what does that mean for her, his wife, whose sole purpose for so long has been him?

She wishes that she had been able to express something like this to Dr. Yu, something of this profound sense of loss, rather than saying what she did about Dr. Yu's father. She glances across the aisle, sees the rigid figure of her best friend seated three rows in front of her. The two of them have not exchanged a word since their heated encounter last night. After leaving the kitchen, Noah's wife retreated to the guest room and lay down on the bed, dizzy and short of breath, the loneliest she has been since her mother died.

They make an odd pair, the minister and the magician. Noah towers over Dr. Yu's father, his dark beard thick and untrimmed, an old charcoal-gray blazer hanging loosely over his gaunt frame. The floodlights Dr. Yu's father attached to the gazebo cast stark and angled shadows across his features. Visibly embarrassed by his own show thus far and determined to succeed at something marvelous before the intermission, Dr. Yu's father instructs Noah to retrieve the aluminum pan from their trunk of props. Noah's wife watches the magician flash the pan at the audience to prove to them that it is solid; she watches him pour a small amount of kerosene into it, senses the people around her instinctively draw back when he drops a match into the oil to ignite it. He claps the lid over the sudden flame and for a long moment he pauses, holds it there, gazing out over the dusky harbor with an expression of triumph. When he flings the lid from the pan, the fire is gone but a bird has appeared—a slender white dove that goes winging over the heads of the spectators, soaring three or four times around the gazebo before darting toward a patch of trees and vanishing from sight. The audience cheers while Dr. Yu's father takes a quick bow and signals for the curtain to fall.

During intermission, Noah's wife leaves her seat, walks to the back of the gazebo, and climbs up behind the curtain. She finds Dr. Yu's father pacing back and forth across the platform while Noah stands to one side, leaning against a post with a deeply furrowed brow.

"Is everything all right?" she asks. "Your last trick was beautiful."

"That dove was a rental," snaps Dr. Yu's father over one shoulder. "I was supposed to return her first thing in the morning."

"We'll get her back," says Noah, lacking conviction.

"How?" demands Dr. Yu's father, halting in his tracks and throwing his hands in the air. "You saw her—right into the sky. She could be miles from here by now!"

Noah's wife sees the long shadow of Dr. Yu rounding the gazebo and crossing the grass to meet them. "I'll go look for the bird," she volunteers, hurrying to descend the platform in order to avoid an encounter with her best friend. "Perhaps she hasn't gone far."

Leaving them to their second act, Noah's wife steps off the back of the platform and into the grass. The night air is brisk, the breeze prickly with salt, and she shivers. She is wearing one of Dr. Yu's dresses, layered beneath one of Dr. Yu's coats. For the first time in her life she feels uncomfortable in her best friend's clothing and wishes she had brought more belongings of her own. Turning away from the gazebo, she begins walking along the harbor in the direction of another park several blocks down. As she goes she tilts her head back and looks up into the branches of the small trees that have been planted at intervals along the sidewalk. A few times she thinks she sees the flutter of wings among the leaves—but first it is only a scrap of paper, and then a torn plastic bag.

Three blocks down, her gaze still raised to the sky, she runs into a man who is taking long, blind steps in the opposite direction with his shoulders hunched and his own eyes on the ground. The collision is hard enough that they both take two or three steps back.

"I'm so sorry," she says with a sharp intake of breath. "Are you all right?"

"Watch where you're going," the man snarls. "I'm fine."

She looks at him more closely, hearing something familiar in his voice. "The weatherman?" she asks, dazed. And then, correcting herself: "Jonas?"

This does not look like the person she saw only last week.

The man has none of his cocky swagger; there is no insolent light glinting from that pair of pale eyes. His coat is damp and his shoulders are hunched, and when he speaks to her his tone is dull.

"Oh," he says. "It's you."

She laughs a little at the absurdity of seeing him here—her first laugh, she realizes, in weeks. There is a rustling in the branches above him and she glances swiftly up, wonders if it might be the missing dove.

Jonas scowls. "I'm glad you're so amused," he says. "That makes one of us."

There is something arresting in his tone—some sense of foreboding that she doesn't understand. She drops her gaze from the trees and looks him in the eye.

"Are you all right?" she asks.

"I was fine until I ran into you and your husband," he spits back. "Then he got under my skin, with all his talk of failure. So I decided to give it one more try."

He glares at her, his eyes glittering, the lines in his face taut with exhaustion. There is a strange energy crackling between them; she feels a rosy heat rise to her face and course swiftly through her limbs.

"You went back," she says.

"Yes," he confirms. "I went back. And you know what? I shouldn't have. I should have followed my instincts and left well enough alone."

Her heart constricts. "Did you get them out?"

He emits an explosive sigh, shoves his hand through his hair. "No, I didn't—but only because I couldn't get close enough to try. The highway that leads into the hills is flooded. No one is getting into or out of that town until the water goes down, and it's not going down anytime soon. As far as I can tell, it's still raining."

"What can we do?" she demands. "Shouldn't we go for help? The police, the coast guard—there must be someone who can get through to them."

"You think I didn't consider that?" Jonas demands. "You think I didn't try? I *went* to the police, and I *went* to the coast guard. That's where I'm coming from." He flings his hand toward a windowless gray tower looming over the harbor. "They took down my statement, promised they'd look into it. First they'd need to send a scout up the coast to assess the situation, determine what sorts of ships can fit upriver and how many of them would be necessary to take all those people. Then they'd have to call in reinforcements from the next major port to the south. They said that it would be impossible to organize a rescue attempt in fewer than four days."

She takes a ragged breath. "What if that's not fast enough?"

His smile is scornful. "It'll have to be," he says. "At the station they told me to go home. There's nothing we can do about that town now—not to mention my career, which is as good as dead, too." He glares at her. "Don't you see? Those people had their chance, and they missed it."

This is what it is to be in shock, she tells herself, unable to speak or move her limbs. What about the town meeting? she would like to know. What about the photographs? If Jonas is not accountable for her neighbors' fate, then isn't she?

"Stop it," he says, reading her mind. "You're not responsible either. They knew the risks, they made their choice. There is nothing you could have done to save them."

He takes a step forward so that he is standing closer to her—so close, in fact, that she must tilt her head slightly back to meet his gaze. No one has looked at her like this since she and Noah left the city; no one has considered her as intensely, as gravely as this man is doing now. For several seconds she stares back at him, his face growing more familiar the longer she looks at it. What would her life have been like if she had never met her husband? What sort of person would she have become? She glances past Jonas to the stars that hang, faintly pulsing, in the evening sky. How she missed them in the rain! she recalls. How dark the sky becomes without them!

Jonas narrows his eyes, watching the slow illumination of her expression. He can see the plan taking shape in her mind.

"Don't think I'm going with you," he says with a grimace.

"I don't," she says, suddenly spotting movement in the tree above him: the quivering of white wings.

"Because I'm not. I want nothing more to do with that town. The people there are willful and thoughtless and sometimes they are downright selfish, just like everybody is, and you will never be able to change them because they have always been this way. Even if you saved them, they would still be this way.

That's how people are. You do not owe them a thing. They deserve whatever comes to them."

She remembers her neighbors, their animals, her fox curled up on the love seat at her feet. She thinks of Noah in the little wooden gazebo, standing behind the makeshift curtain at this very moment with his arms folded across his chest, the skeleton keys tucked within the cuffs of his shirt. It was not so long ago when she thought that he walked with God, when she believed that he possessed a kind of power and authority that no one else ever would, that there was a call in the world that could be heard by him alone. And yet here is the revelation that has been creeping up on her over all those long, gray days as the rain drummed against her shoulders and slid into her boots: there is nothing special about him at all. Nothing heroic, nothing superhuman, nothing divine. He is as fragile as anyone, as frail and as brokenly human as she is, as all the rest of them are. And yet, she realizes with some surprise, struck by the force of the emotion: she loves him all the same.

What Jonas is saying—it is far too simple. The townspeople do not deserve a watery fate any more than she does, or Noah does. No one asked for the rain. No one wanted the old minister to walk into the river, or Dr. Yu's mother to fall ill; no couple wants their son to meet his death on the road before he has a chance to finish high school.

Although it is true that Noah's wife has endured her own fair share of loss, she has spent most of her adulthood marveling over her happiness and asking herself what she ever did to deserve someone like Noah. And yet the truth, she sees now, is that people do not *deserve* their good fortune any more than they deserve their heartache. A person's fate simply comes to her, unbidden—a white dove in the dark—and her only task is to accept it, to reach out and make it her own.

thirty-six

Here they are.

The fragments of their lives have been washed away and there is nothing left to gather besides stacks of canned goods and jugs of fresh water. Nothing left to preserve besides jars of olives and jams.

The remaining telephone poles drop like dominoes. The townspeople can hear the thuds and the splashes as they topple, one after another, to the water. The wires are tangled below the surface, the crackle of voices buried in a roiling silver sea. It is clear to everyone now that the decision to abandon this town should have been made long ago: before the basements filled, before the sidewalks flowed.

"But how were we to know?" the townspeople ask themselves, shivering in the soaked candlelight of the church. They were only being optimistic. They never once imagined that it would come to this. What they see now is that the problem has always been, essentially, one of hope. Of misguided, misplaced, mistaken *hope*—which had bled from their hearts to their organs and then corroded their minds. Hope had affected the soundness of their judgment.

"Hope!" they mutter now in condemning tones. "Hope! How damaging it has been, all this time. And no one ever told us. We never knew."

They know now. They hunker down in their pews and wrap their blankets more tightly around their shoulders while the rain thunders to the roof and the wind howls at their door. Some of them snack on rations of bread or small bowls of pasta while others rearrange their sleeping bags, shuffle and reshuffle their stacks of playing cards, or page through tattered hymnals. Although many of them were baptized or confirmed in this church, it is a long time since they have been up here. They cannot remember exactly when they stopped attending, or why, although some of them do remember trudging despondently home after the last few services when the old minister had them pray for change that never came.

At the organ Leesl plays the opening bars of a song that sounds vaguely familiar to Mrs. McGinn's daughter, although she never came here as a child with her stubborn Quaker mother. When Mrs. McGinn starts humming along, the girl stares at her.

"'Amazing Grace,'" Mrs. McGinn murmurs, below the music. "It's soothing. I used to sing it to you as a lullaby when you were a baby. Knocked you right out."

Mrs. McGinn is lying flat on her back in the middle of the aisle that runs from the altar through the nave. Leave it to her mother to choose the most prominent and obtrusive spot in which to have her breakdown, reflects Mrs. McGinn's daughter, propping another pillow underneath a heap of curls. When her mother heaves a theatrical sigh and requests a tall glass of Communion wine, Mrs. McGinn's daughter takes this as a sign that the woman has begun to regain some of her old spark. There is nothing Mrs. McGinn loves more than a good crisis, after all. As much as she claims to dread her neighbors' anger, the truth is that she will not be able to resist taking control of the situation for much longer.

Mrs. McGinn's daughter rises to her feet and begins to make her way toward the boxes of Communion wine that are stashed behind the altar. Her gaze roves across the church as she goes, instinctively seeking out the zookeeper. When she sees him on the far side of the building she pauses to watch him swing a bale of hay into the nave, feeling a surge of sudden and possessive affection. She is proud of him. Look at what he has accomplished here already!

He has blocked off the perimeter of the room for the animals, leaving the pews and aisles open for the townspeople. Around the walls are portable cages, easily collapsed and bolted back together, for those animals who already had them. The glass terrariums with the reptiles and the tropical amphibians are stacked four or five high in one of the front corners. The zookeeper built makeshift pens for the rest out of chicken wire and wood, which are not the most stable but work well enough to contain the taller, flightless birds, the monkey and red panda, the sheep and the boars and most of the livestock. The eagle is chained to a post near the pulpit. Downstairs are the penguins, the wolves whose prowling is confined to the old nursery room, the alligator on the cold tiles of the bathroom floor. While he has contained as many of the animals as possible, there are not enough cages for all of them—and so the townspeople have had to accept such things as the peacocks roaming free and the tortoise slumbering beneath the pews. The red fox darts from one shadow to another, peering into people's faces as if looking for someone.

The townspeople have been assigned shifts for cleaning and feeding, as the zookeeper cannot do it all himself. Empty rooms downstairs are stocked with hay, canned produce, and grains. The freezer is packed with all the meat that they had time to collect, although there is not enough to last the carnivores very long. Parked on the driveway between the church and the house is a truck that Mrs. McGinn's daughter remembers well from the zoo: a red metal monster with a five-hundred-gallon tank stocked with fresh water. If they go through all of it, she overheard the zookeeper saying gravely to Leesl, that's when the problems will really start. He told her to begin saving spare containers that could be used to collect rainwater.

Abandoning the task of the wine, Mrs. McGinn's daughter deliberately turns her steps toward him. It feels to her as though it takes an eternity to cross from one side of the nave to the other, her steps plodding, her heart thudding in her chest. When the zookeeper hears a sound behind him he looks up from the fence he is repairing, but when he sees that it is her, he turns immediately back to his work.

"Adam," says Mrs. McGinn's daughter. "Hey." He doesn't respond and so she hesitates, placing her hand on top of the nearest pen and shifting her weight to appear as casual as possible. "Is there anything I can do to help?"

The zookeeper's gaze flicks up to her hand. "Don't touch the wire," he growls. "Those fences aren't made to withstand any kind of force." He pokes at a strip of chicken wire with the broken handle of an umbrella to demonstrate how quickly it would give. The wild boar on the other side raises his chin and shows his tusks. The hornbills screech and Leesl's cheetah growls, a low rumble that makes it feel as though the floor of the church is trembling.

"Sorry," she says. She stuffs her fists in her pockets and repeats her offer to help him. "Just tell me what needs to be done," she says. "I'll do it."

At this, the zookeeper glares up at her. "Is that so?" he says. "Is that a promise?"

The left side of his lip is curled in a snarl, and at the sight of it Mrs. McGinn's daughter worries—for the first time—that he might refuse to take her back.

"I'm sorry I left," she says, kneeling down beside him. She reaches out to touch his arm. "I was scared, Adam. It was stupid. I won't ever do it again."

He pulls his arm away. "And what about the rest of us?" he demands. "You think you're the only one who was scared? You think that everyone else in here isn't terrified of what's about to come next?" He flings his hand in the air, taking in the entire nave with a broad sweep of his arm. Her gaze follows the gesture and comes to rest on the worn gray faces of her neighbors. "Of course you were scared, Angie. Of *course* you were. But that doesn't give you any right to take off the way you did. And it doesn't give you the right to make decisions as if you're the only one that matters. You owe us more than that."

"I know," she says. Feeling queasy, she pauses for a minute to take a deep breath and rest her hand on her abdomen. Her tone turns pleading. "I'm sorry, Adam. I said I was sorry."

He shrugs. "Sure you are. I'm not worried about that. What I'd like to know is whether or not you'll try to leave again. Because I can handle the rest of this. I can deal with the animals and the rain and whatever the hell happens to us here. But I don't want anything to do with you if you can't promise me that you'll stick around."

He heaves a sigh and turns away from her, tilting his face toward the window. The light seeping through the stained glass softens the hard line of his jaw. "I want to believe that people belong to each other, Angie," he says, his voice suddenly thick and weary. "I want to believe that you and I and that baby will get out of here somehow and that we'll be able to build something together—something that lasts. But I don't see how that will ever happen if you don't believe in it, too."

He looks her squarely in the eye and waits for her response. Several long seconds pass without her knowing what to say, and after several seconds more, the zookeeper heaves himself to his feet and begins walking quickly, unsteadily toward the back of the church. Mrs. McGinn's daughter cannot bring herself to turn and watch him go. Instead she stares at the space where he had been sitting, remaining there until the wild boar jams his snout into the chicken-wire fence. Startled then, she stumbles up and hurries behind the altar, keeping her head down until she reaches the boxes of wine.

Why didn't she speak? she demands of herself, yanking out a bottle and tucking it under her elbow. Here she had been worried that he would not take her back, and then when he gave her an opportunity to reassure him, she froze. What is the matter with her?

She *wants* to marry him—of course she does. She has wanted to marry him since their second date at the diner, when he explained to her about the penguins and she leaned over their table to wipe buttercream frosting from his beard. And yet over the past few weeks, as their little world has gone whirling off its axis, she has begun to doubt whether there is anything that is permanent or stable. How does she know that their marriage will last, even if they think they love each other now? How does she know that he will not grow tired of her, that he will always be faithful, that the life they build together will not someday be swept out from underneath them?

What Mrs. McGinn's daughter would really like to know, she realizes as she makes her way back with the wine, is why her mother kept getting married, over and over again, when she should have known by marriage two or three that the next would be as likely to fail as the rest. Some people are good at marriage, Mrs. McGinn's daughter had discovered at an early age. But her mother was not one of them.

Her daughter had hated it. She was humiliated by her classmates' questions; her mother was the only divorcée in town. She hated the shuffling transitions from one home to another, the solemn, self-conscious parades down the street with her mother while their neighbors peeked out from behind semidrawn curtains. She hated the scratchy feel of new furniture and the stiff spines of new books and the dizzying scent of fresh paint, but most of all she hated the whole idea of it, the whole attempt: the washing away of their personal history as if it hadn't happened. Mrs. McGinn's daughter used to threaten to run away from home; she used to call her mother spiteful names. Once during one of their marches from old home to new home she had sworn that when she was grown, she would live her life differently.

When she reaches the center of the aisle, she bends down to her mother and props her up so that she can drink. Together the two women survey the church. Pillows and blankets are strewn across the aisle and the altar; dirty dishes are stacked in the corners. The electricity is out and the wicks of the candles are burning so low that even the light feels damp. The air reeks of rotten produce and hay and dung. The townspeople are disheveled, unwashed, and they, too, are beginning to stink of musk.

"Angela Rose," says Mrs. McGinn to her daughter, her voice becoming more resonant, more regal with every swig. "Look at these people. Depressed. Hopeless. No better than the animals who are trapped up here with them. Do you know what they need?" She pauses, as if considering, but the daughter has lived with her mother too long to be fooled. Mrs. McGinn already has an idea.

"What is it, Mama?" she says obediently. She is tempted to take a sip of that wine herself.

"They need something to cheer them, something to take their mind off the situation!" she exclaims. She raises one orange eyebrow, her expression pointed and cunning. "Angela Rose. Why don't you get married up here?"

Her daughter stares. "Are you serious?" she demands.

"I never joke about weddings," replies Mrs. McGinn. "I know it's not as lovely as you might have wanted it to be. But the whole town is here! If we rearranged the potted plants, found some hangings for the walls . . . There are enough canned vegetables and beans to whip up something of a wedding dinner downstairs. Why not?"

"Because, Mama," she says, casting a desperate glance around the church and ticking off the reasons on her fingers. "It's too cold up here, and it's too dark. I don't have a dress. It's raining.

The place smells like swine." She hesitates, stumbles into truthfulness. "And anyway, I don't think that Adam would take me back."

Mrs. McGinn snorts. "*That* Adam?" she retorts, tilting her head meaningfully to the left. Mrs. McGinn's daughter looks in the direction that she indicates, sees the zookeeper standing a few pews away, his fingers gripping the wood and his gaze fixed heatedly, unhappily on her. At the sight of him, her whole body aches—and when their eyes meet, he doesn't turn away.

"He loves you," says Mrs. McGinn simply.

"It isn't that easy," snaps her daughter, turning back to her mother. "You should know that better than anyone."

Mrs. McGinn shrugs. "Whatever you say about me, whatever anyone says about me—I've had a fine life, Angela Rose. I've had some good partners, some bad. Did I expect to marry four times? Of course not. No one does. Do I regret any of it? Well, how could I? I don't believe that there are right choices or wrong choices, only the paths you choose to take, and the ones that you don't." She lifts her right arm, wraps it around her daughter's shoulders, and pulls the girl close. "I know you're frightened, sweetheart. I want to be able to promise you that your life will have no hardship and that your marriage will be happy and that it will last from now until kingdom come. But I can't. All I can tell you is that things happen and plans change and we've got to change along with them or risk being left behind. The world is an uncertain place, that's for sure—but if you've got someone you love and who loves you back, you ought to hold on to him. I've always had you. And I've hung on so tight that the rest doesn't matter."

Pressed against her mother, Mrs. McGinn's daughter turns her head slightly to see if the zookeeper is still there. The light in the church is murky and wet, the figures of her neighbors mingled with the shadows. As everything else tumbles down around her, she longs to make an attempt at something permanent, to attach herself to something true.

thirty-seven

Noah's wife assumes that her husband is on board, and Noah doesn't have the heart to tell her otherwise.

Has he not disappointed her enough?

He has seen the way she looks at him when she crosses his path in her best friend's small and sterile house: her lips pursed with worry, her gaze steady with disapproval. He feels terrible for missing the interviews that she set up for him, but he simply could not bring himself to go. He is Noah, after all—he used to walk with God. And now? For him, the days before they left that town were as empty and as bleak as the sky itself. He feels resentful and alone—as if he has been abandoned, as if all his faith and certainty had grown wings and taken flight. But how could he explain that to his wife? He would rather wait, and bide his time, and hope for everything to be restored. He has always been a patient man. He would rather listen for the rustling of familiar feathers, watching the sky from dawn to dusk until what he has lost returns to him. Is that not a kind of faith, too?

"I thought you were afraid of boats," he tells his wife as she works beside him in the parking lot of the harbor. She and Noah and Dr. Yu are loading all of the magician's gear into Dr. Yu's hatchback in the parking lot. Her father was supposed to help them as soon as he wrapped up the show, but instead he tossed his scarves and cuffs onto the lawn and went flying down the pier in search of his friends who own a boat.

"I don't like them," admits Noah's wife. "But if the roads are flooded, what other choice do we have?"

She turns the full weight of her gray gaze upon him, but Noah can't meet it. Instead he focuses on her fingers, nimbly fastening her coat against the sea breeze. He knows that she is waiting for him to speak, waiting for his reaction to the news she brought back along with the dove; she wants to know if the current crisis in the town has changed the way he feels about going back. This is a chance, at last, to deliver them! Have the old flames finally been lit within his soul?

He stuffs his fists into his pockets, where his knuckles encounter feathers and ribbons and skeleton keys. He loosens his right hand and closes it again around one of the keys, clenching it so tightly that he can feel its teeth digging into his palm. The end of the performance had gone much better than the beginning. It had been Noah, in fact, who deftly stepped in to save one of the tricks when it looked as though it might be going awry. Perhaps he was getting the hang of it, after all. Noah is no fool—he knows that Dr. Yu's father believes himself to be helping the broken-down minister by providing him with some sort of instruction, something to occupy his empty hours. But from where Noah stood on the makeshift stage this evening, he wondered if it is *he* who has been of greater help to the magician. Under the watchful eye of Dr. Yu herself, Noah has learned how to tell if her father has eaten that day, how much he has slept, whether or not he has taken the vitamins that she prescribes for him. During their performances, Noah is the one to lift the trunks, the coffin-box, and the tables when the magician grows weary, and he has begun to take the wheel on their trips to and from the harbor because his companion's driving is often so erratic. As reluctant as he was at first to be roped into the project one week ago, Noah was beginning to enjoy the task. Perhaps he is not praying, or preaching; perhaps he is not saving any souls. But the work is tangible and practical. Yesterday was the first time in a long time when he did not wake up full of that old sinking feeling, his chest crammed with invisible weights, his throat prickly and parched. This morning he rose early, slipping out of bed so that his wife would not awaken, and even whistled a little as he checked on the canaries and prepared a pot of oatmeal. In the gazebo that evening, as he pulled the curtain in front of the coffin to hide it from the audience and headed around the other side to help Dr. Yu's father, he stepped lightly over the groaning boards of the platform and felt more alive than he had in weeks.

And now there was this. When his wife had burst backstage,

her face sharp with fear, he guessed at what she had to say before she spoke. He stood frozen while she called hoarsely to Dr. Yu's father from behind the curtain, his heart sinking in his rib cage as she explained to him and Dr. Yu the situation as she had learned it from the weatherman.

Noah has never seen her so animated. He watches her face light up with recognition when Dr. Yu's father finally reappears, his two friends jogging to keep pace with him.

"This is Stan," says Dr. Yu's father, short of breath, pointing to the mustached man two steps behind him. "And his wife—"

"You must be Nancy," says Noah's wife, smiling broadly and extending her hand to each of them in turn.

"How did you know that?" demands Dr. Yu's father.

Stan smiles. "We met the other day."

Noah keeps his gaze upon his wife, wondering where she has been going while he stays at home. He takes a step closer to her while she sums up the situation for Stan and Nancy.

"So you see," she concludes, "we've got to get there as quickly as we can. And we've got to go by boat." She hesitates. "I wish there were another way, but I'm afraid we have no choice."

Nancy nods. "Stan doesn't like boats either," she says, clasping the hand of Noah's wife warmly between her own. "So you're in good company, my dear. But don't worry! We've been living on this boat for weeks. We know the ins and outs of it by now, don't we, Stan?"

Stan nods, his smile dimming slightly. Dr. Yu's father glances fiercely at his watch. As Noah considers the faces of the hardy souls gathered around him, he is struck by the vision of a sinking ship—imagines all five of them pitching into a turbulent sea and vanishing beneath the waves. What would become of him then?

The simple truth is that he is afraid. He cannot return there; he does not have the strength to witness firsthand the destruction that he was supposed to have prevented. In the days since their departure he has come to believe that he was right about that place from the beginning: there is a darkness to it. It is no coincidence that Noah nearly met the same fate of the old minister who drowned in the river; the clouds that have hung so low over that place for so long must certainly be a sign. He remembers the waters closing over his head, the gentle, insistent tug of the current—he remembers sinking, his body and soul so cold that he could feel his bones throbbing with the chill. He barely survived the town the first time around, and he is only beginning to feel better now. If he returns, there is no guarantee that he will make it out again. There is no guarantee that *any* of them will make it out again.

"When you can see that something is doomed," he says slowly, "what's the sense in going back?"

At first he is not aware that he has spoken the thought aloud. When he sees his wife's stricken expression, he instantly regrets the words. He knows that she loves him because he is confident and unshakable. And he has always taken great pains not to destroy that illusion—not to tell her that he is afraid of stupid things like theme parks and bee stings—but then, what is the sense in hiding his fear now? What right has he to remain silent and let her go when it means that she is certainly going to her death?

He takes a deep breath, parts two chapped lips, and speaks. "This will never work," he tells them in the steadiest voice he can manage. "It's a fool's errand."

"What do you mean?" asks Noah's wife. Her face is unfamiliar in the shadows. "Noah, if we don't go now, it might be too late before anyone else can reach them. What if they die there?"

Noah shakes his head. "And what if you do go?" he says. "You'll never make it there in time. You won't be saving anyone, you'll only lose yourselves in the attempt." He pauses, shudders. "Trust me," he adds. "I know."

Dr. Yu is examining him, her dark eyes narrowed and her gaze as keen as her father's. "Noah," she says, trying in her own way to give him the benefit of the doubt. "I don't believe you mean it. I'm sure you've got a little more faith left in you than that."

The heat rises to his face. He is ashamed at his response to the crisis, which makes him all the more desperate to explain to them what they are too hopeful, too naïve to see. "Faith is nothing but a trick of the light," he says, pulling up his words as if from a great depth. "You think that something can come from nothing, but it's only an illusion. The dove does not vanish or reappear. She is always already there, hidden in the folds of the magician's cloak. Isn't that right?" He glances at Dr. Yu's father. "Isn't that what you've been teaching me?"

Dr. Yu's father stands paralyzed beside Nancy, his expression at once appalled and full of pity.

"Noah," he says, "I think you've got it wrong."

"I know what I'm talking about," replies Noah, his sense of conviction increasing with every word. For a few seconds he feels almost as unshakable as his old self. "This is senseless and dangerous. There isn't any point in going back."

He scrutinizes his wife, waiting for her to waver. In spite of everything that has happened—as if the last few weeks have been nothing but a bad dream—he is expecting her to do what she has always done: to see that he is right and then step swiftly to his side. But her expression remains opaque, and he is so taken aback when she turns away from him that he must place a hand on the hull of the yacht to steady himself.

There is little he can do but watch as she gathers her team around her. It is decided that she and Dr. Yu will take the car and make a quick run for supplies while the others prepare the boat and persuade as many people as they can to join them.

"The more boats we have, the better," Noah's wife explains. "It's not only the people we're worried about, but the animals, as well. There isn't any way they'll all fit on one."

Nancy smiles. "We've met quite a few people in the harbor these past few months," she says. "It's high time we called in a favor or two."

While Noah's wife and Dr. Yu climb into the car, Dr. Yu's father follows Stan and Nancy down to the boats. Nancy kicks off her neon pumps and climbs up the ladder to the deck of her boat to begin untying knots, pulling the tarps from the helm and the controls. Stan and Dr. Yu's father pace up and down the piers, knocking against hulls to see who is on board, looking for fellow sailors who are present and willing to lend a hand.

Noah stands alone, set apart from the action. He watches the shadowy figures emerge from the boats to the dock, scratching their heads or tilting their chins while listening to Dr. Yu's father's passionate account of the situation in the town. He is still wearing some of his magician's gear, and even from a distance Noah can see that the tuxedo lends an air of elegance and authority to his plea. Of course the man has never seen the place, Noah reminds himself ruefully. He has no idea what it will take to get there, or what they will find waiting for them if they ever arrive. Perhaps this is why he and his daughter and the rest of the lot are so willing to climb upon the nearest boat and turn their helms to the north, barreling straight into the heart of the storm. It is easy to play the parts of heroes when they do not know what to expect, when they can imagine the situation as something other than what it is. There is a great power in imagination, in belief, in fiction. It can make a man feel like anything is possible.

Indeed, Noah knows exactly what they are feeling right now, the small crowd of would-be heroes growing slowly but steadily in number as the minutes pass. In the past, he has felt it, too: the rush of adrenaline before a service, before a ceremony; the energy of prayer; the confidence and drive that come from the certainty that he is needed, that there *is* a force for good in the world and that everything will turn out for the best in the end. It's fine to believe that now, here on the docks where the lamps glitter against a navy blue sky, where the stars swing over the harbor on their constellated strings and the boats rock quietly on the waves. It is peaceful here. It is beautiful. But it won't be peaceful there, with the water crashing against the houses and the rain plummeting down to the roofs like hard, translucent stones. People will be wailing, clawing at the walls to get out. Some will be dead; others will be well on their way. There will be nothing left but destruction—and the simple truth is that Noah cannot bear to see it.

As the time nears for their departure, the energy along the docks intensifies. Noah counts at least twelve boats with their engines running and their navigation lights beaming out across the water. Noah's wife and Dr. Yu, having returned from their errand, are unloading cardboard boxes from the trunks of their cars and placing them into the arms of their willing volunteers. People he doesn't recognize are tossing supplies to one another from boardwalk to boat: blankets, tarps, flashlights, jugs of fresh water, crates of bread and crackers. Dr. Yu's father is bent beside Stan beneath one of the standing lamps, their necks craned together over a map unfolded between them.

When Nancy calls out to Stan from the deck of their boat, his head snaps up and he hurries over to join her. Dr. Yu's father glances away from the map and sees Noah drifting in his direction.

"Noah, you've changed your mind!" he cries, clearly pleased. "Are you coming along with us after all? We could use another set of hands on board, that's for sure. I've got no idea what I'm supposed to be doing out there, and there's plenty of room yet with Stan and Nancy." He indicates their extravagant, cream-colored yacht moored to the end of the pier.

"Ezra," insists Noah, his desperation rising every minute, "be practical. You know this is dangerous. Can't you wait another day or two? The coast guard said that they'd be willing—"

"The coast guard!" snorts Dr. Yu's father. "Since when does it do anyone any good to wait for help from on high? No, if you want something done right, you've got to do it yourself. Besides, didn't you hear your wife? We've got no time. It has to be now."

He looks Noah over as if for the last time, compassion shining through damp eyes. "I know what it's like to try to hold on to something," he says huskily. "I know how senseless these little plans, these grand gestures seem in the face of what you've lost, and what you stand to lose. But that senselessness, Noah, that irrationality—that's what sets us apart from the beasts. We've got things like hope and happy endings. We find ways to make a cold world feel warm again." Noah looks down at the boards beneath his feet and suddenly finds himself enveloped in a tight, abrupt embrace. He inhales sharply and smells the singed collar of the magician's cloak. Dr. Yu's father ends the hug as quickly as he started it, swipes at his eyes and holds out his hand, which Noah automatically reaches for and shakes. "Take care of yourself, Minister," says the magician. "Keep your chin up."

At the far end of the harbor, several of the boats pull away from their piers. Dr. Yu's father spins in a half circle and dashes down to the yacht, clambering on board after his daughter. Stan and Nancy are already getting the boat under way, Stan clinging to the helm with his knuckles white and his jaw set in desperate resolve.

"Here we go, Stan!" Noah hears Nancy shout. He sees her fling one arm in the air in a kind of salute, but Noah does not wave back.

"Twelve, twenty, twenty-four," mutters Stan, his gaze fixed on the depth meter. "Oh, Lord. Give me strength." He slides the boat forward to the end of the pier, waiting for Noah's wife to grab the last of the supplies from the parking lot and join them on board.

Dr. Yu calls to her, and she comes. Noah can see her slam the trunk of the car and then spin toward them, taking long strides and gathering speed as she goes. By the time she steps onto the pier she is running, her arms full of plastic ponchos, her feet flying off the ground. He positions himself so that he is directly in her path, so that she has to pull up short as she approaches him—coming to a halt just in time. Her face is inches from his and without thinking, he reaches out to touch her cheek. He recognizes every freckle, every mole; he knows her as well as he knows himself. His breathing steadies and his panic subsides. She will not go without him.

"Listen," he tells her firmly. "If you try going back there, you won't be able to get out again. The rain is too powerful, the winds are too strong." He takes her hand. "You're my wife. It's my job to keep you safe."

"That's what I used to think, too," she says. She has never looked at him this way before—with her expression full of sorrow. "I thought that by loving you, I'd be protected from everything that was painful in life—safe from loneliness, heartache, uncertainty. But I had it all wrong. No one can promise safety or stability, Noah. The world is too unpredictable."

At her words, his chest tightens. He shakes his head, struggling to project the confidence he does not feel. "If that's true," he says, "then why wouldn't you want to stay here, and hold on to what you have—what we have together? Why would you want to go back there? There isn't anything that you can do for them."

"I can try," she tells him gently.

"But they are not your responsibility!" he insists. "They never were!"

She raises her chin. "Then who *is* my responsibility, Noah?"

The answer is obvious. "I am," he says flatly. "And you're mine. We belong to each other. That's what marriage means." He stares at her, his expression dark beneath his brow. Her skin shines bronze in the soft glow of the harbor lights. "I love you," he says.

She hesitates. Her gaze is tender and deep. And in that instant he is certain that he has her; he is convinced that this whole night—the harbor, the sea—has been nothing but a nightmare. He will wake beside her tomorrow morning and all of this will be over.

"I love you, too," she says fiercely. "You have no idea how much. And that used to be enough. I used to believe that it was my role to support you no matter what. But I think you're wrong about this, Noah. I can't support your choice to leave them."

Noah reaches for her—a drowning man grasping at the wreckage of his ship. But before he can wrap his arms around her she has ducked and slid past him and begun again to run.

And why doesn't he go chasing after her? His limbs are numb with fear, his confidence shot and his resolve too weak. His heart thuds in his ears and he tries to call to her, but his tongue will not form the words. He feels the cold water of the river close over him once again and he hears himself gasp for air, hears the strangled cry torn finally from his throat. She cannot, she *will not* leave him here. He calls her name—once, twice, again.

Does she even hear him? She doesn't falter, or turn back. Instead she sprints, her black hair streaming out behind her, her limbs glowing beneath the lights that hang over the pier. She soars from boat to boat, lamp to lamp, until she reaches the yacht that is waiting for her at the end. From where he stands, Noah can see her fly up the rope ladder and leap on board, can hear the goose-like call of the horn as the boat pulls away.

Noah remains on the dock, the scent of her lingering where she stood. He watches as the boats motor forth into the night, falling one after another into line. The fleet grows smaller and smaller, their lights fading one by one, until the last of them has rounded the bend and disappeared. Noah stands on the pier for a long time after, while the stars tumble over the sky and the horizon lightens in the east. He cannot stop expecting that his wife will turn her boat around. He is unable to believe that she has gone.

thirty-eight

The morning of his stepdaughter's wedding, Mrs. McGinn's husband opens the church door to find that the water has risen halfway up their hill.

The rain is slamming down so hard that when he draws back inside the building, the forearm that he extended out into the weather feels as though it has been bruised. He kneads it with the fingers of his other hand, drawing blood to the surface. He turns around to see if any of the townspeople were looking at him, if any of them were near enough to see the situation as he saw it—but most of his neighbors are still asleep and the ones who are not are avoiding his gaze. That's fine by him. He doesn't care if they're afraid of him; his only concern right now is to prevent them from panicking. Death by drowning or death by stampede? he finds himself wondering. Which is the easier way to go?

The end has never felt so close before.

He slides the bolt in place over the front doors and trudges past the owl perched on the railing. The bird opens one eye and turns her head, sleepily, to watch him go. Those townspeople who are beginning to wake, yawning into their sleeping bags and blinking in the cool, gray light of morning, nestle farther down and press their eyelids shut as he passes them by. After all these years Mrs. McGinn's husband remains a mystery to them, a perilous enigma, a firecracker on a short fuse. They are well aware of the fact that Mrs. McGinn has a penchant for matrimony and a knack for weddings, but they have never been able to understand what demon induced her to set her sights on her current husband.

This morning, she is determined to organize yet another wedding. The townspeople assumed that something was afoot yesterday afternoon when they saw Mrs. McGinn's daughter and the zookeeper briefly disappear into the basement, only to rejoin the group with their faces shining and their arms wrapped around each other. They heard Mrs. McGinn's daughter inform her mother that the two of them wanted to be married in the church as soon as possible, and so they were not surprised when Mrs. McGinn marched between the sleeping bags at bedtime, passing out handwritten to-do lists to each of her neighbors with all the things that needed to be taken care of before the service. After they had their assignments, she enforced a lights-out curfew to keep the candles and the light boxes fresh for the ceremony. Her husband slept poorly on the floor beside her—the animals shifted and cried in the night, the rain battered against the stained-glass windows—but managed to doze off before dawn. By the time he roused himself enough to stand and stretch, his wife was already up and gone.

Now he follows the scent of pancakes and the murmur of voices to the basement, where he finds Mauro manning the griddle while Mrs. McGinn bends with great concentration over a spiral-bound notebook she borrowed from Noah's old office. Her husband does not need to look at the paper to know that she's drawing up another series of lists.

"Eat a good breakfast, people!" she calls out. Her voice soars over the rippling conversation and the rattling of cutlery. "The ceremony will be held at seven o'clock this evening. We've got a lot to accomplish before then. Come check in with me if you have any questions about your assignments!"

Mrs. McGinn's husband gives a little wave to Mauro and drops into a chair across from Mrs. McGinn. "Evelyn," he says. He picks up her fork and spears a piece of untouched pancake. "Good morning."

"Morning, Jackson," she says, glancing up from her work. "How did you sleep?"

"Fine," he mutters.

"Good. I have a favor to ask of you."

"Before you do," he says, "I've got to tell you—this is a terrible idea. The water's rising. We should be spending our time building boats or something, not trying to organize this charade of a wedding. It doesn't make any sense."

"Charade?" repeats Mrs. McGinn, her tone a warning.

"Yes, charade. Do we have a minister? Do we have a judge? The judge left months ago—and we should have, too. Who the hell do you think is going to perform the service?"

He can sense the frustration beginning to bubble into his chest. He glances at the plastic syrup container, feels the sudden, unquenchable urge to grab it and hurl it across the room.

Mrs. McGinn sees the look, recognizes the signs, and briskly moves the container out of reach. He glares at her.

"Stop it, Jackson," she says. "Calm down. The wedding is happening. I've got people on cleanup and decorations, Leesl on the organ, a few volunteers to tease the bride's hair into something better than the matted bird's nest it looks like now. If we can rearrange the potted plants, remove the sleeping bags and the buckets of feed, arrange the candles in the windows and the light boxes near the pews, whip up some sort of buffet from this stack of canned goods—well, then we'll have a wedding, and it will be beautiful, as weddings always are. Don't you remember ours?" She takes his hand. "*I'll* perform the ceremony, Jackson."

"A woman minister?" scoffs her husband. "Who's ever heard of such a thing? I'll bet that it's not even allowed."

"Allowed by *whom*, Jackson?" demands Mrs. McGinn, her gaze fiery and her tone defiant. "Who is here to stop me, pray tell? Adam and Angie can find a courthouse and make it legal later. They'll sign the papers some other day."

"There won't *be* another day, Evelyn," he snaps. He removes his hand from hers. "Have you looked outside this morning? Trust me—the end is nigh. This is it."

"All the more reason to throw a party," she says, her chin set stubbornly. "Let's go down dancing, shall we?"

Mrs. McGinn's husband considers his wife. Her face is rutted and pallid without her makeup. Her ears are bare, and as he runs his eyes along their curves he is reminded—as he always is—of the sea, of the spirals of conch shells that he used to whisper into when he found them as a boy on the beach. He decided early on that he would support his wife in all her endeavors, and he will continue supporting her now.

"You said you had a favor to ask of me?" he says grudgingly.

"Yes," she replies, satisfied. "You're in charge of all the lights. And will you walk her down the aisle?"

He hesitates for half a second. The thought had not occurred to him, but who else is there to do it? Besides, he has been married to his wife long enough to know that even if he says no, somehow he will end up performing the task anyway.

Mauro, stopping by the table with another stack of pancakes, overhears the end of the conversation. "I can be helping you with the lights, Jackson," he offers. "So many birds, so many stones! But only first I must be finding the iron for Adam."

"The iron?" repeats Mrs. McGinn. "He doesn't have a suit to press, Mauro."

Mauro shakes his head. "Not that kind. A piece of the iron,

I mean, for his pockets. So that the marriage will be having much luck."

Mrs. McGinn swallows her coffee and takes the superstition in stride. "All right," she says. "I can't argue with that. Go find your iron, and then meet Jackson in the nave. We could all use a little extra luck at this point, I suppose."

Soon afterward the breakfast crowd disperses, each to an appointed duty. When Mrs. McGinn's husband climbs the stairs and returns to the nave, he finds the church full of life. People are dragging furniture across the floor or piling sleeping bags against the wall or stacking and restacking crates and cages. The zebra flares its nostrils and paws at the carpet. The cattle low, deep and mournful. The zookeeper comes dashing around a corner, in pursuit of an ostrich that has escaped its cardboard-fence corral. He curses when the bird pauses to tear a page from a hymnal with its beak. It swallows the song whole.

Mrs. McGinn's husband watches the proceedings, shaking his head and standing silent witness to the chaos. When he feels a powerful wave of melancholy break against him, he drops down without warning onto the organ bench.

"Hey," says Leesl, who is paging through music in a nearby pew. "Are you all right?"

"I'm fine," he says gruffly. She stares at him, making him feel as though he must add more. "The whole thing is such a farce."

Leesl doesn't need to ask him what he means. "I can see that," she says kindly. "Your wife is right—it's good for everyone to keep busy. But I've never understood the fascination with weddings, to be honest. Or the desire for marriage."

He raises his head. The light in the church glints off her glasses and makes her dull hair shine "How do you mean?"

"Well," she says, "people change. It's very optimistic to promise to love someone forever when you know that—in five years, in ten years, twenty—both of you are going to be really different than when you started out. There's a good chance that you'll wake up one day and find yourself married to someone you don't even know anymore, someone who isn't the same person you fell in love with."

She hugs the sheet music to her side. "People fall out of love all the time," she says. "It's terrifying, and it's heartbreaking, but it's the truth. And a wedding contradicts that. It's like everyone is getting together and saying that 'forever' is a thing you can count on, that everything will always be the same. But nothing ever stays the same. One minute your life is routine—you're waking up in the morning and going to work the way you've been doing every day for years. The next, your house is washed away and your entire existence is gone with it."

Mrs. McGinn's husband is surprised by Leesl; he has never heard her speak so much at once. Is she right? Is that why people get married? he wonders, as he sets himself to the task of stringing lights across the ends of the pews. Is that why his wife married him? Is that what his stepdaughter is hoping to find with her zookeeper?

He remembers that when he asked Mrs. McGinn to marry him, she hesitated.

"How do I know you won't leave me?" she asked in a voice that was childlike and wounded. "How do I know I can trust you?"

There it was, he thought to himself. There's the chink in the armor. His wife may be the bravest woman this town has ever seen, but everyone fears being left.

"You *don't* know," he had replied, honest because she deserved it. "Every relationship is a risk. Marriage is a leap of faith."

When Mrs. McGinn's husband remembers his father and his mother, the smashing glass and the flying plates, he feels the ache in his chest of a heart long broken. He learned at an early age that the only people who can truly hurt you are the ones that you love.

AFTER THE LIGHTS are strung and turned on, he spends an hour arranging candles in the windows and around the altar. When Mauro joins him, the peacocks tottering behind, Mrs. McGinn's husband asks him if he found the iron he was looking for.

Mauro shakes his head. "Not yet," he says cheerfully. "But instead I am finding these."

He holds out a fist and uncurls his fingers to show Mrs.

McGinn's husband the two brass curtain rings resting in his palm.

Mrs. McGinn's husband nods and pulls another stack of candles from the box. Why not? he asks himself, doing his best to channel his wife's cheerful determination. The young couple is being married among sheep dung and moldy hay, with wild animals pacing the perimeter and the rain pounding against the roof. Why not have Mrs. McGinn as their minister, why not make their vows while exchanging curtain rings? Never mind the fact that the whole thing seems more than a little absurd. Perhaps that is the nature of the ritual.

WHEN IT IS TIME for the ceremony, Mrs. McGinn's husband approaches each candle with an acolyte's pole, touching his flame to the wick with furious concentration. The candles flicker whenever the townspeople or the animals hurry by, their shadows quivering along the floor, and he must retrace his steps to relight several that go out. Finally the task is complete.

As the townspeople finish up their preparations and their chores, fluff out their hair, and find their seats in the pews, the shadows of the world retreat to the farthest corners and the church shines with a light that will not be contained. The building is filled to the brim and soon it overflows, light pouring from the windows, rushing through panes of colored glass and washing out across the water in waves of blues and greens and deep, rich reds. They stand together within a painted lighthouse, a multicolored beacon that beams across the town and the houses that lie buried beneath the surface, gleaming even through the rain. She always wins, his wife, he thinks to himself as the music starts up and they all draw breath before song. She was right yet again: in the end, they will all go down dancing.

thirty-nine

Noah's wife has never liked boats.

As she swings herself on board she feels her stomach flip and fall. While Stan guides the boat out of the harbor she sways at the stern and grips the railings with sweaty palms, staring back at the shore where the figure of her husband is growing smaller by the minute.

"I think I'm going to be sick," she says.

"No, you're not," says Dr. Yu from behind her. Noah's wife feels a firm hand come to rest on her shoulder. "You're going to be fine."

The boat tilts and heaves on the water. Noah's wife digs her heels into the deck and remembers the whale-watching boat in the rain. She remembers the scent and the strong, solid feel of him as the waves tossed her against his chest—Noah, with his powerful arms and his stubborn faith, with a hope so blinding that in spite of all that has happened she still believes that she could see it blazing from miles away, if only she knew where to look.

As she squints in the direction of the shore, the rest of her little fleet falls into line behind her, their lights beaming forward in the night. She stares at the silhouette of her husband on the dock, keeps her gaze fixed upon him until his shape has been swallowed by the night and there is no sign that he is still standing there at all—only the lights in the harbor flaring softer and fainter until the boats round a bend in the coast and they vanish completely.

The yacht heaves again and Noah's wife stumbles. Is Noah angry with her? she wonders. Will he try to follow her? In the sudden darkness she is angry with herself for abandoning him, for heeding the call of that town when her husband didn't seem to hear it. Must people always *belong* so wholly to one another? she asks herself bitterly. Must it always be impossible to unknot the threads of so many lives? She remembers the light boxes glowing through windows, the animals kept safe in spare bedrooms and bathtubs, the rain blowing in waves across roofs. What if Noah is right, and they arrive too late? What if, in her instinctive, foolish desire to help, she leads her entire crew to their demise? She cannot bear that kind of responsibility; she never could. She has always been content to leave the responsibility to the Dr. Yus and the Noahs of the world, people strong enough to shoulder it.

Another rush of panic leaves her feeling dizzy, unable to tell which way is up, whether their boat is being borne across the waves or is hanging suspended above them. The sky and the sea are the same shade of black, so full and so vast that she cannot help but feel smaller than she has ever felt before, cannot do anything but sink slowly to her knees on the deck as the silliness, the futility of the venture knocks the breath right out of her. She had been running on adrenaline, and now even that has left her. There is nothing to do on this boat except wait.

"Oh God," she gasps. "This was a mistake."

She is not a mover or a shaker. She is not a visionary. What made her believe that she could do this? How many thousands of moments have there been in her life when she was reminded of her own insignificance? It was Noah who was supposed to be saving this town, leading this expedition. How did the task fall to someone like her?

She buries her head in her arms and takes quick, shallow breaths. Dr. Yu slides down beside her, her back resting against the railing of the stern, one leg crossed over the other.

"Hey," says Dr. Yu. "This was not a mistake." She pauses, watching her father at the helm with Stan and Nancy. He whistles to himself with the map unfolded in his hands, poring over the course that they had charted together and talking to Stan all the while. His stance is wide and secure, the tails of his tuxedo flapping in the wind. The water, dark as stained glass, slides endless toward the horizon. "I've never seen you the way I saw you just now," Dr. Yu tells her best friend. "You were fearless."

There is a fine line, Noah's wife wants to respond, between

being a hero and being a fool. It was not that she was fearless; she simply was not thinking. After her encounter with the weatherman, she sprinted down the boardwalk with the dove clasped to her chest, the bird's wings flapping wildly against her coat. She flew back to the gazebo and called to Noah from behind the homemade curtain while Dr. Yu's father struggled with his handcuffs in the harsh glare of the floodlight he had placed to one side and Dr. Yu watched helplessly from the audience. The trick did not go as planned. When Dr. Yu's father finally retreated behind the curtain to ask Noah for the key, with Dr. Yu following quietly in his wake, Noah's wife was already setting her plan into motion.

"The road through the hills is flooded," she was saying to her ghost-faced husband when the two of them appeared. "The only way to reach them is by water."

Was it really she who said that? She shakes her head. Remembering it now, the waves rocking her back and forth like a child, she feels that she had been driven by a nameless force, an appeal that she does not understand. She wishes she felt as certain now, on this boat, as she did beneath the slatted roof of that gazebo.

"It wasn't supposed to be my job to save them, April," she says. "Somewhere along the way, something went wrong."

Dr. Yu takes her best friend's hand, exhales slowly, and instructs Noah's wife to do the same. "Breathe," she says. "Breathe." And then, in a tone that is both clinical and kind: "And what *was* your job supposed to be?"

Noah's wife stares at her. Everything she thinks to say in response to the question seems suddenly weak, inadequate. A good spouse, she might have said if the question had been posed to her several months back—a devoted wife, a pillar of support. She loved Noah more than herself, and she would have gladly followed him to the ends of the earth without a second thought. And yet how is she to balance her duty to her husband with her obligation to those she left behind her? Doesn't she owe something to that town, too?

Dr. Yu is watching her, reading her mind with a faint smile tugging at her lips. "You know," she admits, "for a long time I was jealous of Noah. I felt that by loving him, you had less to give to me." Her words are slow, as if the thought is just dawning on her. "But love is not a loaf of bread. It isn't something that has to be broken into smaller and smaller pieces if you want to share it. It isn't finite—in theory, the more people you care about, the more it should multiply. I think both you and I misunderstood that."

She takes a deep breath. "This wasn't *supposed* to be anything," she continues. "There isn't any greater plan or predetermined path. Noah was always wrong about that." She glances again toward the helm and falls silent for a few seconds. "For years you've tried to divide the world into the ordinary and the extraordinary—but those divisions only keep you from doing the hard work yourself. There are no extraordinary people. Only ordinary people who sometimes do extraordinary things."

Is this what it feels like to do something extraordinary? wonders Noah's wife. Is it always this terrifying, this exhausting? Life had been ordered before—she had done her best to make it so. She had tried to stow her world away, to keep her happiness contained within a box so that she could hold on to it and keep it safe—but perhaps there is no such safety. Perhaps happiness is always fleeting, and joy can never be contained. How can she return to what she was, how can she pretend that she and Noah are unchanged, that their marriage is as secure and blissful as it ever was, when her old sense of order has been turned upside down and nothing is as stable as it seems?

"I'm sorry for what I said last night," she says to Dr. Yu. "I'm sorry if I sounded unsympathetic, or unkind. I was overwhelmed."

Dr. Yu lifts one shoulder and lightly lets it fall. Noah's wife sees the flash of her smile in the darkness. "Of course you were," she says. "But you don't have to do this by yourself. I'm here. I think that's what my father has been trying to say: you've been taking care of me for years, and I've been trying to take care of him—but you and I, we need to learn when to accept help as well as offer it. Sometimes we're given more than we can bear alone."

For a while they listen to the motor and the waves thudding against the hull. The moon is falling lower in the sky, but something in Noah's wife is rising as she goes. As their boat slides along below the stars she leans back against the railing and shoots off wordless prayers like signal flares, powerful bursts of hope up into the heavens and out toward a lonely town that is holding its breath and preparing to go under. She pictures the prayers rising from her boat in long and looping threads connecting earth to sky, her boat to the town, other lives to her own. The water is dark and deep but she is being pulled swiftly across it to them, propelled by the power of their connection.

As the new day dawns, as Stan motors up the coast toward the ominous smudge of a storm on the horizon, the flock of boats soars after them. The sun rises and falls again, and when she is not at the helm Noah's wife paces the deck or tries to nap on one of the beds in the cabin below. They head east through the hills, careening into the mouth of the river. The sun sets behind the clouds and when the boats finally enter the town a couple of hours later they do so on hushed waves, the motors purring and pouring frothy bubbles into dark water, the lights on the bows beaming a few feeble feet forward. The glow is not strong enough to see anything but the wreckage spinning on the surface—bobbing mailboxes, cast-off umbrellas, the empty sacks of broken sandbags, drifting tree trunks and telephone poles—and the occasional gleaming weather vane that marks the spot where a roof lies dark and buried below the water. It is still raining. Noah's wife tightens her hood and peers through the downpour. The stars have vanished behind the clouds and the last of her hope splinters and sinks. They have come too late.

The weatherman had tried to tell her that this town was not her responsibility. He had insisted that she did not owe these people anything, reminded her that he had tried to help them several times already and had only failed in the attempt.

"How many times," he had growled, watching her reach for the dove in the trees, "do you have to extend a hand to help people when they refuse to take it?"

Noah's wife had turned to him before taking off with the bird. The answer was clear to her, and she did not understand how he could not see it. "Again," she told him simply. "And again."

Suddenly Dr. Yu's father emits a cry from the stern. It is only then, turning and following the indication of his outstretched arm, that she notices the light in the distance—the spectrum that arcs in reds and yellows and greens and blues from the stained-glass windows to the water. Stan wrenches his wheel to the right and the rest of the fleet follows, battling against the wind while the rain keeps pummeling down.

forty

The organ swells as the water rises.

The townspeople part their lips and begin to sing, the hymnals spread open across their palms. They turn in their pews and stand on their toes, craning their necks to catch sight of the bride as she makes her way down the center aisle to the altar. Even Leesl looks over her shoulder as she plays, her fingers skipping across the keys. Mrs. McGinn's daughter is wearing a rose-colored dress that one of her neighbors had pulled out of a suitcase. Her arms and neck are weighed down with jewelry that the women in the church had been only too happy to provide. When word had spread about the wedding, they had gone digging through their luggage for bracelets and brooches, had unclasped their own necklaces and hurried over to refasten them around the bride.

"Something borrowed!" they had each exclaimed, and by the

time the preparations were complete, Mrs. McGinn's daughter was wearing something borrowed from nearly every woman in town. Although everyone knew it was too much—really, the bride looked rather ridiculous in the stacks of sterling silver chains, the strands and strands of pearls, the brooches pinned from her shoulder to her hip—Mrs. McGinn had nodded, satisfied.

"Yes," she had said. "That's what weddings are for."

The girl is striding down the aisle on the arm of Mrs. McGinn's husband while the peacocks stalk regally ahead of them. Mauro grins and waves at the birds from the middle of the pews, where he is bustling between the rows and passing out handfuls of torn-up hay for his neighbors to use as confetti. Mrs. McGinn wipes her eyes with her husband's handkerchief and shifts on her feet as she waits for the couple to arrive at the steps of the altar.

The zookeeper, meanwhile, is standing a few feet away from her, his gaze fixed solemnly on Mrs. McGinn's daughter, holding his breath as he counts the number of steps she has left before she reaches him, wondering (perhaps) if there is any chance that she will turn and run. He needn't worry, reflects Leesl, still gazing at the bride. The girl's pace is calm, her face alight and at peace. Her eyes shine at the sight of the zookeeper, his hands folded one over the other, his suit rumpled and worn. She does not seem to notice the animals milling around him—the red fox huddled at his feet, the eagle spreading her wings over the post where she is chained behind him. The sheep are pacing back and forth below the steps, the cattle are lowing, and as they near the altar, the ostrich goes streaking past with her feathers flying. Mauro tosses his basket of confetti in the air and takes off after the bird, having received express instructions from Mrs. McGinn to keep the animals in line during the service. Mrs. McGinn's daughter releases the arm of her stepfather, surprised by the dry kiss he drops ceremoniously on her cheek. She turns, intending to thank him, but he has already stepped unsentimentally away and the zookeeper is reaching out to draw her toward him. Leesl finishes the hymn and lifts her fingers from the keys. The townspeople assume this is their cue to be seated.

"Dearly beloved!" announces Mrs. McGinn. "We are gathered here today!"

She holds the book of liturgy close to her nose, her hand trembling only slightly, while the members of her ragtag congregation lean against the hard backs of their pews and allow the familiar words of this familiar ritual to wash over them, marveling at how long it has been since they set foot in the church. There is a kind of comfort to it, after all, some of them murmur to one another, remembering the days before the rain. But how difficult it had been to think about heaven, how exasperating it had become to climb all the way up here, when every time they looked skyward they got water in their eyes! A few of them, struck with sudden guilt at the memory of their truancy in the days of the former minister, whisper to their neighbors that they might have continued to come, if it were not for the rain. The old man had always been so patient with them. And then before they knew it, he was gone.

At the thought of the former minister, they all shift uneasily in their seats and try their best to focus on the ceremony. The church is beautiful—they must give Mrs. McGinn credit for that. The portable light boxes have been attached with their batteries to a heavy rope that runs back and forth across the nave, swinging and glowing softly above their heads. The candles are flickering at the altar, and the fake flowers that someone retrieved from a closet downstairs have been propped up near the baptismal font. Even the animals are settling down, their gleaming eyes on Mauro as he patrols the perimeter with a bucket full of overripe fruit. The pews are polished, the silver is shining, the walls are newly painted. Noah worked hard on this church—they can see that now. And then he left them, too.

There is so much that the townspeople do not want to think about. They would prefer to avoid dwelling on the real reason they are gathered here today, the real reason why Mrs. McGinn is presiding over them and why the bride and groom must lift their feet from time to time to nudge at the goats and wild birds that are crowding up the steps of the altar. They are trying not to think about what they saw this afternoon as they prepared for the wedding: the water that is beginning to seep under the door and spread across the stone floor of the church. It is clear that the building will not be able to withstand the rain much longer, but what good does it do to dwell on that now?

The telephone lines are down and their cars lie buried beneath the water. What can they possibly do but wait?

Mauro hurries forward with the curtain rings clutched in his fist when Mrs. McGinn calls for the exchange of wedding bands. As he unfolds his fingers he sees the look the bride and groom pass between them and for a moment he feels foolish for standing up there with these cheap pieces of brass, deeply grieved that he has no more to offer them than this. While the zookeeper and Mrs. McGinn's daughter make their promises to each other, while they vow to be constant until death do them part, a collective shudder runs through the townspeople. How much longer does anybody here have? How many hours until death parts them all?

Leesl senses a change in the room and whirls around on her bench. Mrs. McGinn feels it, too, and slams her prayer book shut in an effort to draw their attention back to her. A small cloud of dust rises from the pages, the particles sparkling silver in the glow of the candles. The bride and groom consider her in some surprise, waiting to be told that it is time for them to kiss, while the congregants turn long faces her way and huddle down in their pews. The entire building creaks and groans, sways a little in the storm.

Frightened, the townspeople look to their neighbors. They almost do not recognize each other, so strained are the familiar faces with exhaustion and despair. They do not deserve a fate like this. They are good people; they have tried to live good lives. Perhaps they have not always been as kind or hospitable as they should have been; perhaps they have not always loved their neighbors as themselves. But are they so much worse than everyone else? Some of them scowl and curse the world that they imagine spinning gaily beyond their hills, all its other inhabitants dry and at peace, free of this watery nightmare from which they themselves cannot awaken.

Even Leesl shivers. She is supposed to go up to the altar and sing before the end of the ceremony, but when she sees the small pools of water that have gathered below the pedals of her instrument, she freezes in place with a quick chill of fear. She had done her best to prepare for the crisis, to stock up on food and blankets and batteries, but what good are her preparations if the water sweeps them all away? She had been pained enough to lose the old minister to the river; must she now lose the rest of her town, as well? For the first time in a long time she remembers her long-distance lover. She pictures him under a flat wash of blue sky, his limbs brown, his face warmed by the sun. How glad she is that she let him go, that she did not keep him close. Look at what comes of holding on to things!

Mrs. McGinn's daughter and the zookeeper are still hand in hand, waiting to be told that they are married. But instead of finishing the ceremony, Mrs. McGinn clears her throat and glares up at the stained-glass windows, where the rain is rattling like stones against the panes. "Hold on," she says. "I know what all of you are thinking. And so before this whole thing is over, I'd like to say a few words about the damn elephant that's in the room. Because we may not have much time left, and someone should."

From where he stands below the pulpit, Mauro sees her fingers trembling. He glances around the perimeter of the church and looks into every pen even though he knows already that there is no elephant to be found. The only one they had was carted away years ago.

Mrs. McGinn lowers her gaze, contemplating her congregation. Her face is glistening with perspiration, her hair chaotic in the humidity. "What are we doing here? What are we trying to prove?" She pauses as if to reflect. Her daughter is staring at her, dry-eyed and aghast, but the sight of her only strengthens Mrs. McGinn's resolve to speak. "The truth, you two, is that marriage isn't going to make you happy, and anyone who tells you differently doesn't know what on earth they're talking about. You'll be happy sometimes, sure, but sometimes you'll be frustrated and sometimes you'll be sad or lonely and sometimes you'll be so angry that you wish you could break the whole world into pieces. Because that's what life is like, and marriage isn't any different."

From the front row, her husband nods in fierce affirmation. Well, what do you know? he says to himself in some surprise. She gets it.

While the rest of Mrs. McGinn's congregation grows increasingly distressed, her husband finds himself at peace. His haggard face is serene as he gazes at his wife and looks around the church and marvels at the fact that all his anger has deserted him. What would his anger do for him right now, anyway? What can he destroy now that there is nothing left here but destruction?

"Listen!" Mrs. McGinn continues, gaining volume with every word. "No one ever said that we'd be safe and dry every day of our lives. Most of the time life is *hard.* It's lonely and it's brutal and it's terrifying, it really is, and there are days when you wake up feeling like there isn't any point in carrying on with it at all. And all you can do is hang on through the hard parts and recognize the good parts when they come and hope that there's some purpose behind it all." Her voice trails off.

And what if there isn't a purpose? the townspeople would like to know. What if this is all there is? For a long moment they stare at one another, their expressions stricken and bleak. They remember how pleased they had been about the wedding, only this morning, but now the whole idea seems ridiculous. What is the sense in celebrating a commitment that is bound to be extinguished within hours?

The zookeeper and Angela Rose are holding hands so tightly that it hurts, the curtain rings digging deep into their skin. How silly they had been to argue about staying or leaving! How many hours had they spent battling over that question, when now, as it turns out, the question simply doesn't matter? There is nothing left for them but this, the present: the darkness and the rain beyond the stained-glass windows, the lights swinging over the pews, the promise that they will not have to face the end alone. One of the penguins comes waddling down the aisle with a wedding ribbon wrapped around his foot, and Mrs. McGinn's daughter cannot help but laugh at him before Mauro leaps to usher him away.

The sound of her daughter's laughter seems to change Mrs. McGinn's mood. She shakes her head to clear it, and opens her prayer book as if she has every intention of finishing the ceremony. "Well, I'll tell you why we're gathered here today," she says again to her neighbors without looking down to verify the text. "You may think we're here because we're at the end of something, and perhaps we are—but the end of something always means the start of something else."

She turns to the couple with her skin wrinkled and pallid, her hands steady, her gaze clear. "Your union today signifies a new beginning. And every morning that you wake up next to each other, and every day here on out, and every month and every year for all the months and years you have before you—I wish for your lives to be blessed with ten thousand times ten thousand new beginnings. I hope that you take every chance that you are given to forgive each other, that you help each other grow and change, and that you take comfort in the knowledge that you are not in this world alone."

Before Mrs. McGinn's words have died away, her daughter has reached for the zookeeper, now her husband, and pulled him to her. As he leans down to kiss her, the entire church fills with the sound of a high, translucent voice rising and falling in song. Behind the couple on the altar stands Leesl, little Leesl, with her back straight and her chin up, no longer hunched over her organ or pinched behind her glasses. The soft light of the candles makes her features glow. Her eyes are closed, her lips parted. The song seems to come from the depths of her rib cage, soaring out into the church with the instinctive force and joy of a beast's release back into the wild. Mauro, chasing down the penguin, stops in his tracks and stares back at her.

Had any of them known that Leesl could sing? The melody is a pleading one, not particularly uplifting—but the longer they listen, the more they hear something serene, resolved, even triumphant in the notes. The townspeople picture the restless waves, the foaming deep of the lyrics in the world outside the stained-glass window and mull over Mrs. McGinn's words, wondering where Leesl could have found this song, wanting to believe that someone wrote it specifically for them. Somehow, when Leesl sings, they feel as though they have not been forgotten. They close their eyes and reach out for their neighbors and in that instant they are calm, and strangely at peace. For a minute the music lifts them up and carries them forward, bears them out of the building and into a night that is starry and dry. They press their eyelids firmly shut, unwilling to open them and be reminded of where they are, wanting to believe that they will be delivered, that they, too, might yet be offered an opportunity to start over, a chance to begin again.

Their eyes are still closed when the song ends, when the church door crashes open and the sound of the rain doubles its thunderous volume. The townspeople are determined to cling to the last bit of light at the end of Leesl's song, this final prayer.

They are determined not to see the end as it comes to them, determined to hold fast to their pews while the waves rush in, and so they refuse to turn around. They stand where they are, facing the altar with their heads bowed and their hands clasped tightly together. They do not see the figure stepping through the doorway with her long dark hair whipping to one side, they do not hear her call to them over the sound of the rain pouring into the water, and they do not see the gold lights gleaming from the boats that are idling and waiting for them, floating on the flooded town behind her.

ACKNOWLEDGMENTS

Noah's Wife began as a series of character sketches when I was attending the Creative Writing Program at the University of Notre Dame. The project would never have left the ground were it not for the support of my lively and talented cohort, the counsel of William O'Rourke and Steve Tomasula, and the eloquent, ever-affirming guidance of Valerie Sayers.

I am deeply indebted to my agent, Laura Langlie, who pulled my manuscript out of her slush pile and pronounced it worthy of pursuit. I am grateful not only for Laura's keen editorial eye, but also for her patience, her confidence, and her warmth on the days when the project seemed like it would last forever.

Amy Einhorn, who purchased the book, perceived something of value in the roughest, earliest draft of the manuscript when it landed on her desk. Her staunch faith in a future version of the novel truly propelled me forward.

Liz Stein, who edited the book, consistently impressed me with her talent and her tenacity. She came to know the characters as well as I did, and the novel is stronger and deeper because of her.

Helen Richard, who ushered the final product into the world, has approached my prose time and again with precision and care. I am thankful for both her edits and her generous affirmation, and I am fortunate to have her as a champion of the novel.

Other individuals and institutions that supported this project include Ken Reininger and the staff of the beautiful North Carolina Zoo, where I was invited behind the scenes. Friends-of-friends Cheri LaFlamme Szcodronski and Joe Szcodronski were kind enough to sit down with me over dinner to share stories of the time they spent as zookeepers.

The Department of English and Comparative Literature at UNC-Chapel Hill provided me with the flexibility necessary to finish the novel while also working toward my doctoral degree. I especially appreciate the encouragement of Gregg Flaxman and Erin Carlston, my dissertation directors, and the generous support of Daniel Wallace, whom I feel lucky to count as a mentor, colleague, friend, and reader.

At UNC I had the opportunity to work as an editor of *The Carolina Quarterly*, where I was inspired by the fresh voices we published as well as by my fellow editors' tireless commitment to and advocacy for contemporary literature. I was also energized by the passion, insight, and honesty of my students in Introduction to Fiction Writing (Fall 2015). I am certain that this novel would be ten times stronger if only they had been given the chance to critique it.

Throughout this process, I leaned on friends and family. Lissa Yu provided Dr. Yu's name and served as a model for her intelligence, her commitment to her family, her dedication to medicine, and her faith in her friends. Tasha Matsumoto walked me through the first draft on our morning constitutionals in South Bend. Subsequent drafts took shape over long dinners with Katie Spencer, who mused with me about characters and pairings and who, together with Martha Precup, patiently answered time and again when I wondered aloud: "But who *is* Noah's wife?" I entrusted very few people with the whole manuscript before it was finished, and I am thankful for the insight and forbearance of those rare souls who kindly volunteered to read it.

My father hosted me at the lake year after year for impromptu writer's retreats, pored over my contract, downloaded multiple drafts on his e-reader, and built a bookshelf specifically for my book. He provided love and support in every possible way—often in the form of lattes. To his faithful and persistent inquiry, I can now reply: Yes, the book is finally done.

My mother, Lorelei, has read every single world of every single draft, and yet her enthusiasm for the project has never waned. Throughout these five years, I have been astounded time and again by her generosity, her intelligence, her sense of humor, and her faith. If the book has any wisdom to it, that wisdom is hers; I simply transcribed it.

And to Christopher, who knew when he asked me to marry him that he would be marrying this novel, too, and who went through with it all the same: Thank you for loving me in spite of the book, not because of it; and thank you for sustaining me in this world when my mind was lost in another one. Everything is better with you.

ABOUT THE AUTHOR

Lindsay Starck was born in Wisconsin and raised in the Milwaukee Public Library. She studied literature at Yale and creative writing at Notre Dame. She currently writes and teaches in Chapel Hill, North Carolina, where she lives with her husband and a golden retriever. *Noah's Wife* is her first novel.